To my parents, whose support means everything.

And to Corey Jo Lloyd.

THE MOMENT APE'S HAND LANDED ON HIS SHOULDER, Clay Navarro knew the game was up.

It could have been the look in the asshole's eye that told him, or the way his fingers dug into Clay's muscle way too hard to be friendly. Probably, though, it was that other thing—that elusive animal intuition that told you your life was about to end.

He managed, somehow, to shrug off Ape's hand and veer into the head, mumbling something about taking a piss. As soon as the door closed behind him, he leaned down and spoke into the button mic sewed onto his leather vest. He was frantic. God, was he having a heart attack? Wouldn't that be something, to have a heart attack on the day everything was supposed to go down?

"Shit's hitting the fan here. Whoever's listening, I need backup."

He glanced at the tiny window and considered trying to make a break for it, but there was no way he'd manage to squeeze through. But, man, he couldn't risk the op at this crucial moment, even if it meant saving his skin. Not when they were so close to taking the sons of bitches down. There was no choice but for him to go out and face whatever Ape had in mind for him—try to stall him and bluster his way through. Whatever it was, they'd catch it on the wire.

Back in the hall, however, flanked by three of his Sultans MC "brothers," Clay was pretty sure there'd be no bullshitting his way out of this. There was a sick sort of glee on Ape's face when he shoved Clay into the manky vinyl dentist's chair, brandished his tattoo gun, and said, "Thought you needed some new artwork, *bro*." After a pause, the man smiled and said, "How about your lids?"

"No fuckin' way, man." His heart rate spiked.

"Knuckles, then," said Ape, and Clay knew better than to argue. There was a chance he hadn't been made—that Ape was just being his usual sick self. Considering everything that was at stake, he had to ride out that hope for as long as he could, and if that meant letting the crazy bastard ink him up some more, then so be it. He forced his body to relax, forced a smirk onto his face.

But then one of the other bikers grabbed for him, and it was all Clay could do not to go down swinging. He submitted at the last moment, pulse flying, reminding himself that he just had to make it through a few hours before it was all over, one way or another. The biker grimly held him, head locked so he was staring straight ahead, unable to watch as Ape pressed the tattoo gun to his finger. He tightened his jaw through the inking—a quick, messy job, even for Ape—and broke the hold long enough to glance down at his knuckles.

DEAD MAN, they said in big, thick black caps. *Fuck.* "What the—"

"Sit your ass down and stay put, or I'll pop your fuckin' eyeball," Ape said through gritted teeth. He brandished the tattoo gun at Clay's face.

Clay bolted up, but the two MC brothers were on him in a flash, grappling him back down. One had an arm locked around his neck, holding his head still for Ape and that *damned tattoo gun.* Clay flinched away, tried to push free, but there was no stopping that needle coming straight for his eyes.

He slammed his lids closed and prayed for a miracle.

"What the shit?" Clay managed to spit out before Ape went to work on his eyelids. The only thing worse than the pain was the fear. He breathed through it as best he could, waiting it out as Ape inked him. He didn't open his eyes until he was sure the needle was away—and even then he was left blinking and dazed, eyeballs stinging.

"What are—" Clay began, fighting to sound normal even after all this—until he spotted Ape pulling out that little ax he carried around with him everywhere. He stiffened, fought, expected to feel the deep slice of a blade in his skull, to see Ape's crazily grinning face through a film of blood, his brain matter scattered across the walls.

He should have known better. Ape might be a total lunatic, but he didn't do anything without Handles's approval. The only thing he carved was Clay's shirt. With the sharpened ax blade. The fucker sure had a flair for the dramatic.

So maybe Handles didn't know yet. Maybe there was

still a chance he could ride this out until the end. Or at least until backup arrived.

Something occurred to Clay's crazed brain as Ape picked the tattoo gun back up and leaned in to etch something onto his chest. The asshole hadn't touched Clay's leather cut—the biker vest would have been the first thing to go if they knew for sure he was an undercover agent. Ape was killing time until Handles got back. Nothing more.

I'm not a dead man. Yet.

But if he wanted to convince his brothers he wasn't a cop, he needed to work a lot harder at being Jeremy "Indian" Greer instead of Clay Navarro. And, right now, Jeremy would be pissed as shit.

"The fuck, man?" he bellowed, elbowing one of the other men away, breaking free. The needle slid against his side, and Ape moved closer, pressed harder. He stank of stale booze and old sweat, piss, and blood.

"Think we don't know who you are?"

"Are you out of your mind, Ape?" Clay reached for his KA-BAR—of course Ape would have been cocky enough not to take the knife off him—his mind flying through the options. *Get the fuck out* was foremost among them. He threw a knee to Teller's groin, took a millisecond to enjoy the sick groan he got in response, and slid a hand into Ape's filthy hair before the other man could react. Jesus, it was so greasy, he almost couldn't get purchase. Finally, he managed and pulled the shithead into him.

"You got a death wish?" Clay snarled.

"Do you?" The man's breath was fetid, rotten, like his mouth had never seen the business end of a toothbrush. "We know who you are, you fucking traitor."

"Oh yeah?" He inhaled through his mouth, ignoring the sound of the others gathering, and set his blade beneath Ape's ear, right where the carotid would be in an actual human being. With Ape, who the fuck knew? The bastard probably had raw sewage running through his veins. "Why don't you tell me?"

Beside him, someone moved, and Clay pressed the knife in—just a couple of millimeters, but enough to make Ape gasp and throw up his hand. "No closer, man. He's gonna fuckin' kill me."

"You wanna tell me what's going on here, Ape?"

"Got a call."

Clay waited, the early fog of nerves giving way to the precise, clear-cut vision he got when adrenaline did its job. Energy and strength shimmered under the surface of his skin. God, he was born for this shit.

Clay asked, "Call from who?"

"You're hurtin' me, man," Ape moaned. Clay tightened his hold.

"Shut up," interrupted Clay. "What's this traitor bullshit?"

"Got an informant. Told us you're—"

Something hard and cold was pressed to his forehead. A gun.

"Put it down," said a voice right beside Clay's ear, dark and certain. Fuck. Of all the guys in the club, Jam was probably the deadliest. Ex-military, ex-con, and racist as fuck, Jam had wanted Clay's blood since the day he'd seen his too-dark skin. If Clay hadn't saved his life about a year ago, the psycho would never have voted him in. "Handles's on his way back. Told us to lock you up till he gets here."

"I'm not what you're thinkin', Jam."

"Not thinkin' a goddamned thing…*brother*."

For a good five seconds, Clay waited, the barrel of Jam's gun burning a hole in his temple and the blade of his KA-BAR ready to slice into Ape. Five seconds during which he pictured doing it—ending this man's life in exchange for his. It was almost worth it. Almost.

Except a whole goddamned operation depended on Clay getting out alive and giving his testimony in federal court. It depended on Handles going through with the huge deal that was set to happen in less than an hour—was probably happening right now, in fact. The only way Clay could ensure it went down as planned was by releasing Ape, because if he held on, he was a dead man.

Finally, he opened his hand and let Ape go. The big dude came after him then, of course. All brawn and no smarts, as usual, but with Jam's weapon leveled on him, Clay was powerless to counter. A meaty fist to the jaw, another to the stomach, and Clay waited, doubled over, for his breath to return.

Fisting Clay's hair in a parody of his earlier move, Ape leaned down and whispered into his ear, "You're a dead man, Indian." He spat a fat, sticky wad onto Clay's face, wiped his own, and backed up a couple of steps.

"Grab his phone and his weapons. I'll lock him in his room till Handles gets back," Jam threw over his shoulder before leading him away.

"Not a traitor, man," Clay tried in the hall.

"Shut your face" was all the answer he got as Jam brought him to his room. Jam pulled the key from the lock, shoved Clay in, and locked the door behind him.

Through the door, Clay heard him tell someone to shoot on sight.

Jesus, how the hell was he going to get out of this? He turned to look at the room and found it ransacked. Fine. They wouldn't have found anything incriminating anyway. Giving a hard exhale, he pulled the backup phone from his shoe and made the call.

"Speak to me," said Tyler.

"Wire not working? I asked for backup thirty minutes ago."

"We'll get someone in there soon as we can."

"They've got me in my room, under guard, while they wait for Handles. Did it happen? Did you guys get him?"

"No. He never showed."

"Fuck." Clay ran a hand over his face, surprised to see blood when he pulled it away.

"Bread there with you?" Tyler asked.

"Don't know where he is. Why?"

"If you were outed, stands to reason—"

Beyond the walls, something blew, rattling everything. The air in the room stilled for a millisecond in that strange vacuum of suspension that happened before everything exploded.

When the next wave of chaos came, it was in the form of shots fired outside the club walls, along with agonized screaming and shouts from all over. More gunfire in rapid bursts—club AK-47s, from the sound of it.

Clay put the phone back to his ear and yelled through the dense fog of noise, "The fuck's going on out there, Tyler?"

Silence from the phone. Everywhere else was mayhem.

There was nothing he could do. He was a sitting duck in here. He ran to the door and pounded. "Let me out of here. Let me the fuck out."

No answer from the other side. None from Tyler either when he redialed. Minutes passed, and the fighting continued.

Was that his team out there, forcing their way in? Christ, he hoped so.

The yelling drew closer, and his adrenaline ramped back up. He searched the room for something, anything, to fight with, and came up empty-handed.

When the door flew open to show Handles standing there, pointing that fucking Glock at his face, the only thing he could do was turn and dive.

Too late, though. Too fucking late.

The first bullet tore into his back, pinning him to the bed, and Clay Navarro was a dead man.

2

Five months later

THE DOOR TO THE CLINIC STOOD WIDE OPEN, INVITING IN A way Clay didn't entirely trust. It had all been too easy—the drive into town, locating the place, finding a parking space right out front. The few people he'd encountered on the sidewalk had been friendly, smiles so wide and open Clay developed an uncomfortable itch at the back of his neck—like the buildings were a facade and everybody actors, and he was the only one who wasn't in on it.

He was right not to trust, he decided when he reached the door, only to find a hand-written sign taped to the door. It read: CLOSED—No A/C.

Dead end.

Yeah, well—not good enough. They'd need a road-block to keep him out at this point. He tried the door and found it open.

Inside, the place was dark and stifling. There was a reception area, waiting room—what you'd expect from a doctor's office—all empty. He waited for his eyes to adjust and listened to what sounded like the scratch of pen on paper. He cleared his throat, and the woman hidden behind the reception desk jumped up like a jack-in-the-box.

"Afternoon," he said and walked farther inside, still squinting against the dark interior.

"Hi there," the woman said, her voice bright and warm. "Sorry to say we're closed. A/C's out, and we can't see patients in this heat."

"You the doc?"

She hesitated, looked to the side as if searching for reinforcements, then faced him head-on again. "I am."

"Any chance you could help me out?" He made his voice as light as possible, trying for friendly, even though it never seemed to work.

"Do you have an appointment? Cindy was supposed to call everyone and—"

He sighed. "No appointment. I hear you're the only place around that does what I need."

"Oh." She blinked, big eyes roving curiously over him from beneath blond hair that looked darker along her forehead. From sweat, he realized, before letting his gaze travel down the rest of her—not a large woman, but curvy in a way that he liked. Something about the heat, her flushed face, the way the fabric of her tank top clung to her belly, and her hair stuck to her slick neck woke him up. She swallowed, her vibe slightly nervous. That was no surprise, since he knew exactly how he looked: mirrored glasses; long-sleeved shirt; short, dark hair; ink creeping up the back of his neck. Staring at her like some goddamned creep.

"I don't mind the heat," he said, taking a step back. *See how nonthreatening I am?*

"Yes, but—"

"I'll pay."

"Cindy takes care of paperwork and invoicing, insurance and all that. I'm just not equipped to—"

"Could you just take a look, Doc? Please?" he cut in, unable to keep the emotion out. "I could use your help."

She hesitated another beat, then softened. "What do you need looked at?" she asked, voice gentler. Warmer.

Stomach a goddamned fireball of nerves, Clay reached up and pulled off his aviators. He stood there and let her see what Ape had done to him, what he'd have done himself for the sake of the mission—and waited.

∽❧∽

The man who stood in her reception area didn't *look* like he needed help. But then he removed the glasses, baring eyelids marred by ink, and George squinted over the desk at him. Taking off those lenses transformed him from a hard wall of masculinity into something more appealing, if just as intimidating.

"The eyelid tattoos?" she asked, moving around the desk.

"Yeah. Others too."

Up close, she felt the difference in their sizes more keenly. He was *huge*. "Lean down, please. Let me get a look." Lord, what had the man done to himself? "Ouch."

"Yeah." The word emerged on a half laugh, as if she'd surprised it out of him.

"You haven't had this long, have you?"

He shook his head, and George's brain filled with questions—some appropriate, some not. She went with the former.

"How long?"

"Few months."

"Any idea what was used?"

"Used?"

"What kind of ink?"

"No." He cleared his throat before going on. "Tattoo ink, I guess."

"They protect your eyes while they did this?" she asked, and he snorted in response.

"Not exactly."

"Did you consent to having your eyelids tattooed?" she asked, knowing this wasn't the sort of question you asked a man this big, this badass.

His eyes shot open, and George fought not to step back.

Oh dear God, his face.

"Have we met before?" she asked, wondering where she'd seen those eyes; the high, flat cheekbones; the perfectly shaped mouth outlined by dark stubble that made her fingers itch disconcertingly.

"Don't think so, Doc. I'd remember if we had."

George blushed at what she thought might be a compliment even as she continued to study him.

Those wide cheekbones, a sharp nose, and an obstinate-looking jaw made her think this wasn't a man who'd easily ask for help. Layered over his striking features were the ravages of life: those lids marred by black ink, a scar bisecting a cheek and disappearing into short, dark hair.

But most intimidating—and appealing—of all, were the darkest eyes she'd ever seen, perfectly in keeping with those dark looks. They were wide and hard. Just like the rest of him, she thought, with a hiccup of something sharp and hot and previously dormant in her abdomen.

"You have others?" she asked, ignoring the unwanted twinge with a quick step back.

She wouldn't allow herself even a glance as he unbuttoned his shirt and shrugged out of it. She saw the ink on his arms only peripherally, barely looked at how it contrasted so dramatically with the bright-white cotton of his T-shirt. He reached to take that off too, and she stopped him with a hand on his arm, immediately removed.

His golden skin was covered in tattoos, starting at his hands and crawling over solid shoulders to seep through his tee, dark enough to look like a design on the surface of the white cotton. He was wide, his arms long and strong-looking. She didn't say anything for a time, caught up in ink and muscles and the crisp-looking hair of his forearms.

He finally broke the silence. "You get it now?"

"I'm sorry?"

He fisted his hands, knuckles up. "Kinda urgent. Ma'am."

Ma'am. She hadn't been called that in ages. It made her feel like she'd been bad, chastened—the way she'd felt the one and only time she'd gotten pulled over for speeding.

"I see."

"Can we get started today? I'm on a bit of a deadline."

She considered it, her feelings divided. On the one hand, she had the perfectly normal urge to make him better, to help. But on the other hand was this overwhelming whoosh of something…uncomfortable, disconcerting.

Attraction? Was that it? It had been so long since George had felt anything even remotely physical toward a man that she wouldn't recognize it if it came in and bopped her on the head. Or punched her in the gut, more likely.

She shouldn't bring this man into the back with her. Shouldn't be able to picture him splayed across an examination table, shouldn't feel the need to get a closer look, inviting intimacies with just the two of them here—all alone in the clinic with this beast of a man. Not only that, but once most patients found out how much it cost to get their ink removed, as opposed to put on, they got angry.

Would this man get *angry*? She narrowed her eyes at him, trying hard to picture that.

"I don't think that's a good idea, Mr.—"

"Blane. Andrew Blane."

"Mr. Blane, I'm alone here as you can see and—"

"Look, Ms.…."

"Doctor. It's Dr. Hadley."

"Right. Doctor. I'll pay you. I'll pay whatever it takes. I've just got to get these taken off. The sooner the better."

"I understand it's urgent, Mr. Blane, but tattoo removal is a long process. It's never instantaneous. And, even so, I can't guarantee that you'll—"

"Please. *Please, Doctor.*" The words, even in that low, coffee-rich voice, reeked of desperation.

And George Hadley was a sucker for desperation.

She glanced again at his face and saw, besides the obvious, no real threat there. Yes, he was big, tattooed, and scarred, leaning on the counter, hands thick and capable-looking, but his vibe wasn't threatening.

With a sigh, she stood up and, as much as she could with their disparate heights, spoke directly to him. "You're an intimidating man, Mr. Blane. Forgive my hesitation."

"I won't hurt you."

"Is that a promise?" she asked in a voice too low to be hers.

A corner of his mouth quirked up slightly, and George had to look away from a smile that was positively annihilating.

"Yes, Doctor. I promise you're safe with me."

"All right, then, Mr. Blane. Let's get you taken care of. You can fill in the paperwork while I get things set up."

In an effort to recoup some sense of professionalism, she grabbed a new client packet and pushed through the swinging door, holding it open for him and then going back at the last minute to grab her lab coat off Cindy's chair.

~⚬~

Clay watched as the doctor moved around the room, setting things up quickly and efficiently. That was how she appeared—like someone who didn't waste extraneous time on things. That hair, short and blond, looked easy to maintain rather than stylish, and her face was devoid of makeup. All business, which he kind of liked. And fresh in a way he didn't think he'd ever seen in real

life. Fresh like a shampoo commercial or toothpaste.
Only real.

And the way she looked at him… When was the
last time someone had looked at him like that? Like he
was just a guy. A patient. A man. In the hospital, he'd
been an agent, under heavy guard, riddled with bullets,
fighting for his life. But even the nurses and docs who
knew exactly why he was there gave him a wide berth.
Because of how he looked.

Bullshit. It wasn't his looks; it was his demeanor. No
matter where you came from, spending every waking
hour as a dirty-ass biker rubbed off on you eventually.
But this woman—

With a loud crack, the doctor pulled one of those
sheets of paper over the exam table and tore it, breaking through his thoughts, then washed her hands at a
sink before settling onto a stool and rolling it over to
his side.

Even with those beads of sweat collecting along her
hairline, she looked smart and in control. Not the kind of
chick who'd ever touch him under normal circumstances.

"Okay," she said, gathering the papers in front of her
like a shield. "I'll have the receptionist get anything we
miss here today. She can also deal with payment next
time you come in."

"Don't have insurance," he said, thankful but surprised she'd actually agreed to take him in, alone like
this. "Filled those papers in, but if we could…you know,
keep this on the down low, I'd be grateful."

"Oh." Her eyes flew up to his, full of concern. "Are
you in trouble?"

"I can pay. Just rather keep this quiet." He swallowed,

reading her as too much of a straight shooter to go for it. "If you don't mind."

After a quick scan of his body, she looked at him again, everything about her serious. Whatever she saw must have decided her, because she grabbed the papers he'd just spent five minutes filling out with bullshit and ripped them in half before throwing them into the trash. Clay's brows lifted in surprise. Maybe not quite the Goody Two-Shoes he'd taken her for.

"Okay, Mr. Blane. Let's see what we're working with here." Her eyes ran up his arms. She was clinical now, in charge. "You want all of these removed?"

"No, ma'am. I'm keeping the sleeves." He indicated his face. "But I could use some help with these."

"Right. The eyes." She slipped on a pair of horn-rimmed glasses—sexy ones that framed her eyes, spotlighted the bright-green irises that he only now noticed—and stood, leaning in to stare at the ink on his eyelids. The neckline of her lab coat sagged enough for him to catch a glimpse of the skimpy tank top beneath. He ignored it, instead concentrating on her face, a perfect distraction from thoughts of the two deadly numbers etched onto his lids.

"It's a relief you only want a few of these gone. You've got so much ink on those arms, we'd be here for years." One small, white hand reached out, cupped the side of his face, and pulled at his skin. Firm and painfully gentle.

Trying not to breathe her in, Clay averted his gaze. None of the nurses in the hospital had looked at him with this much kindness. It made his throat hurt.

"These are quite crudely done."

"Ya think?"

She glanced at him, eyes wide with surprise, and he pulled it back. No point offending the person he'd come to for help. Why was he being an asshole?

Because she's pretty and nice, and I'm not used to that.

"Sorry. So, these too." He held up his hands, baring knuckles that had seen better days—knuckles that itched with the ink of his enemies. Ink that couldn't disappear fast enough, as far as he was concerned. One hand went to his neck. "This one and a few more."

"Good. Black is good. And prison-style tattoos like this are generally easier to get rid of than professional work, so...I know it might not feel that way, but it's actually a positive." She smiled, cleared her throat, met his eyes, and held them. "I work with a lot of people who've been through some...hard times, Mr. Blane. And you...are you okay?"

"What? Yeah. Great," he lied.

"I don't want to pry, but if you're in trouble... If you need help at all—" Her hand landed on his arm, soft and comforting, and something tightened in his throat before he shook it off.

"I'm fine."

There were a couple of beats of quiet breathing as her eyes searched his. She was close to him now, lips compressed in a straight, serious line, and he could feel her wondering. Jesus, this was a mistake. He should go, before she freaked out and called the cops, who'd fuck everything up. "Where else, Mr. Blane?"

She sat back down and rolled a couple of feet away. When he caught her eye, expecting judgment, he was surprised to find more of that unbearable empathy.

In response, Clay stood up and pulled off his wife beater, looked straight ahead, and braced himself for the real judgment.

~∞~

Before she could stop it, a startled *oh* escaped George's mouth.

He was beautiful. Beautiful but tragic, his skin a patchwork of scars, old and fresh alike, intersected by ink that ran the gamut from decorative to distressing. After a few seconds, she felt the awkward imbalance of their positions and stood, which still put her only about chest high.

His was a chest unlike any she'd had the pleasure of seeing. Beyond the obvious—the ink and the damage— his shape appealed on a level her brain couldn't even begin to understand, but her body seemed quite eager to explore. She eyed his pectorals, curved and strong-looking, solid and sprinkled with a smattering of hair, and that vertical indentation in the middle, just begging a women to slide her nose in there, to run it up to a finely delineated set of clavicles, where she knew he'd smell like man, and down to the apex of a rib cage and belly carved in bone and muscle and sinew. She wondered how he'd gotten all that strength and unconsciously lifted a hand to touch…

With a start, George pulled herself back to the room, to her job, *to her livelihood, for God's sake*, and felt her face go hot.

Dear God, my ovaries are taking over.

Take George's professional trappings away from her—things like paper gowns and background music and attending nurses—and you might as well throw her into a barnyard or a zoo or whatever uncivilized place her overheated brain had escaped to.

This is a patient, she firmly reminded herself.

Not a man. *A patient*.

She cleared her throat, pushed her glasses farther up her nose, and leaned in. Still too close, too much. She thought she could smell him. Probably his deodorant, although it was more animal than chemical—very light, but inevitable in the stifling heat—and a hint of something less healthy. Alcohol?

"Please take a seat on the table, Mr. Blane." There, that would give her some much-needed distance. Doctor, meet patient. She waited as he stepped up effortlessly and settled himself with a crinkle of paper, perfect muscles shifting under tragic skin.

Burns and battle scars. Even the tattoos.

Most weren't professionally done, except for the arms and one word she could see, curved at the top of his chest in scrolled lettering that skimmed his collarbones. *Mercy*, an oddly poignant blazon fluttering above the mess beneath.

"This one looks professional," she said, reaching out toward the letters before stopping herself, her finger almost close enough to touch the crisp-looking hair. She'd have to touch him eventually, she knew. But better to do it with gloves on, laser in hand.

"That stays."

Good, she thought, with the strangest sense of letting go inside. Just a tiny slide into relief that the man wasn't all blades and bared teeth.

"And like I said, I'm keeping the sleeves. They're…

mine. Except for the clock." He touched his wrist. "We can get rid of that."

His hand moved to his chest, and he rubbed himself there. The move seemed unconscious, mesmerizing, the sound of his hand rasping over hair loud in the quiet room.

Mercy. What a strange banner for a man who looked like he'd been spared nothing.

"Got it. Keep *Mercy* and the arms," she said with an attempt at a smile. She eyed those arms, where death and destruction appeared to play the starring role. A skull, covered in some kind of cowl with a scythe and what looked like oversize earrings, took up his right forearm. Higher, from shoulder to elbow, leered a mask, Mayan or Inca, and perfectly in keeping with his chiseled face. The other arm had darker imagery: a kilted man with a sword, wreaking havoc on what looked like a big wolf. A griffon sat, claws sharp and deadly, and around all of the violence, rooted in the clear-cut line of his wrist, was a complicated design made up of knots and what she thought were Celtic symbols. Crowning it all, an over-size cross covered his entire shoulder, overflowing into the ink on his chest and back, connecting the *Mercy* in front to his back.

"Yes, ma'am."

Doctor, she almost wanted to correct him, because anything was better than *ma'am*. It sounded old, dried-up, sexless, which, on second thought, was probably more than appropriate. Although she didn't feel sexless right now.

Christ, not at all.

For each tattoo, she went through her usual questions:

How long ago had he gotten it? Had it faded? Was it professional? What kind of ink was used?

He didn't know about the ink for two of them—the eyelids and knuckles—which wasn't good. She'd had people come in with tattoos made from soot—a lot of those ex-cons—but his didn't look quite so crude. People would use anything, anything at all, on themselves and each other. She'd once had a patient whose "ink" had been made from melted car tires. The memory made her shiver.

George glanced up to find him looking at her, his attention intimidating in its focus.

She ignored it. Back to his body.

Around his neck curved a black spiderweb, its lines thin and delicate, unlike the heavier areas where no ink had been spared.

"This should be faster than some of the others. The black and the…" She leaned in. "Huh. It looks sketched in. Very light. Interesting how shallow this one is. Looks professional." Which was *weird* for a prison tattoo. She'd seen spiderwebs like this before, and they were all prison tattoos.

He nodded, didn't appear surprised in the least, and quirked that eyebrow again—his version of a smile. "Good eye, Doc."

"And the rest? You want those gone?"

"All of 'em."

"I'm afraid it's going to hurt."

"Don't mind."

Across his body, front to back, her gaze traveled, taking in every pit, every crag, every heartbreaking curve. What a tragic story—she'd seen bits and pieces of ones like it, but this—

Her eyes landed on a swath of discolored flesh marring his side—a burn, if she wasn't mistaken—an elongated triangle, curved at the top like an—

"Oh no," she gasped before her hand flew to her mouth to cover it. An iron. He'd been burned with an iron, the skin melted. "Who did this to you, Mr. Blane?"

When he didn't answer, she went on, cowed and embarrassed at her outburst. She should be professional, should keep her shock to herself. Lord, if she couldn't control herself enough to do that, she shouldn't be seeing patients at all, should she?

Okay. Slow down, concentrate. In an attempt to control her breathing, to rein in her pulse, she closed her eyes.

Now. Open, professional, serene.

She continued cataloging the man's sufferings. On his back were two perfectly round scars. *Don't react. Be a doctor.* She kept her voice calm, steady when she said, "You've been shot." *In the back.* "Are you safe now, Mr. Blane?"

"Yes."

"Do you need help? There are people who—"

"I'm fine," he interrupted, his voice harsh, the subtext screaming that she'd better let it rest.

After a few beats, she continued her perusal. An *S*, as intricate as the letters on his chest, but not nearly as dark, followed by a scrolled *M* along his spine and a *C* on his right shoulder blade, with a complicated set of symbols in between—a triangle, arrows, an eagle, a river. A skull. The whole thing making up a deadly coat of arms.

"They really laid it on here." Her hand skimmed the picture, gently, barely touching. With a shake of her head, she went on. "I'll be honest with you. This is a lot of ink. It's going to take months, with gaps in between to heal. And it's going to hurt. This red here, that's not good. Red's a lot harder to get rid of. The particles don't break down as easily and—"

"How long?"

"Several sessions, definitely. A few months, certainly. I would venture to say close to a year. Possibly longer." She'd seen tattoos take ages to fade. And some…some never went away. "There'll almost always be remnants, Mr. Blane. I just need to make sure you understand that. Your skin's never going back to how it looked before."

He nodded and sighed, that big back curving slightly, as if in defeat. Were he a woman, she'd put a hand on his shoulder, comfort him, but this man… No. Better keep that to a minimum.

"I've got a couple farther…uh…farther south." One wide, ink-blackened hand gestured vaguely to his legs, and she smiled nervously, nodding as if this were all just par for the course. As if she hosted half-naked bad boys in her office every day.

"Yes, well. How about we start with one session whenever we can fit you in, and we'll—"

"Start now."

"Oh. No. There's prep that needs to be done. We need to numb you for big surfaces like this. And then when you come in, we'll also ice you down. For the pain."

"Doesn't matter." He swallowed, his Adam's apple bobbing visibly, and she could feel his nerves or fear or whatever that edge was. "Clock's ticking, Doc." His expression grew impossibly harder: jaw tight, lips curving down into a sharp, pained sneer. "Just…" One of those big, rough-looking hands skimmed his chest. "At least my face and knuckles. Here too. Whatever a suit can't cover up to start with, but—"

That surprised her. "A suit?" she asked before she could hold the question in.

He gave a tight smile, one brow arched high. "Yeah. Can't picture that, huh?"

"Oh, no, that's not what—"

"I know what you meant, Doctor." He caught her eye, held it, intimidating, but also human behind the markings. "Not offended."

"Look." She glanced at her watch, trying not to think of the parody of a timepiece etched into his wrist. "It's late on a holiday weekend and—"

"I don't need pain meds. I can do this. And I know you got family waiting. But maybe you could just…" He looked away before nodding once and turning back to her with a harshly expelled breath. "You're right. Not the best time. I'll let you get back to your life." He stood, swiftly and smoothly, and George couldn't help but stare at the mess of his skin, contrasted with the perfection of his body—the mystery of the man within.

All sorts of bodies came through her clinic, young and old, tight and saggy. She'd examined some whose scars were hidden and others whose damage was obvious. There'd been babies, fresh and new and already marred for life, and yes, there were sometimes men she admired. Next door, for God's sake, was a plethora of hard bodies to choose from. The MMA school overflowed with them—men who lifted and punched and fought and worked, but this…this was masculinity in its purest form. This man didn't primp in the mornings or even look in the mirror. He got up, he washed, he walked out the door. Only there wasn't a door in her musings. There was nothing but the great outdoors, savage and unkempt, or the mouth to a cave.

Hard and dark, his hair almost black, with brows that arrowed straight out from three deep frown lines. And his body—she stared, caught up in the *realness* of this man, which was the oddest thought, as if the rest of her patients were somehow *less* than this one. This wasn't just another epidermis to examine. This was muscle, undeniable in its curves and hollows. And even the damage was heartbreakingly appealing, layered as it was on top of that firm flesh, his energy palpable, tensile strength, so real that she could almost feel him vibrate with it.

Beneath her gaze, under the harsh, white light, she could have sworn his nipples hardened, and viscerally, her body felt it, reacted as if separate from her doctor's brain.

Keep it in your pants, Hadley! The man is probably dangerous, possibly in trouble, and, if nothing else, completely inadvisable.

Out of guilt, as if to make up for her rogue brain or overactive hormones or whatever the hell was pushing her to skim the line between brazen and professional, she put a hand up to stop him.

"Fine. We'll do your knuckles and your eyes and see how it goes from there. Your face is… You'll need injections and metal eye shields. Would you like something to drink? Water or tea?"

"Tea?" he asked, that brow up again, and she felt herself flush.

Right. Not a man who drank tea.

"All right, well, I'll need to numb your lids first."

"No numbing."

"It'll be painful, Mr. Blane. Like being splashed with hot bacon grease." *I know firsthand*, she almost added but decided to keep that detail to herself. "And if you accidentally open your eyes, it's… Look, I don't recomm—"

"No numbing," he repeated firmly.

"Okay, then. But I'll have to insert eye shields. They're like big metal contact lenses."

"Sounds sexy." His voice was low with what might have been humor—an apology, perhaps, for his abrupt words before.

George's eyes flew to his to find him watching her, and rather than dwell on the way his gaze affected her, she looked quickly away and busied herself by collecting supplies. If nothing else, she could at least pretend to act professional.

She was, after all, a doctor.

3

JESUS CHRIST, THE DOC WASN'T KIDDING. THIS SHIT HURTS.

Like poison, the Sultan ink hurt worse going out than it had being put on. There'd been other shit happening on the day Ape had gotten him, of course. Stuff like adrenaline. Fear too. Fear had been a distraction. Ape's whispered words rushed back to him: *I'll pop your fuckin' eyeball.* He was still shocked the asshole hadn't blinded him.

He'd been the traitor, after all. He'd deserved it in the eyes of the Sultans.

Here, Clay could feel the ink splitting apart with every painful pass of the laser, flooding his bloodstream, and one day soon, leaving him forever. Months. Months of this treatment, she'd said. It couldn't happen fast enough.

Besides, what was a little more pain? It didn't bother him. In fact, the burn helped center him.

A good thing, considering the goddamned racket the machine made. A fuck-ton of noise for such a small piece of technology. He eyed the big red Emergency Stop button on the machine's console, wondering about the circumstances that might lead to pressing it. It let out these rhythmic beeps and zapping sounds that brought him right back to his room in the clubhouse, where he'd been caught like a rat. That feeling of being trapped and useless and alone, with the sound of gunshots tearing through the place. It was all he could do not to get up and bust the hell outta here. Or, more likely, cover his ears and curl into the fetal position, right there on the paper-covered table. He shut his eyes, tight, remembering Handles's face just before that first bullet tore into his back. It was that face he saw over and over again. That look that told Clay the man wasn't there to protect himself or his brothers. No, this was an execution. Pure vengeance. For taking them all in. For making them believe he was one of them. For making Handles like him, even love him, maybe, like a son.

But the woman—Dr. Georgette Hadley—kept Clay from losing himself in memory with calm, gentle touches. She moved his hand into place, held his body where it was, and kept his mind right there, in the room. Mostly.

He'd been fighting this thing for a while now, this compulsion to disappear into his head. Had fought it in the months at the hospital and the single week at home before they'd torched his place. He'd fought it while talking to that lawyer, Hecker.

Get that shit off your face, Navarro, the assistant U.S. attorney had said at their last meeting. *You've got seven months to prep, and all you've gotta do is get your goddamned story straight, stay the hell outta sight, and get rid of the ink. I don't wanna see a hint of that shit in the courtroom, you got it?* At Clay's resentful nod, the suit had headed to the conference room door before turning around and barking his last order. *And for God's sake, stop talking like a fucking biker.*

I am *a biker*, he'd thought at the time. Although he didn't feel quite so much like one without his chopper thrumming between his legs.

The laser skimmed over the knuckle of Clay's middle finger, and he held back a groan, forcing his body to stay seated. Not an easy task, despite his claims of immunity to pain.

Not immune. He just knew there were worse things in life than physical suffering.

"Need a break?" the doctor asked, focusing the numbing blast of cool air on his hand.

"No," he managed. "Don't stop." *I'll keep it together.*

"I've got the levels low for today. But it's still going to burn. That's inevitable. You'll blister before scabbing up. And I can't guarantee you won't scar, especially with the hands. We wash them and work with them. They're the most painful, usually. Well, besides those eyelids. I don't know what kind of work you do, but it could be a handicap. At least temporarily. Let me know if you need a note or—"

"Off the books, Doc."

"Right."

Two more knuckles, then the clock face on his wrist before she stopped and leaned over to shut down the machine. Silence, as loud as the buzzing had been, engulfed the room.

"You got good aim," he said.

"Excuse me?"

"You never miss your mark."

Although he couldn't see her eyes behind the dark,

protective glasses they both wore, he noted how her brows lowered briefly before they lifted, understanding dawning. "Oh, you mean the laser? No, no. This is an Nd:YAG laser. It follows the ink. Kind of…ah…hunts it down."

"So what happens if you accidentally get yourself?"

"Nothing," she said with a smile, tugging off her glasses and revealing those eyes again. "And the treatment gets easier as we go. The less ink you have, the less pain. Next time, it won't hurt as much."

"Good deal," he said before she tightened her lips in a smile and moved on to his face—the numbers on his lids that weighed on him the most, that made him a target, that meant he could no longer do his job.

The ink he hadn't agreed to.

"How's it feel?"

The air was thick with the stench of singed hair and maybe burning flesh too. He swallowed and stretched out his fingers. "Burns, I guess." Understatement of the year. But better than Ape doing it. Anything was better than Ape with his tattoo machine.

"Okay. Let's do the eyes now, Mr. Blane."

"Sounds good."

"This is dangerous. And without the anesthesia, it won't be easy."

"I get that, Doc. But I was told you're the only one around who'll do the eyes."

"That's true."

"It's why I came to you," he said with a big, fake grin. Anything to put them on even footing. What was it about this woman that made him so off-kilter?

"Good." Her smile echoed his, only it looked real. It shamed him with its warmth.

When the doctor slid the eye shield things in, they were uncomfortable and almost impossible not to blink out. His eyeballs felt strange—thick and paralyzed and blind. Worst of all, it reminded him of corpses, those cotton balls morticians slid under the lids to make the eyes look full and alive again.

Full and alive. With a detached, self-deprecating sort of humor, he wondered how that would feel.

In the short time it took to do the eyelids, the man on George's examination table transformed...or went somewhere. She could see the moment it happened. The moment his soul left his body, she thought, before realizing how absolutely odd that was. He wasn't dead after all. He was just...gone. Narcoleptic, perhaps? She'd gone to school with a man who suffered from that.

Narcoleptic or not, she couldn't imagine falling asleep mid-treatment. She'd undergone it herself and knew exactly how painful that laser could be. And on the eyelid... Not something she could imagine sitting through without proper numbing.

After finishing up, George removed the eye shields and applied a thick layer of petroleum jelly to his eyes and hands, up to his wrists. After a brief hesitation, she cleaned up around him, ignoring the strange brew of feelings that had replaced her initial wave of fear: curiosity, empathy, and attraction that worked away inside of her as she wondered how on earth she was going to get this big, slumbering man out of her clinic.

Finally, she laid a palm to the warm flesh of his shoulder with some notion that she'd shake him awake.

Fast and hard, his hand gripped hers, squeezed, held her there, and his eyes opened, cold and unfocused but violent. Oh, she could *feel* the violence in that hard, shaking grasp, see it in those cloudy eyes.

For a split second, she froze, eyes glued to his unseeing ones, adrenaline coursing through her.

"What the fu—"

Her squeak interrupted that no-nonsense snarl, brought his hard gaze to hers, and as she watched, the man came back, his return as clear as his leaving had been.

His eyes took a quick inventory of the room before landing on his hand trapping hers. Finally, his hold loosened, his confusion disappeared.

"I…I'm sorry I frightened you. I'll give you a minute to…" She let her words trail off, extricating her hand from his before rushing out of the room, her heart too big for her chest, her skin hot where he'd squeezed her. What if he hadn't let go? A man like that—so big and rough, his body packed full of muscle—could do whatever he wanted to someone like George. What had she been thinking coming back here alone with him? She stopped in the hall and leaned against the wall, working to catch her breath.

He could have hurt her badly. He hadn't looked like someone who wanted to hurt her, though. More desperate, like that initial instinctive response that made dogs or bears attack at the first hint of a threat. What kind of life made a man react like that?

By the time he emerged, Andrew Blane appeared to have recovered.

"I'm sorry" was all he said before she led him out to the reception area, turning lights off as she went.

"You'll need petroleum jelly. Thick layers, reapplied often. Like I said, it'll blister and then scab, but whatever you do, don't pick at it. You don't want to scar."

"Right. Don't need any more of those."

"For the…" She swallowed, remembering the skin of his back. "For the rest, I recommend that patients purchase a pack of cheap, breathable cotton T-shirts, because you'll need the jelly all over, and you don't want to ruin your clothes."

Night had almost descended when they finally made it outside, Andrew Blane holding the front door open for her and waiting as she locked it behind them.

"Have to pay you," he said.

"No need."

"No way, Doc. You've gotta let me pay for your services. I'm not a—"

"You wanted this off the books?" she cut through.

"Yes, ma'am."

"If you're off the books, then you're pro bono, which means—"

"On the books, then. I'm not a charity case."

"Look, Mr. Blane, I can't accept money from you and not include it in my accounting. It's just not ethical."

He looked to the side, shook his head, and shut his eyes hard on a sigh. "I appreciate it, Doctor. And I apologize for scaring you earlier."

"You didn't—"

"You were a woman alone and I pushed you to take care of me. I appreciate that."

"You're welcome, Mr. Blane. Look, if there's anything you need, anything else I can do…"

"Just need the tats gone."

"That I can do."

"That's it."

She wanted to argue, wanted to ask him if he had a place to stay, give him dinner, make sure he was okay, but he clearly wasn't the sort of man who accepted help. Besides, he was big and he could be frightening—she shouldn't *want* to be around him, no matter how attractive he might be.

"So, you'd like to come in again, I imagine?" she forced herself to ask.

"Yes, ma'am."

"Why don't you call the office on Monday, and Cindy can—" She stopped herself, remembering. "Actually... we need to get you in after hours, don't we?" And something about that idea had her pulse picking up.

"Whatever you can give me," he said, sounding so eager that she had to flush. *What on earth is wrong with me?* "The sooner the better."

"Monday?" she offered. "Five p.m.?" She pictured Mrs. Venable running into him in the waiting room and amended her offer. "Actually, make that closer to six." She'd do paperwork while she waited. "Oh. Wait." She pulled out a card and found a pen, then scribbled her cell on it. "I give my cell to after-hours patients. It's easier to call me directly, once the answering service kicks in."

"Monday. Great." He took the card, and when he reached out with his other hand, she thought he meant to grab her arm. The few seconds he waited were awkward before she finally understood.

Gently, avoiding his gel-covered knuckles, she clasped it. Warm and firm around hers, his grip reminded her of why she did this, why she'd gone into medicine, why she offered these services: to help people.

And more than almost anybody she'd ever treated, George knew this man was in trouble.

The other thing she felt, the shimmer of excitement, she chose to ignore.

∼୧∼

Clay watched the doctor's Subaru disappear down Main Street. He was tempted to follow her, which made no sense whatsoever. Then he dug deeper and recognized the urge: protectiveness. Curiosity. Maybe a little something else thrown into the mix.

Instead of tailing her, he slid her business card into his pocket and swung his rental car out of its parking spot and onto the road. Traffic was nonexistent here, but what vehicles he saw were mostly trucks, dusty and old. And everyone went slow. Man, he couldn't imagine a life where you didn't run around all the time, where nobody was in a hurry, and—

From somewhere close by came the low thrum of a motorcycle, and every hair on Clay's body pricked up in response. Oh, Christ, they'd found him—the MC members that had gotten away. How could they have found him when he hadn't even known where he was headed?

A shitty Tempo pulled out in front of him, yanking him from his rising panic before cutting him off. He turned the wheel and came to a grinding halt on the side of the road as the asshole drove away in a loud, aggressive burst of exhaust. With an effort, he battled the urge to take off after them. Not his problem, not his business. And also not the best way to handle the stress of these…

episodes or whatever they were. Because that's what this was, right? Just him getting lost in his head again.

He sucked in a long, painful breath and waited just to be sure. No Harley. No sound of bikes at all. Just the ridiculous grind of the Tempo's engine, still audible in an otherwise quiet country night.

It was nice to know there were tweakers everywhere, even in this perfectly sleepy town. Felt right at home.

Now he just needed to find a place to crash—preferably far from everyone else, because he didn't think he could stand too many more wakeful nights waiting for another bike to rumble toward him.

Even before he'd left Baltimore, he'd had this urge to disappear, alone—like some fucking hermit—into the wild. Not, he thought looking around, to a painfully quaint, lost town like this, but to someplace more savage.

Yeah, well, Alaska was a bit far, so the wilds of Virginia would have to do.

Crisscrossing the small downtown area, he thought about the other option he'd been given—WITSEC—and the trapped feeling he'd had ever since he'd awakened to find himself heavy and unmoving in that hospital bed.

Three shots, one to the leg and two to the back, the doctors had told him when he'd been lucid enough to understand. *Lucky to be alive*, they'd said over and over and over. Tyler had said the same thing when he'd come to visit. Then Hecker, that lawyer, and the special agent in charge, McGovern, had woven in and out of his spotty memory. Tyler had brought his wife, Jayda, with their kids, lugging huge bouquets of flowers. Even McGovern had brought him flowers, which was weird, getting flowers from your boss. Fucking flowers and goddamned teddy bears, every time he'd pulled himself out of the drug-induced stupor, as if all that crap was supposed to cheer him up. He'd lain there, incapacitated, as the Sultans were indicted, one by one—almost two dozen in all.

But more were out there—guys like Jam and monsters like Ape, who'd fallen off the map before the Feds could catch up with them.

Driving around the deserted town, Clay thought of all the other places he could have gone. Places like Richmond or DC. But he couldn't go anywhere he'd worked. At this point, there was hardly a place in the eastern United States where he could disappear.

Jesus, where were the goddamned motels?

Just his luck to have landed in a tiny nothing of a town with a library the size of Tyler Olson's three-car garage, a skin clinic, and possibly no motel? Anxiety tightened his chest as he wondered what the hell he'd do without a place to stay. Sleep outdoors, under the stars. No walls, no bed. No protection.

It wasn't until he turned off the main drag, with its antique shops, frilly B&Bs, and fancy coffee places, into a shittier area, that Clay started to breathe again. There, a sputtering neon motel sign advertised vacancies, its blue jarring against the lush green backdrop of the sleepy mountain town.

In his room, there was almost nothing to unpack, since his belongings had been destroyed in yesterday's fire. Not that he'd acquired much in the manner of personal junk over the past few years. Just his bike, which the Sultans had also destroyed in a big, final fuck you. Bastards knew how he felt about his bike.

Just one more lesson in letting go, wasn't it? Now, his entire existence was pared down to the wad of cash he'd withdrawn before leaving Baltimore, toiletries, underwear, and a bottle or two to help him get through the night. That and the rental car he'd have to return at some point. And, of course, the thick sheaf of papers he'd grabbed at the office before leaving town. A bunch of legal shit he'd need to look at before heading to court.

Twisting open the first bottle of vodka, he went to the window, pulled back the curtain, and looked out at the blue-washed parking lot. He should eat, but he wasn't hungry. He glanced back at the papers and thought about going through them.

Fuck that. He took in a painful slug of vodka and thought about the day he'd first walked into the Sultans' watering hole, sporting his freshly inked prison tats— the clock and spider web. They'd ignored him at first, had treated him like nothing, until he'd brought them some valuable intel on a rival club's drug shipment. They'd accepted him after that, had taken him on as a prospect, treated him like one of their own.

Just one big happy family, he thought, missing them and hating them and wondering how the hell he'd pass as regular Joe Citizen down here in Rednecksville, Virginia.

He took another swig and threw another glance at the stupid legal brief.

Get your goddamned story straight, that lawyer, Hecker, had said, which almost made Clay laugh, because every single thing that had happened since the first day he'd ridden his Harley into Naglestown, Maryland, was imprinted on his brain, as indelibly as their club emblem was emblazoned on his back.

Not that indelible, he realized with a jolt of surprise. The perfectly pristine Dr. Hadley would be removing all traces of the Sultans from Clay's back and face and hands. Despite the pain involved, it was good to have something to look forward to. With his third pull of booze, he squinted out at the parking lot and let his vision blur, trying to get back that image he'd conjured of the woman wearing next to nothing. Instead, his weird-ass mind fixated on the lab coat, the horn-rimmed glasses, and the way those green eyes had looked past all the ink to the person beneath. He remembered the feel of her hand on his skin, so careful, as if he were fragile, and he felt something other than empty. Something other than the pain in his back and the tweak of his thigh and the burn of his eyes and knuckles.

He felt alive, unexpectedly, after all these months—even years—of surviving. And it was almost too much to bear.

4

INDEPENDENCE DAY DAWNED HOT AND HUMID, LIKE EVERY other day in recent memory. And like every other morning, George rose, showered, and went down to the kitchen, where Leonard tried his best to herd her toward the food bowl. She doled out a quarter cup of pellets with a metallic rattle, set a pan of water to boil, slid her feet into her rubber boots, and tromped straight out back to the henhouse. Feathers flew at her arrival—her ladies just as excited to see her as the cat had been. Feed and caresses dispensed in a flurry of clucking, she returned to the house just in time to drop two fresh eggs into the water and slice a miniature battalion of perfectly straight soldiers to dip into the yolks in the three minutes it took to soft boil them.

These rituals were the bones of George's life. No, perhaps not the bones, but the ligaments, holding the bones of work and sleep together.

Today, sparks of something else peppered what would otherwise have been a normal morning. A heaviness in her belly, a shortness of breath. It felt like excitement, but she couldn't pinpoint its origin.

Since it was Saturday, she packed up a basket with eggs, veggies from her garden, and quiches she'd baked earlier in the week. After a quick stop at the gas station, George made her way to her parents-in-law's home—a brick rancher in one of Blackwood's older, leafier neighborhoods.

The door opened before she'd made it to the stoop.

"Georgette, darling!" Bonnie Hadley was not her mother, strictly speaking, but the closest she still had to one. As usual, the woman hugged her hard, and George soaked it up.

"How are you, Bonnie?"

"Good, good!"

"And Jim?"

"Oh, you know, he's the same."

"But not worse?"

"No, darling, not worse. He's in the back, weeding."

"Uh-oh."

"We're doing okay today. I managed to stop him from pulling out most of my hostas."

"*Phew*. Lucky." George walked straight to the kitchen—eyes avoiding the school portraits and family pictures on the walls. What was essentially a shrine to their son—her wedding photo at the center of it. "I made a bunch of quiches to freeze this week and thought you might like some," she said, forcing her voice to be breezy and light.

"Oh, you didn't have to do that."

"They're left over from a dinner party," she lied. George hadn't seen the inside of a dinner party in a decade. "And the trout's from the fish man at the market. Here, I'll put this stuff away."

"Nonsense," said Bonnie. "Leave that. I can do that anytime. Come out back and say hello to Jim. He'll be so glad to see you." That, George knew, probably wasn't true. The last few Saturdays, he hadn't known who she was. George gulped back a wave of sadness and pushed her way back out into the blinding sunlight, wishing herself somewhere else.

"Jim," said Bonnie, her voice loud and artificially bright. "It's Georgette, here to visit!"

"Mmm?" came her father-in-law's voice from somewhere beyond the edge of the blue-painted deck. The women exchanged a look and descended the stairs to find the tall man digging a hole in the dirt, up against the house. His white button-down shirt was filthy, as was his face, and George had to swallow hard to keep the melancholy at bay. Tears, she knew from experience, served no purpose but to sow more tears. If she started now, she'd never stop. Best to just get things done here and head back home. Or to work. Work would be perfect.

"Hello, Jim!"

He paused, glanced at his wife for confirmation, and then rose, his smile unsure.

"Oh, oh. Hello, hello," he said. "Hello, hello."

After an awkward moment where no one spoke, George said, "I'll just…get the gas from my car and mow the lawn now, Jim. If that's okay with you."

He gave a vague sort of nod, so she gassed up the mower, got it going on the third try, and started cutting the grass.

A couple rows in, the hum of the motor dulled her conscious thoughts, and George let her mind wander.

Flashes of memory—bronze skin, black lines, burn marks, vestiges of pain scattered across a body so beautiful she could cry. An unexpected shiver of excitement, another flash of sharply pebbled nipples, her own hardening sympathetically, warmth in her abdomen a pleasant weight and then… Oh crap. She was wet. Actually wet, thinking about the stranger—her patient, for God's sake.

George stilled, lifted her shirt, and mopped her brow, shutting her eyes hard and pulling in a ragged breath. *Stop it. He needs help, not…whatever the hell this is.*

For the next hour, she battled her stubborn subconscious, shutting it down every time it fed her another drop of him, another memory, a smell, a shiver.

An hour later, sweaty and grass-covered in the frigid living room, George accepted the usual lemonade and sat beside her mother-in-law on the sofa, feeling caught and guilty in the worst possible way.

"You sure you don't want me to fire up the grill?" George said. "It's the Fourth of July, after all. We should celebra—"

"No, no. It's too much for Jim. Besides, didn't you say you'd been invited to a party this afternoon?"

Oh, right. A party. A fresh wave of dread rolled up, and George wondered, not for the first time, how upset Uma would be if she canceled. "You're right," she said, voice small.

"So, how are…*things*?" the older woman asked, keeping it vague, but her eyes so bright and excited, she could only be referring to one thing.

George swallowed. None of this was normal. It wasn't normal to be a widow at her age. It wasn't normal to be caretaker for your in-laws—though she'd never begrudge them that responsibility—and it most certainly wasn't normal to use your dead husband's sperm to try to get pregnant. "Good. Good. The hormones seem to have…kicked in."

"Yes?"

"I'm feeling…something."

"So, you'll be…" *Ovulating* was the word Bonnie wouldn't say. And neither would George—not with her mother-in-law. She glanced at the door. How soon could she get out of here?

"Soon, I think, Bonnie. Soon."

"That's… It's wonderful, George. You truly deserve this. You've wanted a baby for so long and—"

"Yes. Yes, I have. Thank you, Bonnie. Thank you for supporting me."

"Of course, dear. Of course." Bonnie's eyes filled with tears.

Though George wanted to look away, she forced herself to reach out and put her hand over the other woman's frail, knobby one, the papery skin dry to the touch. How many times had she held this hand? Certainly more often than she'd held her husband's. "Have you been using the cream I brought you last week? You really should—"

"Oh, do you know, I forgot about it? I'll have to go find where I've put it. I don't want you to think that I—"

"It's okay, Bonnie. It's okay," George said, clasping the woman's hand more tightly and wondering how soon she could escape.

⌇⌇⌇

Clay's eyes flew open, but he couldn't move. Fear choked him. No air. Arms like lead. They'd found him. Ape's needle to his eyeball, his ax cleaving his head. Oh, fuck, he was bleeding out.

His mouth opened, gaped like a fish out of water, and finally, finally, found air. With it came the flood of memories. The pain, scorching, fire, Breadthwaite— Bread—pulling him out. The rest of the team getting inside late—*too fucking late*. White bed, voices, fuzzy, heavy pain, blinding flashes, muddled memories. His sister, Carly, too. Clean, fresh Carly, not the bruised, battered body he'd identified in the morgue. No, wait. *Not* Carly. Carly was gone. Other faces. Questions, pain, always the pain.

His moan was the sound that brought him back, his eyes slitted to see a cracked ceiling, a landscape on the wall, faded and blue.

Mountains.

Virginia. Blackwood, Virginia. Where the skin doctor was.

The motel. He was in the motel. White-and-peach bedspread on the floor beneath him, blinds closed, curtains pulled, A/C set to frigid. Against his face rested an empty fifth of vodka.

Last night, like every other night since that day, Clay had succumbed, not to sleep, but rather to a self-inflicted, booze-induced near coma, which didn't qualify as sleep no matter how long his eyes stayed closed. It left him tired and dizzy and nauseous, with a head the size of Maryland, but at least it gave him those few hours of oblivion.

Painfully, he creaked to standing, each joint making

itself known in ways it hadn't before the shooting. He got up, popped the usual six ibuprofen, his hands tight, and moved to the bathroom, blinking at the heaviness of his eyes. It wasn't until he caught sight of his puffy, red face in the mirror that he remembered why his eyes hurt so bad.

After a shower, he hit the road, crawling through downtown Blackwood, which appeared to be celebrating Independence Day in style, and finally hit the open road.

In his Toyota. Yeah, not the quite the hum of a Harley.

He drove three hours to the coast, where he scoured craigslist and made some phone calls and bought a truck, dented and dusty with a sprinkling of rust. He hoped to God the thing took him back to Blackwood, but it was safer to do this here or in West Virginia, and he figured he'd stand out less at the beach.

After parking in a spot with an ocean view, he powered up his phone and hit Tyler's name, noticing the holes in the upholstery and the missing radio knobs. Local color.

"Hey," he said when his friend answered.

"Clay? Where the fuck are you, man?" Tyler asked. "I been calling you like crazy. Jayda's asking me if you're coming today, and I don't even know. What the hell's going on?"

"I refused protection, Tyler. Left town."

"Seriously? You can't do that, man! They found your house! Got your damned bike! You've got to—"

"How'd they find me, Ty? No one else will say."

"I don't know, man. Weird shit's been going down."

"Boss tried to force me into protection, but that's not happening. Second best choice, she said, is I get the hell outta town until trial. Got a shit-ton of PTO. It's an extended vacation. *Away.*"

"So, where you headed?" his best friend asked. The man who'd been his lifeline for two long years undercover. The last man he'd spoken to before getting shot. The only person he trusted his life with—except maybe Bread, who'd gotten him out of the burning clubhouse.

After a long sigh, Clay said, "Can't say."

"The fuck?"

"Look, I trust you. It's the phones and the… Yeah. Not telling anyone."

"You tell the boss?"

"Not even the boss."

"She is gonna kill you."

"Yeah, well, she'll get over it. She's the one who told me to disappear." He let out a pained groan. "This shit is bad. If they know where I live, man, who's to say they can't find everyone else who worked on the case? No way I'm putting you and Jayda and the kids in danger, okay? I'd rather listen to the boss—"

"For once," interrupted Tyler.

"Yeah." Clay grinned. "For once."

"So, it's R & R for you, and what? Catch some waves at the beach or…"

"Just leaving town, bro." After a pause, he went on. "Found a dermatologist here who'll take care of these tats. Boss wants me to lay low? Fine. I'll goddamn disappear. Go so far off the grid it'll be like I never existed."

"But you're coming back for court, right?"

"Wouldn't miss it for the world."

Clay heard a female voice in the background and could picture Tyler's wife, Jayda, asking him something or calling him in to lunch. Man, things had changed since they'd gotten married and had kids. Different, but good for Tyler. Probably. Family life just didn't hold much appeal for Clay: the house and mess and all the other stuff.

"Any word from Bread?" he asked, knowing Breadthwaite had opted to go into witness protection, rather than hunker down on his own. Yeah, well, Bread didn't have three bullet holes in his hide, so their trust issues might not be exactly on par.

"He's gone. Flew out yesterday with a couple of marshals and a bunch of fucking suits from Justice," Tyler said, and Clay gave a sigh of relief.

"Jesus. But good. Good." Bread was one of those dudes you just had to like. A hippy in real life who'd done a kick-ass job of passing as a biker—a good man to have on your team. The best.

Clay eyed the slow-moving beach traffic nervously.

"Get yourself into protection, like Bread, ma—"

"You think they don't have rats at DOJ, Ty? I gotta go."

"Right, well, enjoy it for me. Laid out next to the water, drink in hand. On your own. Man, that sounds like the life. Maybe I'll come find you, bring the boat, and we can—"

"Jayda'd cut off your balls," Clay said, picturing the throw down between Tyler and his wife. "Then she'd come after me."

"Yeah," Tyler said, only it didn't sound quite as light as it was probably meant to. Clay didn't want to know about whatever trouble was in Tyler's paradise right now.

"I gotta go, man. Give my love to Jayda and the kids."

"Will do, Clay. Will do," Tyler said, then quickly followed up. "But keep me—"

"Thanks, Ty," he said, ending the call and placing another.

"McGovern," came his boss's gravelly response. Always on, nights and weekends, holidays. He'd never heard her be anything but curt and professional.

"Navarro here, ma'am."

"Navarro." In typical McGovern fashion, she gave nothing. Not an extra word.

"Just checking in."

"Good. From where?"

"I'd…" He paused, unsure how to go about saying it. How did you tell your boss you didn't trust anyone, not even her? "I'd prefer not to say."

"Wh—Hold on." He heard a muffled sound, then voices, followed by what was probably the door closing. Probably at home with family on this sunny Fourth of July, like everyone else in the whole goddamn nation. "Where are you, Navarro?"

"With all due respect, ma'am, I'd rather not—"

"Cut the crap. I told you to take time off, lay low for a while, not to drop off the face of the earth. What am I supposed to say to DOJ when they need you to—"

"I'll check in every week or two. This case matters to me, you know that. But my life matters even more."

"That's not gonna—" She paused, cleared her throat, and appeared to change tacks. "You checking in with the shrink?"

"I'll be fine, Boss."

"Don't mess around with PTSD, Navarro. Dr. Levitz said you need meds, therapy, and—"

"I'm *fine*."

"You're not fine. You're a—" She gave a *harrumph*, then a resigned sigh. "I understand it's been rough, Navarro. Recovery and trying to get back into the swing of things. But you're not undercover anymore. You've got to stop acting like one of those bikers and be an agent again. Just tell me where you are, and I'll—"

"Sorry, Boss," Clay said before ending the call and pulling the battery out of his phone.

There, ties cut. Clean slate.

Sort of.

~∾~

George took in a big, fat breath, pasted a smile on her face, and dropped the knocker on the door. The sound was full and warm, like the woman who welcomed her with a smile.

"You came!" Uma Crane said, throwing her arms around George in a way George both loved and didn't quite feel comfortable with.

"I came!" she couldn't help but blurt out with a laugh. Uma was… She pulled back, admiring the woman's smile, her face round and glowing and so clearly happy. Her arms, nearly clear of ink, were pale for midsummer. "Thanks for inviting me."

"I was sure you wouldn't come."

"It's not like you gave me a choice this time, Uma," George said, smiling.

"No. Three times, you've refused me. No way you were getting away with this one."

"Yeah. I kind of got that."

From the back of the house, a child's voice whooped and someone laughed. Down the hall, a large figure emerged, massive and intimidating, and George's breath caught in her throat—until she recognized the man. Ive. Ive Shifflett, Uma's boyfriend.

Not Andrew Blane, her new project. George wasn't sure if the big breath she expelled was relief or disappointment, although it felt more like the latter.

"You remember Ive, right?"

"Yes, of course. Hi there. Good to see you again," she said, letting her hand be engulfed in the big man's.

"Doc."

"It's George. Please call me George."

"Right. George."

"Come on in." Uma grabbed her arm. "Let's get you set up with a drink and introduce you around."

She followed the couple into the house, taking it all in and girding herself. A party. So very different from the way she managed to deal with people at work. Social situations did her in. The constant smiling, the small talk, the personal side of things was exhausting. She was so painfully bad at it. When Tom had been alive, he'd been her buffer, the social one, the guy who knew how to charm, but now…

After a quick round of introductions, George settled into a corner of the kitchen, bottle of beer in hand, and watched.

As they prepared things for the barbecue, her eyes kept returning to Uma and her man. Ive Shifflett smiled at his girlfriend, and anything that may have seemed scary in him disappeared, leaving George to gape for just a second at this man's surprisingly sweet, handsome boyishness. He slid one big arm around Uma's shoulder. She leaned into him, looking... Oh, what a transformation. The woman looked content. Unlike the first time she'd come into George's office, almost a year ago, when she'd been so...hunted.

Hunted and frightened and clearly in the throes of something terrible. What chilled George now, as she recalled it, was the uncanny similarity to Andrew Blane's demeanor yesterday. That was it, wasn't it? That was why, when it came down to it, George hadn't kicked him out or run screaming from his presence.

Right. She was fixating on him because he'd looked hunted. Not at all because of how he'd affected her.

My God, she had to stop thinking about him. All morning, she'd dwelled on the man. What was wrong with her?

A woman sidled up, beer in hand, and leaned against the wall beside George. "Don't they just make you sick?" she said quietly.

"Hmm?" George said, eyeing the scattered freckles over the newcomer's sun-browned nose. She'd have to watch that.

The woman smiled and lifted her chin at Uma and Ive canoodling on the other side of the room.

"Oh. Yes."

"I'm Jessie Shifflett, sister to Ive, the massive lovesick puppy over there. I hear you're the woman with the magic wand."

"Magic wa... Oh. The laser." The description surprised a chuckle out of George, who reached out and shook Jessie's hand. "George Hadley. Good to meet you."

"Well, George Hadley, you're a miracle worker. Also hear you do a ridiculous amount of pro bono work for people around here."

"Oh, I'm…" She wasn't quite sure how to handle a comment like that. Praise wasn't really her thing. "Thank you?"

Jessie laughed, the sound easy, casual in a way George admired. "Seriously, though. I hear you're just about the nicest person on the planet. I should be thanking *you*." The woman indicated the couple again, and her smile softened. "For that."

"Not sure I can take credit for what's happening over there. But…" George narrowed her eyes at the other woman. "I feel like we've met before."

"We have. I work out right next to your office. At the MMA school. Teach there too. Monday nights." Of course. George recognized her now. She'd seen her arrive at the gym in the evenings, usually around the time she was closing up the clinic. "You should drop in sometime. Check out my women's self-defense class."

"Oh, right. Uma mentioned it. I keep meaning to stop by." Which was a lie. George didn't need self-defense. She wasn't scared of people. No, the dangers in life were invisible, microscopic things that snuck up on you before you knew it, killing indiscriminately.

"You should," Jessie went on. "Come on Monday. Lots of great gals." George tried to picture it— herself in a room full of women—and couldn't manage. Jessie leaned in, smiling, and said, "If you're really good, we let you beat up on a couple of guys. Including my brother and…hmm. Where's Steve?" She looked around, apparently didn't see the man she was looking for, and grabbed George by the arm. "Come on outside. I'll introduce you to the others. You should know Steve, after all. He owns the MMA school. Good neighbor to have, actually. Never have to worry about anyone bugging you as long as he's in business right there."

Outside, less than a dozen people hung around the grill, drinking, chatting, and playing badminton. George eyed them warily, wishing she could leave, itching to head back to the office. She usually stuck out like a sore thumb at things like this—the stiff, pale-skinned woman who had no clue how to mingle.

Jessie, it turned out, was the perfect icebreaker, if somewhat embarrassing.

"You single, Doc?" she asked over her shoulder as they went down the back porch steps.

"Uh…yes?"

They approached a group of adults, and Jessie's smile turned mischievous. "Excellent. Someone to take the pressure off."

"What are you—"

"Hey, everybody. Meet George Hadley. Owns the skin clinic over on Main Street." Hands reached out, names were given, and George shook blindly. "She's single too, so you can set your friends up with her now instead of harassing me all the time."

"Oh, I'm not—"

Cutting her off with a wave, Jessie winked and led her a bit farther away, to where a black man with salt-and-pepper hair led a couple of kids in a game of badminton.

"Steve! Want you to meet your neighbor."

The man looked up and smiled with a wave before

whacking the birdie hard at the biggest of the kids. "I've seen you. You're the doc next door."

"Yes. George Hadley. And you're the sheriff."

"Yes, indeed. Good to meet you, ma'am," he said, and George got the strangest twinge of déjà vu. First Andrew Blane and now this man, making her feel so official.

"Please call me George."

"Well, please call me Steve," he said, finally leaving the game long enough to come over and shake her hand. "Glad to finally meet you. We've been wondering when you'd come over and see us."

They had? "Oh. Business is—"

"He's just bugging you," said Jessie, who must have felt George's discomfort.

"You got that big place on Jason Lane, right?"

"Um…" How did he know that?

Jessie leaned in again. "Cops. They know everything."

George breathed again. "Yes. That's my house."

"I just rented a place on Jason Lane," Jessie went on happily.

"Yeah?"

"End of the cul-de-sac."

"Oh. I'm in the farmhouse."

"Hey! Right down the road! Awesome!"

"Like Dr. Doolittle over there," Steve said. "One hell of a setup you got. Like a jungle."

"Um. Thank you?"

"Yes, you should take it as a compliment," said Jessie, leaning in to swat the man on the shoulder. "Right, Steve?"

"Definitely. Compliment. Being a widower means you can say whatever you want."

Funny how being a widow had never brought that out in her.

Jessie shot Steve a look. "Shouldn't you be working tonight? Independence Day and all?"

"Yep. Down a couple of deputies right now and can't find a replacement to save my life," replied Steve with a weary sigh and a glance at his watch. "Gotta take off."

After the sheriff left, George's eyes swept around the party, the people laughing and playing, lazing around and talking so naturally. First Uma and Ive's closeness, so intimate she'd felt almost dirty watching, and now these uncomplicated-seeming relationships, people looking so companionable and natural together. A chest-squeezing burst of envy surprised her with its strength. This, exactly this, was why she never went anywhere. She'd forgotten, after so long, how very much it hurt to see so much happiness in one place.

She turned to Jessie. "I…I've got to go."

"Yeah?"

"Thanks for showing me around. Would you mind giving the uh…the lovebirds my regards? Or regrets or whatever?"

"Regards. Sure."

George extricated herself from the party and headed back into town, to the clinic. To escape, get some work done, maybe some research. She wouldn't admit to herself that what drove her was an unhealthy curiosity about a six-foot-something man whose sordid story was etched into his skin.

Clay noticed the tail as soon as he pulled back into town. He couldn't believe it, actually, had been so sure his new old truck would offer him a sort of force field in a community like this one. Virginia plates and all.

Apparently he'd been wrong, because as soon as he hit Blackwood city limits, he acquired a police escort.

There was nothing wrong with the truck. He'd made sure of that before taking it off the dude's hands. And there shouldn't have been anything wrong with his credentials, but that was something he hadn't wanted to risk—a bumbling country cop plugging him into the system was the last thing he needed at this point. Fuck. The sooner he got rid of Ape's goddamned gift, the better. He glanced in the mirror, wondering if he wouldn't have been better off in some anonymous urban setting like Richmond or DC, after all.

No, they knew him there.

As if on cue, the blue lights went on behind him, and the siren bleeped once, twice. Okay, good, at least they were keeping it subtle. He hadn't thought about the possibility of this happening, hadn't considered how he'd play it, but he'd been around law enforcement long enough to know how to avoid setting off the worst alarm bells, so he pulled over, rolled down the window, got out his wallet, and waited.

"Afternoon." The man approached cautiously from behind, kept his distance, clearly eyeing him through his mirrored sunglasses—precisely the same ones Clay wore, although this man was small, wiry, and African American.

"Afternoon, sir." Well, Clay knew how to play the game too, if he had to. He didn't want to antagonize, but neither was he going to give the cop the upper hand. He kept his aviators on, wishing he'd asked the doctor for some kind of bandaging. Now would be a great time to hide the 5-0 on his eyes and the DEAD MAN on his knuckles, with their sickly smiling skull.

"License and registration, please."

Clay lifted his wallet slowly, keeping both hands in sight—palms up in an effort to hide the ink—pulled out Andrew Blane's license, handed it to the man, and reached for the newly signed title.

"You got insurance for this vehicle?"

"Yes, sir."

As Clay handed it all over, he pretended not to see the man examining the back of his cab.

"Didn't you have a different vehicle yesterday, son?"
Son? Jesus, I'm not in Kansas anymore, am I?

"Yes indeed." He craned his neck just enough to read the name tag pinned to the man's uniform. "Sheriff Mullen."

"You just purchased this truck, Mr....Blane?"

"Just today, Sheriff."

"Any reason you decided to trade the old one in?"

"It was a rental, sir."

"What's your business here in Blackwood?"

"My business?"

"Yes. How long do you plan on staying in our town?"

What was this, the fucking Wild West? "I'm not entirely sure about that, Sheriff. Might be a few months, I suppose." He looked over his shoulder, then back at the cop. "What was it you pulled me over for, exactly?"

"Flickering taillight." The man backed up a step, looked the truck over, and returned to the window, looking cocky for such a small guy. This must be the kind of bullshit they used to rid their town of undesirable visitors such as himself.

"Could you remove your sunglasses, please, sir?"

Fuck.

Forcing himself not to hesitate, Clay pulled the shades down, baring his ink to the lawman and sitting through his slow perusal.

"Hmm. You hold tight. Be a few minutes."

He kept a wary eye on the rearview as the man disappeared behind him and slid into his cruiser.

Hopefully, the ID would check out, and everything would be fine. If it didn't...no point worrying until the worst happened. And nobody knew about the Andrew Blane identity. Not his boss or Tyler. Nobody.

A few minutes later, the sheriff returned and handed everything back to Clay.

"Check out?"

"Yes, sir." The man turned as if to walk to his vehicle and then turned back, eyes narrowed with a tight smile on his lips. "Welcome to Blackwood, Mr. Blane."

Clay watched the cruiser pull a U-turn and take off in the other direction before he started his new truck and slowly drove into the quaint downtown area.

Already on the cops' radar. Great. *Why the hell did I choose this place?*

Okay, so maybe he'd head to Miami or Atlanta or someplace where he wouldn't stand out like such a sore thumb. He could get his ink taken care of there, prep for court, and lay low until he had to testify.

As he drove through town, the skin clinic appeared on his right, and just as he passed it, Dr. Georgette Hadley got out of her car, dressed in a light, flowery dress instead of the jeans she'd worn the evening before, and he couldn't help but slow down to watch her. Her legs were sexy, curvaceous, strong-looking, and…man, they were pale almost to the point of translucence, lending a fragile quality to her that he hadn't noticed behind her serious doctor facade. He knew he should keep going— not stare at her like some kind of creeper—but the way she moved kept drawing his eyes.

In the rearview mirror, he watched her walk from her hippy car to the clinic, unlock it, and enter, her skirt swirling as she pulled the door closed behind her, exposing a swath of clear, white thigh—before he rounded the bend and lost sight of her.

Fuck, that thigh. Not a mark on it. No ink, no scars, track marks, or bruises. He didn't think he'd seen such a pure stretch of body in… He blinked at the ghost of the doctor's reflection in the mirror and focused on the road. *Ever.*

After that, Clay drove on to his motel and holed up, ready for a long, vodka-infused night inside, all thoughts of small-town cops and curious locals wiped away by that one, vulnerable peek of the doctor's soft-looking thigh.

∽ଚ∽

Back at the office, close and still and sweltering, George booted up her computer. Only rather than catching up on patient files as she normally would on a night like this, she walked back to exam room 2, reached into the garbage can, and pulled out a sheaf of paperwork—torn in two, but still completely legible.

I want to help him, she thought. *He needs help.*

Guiltily, she scanned the sheets, only to come up empty. Nothing. They told her nothing.

Name: Andrew Blane
Address: None
Phone: None

Homeless? Was he homeless?

But he'd stood so straight. Smelled so…good. Really good. Not like a man who didn't wash.

When he'd pleaded with her, even then, he'd been strong. He didn't have that hopelessness to him that she associated with people who didn't have a place to call their own. Although, what did she know about homelessness? He could be a nomad, for all she knew. Plus, there was that wad of cash he'd tried to give her, which spoke of an unsettled existence. Who used cash anymore?

So, not homeless, she concluded, turning back to the otherwise blank page. Just squirrelly. He had reason to be, considering the way he looked. What on earth made a person get tattooed like that? 5-0 on his face? Announcing what? That he was law enforcement? But he didn't look it. In fact, he looked the furthest from law enforcement she could imagine, especially with the other things inked onto him. The spiderweb and the clock.

She'd removed enough spiderwebs, pro bono, to know what those tattoos meant—the man had done time. A felon. Possibly—probably?—a murderer.

She reached for her mug of tea, took a gulp before

setting it down, remembering the largest tattoo, the one on his back. Some kind of crest, like you'd see on a dollar bill or a modern-day coat of arms.

She typed *triangle*, *arrows*, *eagle*, *river*, *skull tattoo*, and the letters *SMC*.

The results, once she'd sifted through them, were disheartening, but no real surprise. Photos of an outlaw motorcycle gang out of Maryland. *The Sultans MC*.

Arrests, images of outlaw bikers. More arrests. Drugs, guns. Racketeering. Arrests earlier in the year, again in Maryland. Men in black leather vests with patches on the back. She clicked on that one, then magnified it until the image was clear—and there it was. Exactly the same as the tattoo on Andrew Blane's back.

Quickly, she shut down the page and rolled back a foot or two from the reception desk. She'd worked with gang tattoos before. Ink on men who wanted to get out. She'd also helped ex-cons who had chosen to erase their old lives—erase their mistakes. She'd done a few of those pro bono, because everybody deserved a second chance.

But did this man? Did he truly deserve a second chance if he was as bad as these people appeared to be?

She thought of the Latino ex-gang member she'd helped. She'd been perfectly willing to help that kid, but…he'd been a kid, whereas this man was older. Old enough to know better.

Crap.

George let her head fall on her arms. She wanted him to be a good guy. Was that too much to ask? That the man she couldn't stop thinking about be a nice person, instead of a stone-cold killer?

Because this attraction, this stupid attraction, would have almost been acceptable if he'd been a good person, instead of a man who'd done time, quite possibly for murder, and who'd chosen to advertise it on his skin. And some of the tattoos were recent, if she wasn't mistaken.

Yes, but now he wants it gone.

She rubbed her belly—the name she'd gotten inked there and again on her arm in her youth. A lifetime ago, when she'd made her mistake—mistakes. Bad boys, fast cars, fumbling in backseats.

Everybody deserves a second chance.

She rubbed, remembering. She'd had a bad phase after losing her parents—more confused than rebellious. There had been a pregnancy, an abortion, and years of doubt.

Yes, all of that should be a lesson to George, who'd gone the bad-boy route once before. And that hadn't gotten her anywhere. Thankfully, she'd met Tom and… well, the rest was history, wasn't it? Just history.

She sighed, coming back full circle. *Ah, stupidity— the prerogative of youth.*

So, Andrew Blane was erasing a lifetime of transgressions, possibly youthful mistakes. Who the hell was she to judge?

ﾠﾠﾠ✧

It wasn't until Clay'd stripped down to underwear that he realized he'd forgotten to buy Vaseline. And seeing as his knuckles and eyes burned like shit, he figured he'd better head back out to find some.

He dressed, went back out to his new truck, and drove through town, surprised, on this Fourth of July, to see the lights on in Blackwood's only grocery store—a dinky-looking place called Blackwood Grocery.

He parked and watched through narrowed eyes as people went about their business. Naglestown, Maryland—the Sultans' fiefdom—was just a small town too…on the map, at least. But unlike this place, there'd been no antique stores, no cozy cafés, and you sure as hell wouldn't find it in a guidebook. This little town, however, had one of those proud *Welcome to Blackwood* signs, complete with bright flowers and a stone accent wall, inviting you into one of America's most picturesque villages.

Village. Ha. Like one of the books Grandma used to read to him and Carly as kids, with mice and gardens and porcupines in frilly aprons or whatever. But Clay knew, in absolute certainty, that what happened behind closed doors, even in places like this, was just as bad as what happened anywhere else. Sometimes small towns covered up big, bad goings-on. Naglestown had just been more obvious about it—the biker gang so ingrained that they hardly bothered to cover their tracks.

The local cops so entrenched in the MC's racket, they were as bad as the bikers themselves.

As the doors slid open, all heads turned his way, and he was thankful for the aviators and ball cap, along with his long sleeves. What folks could see of his skin was minimal, and odd though he may appear in his Unabomber garb, there was no way any of it was coming off—even indoors. As unidentifiable as possible; that was the goal. Don't give them anything to remember you by.

As if the sheriff would forget a single goddamn detail. *Like, say, the 5-0 etched into my face.*

Eyes followed him to the pharmacy aisle, where he startled an old lady and her little white dog, whose barks followed him long after he'd found razors and Vaseline. Fucking Vaseline, like that didn't look bad. As he headed down to the end of the store, his eyes caught on a display dedicated to local produce, and he salivated—literally.

By the time he arrived at the checkout, he'd gathered chips and dip, apples, peaches.

"Evenin', sir," the cashier said.

"Evening."

"How you doin' today?"

"Uh…" Clay glanced around. What was this, 1954? How long had it been since he'd been asked that? "Good, thanks."

"Great! Hopin' for a storm later this week. Need somethin' to break this heat wave. Always sorry when folks come to visit us, and all anyone can do is stay in the A/C. Y'know?"

"Yeah."

"That'll be fifteen dollars even. Cash or credit?"

"Cash," he finally answered, handing over a couple of twenties, the bills slightly damp against his palm.

"It's only fifteen, sir." The woman smiled at him, and Clay wondered if she was flirting. No. He didn't think so. Just being friendly. She handed him his change and a paper bag filled with his purchases.

"Can you tell me where I can buy clothes? You know, like T-shirts and stuff."

"Oh, you'll have to drive into C'ville for that, sir."

He nodded his thanks and lifted a hand as she called,

"Happy Independence Day!" to his retreating back. "And welcome to Blackwood!"

God, he needed exercise or he'd go crazy in this place. Maybe he'd go for a run when he got back to his room.

Back in his truck, he started up the engine and drove down Main Street with a sense of relief, so out of place here, it was like having a target etched onto his back instead of the Sultans' emblem.

❧

A glance at the clock showed George that she'd spent more time investigating her patient than she should have—especially since she shouldn't have done it at all. Slow and stupid from the heat, she stood up, shut everything down, and headed outside.

It was nearly dark and Blackwood crackled with energy—muggy and sultry with air that felt like it hadn't moved in months, but tonight an extra jolt of electricity seemed to spice it up. The few steps to her car, so familiar, were done thoughtlessly, no attention paid to her surroundings, to a voice a bit farther down the road, yelling something. The sound didn't sink in until she'd opened the door and realized it was a woman, her voice shrill and then sharply cut off with what might have been a slap.

There, across the street, silhouettes closer now, running, a scuffle, one person down.

"Hey!" George yelled, protective instincts kicking in. "What's going on?"

A shriek, a thud.

She dropped everything and ran.

Weird, in those moments, how things sped up and

froze all at once. She was aware of furtive movement and an unnatural stillness, the buzzing of the streetlight above, the crunch of grit under her sandals.

The couple on the sidewalk was closer now, things still murky, but it was a man, definitely a man. Attacking a woman?

"Hey!" George yelled, slapping at his arms.

I'll run and get my phone was George's last thought before the man struck her, right in the stomach, doubling her over and stealing every last bit of breath from her body.

"The fuck off me, bitch!"

My phone, George thought with a glance back at her car, and then *thwack*. She was down. Suddenly, the blond woman was up, yelling and hitting her—the woman who'd sounded so scared... And another man appeared from out of nowhere.

Ungffff. A kick to her leg. *The woman*, she thought.

"Fuck you!" yelled the woman. "Hittin' my man."

There were three of them. Two men and one woman. George caught flashes of bodies and faces, more screaming, directed at her this time. Harsh words interspersed with flashes of bare legs, shorts, sneakers, explosions of color overhead.

Young. No wrinkles. More words hurled at her. Another glimpse. A face covered in lesions. George curled in on herself.

Drugs, her mind supplied, slow but catching up. These people were on drugs.

Adrenaline and fear went into overdrive. Too late. She writhed on the ground, holding her tender belly, strangely aware of the gritty surface of the gutter beneath her, the odd grain of sand shining brightly despite the late hour. All she could do was protect her face and her abdomen. Who'd feed Leonard if she didn't make it home? Who would put the chickens to bed? Trying not to think of the baby she'd never have if she died right here, she groaned. Not from the dull ache in her womb, but from regret.

Something changed in the air then. She felt it, even folded in on herself. Somebody grunted—an unpleasant sound. With an effort, George maneuvered herself into a tighter ball against the curb and lifted her head. What little breath she'd managed to gather escaped in a whoosh.

It was Andrew Blanc. She'd conjured him, probably, and here he was, saving the day with a strangely quiet, grim, hard-edged concentration. One of her attackers was already halfway to the ground, the woman running away, fast, by the time George cleared the fog from her eyes. As she watched, Andrew dealt with the third person in a move that was quick and violent. Efficient—no, *surgical* was a better word for the punch to the neck, the echoing kick low on the man's leg. Oh Lord, but it looked barbaric, frightening for the speed and ease with which it was delivered.

A final blow to one of the kids' faces had blood spattering in a tall, almost graceful arc, and George couldn't stop the scared whimper she let out.

When he turned to her, her savior's breathing looked normal. How could he be that way after the bloody havoc he'd just wreaked? She thought, for a crazed moment, that he was some kind of spy—a Jason Bourne type, an unfeeling psychopath, whose only external mode of expression was through the writing on his skin.

But then he looked at her, and she knew, with absolutely certainty, that he wasn't some instrument of
aggression. He might move like a man who knew how to
hurt another human being, but when his eyes met hers,
she saw that the one who was hurting was him. And how
messed up was it that all she wanted to do was make him
feel better?

5

OKAY, SO MAYBE CLAY WASN'T ENTIRELY DEAD, AFTER all. His muscles still seemed to work, weak though they were, his synapses fired excitedly, and if the adrenaline seeping through his veins was any indication, he'd held on to some of his protective instincts, as well. He was shaky, which was to be expected after all that time spent in recovery, but the physical therapy and the strength training had worked, apparently.

Right now, though, it wasn't himself he was concerned with. It was the doctor. And God, it felt good, this sensation of standing above her, keeping her alive and well, with those two crank-cratered fucknuts moaning at his feet.

It was a damned good thing he'd decided to come back out for a run tonight.

"The fuck outta here," he told the addicts, and though it was clear they hurt, they obeyed immediately. That was one advantage to looking like a tough motherfucker. It had been a while since he'd used force, given orders. Done anything useful, in fact—and it felt good. Better than good. It was life-giving.

"You okay?" he asked, stepping over to the doc, who had pushed herself up to all fours. She looked at him kind of squinty eyed, like she didn't quite trust him, but took his hand, eventually, and let him pull her to sitting on the curb, where he squatted beside her.

"How many hands I got up?" He held up three fingers.

"You mean fingers?" she asked, smart as a whip.

"Yeah," he said with a smile.

She gave one back, a smile at the edges of a mouth so pink he could see it under the streetlamps.

Shit, that was sexy. He put a hand on her shoulder and felt her lean into him, just a little. "Good. Anything hurt, Doc?"

Gingerly, she turned her head, stretched her neck, rolled her shoulders, then made as if to get up, but he tightened his fingers, stopping her. He ran his hand from her shoulder down her arm to pick up her hand and check the palm for scratches.

It was a weird moment right there, under the busted-out streetlight. Clay couldn't quite muster up the energy to let her go, and she didn't seem anxious to get rid of him. Instead, they sat, looking for all the world like a couple waiting for a parade that had passed a good twelve hours before.

She leaned on him for a few seconds and then rose with him. After a brief tightening of his fingers on hers, he finally let her go, and the connection was broken. After that, the calm seeped out of Clay's brain.

Actual calm. How fucking strange. He wanted to grab her hand and get it back.

"Wanna call the police?"

She shook her head, and he sighed with relief, not

questioning the decision. "I recognized them. Local kids and… The girl needs help, and I don't think putting them all in jail is the way to do that right now."

Clay tended to disagree, but he also didn't need to get involved with the law right now, so he kept his mouth shut.

Pop! The sound hit Clay with a start. He threw an arm around the doctor and ducked before he could identify which direction it came from. *What the fuck?*

Another pop, more aggressive this time, had Clay's pulse revving uncontrollably.

"I can't…" He squeezed his eyes shut, then turned, attempting to locate the shooter. "Stay down. We're under—"

"Mr. Blane."

He pushed her behind him, reached for a weapon that wasn't there, turned again. *Fuck.* He'd heard a Harley in town earlier, had told himself it was nothing, and had done his best to ignore it. And now the bikers were here. Where the hell were they hiding?

"Andrew," the woman said, looking totally unafraid. "It's the fireworks."

He blinked a couple of times before taking it all in: the wash of blue, the spray of color piercing the night sky.

Fireworks. Fucking fireworks on the Fourth of July. Jesus, was it possible to overdose on adrenaline?

Like those ravers from the nineties, whose repeated use of ecstasy had depleted their serotonin levels, Clay's mind insisted he'd had too many rushes to be terrified, and yet, here he was, shivering, again, in the aftermath. And then he wondered if it wasn't the opposite; maybe repressing the fear for so long, pushing it into places it shouldn't have to hide, had given him an overabundant supply of the stuff. For all those times he'd stared down some trigger-happy speed freak, the cold barrel of a gun burning a hole in his temple…

The doctor stood, watching him, her quiet stillness notable in a world that trembled so desperately.

"You okay?" she asked, putting out a hand to…touch him, maybe? He stepped out of her reach.

"I'll take you home," he said firmly.

After a few long beats, she glanced around. "Where's your car?"

"I'm on foot."

"You live around here?" she asked.

Rather than answer, he said, "I'll drive you home and jog back."

"No. No, you can't do that. I couldn't ask you to, not with your—"

"I'm fine. And you can't drive after what just happened," he said. "Come on."

After a brief hesitation, she nodded, and he walked her around to the passenger door, which was unlocked, and went to get in the driver's side. She was one of those women whose car was full of random shit, so it took her about three minutes to clear off her seat, but he kinda liked that. It meant she didn't have passengers often. He figured between that and the lack of a ring, she probably wasn't married.

She handed him the keys. "Okay," he said before starting the engine. "Where to?"

With the turn of the key came low, modulated radio voices and a squealing fan belt.

"You need to get that looked at," he said.

"What?"

"Fan belt."

"Oh. Right. I don't… I mean, I never…"

"I could take a look, if you want."

"You?" She looked at him as he pulled out, her shocked expression almost comical. Or it would have been if it hadn't hurt just a bit.

"Sure." He lifted his shoulders in a shrug. "It'd be a pleasure."

"Oh."

He stopped at the sign and turned to catch her watching him.

After a few seconds of silence, he asked, "Which way?"

"Oh." She blinked. "Sorry, left here."

He turned and drove on in silence as she guided him down a few more streets.

"Look, I can't ask you to walk home from my place. It's out of the way and—"

"I'm at the motel in town. 'S it far from that?"

"About a mile," she said.

"That's fine. I was jogging anyway so it's actually perfect."

"I feel bad, Mr. Blanc. You…" She hesitated, and he glanced over at her. "You appear to have a limp."

"It's nothing," he said, his voice as hard and final as he could make it.

After a turn onto Jason Lane, she spoke again. "The motel. What… I mean…you're *living* there?"

"Yeah."

"For how long?"

"Long as it takes you to finish with me."

Her mouth opened, and she looked like she'd say

something but must have changed her mind; the next few seconds passed in silence.

"It's right here," she said, and he pulled into a driveway on a pleasant dead-end country street. Her house—what he could see of it—was dark.

"You got no lights on."

She turned and looked at the house before answering with a shrug. "I don't like to waste."

"It's not safe."

"In Blackwood?" she asked, brows raised.

"Yeah, Doc," Clay said, letting the sarcasm seep through and feeling just a bit bad for it. "D'you already forget what just happened in good old Blackwood?"

"Oh. That wasn't… I think I stepped into a domestic violence situation and…" She sighed, fidgeting with the hem of her dress, and went on. "You're right. I guess I…I just don't have much to steal."

"Steal? You think it's about stuff? Those little shits tonight, maybe. Maybe they'd go for a purse or the keys to your clinic or something. Maybe meds, you know? But a woman like you, Doc? You'd do well to protect yourself. Not just your stuff. *You.*"

He got out of the car, walked around to open her door, and purposefully locked the doors behind her before following her up the dark porch stairs and handing her the keys.

"Thank you, Mr. Blane. Would you…?" She swung her hand toward the door to her house and looked back. "Would you like to come in, maybe for a coffee or…?"

Clay hesitated, standing there on the dark front porch of this near-stranger's house. He wouldn't mind, actually, going inside and having a cup of something warm.

A glance at her face showed nothing but the vague shape of her skull, hollows where her eyes were, a cap of hair gleaming only slightly more than the rest. The night air was hot and loud with celebratory explosions and an underlying buzz he couldn't seem to identify.

"Gotta get back," he lied, because really there wasn't a damn thing to get back to besides an empty room, a full bottle, and the never-ending story running loops through his brain.

"Thank you," she whispered, lifting her hand and letting it settle on his arm, steady and sure in a way it shouldn't be after that attack.

"You sure you'll be okay?" Clay asked, his eyes glued to that hand.

"Yes. Yes, thanks to you." She went to open her door, pulling that hand away so nonchalantly she couldn't possibly have any idea how deeply he'd felt it. That touch—like a goddamned anchor on his body.

He watched, blinking when she went inside and turned on the light. He then waited until she'd locked the door behind her—one of those old wooden doors with a god-damned glass panel you could see right the hell through, all the way down a hall to what appeared to be the kitchen, which made him even crazier. Finally, he returned to the street, fighting the urge to camp out in the woods across the way and keep an eye on the house, before taking off at a painful run, unexpected reluctance clogging his throat and the ghost of her touch holding him together.

Home. Finally. George dropped her purse and keys into the bowl by the front door and hesitated, a shiver running up her spine. No. No, she would not let those kids make her feel unsafe in her own home. She wouldn't change a thing. To prove it, she went out back to put the chickens to bed and turn off the water. What she found there brought her up short: a gaping hole at the bottom of her garden gate.

Throat tight and palms sweaty, she headed straight for the far corner of the yard, where the hens generally congregated, only to find feathers strewn about. But no chickens.

She'd seen a fox a few days before in the woods across from the house. There were raccoons too, wily enough to bust through that gate. With a hot rush of fear—not for herself, but for her girls this time—she turned to the henhouse and stuck her head inside.

Angry clucking greeted George, and she let out her breath on a wave of liquid relief, every joint aching with the suddenness of it. She counted five, six…seven hens. The only notable losses seemed to be a smattering of tail feathers and a good dose of avian pride. The ladies didn't enjoy being stalked.

Holy hell. Too much. It was all too much in one night.

After briefly checking her charges, she shut the coop up, leaving them to cluck among themselves—seeing that hole had scared the hell out of her. The chickens held an important place in her life—in her heart, really—and she couldn't imagine who else would ever fill it.

The sky exploded above her, coloring the tomato and basil plants pink and, for a few seconds, giving her yard an artificial movie-set light. Rather than go immediately back inside, George collapsed heavily onto her wooden porch steps and tilted her head back, staring at the show and listening to the animals' agitation. Were fireworks even safe right now, with the lack of rain this year?

A wet nose pushed at her elbow, and she raised her arm to let Leonard climb onto her lap. The big black-and-white cat took up more room than he'd probably been allotted at birth, but George just couldn't stand to put him on a diet. Why deprive him when he had, at most, another few years on this earth?

Tonight was… It had been…

She swallowed.

She was supposed to feel fear right now, she thought, for herself. But she didn't. Other than a throbbing on her face and pain where she'd landed on her hip, she felt an oddly thrumming excitement that was so wholly inappropriate, she wondered if she shouldn't consider turning herself in to some kind of ethical committee or getting in touch with her mentor from when she'd been a resident. Or going to see a therapist. How on earth was it possible to come out of an attack like that—one that had left her battered and bruised—and feel nothing but regret that the man who'd saved you hadn't agreed to come in for a cup of coffee?

How pathetic am I? A complete mess, and—

With a gasp, she touched her face. Was there blood? Did she look horrible? Was that why he'd refused her offer, looked at her hand on his arm like it was poison, and—

What the hell is wrong with me? I'm out of my mind.

Shifting Leonard off her lap, she stood, went inside, and tromped up the stairs to her bedroom, shutting lights off as she went. She went into the bathroom and looked at herself in the mirror. *Crap.* There were scrapes on her face, and grit was still embedded in her knees. She'd need to disinfect, but she didn't want to. No, all she wanted to do was sink into sleep and forget about everything. Especially that last bit on her porch.

How had things turned upside down so quickly?

Instead, she settled for a stinging, lukewarm shower, a clean nightgown, and bed, where even the weight of Leonard purring on her belly was too much to handle.

Between her sheets, though, sleep didn't hold the blissful nothing she'd hoped for. No, instead of oblivion, she lay awake in bed, eyes wide open. But there was clearly something wrong with her. A normal person would rehash tonight's attack, not dwell on the man who'd saved her. A normal person would be scared, not…titillated. Instead, she sailed along on a strange blend of excitement and guilt, along with something supremely tender that she hadn't been able to tamp down since Andrew Blane had found his way to her office.

⌇

It was the polygraph test that did it, every fucking night. As if living through it once hadn't been enough—

No, *twice*.

He'd had to take two life-changing poly tests—one when he'd applied for a job with the Bureau of Alcohol, Tobacco, Firearms and Explosives and once for the Sultans. The first had been nothing—child's play— compared to the one in the club, Ape and Handles and a couple of other guys hovering around him. Ape with his signature ax in his hand.

"We trust you, bro," Handles had explained. "Just gotta keep our guys safe, man. Fucking cops are on us like flies on shit, and you never know who you can trust anymore. Never know."

Clay, in deep sleep, relived that conversation every night, saw the smile on Handles's face. Handles, the national club president, who'd taken him under his wing, had been like a dad to him.

Clay'd been nervous the first time he'd gone to the Sultans' bar, the Hangover. He and Lil Dino, the confidential informant who'd vouched for him. Dino'd made a deal with the prosecutor and now had to tell the club guys he'd done time with Clay—a job made a hell of a lot easier by the ink Clay'd gone out and gotten done the week before.

That first day, he'd walked in with Dino, waited for his eyes to adjust, and slowly taken the place in, wondering if any of them would recognize him.

They hadn't. Not one of them, but that feeling of being a lone sheep in a den of wolves had never quite died down.

After that, it had been a slow, slow game. Riding into Naglestown every few days, eventually getting a job there, then making his trips to see the guys a daily thing until he'd given them that game-changing intel.

He remembered other things, in flashes. Like the day he'd made initial contact with his targets: Handles and Ape, the club's national sergeant at arms, who, it was quickly apparent, was a psychopath.

Handles and the others had been wary of Jeremy "Indian" Greer from the beginning, as they were of most newcomers, but Ape had hated him on sight—had beaten him and played with him to prove it. Funny how that fucker's crazy instincts had been so dead-on.

There'd been no warning the day of the polygraph—just a tap on the shoulder and a beckoning finger. Clay'd set down the glasses he was cleaning behind the bar, glanced around to catch every eye on him, and followed Handles into the bowels of the building.

It was like a goddamned fort, that place, an impenetrable fortress in the middle of these big, open fields in Nowheresville, Maryland. You couldn't get a jump on the Sultans. Not with their insane security and paranoid business dealings. Not to mention the firepower those guys had.

Halfway down the inner hall, where the Sultans kept their private on-site quarters, he'd started to feel the cold sweat of anxiety. It wasn't just a normal event, being summoned like that. No, it was fucking *serious*.

"Ever taken a lie detector test, Indian?" Handles had asked.

"No," Clay had lied.

"Me neither," Handles'd replied, gold-toothed smile destroying his bearded, bald, Daddy Warbucks look.

Fuck. Fuck, fuck. Nobody'd warned him about the test. Thank God he'd trained for this, but fuck, it had been years.

This is good, he realized. Home stretch. McGovern had been threatening to pull him just the other day, and now, if the club was doing this, he had to be close to being a full-patch member. Close to getting in.

Sucking in his belly to quell the nausea brewing there, he'd forced a grin. "Fuck, man. You guys are paranoid."

"Just keeping the family safe. You seen what happened to the Mongols?"

"No."

"Got screwed for trusting one asshole too many."

"Hmm" was all Clay said, but internally he was on fire—equal parts fear and excitement—that feeling he'd gotten addicted to undercover.

They headed down a long set of shallow steps, to what appeared to be a bunker in the basement, through a hall wide enough to drive a car, and then into a dank room where four guys stood around, waiting.

For him.

Beside an old-looking lie detector kit, a chair sat empty, waiting.

Clay offered a quick, cool nod to the occupants and then sat, heart beating a million miles a minute.

Slow. Breathe. Ignore them.

He grinned and looked around.

Jam and Boom-Boom didn't worry him the way Ape did, standing behind Clay's chair, casually swinging that ax in his hand. Clay'd heard stories about that fucking ax. He'd seen the goddamned stains it bore a time or two when the guys came back from some trip. Some mission. Those times, Ape had always been wilder than usual, extra sadistic. It'd been after one of those trips—just the week before, in fact—that he'd challenged Clay to a fight and gotten pissed when Clay started to beat his ass. Clay'd had no choice but to cave when the big fucker had grabbed a bottle from a brother's hand, smashed it on the bar, and come after him with the sharp end. Getting that slice, though, across the face…that, he realized now, may very well have been just the thing he'd needed to get in.

Fucking club scars, he thought, ass glued to the seat that could become his throne of execution.

Fuck it. He shrugged, cleared his throat, turned, and spat not five inches from the big asshole's feet.

You wanna kill me, fucker? that gesture said. *Do it.*

Then, cool as ice, Clay breathed while the polygraph dude wrapped the cuff around his arm, twined the two long pneumograph tubes around his middle, fiddled with some settings on his laptop, and slid the sensors onto his fingers.

Remember your training, he thought over and over. A mantra, something to hold on to. Feet down, ass squeezed, breathing deep as the stranger cleared his throat and began.

"Are you known here as Indian?"

Big breath, thinking of Carly, getting that pulse up, up, up for the control questions. "Yeah."

"Is today Monday?" Carly, bruised, those weeks before she died.

"Yeah."

"Are you wearing a black T-shirt?" Carly, her face beaten in.

"Yes."

Handles asked, "Did you clean behind the toilet this morning like I told you to?" and Clay decided to lie, letting the stress rise, using it, eating it up, making it his, and remembering that feeling for the big questions.

"Yes," he said, his voice reflecting the shit spewing in his stomach.

"Do you love slinging booze upstairs?"

He reached for another bad thought and didn't have to look far for this one—Ape behind him was good enough. "Love it."

A chuckle from everyone but his nemesis.

"Is your real name Jeremy Greer?"

Happy thoughts—not easy for Clay, since there wasn't much to be happy about, was there? Calm, blue water. A mountain lake. *Carly alive.* "Yeah," he said.

"Have you ever worked in law enforcement?" No longer control questions now. The real deal.

Mountains, a breeze, a brook. "No."

"Are you currently working with law enforcement?"

"No," he said, inflecting his voice with a strain of offended irritation, but he couldn't stop the sweat from dripping out of his hairline, right over a week-old scab and down his cheek.

"Where'd you do your training?" Ape broke in. God, the man had always had a hard-on for him.

"My training?"

"Your fucking law enforcement training? Where'd you do it?"

"What are you talking about, man?"

"You know what I'm fucking saying, you fucking pig. I've seen the way you watch us."

Clay's body had gone numb then, tingly at the extremities, his limbs cold and his face hot, constricted, no air. He'd fought for air.

No sound except breathing. It went on forever, that quiet, Handles and Ape and everybody else just waiting for him to give himself away. It was one of those moments where his skin felt tight, but the persona felt floppy. Surely they could see the real him peeking through the eye holes?

Another few seconds, and Handles leaned in, a half smile on his face. "We've got a deal goin' on next week. Might have to take care of a couple of people—woman and a kid." Clay held it together. They wouldn't kill a kid. He wouldn't kill a kid. *Hold your shit together, Navarro.* He breathed deeply and waited for the question. Interviewing 101. Say nothing until you have to. "Would you do that for your club? For your brothers?"

"Yes," he said, calm, calm, calm. And on it went, Ape breathing down his neck, Boom-Boom watching, eyes devoid of emotion, and Handles staring him down, cold but fatherly in the weirdest fucking way.

"Would you die for the Sultans?" Handles asked, and the door opened, and *Carly* walked in—and like always, the dream exploded everywhere. Blood, gore, loud, loud, the report of a weapon, Boom-Boom's hands on his sister's corpse, her dead eyes turned to Clay, accusatory white globes of hate, Ape's ax through Clay's head, hurting like hell. He dove to the ground, into the stink and shit of the dungeon floor, where the blood of millions soaked into his clothes, up his nose, and he gagged, fought, kicked, screamed himself awake.

Awake. Alive. I'm alive.

But not Carly. Carly was dead. Every time he woke up, his little sister was still dead.

◈

"He's gone." Ape ended the call. He was about to lose his shit, which was precisely the reason for his fucking nickname to begin with. When things went wrong, he went apeshit. Sometimes even when things went right.

"What? He didn't go into witness protection like Candy Lan—"

"Don't call him that," Ape cut in, needing something to pummel. Somebody's face would do just fine. Jam's

if he had to. "His name's Breadthwaite. Special fuckin'
Agent Nikolaj fuckin' Breadthwaite."

"Fuck kinda name is that? Fucker ain't even
American." Jam hated anyone who wasn't American.

"Neither's Navarro."

"Shoulda killed him when I had the chance."

Ape almost laughed. Jam especially hated spics.
And it turned out that was precisely what Special Agent
Clay Navarro was. A spic from South America. Christ,
how the hell had he ever made it into the club? Into the
goddamned ATF for that matter? They just hire any old
asshole off the street now?

"We'll get him." Ape was absolutely certain of that.
He had yet to miss a mark. It could take him months.
Years, even. That ATF bastard had taken down the lead-
ership of the Sultans. But he still had to testify.

Ape knew he'd stop the cocksucker from taking the
stand if it was the last thing he did.

MONDAY MORNING, GEORGE MET THE HEATING AND cooling guys at the office at six thirty—thankful they'd come out so early—and sighed with relief as her first patient arrived to a decent temperature.

Along with the cool air, her nurse's return from vacation gave George the sensation of coming back down to earth after a few days spent someplace very, very strange.

Ah, boring normality—her wheelhouse.

Some people craved excitement and change, but George needed things to be the same, predictable. She preferred *fine* to *good*, *nice* to *wonderful*. Nothing to upset her status quo.

Let her patients be turbulent. George was the calm one. The island in the stream.

Who'd have thought that dermatology could be anything besides sedate?

Purnima arrived with that healthy glow she got every time she went home to India. George assumed it was the diet: real food instead of the hormone- and pesticide-filled crap that masqueraded as nourishment around here. But it was more than that, she knew. Purnima's eyes looked clearer, her smile centered. God, how George admired that in her—how together the woman was. She might be George's employee, but she'd always thought there was a ton she could learn from her.

"You've been busy, I see," Purnima said from her spot in front of the computer. "I thought you said you'd take it easy while I was gone? Wasn't there mention of a mini break or something?"

George just smiled and hesitated. Should she hug her? She'd been gone for three weeks, after all, and... No. Hugging was inappropriate.

"And then the A/C..." George said with a sigh. "You have no idea."

"Feels good this morning. Did you call Carmichael's?"

"Yes," George said, her face reddening with shame. "I hated to call in a favor, but—"

"You caught his melanoma, George. He *wants* to help. People are happy to thank you, however they can."

"Yes, but it's my job."

"Sure." Purnima raised her hands, one on either side, like a scale weighing the difference. "Fixes A/C, cures cancer. I'm sure they come out even in the end." The woman laughed and clicked a couple of keys before looking up and catching sight of George for the first time.

"My God, what happened to your face?"

"Oh, nothing" was all George said, self-consciously touching the bruise on her cheek. Thankfully, Purnima was discreet enough that she wouldn't pry after being rebuffed. But then guilt won out, of course, because if it wasn't safe for her, then… "I was attacked. Outside."

"No! Who would do that?"

"It was the Fourth of July, and I think they were on drugs, perhaps? There was a scuffle and I intervened and… They were young."

"What did the police say?"

"I didn't call the police."

"Whyever not?"

"I…" George thought about it, suddenly unsure. "I…I suppose I didn't need to. Someone came to my rescue, and they left."

Purnima's brows rose at that, but George didn't feel like going into it any further. She didn't quite understand herself why she hadn't called the police. Maybe something about Andrew Blane made her think he wouldn't want that. No. He definitely hadn't seemed to want that.

Whatever the reason, she felt shaky enough as it was today. She was done talking about it, which wasn't something she cared to examine, especially after spending all day Sunday hunkered down at home, thinking—or rather *not* thinking—about *him*.

"So, no patients Friday afternoon, then?"

She debated how to answer but, as usual, gave in to the truth. "There was one."

Purnima turned back to the screen and keyed through charts for a few more seconds, until she eventually turned back to her boss. And somehow, for some silly reason, George had to force herself, with difficulty, to look her nurse in the eye.

"I don't see it on the books," said Purnima.

"No."

The woman's brows rose.

"Pro bono?"

"I…" George swallowed, wondering when she'd ever been this conflicted about a patient. Never. Never was the answer. "Yes," she finally whispered.

Uma popped into her head. She was the only other patient she'd had come in like that, off the street, looking like a victim. No, not a victim. A survivor, maybe.

And not weak at all. Andrew Blane was strong, frightening, compelling.

So compelling I can't get him out of my head.

"Tattoos," she said, a little ashamed at how curt she must sound but unwilling to feed the obvious curiosity in her employee's eyes. "He needs them removed."

Purnima nodded slowly, twice, before lowering her eyes to the screen. "Interesting" was all she said. As always, a mistress of subtlety.

As she continued down the hall to close herself in her office, George looked deep down inside and recognized an embarrassing truth: she didn't want to discuss Andrew Blane with her nurse or with anyone. She wanted to hide her new patient away, to keep him all to herself in a way that felt shameful. There was something else warring with the shame, however: a thread of titillation or excitement or whatever buzzy spark of interest this was, vibrating through her body.

She had patients to see, but all her wayward brain could think about was that man. This wasn't healthy, and it wasn't right, but George couldn't seem to stop counting the minutes until Andrew Blane walked through her door again. She glanced at the clock.

Maybe he wouldn't come back at all.

Too many hours spent hunkered down in the motel room, trying hard not to drink, with only the shitty-ass TV to distract him, was more than Clay could bear. After weeks in the hospital, then months of PT and brain-numbing television, he'd developed a hatred for the device—especially shows that glorified the bad guys. Those were the worst. He'd destroyed his television the first time he'd come across one particular show on bikers.

That had led to his new rule: no vodka during the day, and no TV ever.

Breathing hard and still sore from running the past couple nights—that and beating the shit out of those two kids—he grabbed his keys and headed out the door, needing air, space, anything to distract from the new set of memories working through his mind on repeat.

The doc on the ground, rolled into a protective ball, those *fucks* kicking her. He'd wanted to kill them, had barely held himself back. Because, yeah, if he killed a couple of tweakers right now, he'd sure screw the *hell* out of the Sultans case.

But he *was* a Sultan, now, wasn't he? More Sultan than cop, that was for damned sure. He'd seen the way everyone looked at him back at the field office after his discharge from the hospital. Jesus, his colleagues had eyed him like he was scum.

Course then Tyler'd caught sight of him, and everything had changed. What a shock it had been when they'd eventually stopped typing and set down their phones, and stood up for him. A few of them had even clapped. A huge case. With him at its center.

Didn't matter that he didn't feel like a hero.

In his truck, he looked both ways before pulling away from the downtown area, where traffic had thickened only slightly during what passed for rush hour in Blackwood.

Ahead of him stood the first small foothills before the slightly grander line of the Blue Ridge Mountains. He knew, looking at the beauty of their bluish-purple crests, that he should feel something. He'd spent so much time in slums and projects, filthy biker clubhouses and run-down police stations that he hardly recognized the power of beauty anymore. Maybe it was gone forever—that ability to see the good in things.

He drove on, unsure where this road led, and enjoying the lack of control. Well, not entirely that, maybe, because lack of control was something he'd felt time and again in situations where some psychopath held the reins. That wasn't what he sought.

No, what he needed right then was to feel like anything was possible.

Up he drove, over asphalt, then gravel, then just dual, overgrown tracks in the dirt leading higher and higher.

Finally, long past the *End State Maintenance* sign, he parked, truck facing back the way he'd come, and got out. Up a path he walked, ignoring the way his steel-toed boots rubbed his feet with every step, until the trees thinned, the trail grew rockier, and finally, finally, he emerged.

It was high here—the top of a mountain. The air had lost some of its oppressive humidity and heat, and here…oh, here, he could breathe.

And the view… Jesus Christ. He turned around 360

degrees, an action that forced him to take it all in until he couldn't do it anymore and had to bend, drop his hands to his knees, and breathe.

Just breathe.

Survive.

The polygraph had been about survival. Animal instinct and training had gotten him through that. Later, they'd given him his colors, the Sultans patch sewn onto the sleeveless leather cut he and the other guys wore every single day of their lives. He remembered the feel of Handles's arm around him—fatherly, welcoming, warm. Jesus, that was almost the worst part, how good it had been to have brothers—a family. The only thing that had come close in years had been finishing Special Agent Basic Training with Tyler. They'd been like family back then too.

Nothing like Handles and the club's acceptance, though. The cut, the rides, the way he could do no wrong with them, now that he'd beaten the box, survived the hazing, accepted his patch with tears in his fucking eyes, gotten his ink, and been proud—truly proud—of it.

Jam had hugged him, hard, and Clay had felt it deep in his soul. *Brothers. Family.*

He remembered Ape's scowl when the asshole had taken him in back for his club tat—the big one on his back. But while the dude had always hated him, he sure as fuck had enjoyed tattooing him. Jesus, Ape loved that shit, didn't he? The light in his eye confirming he was one hundred percent sadist.

Ape, who'd disappeared the night of the raid—one of a handful of guys they hadn't managed to pin down. How the hell had he known?

On a deep sigh, Clay pulled his brain back out, let himself see the mountains instead of memories.

He wasn't sure how long he stayed up there, ignoring the majesty of his surroundings and just trying to locate a new well, a new vein of hope he could tap into. It took some time for him to realize he'd just about used it all up. He was all dried out. It would take one hell of a dowsing rod at this point to locate unplumbed depths he was pretty sure he didn't have.

No. Focus. Find yourself here.

Clay drew in a big breath and opened his eyes to the view and… *Whoa.* As far as the eye could see, a hazy, blue-and-gray landscape, surreal like some kind of painting. Artsy shit you'd see tattooed on the arms of hipster kids who didn't know better. Lush, yet almost colorless in the cloud-covered morning. The details smudged out, the edges softened like the view after a couple of beers or that first hit of weed.

Above him, a bird flew—big, dark, huge wingspan. A hawk, he thought for a second and then knew, somehow, that it wasn't.

A vulture. The perfect addition to this colorless, gray panorama. It landed on a lone, brittle-looking tree fifty yards away and regarded the world around it with quick, unimpressed moves of its head.

A hawk or an eagle, he could have gotten behind. A symbol of hope or something.

But a vulture?

And then it hit him, with an ironic twinge of humor, how right it was.

He stood straighter, like that scavenger on the branch, wanting to feel above it all.

So, fine, Clay Navarro was no eagle. But there were other things he could build on. His strength had always been his ability to see past people's exteriors and get a line on what it was they really wanted. Not what they showed the world, but the petty things that made them tick. In recent months, he may have lost that ability, seen it drowned out by the constant white noise in his head, the pain in his body. But it was clearer up here; this high, he could even trick himself into thinking he'd get it back one day.

Like that creature up there, his career had flourished off the flesh of others—on what they'd left behind, untended. So, he'd just have to view himself the same way and live on the bits of rotting meat still clinging to his bones. The shitty bits still left after all the good was torn away—vengeance, hate, anger. Yeah, he had lots of that. Enough to fuel an army, in fact.

And that thought, that realization, sent Clay back down the mountain, into town, with the strength to keep up this charade of a life. For the time being, at least.

This time, George was ready when he arrived. Sort of.

It had been a busy day spent trying to catch up on Friday's missed appointments, which was good, since her mind had spent an uncomfortable amount of time going back to him. All day, she'd fended off questions about the bruises and anticipated his arrival with the most unwelcome combination of excitement and apprehension, building it up so that, by the time his form blocked out the low evening sunlight, she had decided more or less how to proceed. No casual talk and no mention of Saturday night, besides a well-deserved thanks. Professional, strict.

That, of course, translated to stiff, which probably only made her seem nervous. A complete failure in bed-side manner.

"Evening, Doc."

George shivered. *That voice.* Rougher than she was used to, lower, without any hint of local Virginia twang.

"Mr. Blane." He loitered in the doorway. "Come in, come in." Great, now she sounded like a little old woman, enticing him with tea and cookies. Or something.

"How you feeling tonight, Doc?"

"Wonderful."

"That's quite a shiner you got there."

"I'm fine," she snapped, tired of explaining the thing all day and not wanting to relive it with him right now, either.

The man moved inside, limping—which reminded her that he'd run back to the motel the other night—and finally pulled off his glasses, baring sharp, assessing eyes beneath two bright red, puffy lids, greased up.

At least he followed directions.

He stepped forward, hand out, and George hesitated, thinking for a second that he might… What? Kiss her? Hug her? Lord, she was messed up.

"I owe you some money, Doc."

"Oh. No. Thank you," she said. "You saved me from…from a world of hurt. I can't accept your money."

"Look, Doc, I—"

"Mr. Blane. Please," she said, her breathing loud in her ears.

His eyes flicked between hers, measuring, weighing, and finally, apparently, deciding she wasn't bluffing.

He gave in, lowered his chin in a single quick nod, then asked, "Where d'you want me, Doc?"

"Come on back," she said, trying so hard to sound like the doctor she was, suddenly wishing she hadn't insisted on seeing him this late, all alone, with her staff long gone.

As she led him to the last exam room on the right, George pretended he was just another patient—an urticaria needing steroid cream, a full-body skin check, or a mole to biopsy. When she turned back at the door, though, and caught him eyeing her bottom or her legs, hidden though they were by her trousers, her body reacted in a way that showed *it* knew the difference between him and everyone else, even if her mind didn't care to. Just that look, that slide of his eyes over layers of clothing, dragged her into a morass of sexuality that she'd managed for years to avoid.

His gaze went up to her face, and she saw his eyes change, watched their warm brown darken to black, and the muscle in his jaw tighten. "Didn't realize they'd got your face so bad."

"Oh," she said, her hand flying back to the telltale bruise. "It really is fine. No big deal."

"You call the cops after I left?"

"No. No, I didn't." And then, because she didn't want to talk about it any longer, she said, "Your eyes look good."

"You call this good?" He shook his head wryly. "You're one weird lady."

"I know it hurts, but it's doing what it should. Red, blistering. Now, let's get your shirt off, Mr. Blane," she said, dodging his gaze. And that sentence—her stupidly chosen words—heightened her body's fall into unwanted sensuality.

Wonderful. Just great. After all her careful planning and preparation. Rather than look at him as he stripped, George busied herself prepping the already-prepped room, her mind hunting for words that didn't contain subtext within subtext, with even more subtext lurking beneath.

"Remembered the burning hair last time, Doc." Behind her came the sound of clothing being removed. "So I shaved my chest."

Oh, that did it. Her eyes, evil creatures, bypassed her brain's directives entirely and slithered right to where her body wanted them—on that chest. Good *Lord*, that chest. She'd spent all weekend thinking about that chest. Below his clavicles, he was so unfeasibly flat and broad, she'd need a half-dozen hands to span it. And *strong*. Still lower, the muscles curved out, hard and male and sexual in a way that pectorals shouldn't be—they really *shouldn't*. And then the thought of her bare hands, right there, touching his freshly shaven skin…

George swallowed audibly in the quiet room and reached for her gloves. A barrier.

"'S that okay? You hadn't mentioned body hair last time, but I figured it'd make it easier."

"Oh, yes, that's *wonderf*—" Another attempted swallow over dry, dry throat. "I mean, you did the right thing. In fact, I should have told you." Her throat clicked again, and before her tongue managed to talk her straight into some sort of absurd 1980s porn scenario, George threw the switches on the machine. It would drown her out. And him, thank God.

༄

He'd blocked out the memory of that fucking *noise*. Louder than the sound of Ape's tattoo machine and just as insistent, like being too close to an airplane right before it takes off.

The doctor put a hand on Clay's arm, and he sighed.

"Sorry. Kinda forgot about that sound." The mother-fucking sound.

"Need a minute?"

He shook his head. They'd done this just a few days before. He could do it again.

Her hand lingered on his shoulder for another beat, and he willed it to stay there. To touch him, ground him, make him real.

That didn't happen though. Instead, she moved, handed him a pair of big, dark glasses, which he slipped on, and picked up that laser thingy.

"Okay, so. Chest today." She sounded as breathless as he felt.

"Yeah."

"Great."

The clicking started, and Clay closed his eyes, girding himself for the pain. When it registered, though, he opened them again. He needed to see what was happening. There was nothing worse than being blind to your fate.

She held the metal arm contraption out, focusing the point on his skin, and pulled the trigger mechanism. With her head down, with those glasses on, the woman looked focused, serious, professional.

Fuck, that hurt. And not one big pain, but a series of tiny, minute burns, one after another, like rubber bands snapping, snapping. He watched his skin change in the laser's wake, a hazy, slightly puffy white frost over-laying his ink. He'd been disappointed to see from his last session that the white disappeared eventually. False hope that the process would be faster than expected. But no. Once the white burn faded, the ink was still there, only—

Oh, hell, it hurts.

"I'm so sorry. That was your…" The woman cleared her throat. "Your nipple."

No shit, he thought, pasting on a smile for her benefit.

"The rest should be easier." Again she hesitated. "Your stomach and…hips."

Clay's eyes stayed glued to the doctor. What the hell she must think of him, this big creep with his contradic-tory stories scrawled all over his outside—and his one, drunken attempt to rid himself of the worst of the ink.

Yeah, he bet she was impressed by that. Her expression, though, was hidden behind those ugly-ass glasses, so he had no clue. No fucking clue. She bit her lip, leaned in, and went to town on his belly, one hand resting lightly on his. Clay closed his eyes at her touch—soaking up the pain the way his bloodstream would soak up the particles of pigment—and let his mind go away.

Ape, marching him into the back that day, sur-rounded by their brothers. But what could he do? What could he fucking do, with the entire fucking *multi-agency task force* poised outside, waiting to descend on the place?

Into the back, the stress of that quick stop in the head, whispering into the wire and those ridiculous Hail Marys as he waited for Ape to pop his eyeball. Because when Ape wanted you in back, you fucking went, and you let him ink you. Brotherhood and all that.

"Mr. Blane? Andrew? Are you okay?"

"Mmm?" Clay shook his head. It was fuzzy, wrong.

He opened his eyes to find that the noise had stopped, which was better, since it meant no more tats. Ape nowhere in sight. Or behind him with a fucking ax.

The quiet left a hollow in his head, a vacuum where he should have found relief, but instead he seemed to have lost sight of himself.

From the hazy depths, he saw a woman's hand on his. He frowned at it, the way the fingers looked over his dark ones. She was talking to him, and he tried nodding, wanted to smile.

Be a cop, not a biker.

Stuffing the biker deep, deep inside of him, Clay attempted to listen to what she was saying.

Her other hand reached out and touched his shoulder lightly before trying to pull away, but he stopped her, grabbed her, held her against him, hard.

"Stay here," he slurred. Was he drunk?

"May I…" A thin, white hand hovered close to his face, and he almost flinched before she reached out and removed the foggy layer covering his eyes.

Oh. Oh, right. Glasses. Protective glasses. He blinked in the bright, sterile room and let it come back to him. Or rather let himself return. Shit. The doctor. Had he hurt her?

"I'm…I'm sorry, Doc."

He should thank her.

He would. In a second. Just as soon as he got out of this fuzz. He sat back on the table, sank down, heavy.

Shit, he'd done it again, hadn't he? Gone somewhere ugly, from the looks of it.

"Did I…?" He closed his mouth, trying to get enough saliva to speak. "Are you okay?"

"Am I…? Oh, I'm fine, Mr.… I'm fine."

The woman, clearly not in her right mind to trust him, reached out, and he caught those gloved fingers with his, almost brought them to his mouth, but saw the freakiness of that before it happened. The arm of his protective glasses snagged between them, hard edges pressing grooves into his flesh.

"Thank you," he said in a voice that wasn't even remotely his. It was too low, too grainy, too breathy and bare.

For a handful of seconds, she squeezed him back, and all he could see were the kaleidoscope layers of her eyes.

It took some time for him to come out of his haze, the air still snapping with electricity.

"You Irish?" he asked, and she squinted, not seeming to understand. "Green eyes," he explained.

"Oh. Right. Actually, yes. I'm half Irish," she finally answered, and he nodded. And there were their hands again, still pressed together into a stark, spidery sculpture of black examination gloves, tattooed fingers, and dark glasses. The longer he looked, the less it felt like *him*. He squeezed and felt nothing. After a moment, she squeezed back, and that, *that* he felt, like a vise. A warm, solid vise. He let a finger loosen, ran it over hers, and shivered when she again tightened her hold. He moved his eyes back to her face, and she looked— what? Shocked? Scared?

Don't be scared.

"Are you okay, Mr. Blane?"

Blane? His mouth groggily attempted to correct her, but the woman talked right over him.

"Is there someone I can call to come get you?"

He chuckled at that. Just a half laugh, which eventually turned into a real one, strong enough to finally pop this goddamn bubble.

Clay needed to stop this. Now. He considered calling the shrink, whose wrinkled card lay back in the motel, at the bottom of his duffel bag. He wondered if he should, in fact, be taking the meds that had been given to him—and then shook his head.

"No. No, Doc. There's nobody to call." He had to smile then at the woman's concerned expression. How was this person so nice? Couldn't she see that he was absolutely the last person on earth she should be bothering with? Had she no survival instincts whatsoever?

"Well, I could bring you—"

He swung his legs over the side of the table, wincing as his thigh got to that crucial angle, and then covering up the expression as he realized what Dr. Do-Good's reaction would be. He let go of her hand, immediately wanting to take it again, then hopped down, ready for the pain this time, and reached for his shirt, which he pulled over his head.

"Oh. I haven't applied the petroleum jelly. You need—"

"I'm fine."

Her eyes roamed his chest in a way he could almost feel, and fuck, he hated slimy crap, but he wanted her to spread that shit all over him. "You should really let me…"

Fuck yes, touch me.

"No," he heard himself say. Firm almost to the point of rudeness. "I'm fine, Doc. Seriously. I got it." He smiled at her again, made the expression hard and self-sufficient. "When can I come in again?"

"Oh. I'd better look at the…" He caught her eyes, let his gaze take in the smooth skin of her face, broken only by the unnaturally rosy flush of her cheeks and that fucking bruise that made him want to kill.

Farther down, her lab coat blocked his view of the rest of her, but he *knew*. He remembered, from those brief, stolen snatches, her pale legs in that dress and—

He glanced back up and found her watching him watch her. Her words had trailed off, and there was awareness here between them. Awareness he might not have given her credit for before. She looked so innocent that he'd thought she might be oblivious too. But the flush crept farther up her ears, and he knew she'd gotten at least a tiny bit of what his thoughts were.

Clay considered stepping forward, doing something inappropriate. He considered it and then threw it away, because his track record with ladies was pretty grim. Not only that, but this woman was the only person he'd found who'd take care of him. And that was the priority.

Priorities. Right.

"Can you take me tomorrow? For my back?" he asked, cutting through this absurd fantasy they appeared to be sharing. Synchronized hallucinations. *Folie à deux*, he remembered a psychiatrist calling it once on the stand, and he'd gone and looked it up—shared insanity. That was what this shit felt like.

"Yes," she said without hesitating. And he liked that. He couldn't help but enjoy that she wanted him to come back, but he also knew it was bad. Attachments were bad. Anything that distracted from his goal. Anything that risked his cover, his anonymity. "We'll need to numb your back. You'll need an injection."

"No."

"It's too big a surface, Mr. Blane. The pain—"

"It'll be fine. No injections."

"Then we'll do one section at a time."

"I want to get it out, Doc. All of it."

"There's so much solid black. I really can't…" She stopped, appearing to reevaluate. "Fine. We'll use a numbing cream. The treatment won't be as effective. The research proves it. But I won't do it otherwise. Not with that much ink."

"Got it. You're the expert."

"See you tomorrow, then?"

"Yes, ma'am. Although"—he glanced at the door—"maybe I should wait for you to finish up here. Walk you to your car."

"Oh, no. I'll be fine."

He wasn't sure he agreed, but her expression didn't leave much room for argument.

"See you tomorrow, then. Same time" was all he said, before turning and limping out the door.

As he made his way up the hall, through the waiting room, and out into the hot, humid evening, he considered, not for the first time, what his future consisted of.

And, try as he might, he couldn't get past the first few steps: federal court, testify, put those fuckers in prison for life. And then… Christ, he didn't know. He tried to picture his next gig. Tried and tried and…*nothing.*

There was nothing for him but empty road.

George didn't follow him out, didn't lock the door behind him. Hands shaking, she pulled the paper off the examination table, wiped everything down, and walked the trash straight out back, since everything had already been cleaned out once that evening.

Outside, the air was rank with the stench of a week's worth of summer sun beating on the Dumpster—and no rain. A glance farther down showed the lights on at the MMA school. Time to head home to her crew. Leonard would no doubt be angry.

Still her pulse beat like a jackhammer, and she refused to think about why. Why did she feel so compelled to comfort that man? Why couldn't she keep her damned hands to herself?

She had no answers.

George had hung up her lab coat, grabbed her keys and purse when her phone rang. She fumbled it out and to her ear, almost expecting… What? *Him* to be on the other end?

"Hello?" she said, out of breath.

"Dr. Hadley?"

"Yes?"

"Hi there," replied the chirpy voice. "I'm calling from the Charlottesville Regional Reproductive Medicine Clinic."

"Oh." She stopped, heart thumping harder. "Yes?"

"Dr. Sternberg took a look at the ultrasound, and

everything's ready to go. He'd like to put you on the books for a week from Wednesday. The…uh…fifteenth."

"Oh. Wednesday the fifteenth. Okay, great."

"How does five sound?"

"Wonderful. Five. Perfect."

"Did you have any questions about the intrauterine insemination procedure before you come in?"

"No, no, I'm good."

"And you've got the HCG injection for Monday?"

"Yes, I've got it ready to go."

"Great, well, we'll see you next week, then."

A week from Wednesday. Somehow, through the ultrasounds and endless medications and self-administered shots, George had managed not to think about what she was preparing her body for.

They'd take her dead husband's sperm and put it inside her cervix, and she would, hopefully, get pregnant.

Treatment. Pregnancy. Baby. Child.

She should be excited, over the moon, but something was missing here. The husband, perhaps, to go with that vial of washed sperm the lab had kept on ice this past decade? A vial of sperm that she had to use or lose at this point? A daddy for the baby she planned on bringing into this world? Someone to love her?

For almost a decade, she'd let that vial sit, an unexpected second chance left untouched in that sperm bank. A decade spent picking up the pieces of her shattered life, creating the perfect nest for the baby she'd one day have, putting it off and putting it off. A decade spent eschewing fun in favor of responsibility. Because this was what she wanted: her clinic, her house, and now her baby.

Why on earth didn't it feel like enough anymore? She didn't trust it—this feeling that suddenly there might be more to life, just out of reach—but she had no idea how to make it go away.

Clay let his eyes scan downtown Blackwood, taking in the cars parked nearby. The martial arts place next door to the skin clinic was holding a class for women. He squinted, watching the ladies go slowly through a series of defensive moves before practicing them on a couple of guys. He surveyed the rest of the block—it was quiet, so quiet he had a hard time trusting this place. Time and again since he'd gotten here, he'd had to remind himself that it was a small town. Quiet was the norm, not the other way around.

Except it wasn't like that, was it? There was bad everywhere, people like those junkies who'd attacked the doc. Because under the quiet, in every bumfuck corner of this godforsaken country—probably the world—evil lurked.

Back to the martial arts place, where the women were beating the hell out of the guys. Or pretending to, because Clay knew from experience that big guys like himself, like the giant inside, could take a woman down with one hand tied behind their backs. It wasn't some half-assed fist block that would make a difference.

Cynical. So fucking cynical.

Farther along, he spotted the sign for the town's one and only bar. It looked kind of old-fashioned, with lettering that should read *Ye Olde Pub*. Instead, it read *The Nook*, which made him think of dim lights and knitting.

He watched as a group of people pulled open the door and went inside, laughing.

Minutes passed, and Clay's pulse slowed to normal. As he watched the self-defense women, they wrapped up their class and started spilling out onto the sidewalk, which felt like his cue to leave—best not to be accused of being some kind of creep. Surefire way to get his ass kicked out of town.

Just as he turned the ignition, the clinic lights went out, the door opened, and Dr. Hadley stepped outside. She locked the door without looking up once—Jesus, even after the other night, the woman had no sense of self-preservation, which drove him completely nuts. Didn't she know she was a sitting duck for all kinds of predators?

She needed to take that class. Because, although the moves were pretty Mickey Mouse, they'd at least teach her to look before heading out into this fucked-up world. He'd seen the shit people did to women. He *knew*.

Clay watched as she stepped off the sidewalk, not appearing to even notice the women walking out next door, moved to her car—unlocked, which sent his blood pressure through the roof—and finally drove off.

From somewhere close by, an engine fired up, and Clay almost jumped out of his skin.

Breathing too hard, he waited a few seconds for his anxiety to dissipate and, when it didn't appear to abate at all, put his truck into drive and followed the doctor at a respectful distance.

Too many women had suffered because he'd given them space or looked the other way. He was done looking the other way. He didn't care how small a town this was—there was evil everywhere, around every street corner. He'd seen it in guys he'd taken down; he'd seen it in the smiling eyes of psychopaths; he'd seen it in the eyes of men he'd called brother.

God, he knew how fucking weird this was, following the doctor home. He couldn't stand to see another woman get hurt on his watch. Especially one this soft, this caring.

Creeped out was better than dead.

George wasn't generally one to partake in excessive alcohol. Not that she hadn't back in her wild days, when she'd let herself get coerced into situations by bad boys, done wild things, and gotten pregnant in the process. She regretted those times, the manic fun, the stupid decisions made out of sadness and desperation. Bad boys, tattoos, and all the rest of it, she reminded herself, were nothing compared to adult decisions and everything else that had eventually made partying seem not quite so fun anymore.

Bad boys were a bad idea.

Andrew Blane was a very bad idea.

And so was stopping by the fancy country store on the way home to buy herself a bottle of something. Anything would have satisfied her, but she wound up getting a six-pack of cider, because beer felt too casual and champagne too expensive, but she wanted a drink, something to cap off this strange, strange night.

What she really wanted was to call someone—a friend would be nice—and tell them what was going on. She wanted to spill everything. Her need to have a baby—a family. Someone to call her own. Her fears that she was doing something very wrong here. That this wasn't how these things were meant to happen. And D-Day just a week away. It was all too much, this last-chance pressure.

Added to that, the entire weird story about the big, broken man who had suddenly encroached on her every waking thought, his rough hands holding her so tightly, leaving her afraid for rather than of him. And she wanted that friend to *understand*. That was the toughest part, beyond obvious things like ethics and HIPAA violations. More than anything, she wanted to be told that she wasn't absolutely out of her mind for feeling the way she did about him, which was…unclear.

Pulling into her driveway, she glanced at the house next door—it had been empty for the past six months, but Jessie and her son appeared to have moved in yesterday, which was good. Neighbors were good. Someone she could count on when she ran out of sugar. Or whatever.

She smiled at that. Sugar? No. She wouldn't run out anytime soon. George didn't run out of things.

On her way inside, she cast another glance at the cottage and thought about the six-pack of cider she held. She wouldn't mind sharing…

Down the relative coolness of the long hall, into the kitchen, six-pack in the fridge, then straight through the back door and out into the hot, hot humidity of a Virginia summer evening.

The usual sounds of home greeted her: calm clucking, which meant her patching job on the fence had worked; lazy birdsong, gaining in intensity at this time of day— like children at bedtime, the creatures got worked up before the bats took over as kings of the night sky. Beyond that, she heard the far-off drone of a mower. Always mowing in Virginia. Lord, with the in-laws' grass to do every weekend, she had enough mowing to last her a lifetime. George preferred livelier plants, their bursts of color and meandering stalks much more her speed than flat, boring plains of green. And here was the sound of crickets. Loud and intense, but somehow always in the background. Although…no. She cocked her head.

Not crickets. These were cicadas.

She remembered a discussion she'd overheard that day in the office. Cindy and Purnima had come in from lunch talking about the insects' seventeen-year cycle and the noise they'd make this year—not to mention the empty exoskeletons they'd leave behind. George hadn't lived in the area for the last cicada visit, and she didn't seem to have any around her place, so she could only guess how loud it would get.

Someone had left a copy of the Gazette in the waiting room, and George had read through the feature, headlined CICADAS: SEVENTEEN-YEAR ITCH. She was fascinated. To live for such a short time, only to plant your seed for the next generation and die off…

A wave of sadness overcame her, heavy and familiar. A glance at her watch showed it was too late to call the in-laws.

Somewhere close by, a car door slammed, and she heard voices. Jessie and her son. It must be, since nobody else lived that close by.

Behind her, Leonard announced his arrival with a trilling meow before butting his head against George's leg. She bent to pick him up just as the cottage screen door squealed open, then slammed shut, only to open again before someone went barreling out into the yard next door.

A second later, the door opened, and a woman's voice called out. "Gabe! Put your shoes back on! The yard's a mess!" George craned her neck to see past her landscaping and the tall wooden fence. There was no response. "Gabe Shifflett, you get in here right now, or I'll... Oh, whatever." The woman's voice trailed off, and as she turned to go inside, she glanced at George's place. Their eyes met with recognition. "George?"

"Jessie!" George called. "You all moved in?"

"Hey, yeah! Wait, *this* is your house? I thought you were farther down. I thought this place was—" The woman interrupted herself, and George wondered what she'd been about to say.

"This is me."

"What're you up to? Wanna come over for pizza? We can sit on the porch and watch it *not* rain."

"Well, I..." George searched for something to say, some reason to refuse. And then, suddenly, it occurred to her that she didn't have to. Jessie was nice. This could be good. *A friend.* A wish come true. "Why don't you come over here, instead? I imagine you're not all unpacked and... Oh, hey, I've got cider!"

"Cider?"

"Hard cider. Like beer, only"—George shrugged—"for lightweights."

"Can I bring my monster?" Jessie asked.

"Of course!" George said through a bubble of excitement.

Inside, her eyes took in her house, wondering what someone like Jessie would think of the bright-colored, barely controlled chaos. *It's fine*, she decided, ignoring the self-doubt. Her house was hers, and if people didn't like it, they didn't have to come over. On that thought, she pulled out a cider, searched frantically for a good minute and a half for something with which to open it before realizing that her can opener had the right attachment, and took a calming swig.

Okay. You can do this. You can have someone in your house. You can be friendly. It doesn't have to be a big deal.

No big deal, she thought, throwing seed packs into drawers, straightening up random piles of catalogues and medical journals, in a frenzy of last-minute activity. No big deal having actual friends and an actual life after so many years without. Only it *was* a big deal.

Having a life—*being alive*, in fact—was a very big deal when you'd put a husband in the ground and had assumed you'd live the rest of your days alone.

◈

The liquor store was still open. Clay breathed a sigh of relief.

"Can I help you?" the cashier asked when he made his way inside, and Clay tried his hardest to appear innocent.

"Vodka?"

"Sure. Back corner," she said in a voice that was friendlier than he'd expected.

He grabbed the biggest, midgrade bottle he could find—just one bottle, he decided; he'd stop after this

one—and headed back up front, head low and cap down
to shield him from the cameras above the register.

"That it, baby?"

Baby? Clay glanced up in surprise. Nothing, just mild
friendliness. Christ, he'd never get used to the South.

"Yes, ma'am."

"Thirteen oh seven."

He handed her a twenty and watched her chubby hands
deftly handle the change, despite the half-inch false nails
tipping her fingers. He'd never understand stuff like that—
why someone would purposely handicap themselves.
His eyes flicked to her face, round and bland-looking,
then up to sprayed-up blond bangs, then back down over
a lumpy body. So, decoration. Harmless peacocking from
a woman who hadn't been dealt the best hand. With
a mental shrug, he took his change and gave her a smile.

Making the most of what you had. Yeah, he could
relate.

"Night, baby."

"Good night, ma'am," he responded, waving in
response to her bright "Take care" before pushing back
out into the night.

Back at the motel, his room stank of mold, despite
the frigid temperature. He checked the A/C, which he'd
left on low but which appeared to have a mind of its own
and had taken the room to glacial. Damned thing.

Hit by a sudden wave of uncontrollable…some-
thing…he punched it, hard, his knuckles still suffering
from Friday's laser removal. It didn't dent the machine,
of course, which looked like a throwback to those pre-
historic units he remembered from elementary school,
but it felt good to hurt.

Am I fuckin' crazy? he wondered as the burn all over his front throbbed in time with his knuckles. Not to mention the rest—his thigh, his back. Those hurt pretty much all the time. Especially with this humidity, although it was nothing compared to the way he ached before a storm.

"Goddamn weather vane," he muttered as he grabbed the vodka on his way to the bathroom. Shit, he should have bought bleach. This place was gross, the grout black with fuzzy mold. He glanced at the booze, considered using that to clean with, and decided he was better off using it for its God-given purpose. Fuck all that Valium crap the shrink had given him. Vodka worked just fine.

It didn't matter what the shit tasted like anyway, did it? As long as it did the trick. In fact, he'd taken to drinking the clear stuff because it didn't hide behind smoke and caramel or any of those other cushioning screens. No, he drank the closest thing to rubbing alcohol that he could find—it wasn't about pleasure, after all. Far from it.

Take your meds, Clay.

Girding himself for what he'd see, Clay unbuttoned his shirt before pulling it off and peeling away the T-shirt beneath. Oh fuck, it hurt as the cotton unstuck. Not at all like a fresh tattoo. Hot and raw. More like a burn. Which was pretty appropriate, considering what that friggin' laser had done to him. He stretched his hand at the ache there, ignoring the pain on his eyelid, and stared at himself, hard. He'd put another coat of Vaseline on in a second.

Every fucking inch of the man before him was

ruined—by experience, by life, by choice. *Yeah, I chose this.*

He'd chosen some of the ink, at least. The arms, the story they told of his family tree, stunted by the early death of his baby sister. There was the Santa Muerte, symbol of a vengeance he was close to reaping. Farther along was the Inca death mask, in honor of his dad's people in Peru, whom he'd never get to meet, and their ancestors. Then there was the first tattoo he'd gotten— the one he'd never let anybody touch. *Mercy*, it said, and he stared at it to hold on to the good parts of his life. Carly—whose spirit had kept him going all these years. After a couple of seconds, he had to look away from it and return to the shit he'd done to avenge her.

He'd have done anything. *Anything.* To get her back? Fuck, he'd sell his soul.

⁓∞⁓

"Oh my God, I can't believe you punched him!"

"Punched him? Are you *kidding* me, George? I bitch-slap—" Jessie broke off, hand to her mouth, before noticing her son's closed eyes, where he lay in the corner of the wicker sofa.

"He's down," said George. She sat back with a sigh, reached for her bottle, and was surprised to find it empty. "Oh my God, I never drink. This is…"

"Fun?" finished Jessie. "This is *fun*. Thank you for having us over. And…I don't think he's fallen asleep that easily in ages. Not to mention the fact that he ate carrots and salad without argument, which is a minor miracle. We're coming over every night."

"I wish you would."

"Once a week, at least, just to get his veggies in. The pediatrician said that's all you need, really. I'll be golden." They smiled at each other for a second or two, a little dorky, a little embarrassed, until Jessie went on. "No, but seriously. He'd be lucky to have someone more like you for a mother," she said, her face losing all trace of humor.

"He's a wonderful kid, but you're a good mom."

"Nope. Can't take credit for that. That's all him."

It was loud where they sat out on the porch, night creatures chirping from the dark garden beyond the screens. In here, they were enveloped in a warm, orange candle glow, with the occasional tap of insects trying to get in. Funny. George must have had those candles for years, and this was the first time she'd lit more than one or two—the first occasion special enough to warrant a larger glow. Geez. It felt almost ceremonial and was most decidedly silly.

"Of course you can, Jessie. You're his mother."

Jessie sighed loudly, unapologetically, dramatically.

"You've built a life for the two of you. I'm impressed by how together you are, after…everything."

"So, you've heard my story?"

"Not really. Uma admires you. She told me you'd had it rough. I remember she said you were a fighter." George giggled, lifted her empty bottle, and reached across the coffee table to clank it against Jessie's. "Which appears to be true."

"Yeah, literally!"

George stood. "One more for the road?"

"What the hell. Why not?"

George walked inside to the kitchen for another pair

of ciders, her bare feet avoiding the squeaky boards out of habit, but the rest of her floating on an unfamiliar cloud of happiness.

She opened the bottles and stepped back out, handing one to Jessie—her new friend.

"You wanna know what she said about you, George?"

"I don't know. Do I?"

"Yes."

"Okay. Go on, then."

"She said you're a…vampire."

"Wh—"

"Just kidding." Jessie lost her smile and caught George's eye, held it. "She said you saved her life. Ive was there for her too, I know, but she says you're like this rock, and she couldn't have done it without you." George lost a bit of her breath on a dry huff of air. "She said you're the kindest, most selfless person she's ever met and—"

Jessie stopped herself, and George waited before prompting. "And?"

"And she's worried."

That hit George in the gut. A hard weight in her middle that tried to fold her in half. "W-worried?"

"She wants you to be happy and doesn't think you are."

Something occurred to George. "Is that why you came to get me at the party?"

"No! Jesus, George. You're delightful. It's been awesome hanging out with you." She looked around. "But this place…man."

"What about it?"

"It's…" Jessie opened her arms to encompass the house

behind them, the dark garden beyond the screen door. "I guess… Don't take this the wrong way, but I figured some old lady lived here, you know? The chickens and all the furniture and the garden and the cats and… Geez, how do you even have time to do all this with your job?"

George shrugged, feeling the truth of it—the weight of her existence. Add to it the baby she was going to make and—

Overwhelming. It was overwhelming.

Jessie leaned forward but turned to look at the snoring boy beside her. "I don't get out much, either, you know. Nine-year-olds aren't exactly conducive to active socializing."

"Yeah. So what's my excuse?"

Jessie lowered her brows at her and leaned even farther. "Uma said you switched to dermatology halfway through med school. She also mentioned why."

George gulped. She didn't realize Uma knew. How did she know about Tom?

"Pediatric oncology? I can't believe you were even considering that."

"Oh." George gulped, unsure if she was more relieved or disappointed. "I couldn't take all the babies dying. After seeing my husband go that way."

"And yet you're offering your services free to people in need. You can't help but do good."

George shrugged at that. "My parents were old. They had old-fashioned values or something."

"Yeah. Not mine." Jessie smiled. "That's probably how I ended up in my job—I was brought up kicking and fighting, so I figured I'd continue my rampage by fighting for the underdog."

"You're the first probation officer I've ever met, Officer Shifflett. Do you carry a badge and gun and all that?"

"A badge, yes. Don't carry a weapon, though. I own a handgun, but…"

"Oh, I thought—"

"Some people choose to. That's not the type of probation officer I want to be. Less force, more psychology."

"So you're more of a hand-to-hand combat kind of gal."

"Indeed." Jessie narrowed her eyes at George and cocked her head. "Wanna take my class?"

"Self-defense?"

"Yeah. Monday nights. You should come. You can close up shop and just swing by next door. I know you don't wanna talk about those bruises, George, but… whatever happened to your face is—"

"Independence Day insanity," George replied. "A couple of kids. I thought they were hurting each other and got in the middle and…" She pointed at her black eye. "Well, this happened. Anyway," she went on, thinking of Andrew Blane in her office earlier. She wouldn't have been able to see him tonight if she'd done the class. Stupid, stupid thought, since it wasn't like they were "seeing" each other anyway. He was a patient. *A patient, George.* "I don't think self-defense is really my thing."

"You sure?" Jessie tipped her bottle to her mouth with a wicked smile. "You'd get to kick my brother's ass."

With a laugh, George sat back and soaked in this woman's company and conversation, the back of her mind still caught up on a memory of fathomless dark eyes, heartbreakingly battle-scarred skin, and the way his hand hadn't wanted to let go.

∽◈∼

There was nothing better, as far as Ape was concerned, than the wind in your face, the hot rays of the sun setting on your back, and the highway under your tires. Especially when you added all that to the satisfaction of a job well done.

Tying up loose ends felt good. Better than good. It felt right, like this was exactly what he'd been born to do. Him on the road, taking care of business with a few good brothers behind him. Guys like Jam. Brothers you could count on.

He shoved back that itch of irritation at Handles. The guy'd had everything, as president, and he'd gone and let cops into the club.

No way that would have happened on my watch.

Ape hadn't trusted either Indian or Candy Land from the moment they'd started showing up at the bar.

Man, Handles had fucked up. A lot. It made Ape wonder, once Handles got out, what other mistakes he might make. What if Handles wasn't the right guy to head up a club like the Sultans? Maybe it took someone harder, more decisive.

Someone like me.

He glanced back at the two guys behind him and gave a nod before pulling back on the throttle and passing the row of slow-moving cars hunkered down in the right lane, like sheep. Man, it felt good to leave those fuckers in the dust.

Things would feel even better once he'd taken care of Agent Clay Navarro. And they were close. So close he could smell it.

7

SMALL-TOWN LIFE WAS BORING AS HELL. WELL, IT WAS
if you had nowhere to go, nothing to do. Clay had never
been very good at just sitting around, waiting. He'd
awakened early that morning, wishing he had a job to
go to. A job. He *had* a fucking job, but he couldn't
actually do it right now.

In his room, the vodka bottle shone, half-full, from
the bathroom counter like a clean, white obelisk, offering blissful oblivion.

But Clay knew better. He didn't need that shit, he
decided. Beneath the ink and the scars, his body was his
best tool. *My temple*, he thought wryly. The last thing
he needed to do right then was ruin it any more than he
already had.

Hunger beyond what he could satisfy with his col-
lection of local farm fruit finally got him outside, where
he'd spotted a diner just off the main strip.

It was early afternoon, and the place was pretty
empty, for which he was thankful, because the stares
were over the top. *Yeah*, he felt like saying, *not your*

usual small-town fare. Well, don't worry, all you inno-cent people—I'll be gone as soon as I can.

He sat in the far booth, back to the wall, and snagged a menu along with the newspaper spread across the middle of the table.

"What can I get ya?" asked a line cook from behind the counter.

"Burger. Provolone. Bacon. Whatever else you got to put on it." Anything to give it flavor.

"Drink?"

"Coffee."

"Be right up."

The whole exchange had been done in the relative silence of the place, with an unabashedly interested audience and Clay's irritation ramped up a notch.

It wasn't until another customer came in, with a repeat of the whole rigamarole, that he realized he wasn't as special as he thought. *Everybody* got stared at.

The coffee, when he tasted it, was bland. Like everything he'd put it in his mouth these last couple of months. Even with the ten sugar packets he added, it tasted like nothing, which didn't bode well for his lunch. He reached for the paper.

Giving it a good shake, Clay skimmed a sports page to see that the World Cup had trumped baseball in the headlines. Not that there was much going on for the Orioles, but he could give a shit about what the U.S. team did in th—

His gaze caught on a photo and a headline at the bottom of the metro section:

ATF AGENT DIES IN FATAL CRASH

The few lines beneath gave zero details, mentioning

only that Breadthwaite was dead—not where or how. Clay sat up, the coffee cup clattering to the Formica with a dull thud. Tunnel vision, heart beating visible *wumps* in the corner of his eyes. Tightness in his chest. *Shit. Heart attack.*

He stood, head wavering but feet slow, stuck in this morass with fuzzy blinders on his eyes making everything too far away.

"Take the check," he managed, mouth moving, voice emerging in a rush, like water. No, not water. Hot puffs. Hot lips, dry mouth. More like lava. Magma? Was that the word? Was that even a word?

"All right, son?"

"Fine."

"You want yer burger wrapped up?"

"Sure." The path of least resistance. *Outside. Get outside.*

Clay pulled his wallet from his pocket, set a twenty carefully on the table, and picked up the paper.

"Here." The guy handed Clay a Styrofoam box, eyeing him carefully. "You sure you're—"

"Good."

"I'll get your change."

"Forget it," Clay said as he walked to the door, stiff and straight with ten pairs of eyes heavy on his back. It wasn't until he made it outside that he remembered he didn't have the truck. He'd have to walk back through town to his motel.

This didn't bode well. Not at all, with the heaviness in his limbs and what looked like dust motes dancing in front of his eyes. His chest was tight, too tight.

He set off, breaths like hard little bullets in his

lungs, hands grasping the box and the paper but feeling nothing.

Nothing.

He passed the coffee shop, then backtracked, blinking. *Internet.*

A look around showed no public computers.

At the counter, he asked one of those pierced kids, "Got computers here?"

"Um…" The girl stared thoughtfully at him, twisting one of those tunnel things below her bottom lip. In a surreal flash-forward, Clay pictured how that'd look in a few years, if she ever decided to take it out— skeletal teeth and gums a grisly peekaboo. The weird shit people did to their bodies. He almost laughed out loud at that—hysterical laughter. Not good. "Library, I guess?"

"Thanks," he said, already halfway to the door.

"Nice tattoo, du—"

He walked outside, letting the door shut on her words. *Stupid kid. Stupid, stupid kid.*

And who would make sure nothing happened to *that* kid? Huh? A kid like that, stupid enough to put one of those things in her lip, wouldn't know how to take care of herself.

Focus.

The library. He turned a half circle, noticed the to-go box of food in his hand, got a whiff of greasy steam, and dropped it in the nearest trash can on a wave of nausea. The library was in a tiny building that looked old, he remembered, over by the tracks on Railroad Avenue. He headed that way, feeling sharper. On a mission.

Inside, the woman behind the counter lifted her brows

at him but didn't say a word when he settled in front of one of the computers.

ATF Agent Nikolai Breadthwaite, he typed into the Google search bar, his shoulders and back tense to the point of pain.

Only a few hits appeared, all recent news pieces covering Bread's accident. Clay tried to loosen his shoulders, but it felt like the tension was the only thing holding his bones together.

There was one photo, the same one over and over, released only after his death, no doubt. It was his official ATF ID shot. Bread was like him—eternally undercover. *Had* been like him. Clay had seen that badge. He'd made fun of Bread in the shot, called him a googly-eyed motherfucker. There wouldn't be any more photos now. Because Bread was dead.

Clay stifled a laugh. Not the time to lose his shit. Again. *Shit. Shit, shit, shit.*

Only an insider could've figured out where Bread had been placed as he awaited trial. Only an insider could've gotten to him. Somebody with links to DOJ at the very least.

After half an hour spent sifting through articles that all said pretty much the same thing, he leaned back.

An accident, they said. But Clay knew it was bullshit. He pulled out his phone, ready to call Tyler, but stopped when the woman behind the counter cleared her throat.

Right. Library.

After shutting everything down and deleting the browsing history, he limped back outside, into the too-bright day. He wouldn't call Tyler. He couldn't do that, couldn't reach out at all, especially now that the only other guy who'd known what Clay knew was dead. The only other person who could testify. His safety depended on no one finding out where the hell he was. He was supposed to check in with McGovern, but he wouldn't. Not if shit was going down like this.

Fuck. Maybe he should leave, go farther south?

No. He wasn't running. He'd stay here, get these piece-of-shit tattoos removed, and wait. Because fuck if he'd become a fugitive. He was the law, for Christ's sake, not the one on the run.

He stood up straighter, pulled his glasses back down over his eyes, and turned in a half circle.

The town sat, quiet and quaint. Hot and humid as hell. The buzz of summer insects tickled the back of his brain.

What should he do now? Get in touch with Tyler after all? No, Tyler might have a tap on his line. They might be watching him. What about McGovern? Could she be the rat? Weirder things had happened. She had family, which made her prime picking for ruthless bastards like the Sultans.

But no, she was the biggest stick-in-the-mud, straight-arrow agent he'd ever seen. He didn't believe she could turn for a moment. Besides, she'd been the one who'd fought for him with the big guys, the one who'd understood that to be truly undercover, you had to live like your quarry. She got that. Not her.

Who the fuck was it?

Someone had given them his name the night of the raid. Some fucker had told the Sultans he was a cop and set them on his ass in ways nobody could've fucking imagined. Ape calling him in back, Jam and the others watching as Ape did his eyes, then knuckles, branding him.

Handles's out, but when he gets back, you're a dead man. Those fucking words.

Then the needle against his face, his lids screwed shut against Ape's threat of popping his eyeballs with it.

Here, in sweet, innocent Blackwood, Clay stood and breathed, waited, watched as a couple in pink and white emerged from an antique place, arm in arm, and moved along the sidewalk to the ladies' dress shop next door.

Leafy green trees lined both sides of the street, shading the red brick and white clapboard facades of one cutesy place after another—coffee shop, more goddamned antiques, the diner he'd always associate with Bread's death. Beyond that, an indent and that pub —the Nook.

A drink. Yeah. He'd go for a drink. Anything to obliterate the guilt at being the last one standing—and the knowledge that if he fell, there'd be nobody left to make those bastards pay.

Clay Navarro had never in his life felt quite so alone.

George waited for Andrew Blane to show up for an hour and a half that evening. She would probably have stayed even longer if the animals hadn't needed her. That and she'd caught up on every bit of paperwork she could find, so no more excuses. No reason to stay at the clinic.

As she locked up and made her way to her car alone, she realized two things—both pathetic. One, she'd been looking forward to seeing the big man again. And two, his absence made her feel jilted, which was patently ridiculous.

Great. I need to feel needed. And then, when I'm not needed... Lord, did she truly have no life at all?

As she pulled into her driveway, rather than continue thinking about Andrew Blane, she decided to concentrate on home. Home, where things didn't go smoothly unless she was there.

Which wasn't entirely true, either.

Her place was all moving parts. No, not moving parts, but bits and pieces that, together, made up an ecosystem. Almost self-contained, her garden depended on three things from the outside: sunlight, rain, and George.

She liked that dependence. She *liked* being needed.

When she found a bright-purple sticky note stuck to her front door, she initially assumed it was some erroneous delivery—because no one ever visited.

She read it. *Come over for dinner! I got wine! ;)* Something inside her did a strange, unexpected flip-flop.

George rushed guiltily through feeding the animals. She should have watered the garden too, since the leaves were yellowing and there was no hint of rain on the horizon, but who had time when you had a dinner invite stuck to your door? Out back, she locked the chickens up, spared thirty seconds for Leonard's belly rub, and paused on the steps.

Laughter drifted over the other side of the fence and then words. "Hey, George!"

"Gabe?"

"Yeah! Mom says you might come over for dinner."

"Yes. I'm on my way."

"Good! I wanna show you my egg baby. Maybe you can tell Mom to get me a puppy."

"Oh, I'm not—"

"I can hear you, you know!" Jessie yelled from some-where inside her house.

"I'll be right over!" George said in return. "Need me to bring anything?"

"No. I'm defrosting a bunch of crap from the store. That's as fancy as we get around here."

George smiled.

～⌒◦⌒～

"'Nother one, mate?" the British bartender asked, and Clay nodded. Nodding and drinking—about all he'd done for the past couple of hours. Or... He looked around for a clock.

"Time is it?" he asked.

"Half eight."

"*Seriously? Shit.* Cancel that. What do I owe you?"

"Sure you don't want something to eat?" The guy's eyes narrowed strangely on him, and Clay had a moment of clarity—*I must be drunk.*

"Nah. Thanks."

"Here," the guy said, sliding his tab onto the bar in front of him. Jesus, this place was cheap. He'd been drinking for hours, and the check was just around twenty bucks. He threw a couple of bills onto the bar and got off the stool, catching his foot in one of the legs before righting it. Too loud. Clumsy.

"You all right?"

"Good."

"I'll get your change."

"Keep it."

The guy's brows raised. "Thank you." He smiled and did one of those half-bow things dudes like that could pull off. Clay turned. Another step, and Clay stiffened when a hand landed on his shoulder. The Brit had come around the bar, apparently. "You all right to drive, mate?"

"Not driving."

A nod, and Clay walked to the door, then outside into the oppressive heat. He turned toward the skin clinic. Dark. She was gone. *Fuck.* He'd missed his appointment, which meant… He swallowed. Had she waited for him?

Nah. She wouldn't do that. She was nice, but she had a life, a job. Not like him, whose sole purpose right now was those fucking appointments.

Right. And then I go and miss one.

At the clinic, he tried the door, just in case, but there was no point, was there? He knocked a couple of times, pounded the door for good measure.

"Doc left a while ago," a deep, lazy voice drawled from somewhere behind him.

Clay turned, squinting until he saw a man—the sheriff who'd pulled him over his second day here. Small but strong-looking—sitting on a bench right in front of the MMA school. Fuck if he hadn't just passed right by him and not seen him in the night.

"Yeah. Figured."

For a few silent seconds, the two men sized each other up. Whatever he saw, the other man decided to keep the conversation going.

"See you're still here, son."

"Yep."

Clay sucked in a lungful of thick, heavy air, which didn't even begin to clear the booze from his head.

"Blane, right?"

"S' right, Sheriff."

"You hidin' out in Blackwood, Mr. Blane, or you come to make trouble?" Clay opened his mouth, and Sheriff Mullen shushed him. "Nah. Don't say it. Don't need to hear whatever story you've cooked up. I'm in charge here, though, and I'd rather you keep your brand of trouble outside of my town."

Clay nodded, with a quick look around. Where were the TV cameras filming this ridiculous cowboy banter? "Not looking for trouble…sir."

"Good."

He sucked in a few breaths and felt his back loosen when the other man stood up and turned to walk away. Clay watched him go a few steps, then swing back around.

"Noticed you doing that limping jog around town." He indicated the gym behind him with a thumb. "If you're looking for a workout, you should check out the gym. Wouldn't be so hard on that bum leg as all that running."

Clay's brows rose. His eyes flicked to the glow of lights coming from the gym.

"Don't think you'd like my kind of fighting in there."

The sheriff did a scoffing laugh, managing to come off as both wise and condescending, which was really a pretty good trick.

"Don't worry. We've got our share of assholes who think they're tougher than they are. You sober up and come on in tomorrow, son. We'll see what kinda fighter you are. Tell whoever's at the door you're my guest."

"Why?"

"Hmm?"

"Why are you inviting me?"

"It's like I tell the parents around here: know where

your kids are. They're gonna get shit-faced no matter what you do, so you might as well keep them at home." He smirked. "Or at least in the field out back. And, I mean, look at you." He waved at Clay's face, taking in the rest of him with a lazy move. "Don't know when you got out, no idea why you've got 5-0 inked onto your face, but I'd say you belong where someone can keep an eye on you." The man's smile widened again, revealing a perfect, artificial-looking line of bright-white teeth. "'Course, a little birdie told me two of my favorite local meth heads showed up in the hospital Saturday night all broken to bits, tripping their asses off and spouting some bull about how a tattooed giant tore 'em apart."

Clay felt a wave of respect for this small, tough-looking man. "Better the devil you know."

"Exactly. You clean us out of weekend entertainment, and there won't be a damn thing left for the sheriff's office to do anymore. So, you see I might be a little confused as to just who the hell you are, with your prison tattoos and that death sentence on your face. And I'm curious as to what you might be doing in my town. But I'm not entirely sure I want you gone just yet."

"I'm not going anywhere."

The sheriff's eyes flicked up to the clinic sign and back down to Clay; his smile turned smaller, sly. "Figured as much. Anyway, you come on in and show us some of those fancy moves you might or might not have used on our local cranksters, and I'll give you something to occupy yourself with while you squat in my town—keep you from breaking a nail trying to hold off my other local troublemakers. Mutually beneficial."

Jesus, the man had attitude. Old and small, but showing absolutely no fear. Clay smiled, his first one of the day—or was it year?—and, surprising even himself, nodded. "What time?"

"Come in at noon," the old dude said before starting off. "You can kick my ass for lunch."

∽◦

On her way to Jessie's, George grabbed a jar of home-made strawberry jam, some brown paper, and raffia, then ran outside to pick a few zinnias from the back of the garden.

You didn't go anywhere empty-handed. That was something her mother had taught her early on. Hastily wrapped gifts in hand, she rounded the house from the side and headed over.

Inside, the place was sparsely furnished—short, brown coffee table, its veneer cracked; a fat, tan sofa, with worn patches on the arms and stains on the cushions. The floor was covered with carpeting, which she wouldn't have guessed before coming inside, and the fireplace appeared to be sealed shut. Too bad. Pull up the rug and open up the chimney, and the place could actually be quite picturesque.

"Happy new house!" George said, handing the jam and bouquet to Jessie.

"Oh. Wow. You didn't have to do this. Thank you!"

"Don't be ridiculous. So, you're all moved in!"

"Yeah." Jessie looked around, lips compressed. "We don't have all that much."

"Better clean and neat than a hoarder like me."

"You're not a hoarder."

George raised a brow at Jessie.

"Seriously, your place is awesome. It's got character."

"Yeah!" Gabe chimed in. "Candles and cushions and rocking chairs and stuff. You've got all those blankets and those owl statues and the lamp of the Chinese woman and those paintings and—"

"Okay, G. Let's get you in pj's."

"But George just got here."

"Yes, well, remember our deal? Pj's first, then dinner, then teeth."

"And a game?"

"I don't believe video games were ever mentioned."

"Aww, Mom!"

"Look," Jessie said with a sigh. "I'll read you a story, okay?"

"*George* can read to me tonight." The child looked at George, and she could do nothing but smile. He was adorable. Really, truly adorable, with his sprinkling of freckles and amber eyes, just like his mom's. He may be manipulating her, but she loved it.

I want what they have, she thought, pushing back a rogue wave of envy. "I'll read to you."

"No. No, actually, I want you to tell me a story."

"Tell you one?"

"Yeah, like from your head, not from a book."

George blinked. She didn't think she had any stories in her. *Did she?*

"Um." She cleared her throat, caught Jessie's eye roll, and went on with a laugh. "Sure."

Dinner was an odd assortment of appetizers, all

thrown together on a platter, with a bottle of cheap white wine. Unfamiliar though it all was, George loved it—every second of it.

"All right, G, you gotta get those teeth brushed."

"Come on, Mom. You said I could stay up and—"

"No way! Brush your teeth and—"

"Fine. But I want that story."

George smiled. "Just come get me when you're ready."

She watched mother and son traipse off down the hall, her heart a little tight in her chest as she listened to the arguments, brushing, and splashing. Finally, a door opened, and Jessie came back up the hall to whisper, "Not sure what's going on. Usually, he reads to himself, but…maybe it's the new house? Anyway, you don't have to do this."

"It's fine," said George, meaning it. "I want to."

Gabe's room was the only fully furnished room in the house. This was where money had been spent. Kid stuff all over, bright colors, comic book characters. Spider-Man sheets and Pixar posters.

George hesitated in the doorway, unsure where she was supposed to sit, until Gabe patted the spot next to him on his bed. She walked over and settled carefully beside him. Little boys were not something she knew much about, but this one seemed to like her, which was strange in and of itself.

"Okay. I'm ready," he said.

George had no idea what she was going to say. Crap. She hadn't planned for this. "Um, so what kind of story do you want?"

"A monster."

"A monster?"

"Yeah, you know. Maybe a monster nobody wants."

"Oh. Okay."

She thought about it for a few seconds, ignoring the image that rose up out of nowhere—Andrew Blane, haunting her mind's eye, *again*.

"So, um…Bob. Bob is a monster. And he arrives one day in a small monster town." She paused, cleared her throat.

"Wait. They're all monsters?"

"Yeah. And nobody wants to be friends with him. He's just another monster, but he looks different. He looks scarier."

"How? What does he look like?"

Oh. God, George wasn't good at this. No imagination. At all. "He has paint all over him."

"Paint."

"You know, like…tattoos. His paint tells bad monster stories." She groaned inwardly.

"Ooh," said the child, apparently understanding something that George didn't quite get herself.

"Yes. He's got these marks all over his skin. They tell a story about him, where he's been, who he is, what he's lived through. And Bob wants those marks gone."

"Why?"

"Because he doesn't want anybody to know his story. He wants them to think he's just like them."

She paused, waiting for another question, and when none came, she went on. "The thing is, monsters like other monsters who look like them. They don't always accept different-looking monsters."

"Yeah," Gabe whispered, his warm, little body curled up into George's. "Sometimes monsters are alone. With no friends."

"So, Bob came to Monsterton, looked around, and then found one monster who knew how to take the monster paint off."

"The monster-toos."

"Yes. And slowly, Bob's monster paint starts to disappear, leaving him with perfect, clear-blue monster skin."

"Do the other monsters like Bob now?"

George sighed, snuggled deeper into the bed, despite the heat, and wondered, *Do they? Good, good question.*

"I mean." Gabe turned onto his side and looked up at her. "Does Bob have friends now?"

"No. No friends. Because they all saw him before, and they don't trust Bob," George said. But then her forehead wrinkled with worry. What kind of story was she telling this child? This wasn't a lesson she should be teaching. "But then something happened."

He sucked in a breath. "What?"

"One day, one of the monsters from Monsterton falls into the lake, and she can't swim."

"Monsters can't swim?"

"Only some."

"And Bob? Can Bob swim?"

"Yes. So he dives in after the monster and saves her." George paused, waiting for Gabe to interject. Nothing. "And they throw him a party."

"To thank him."

"Yes."

"Bob's a hero."

"Yes. He's a hero."

Gabe yawned, his mouth creaking. "Bob's gonna be like a superhero now, isn't he?"

With a smile, George reached out and turned off the lamp. "Pretty much."

"Yeah, superheroes are always different from everyone else, like freaks. But they save people, and then everyone loves them."

"Right." She put a hand on Gabe's soft hair, looked up, and saw Jessie silhouetted in the doorway. "Good night, Gabe."

"Night, George. That was a pretty good story."

"Glad you liked it."

"Superheroes always look like bad guys first," he said, turned over, and snuggled into his pillow, leaving George in a sort of dull shock. What on earth was she doing, telling a story like that? She'd had no idea where it was going, no idea that she was, in fact, giving her version of someone else's true story.

And good Lord, what was wrong with her that she couldn't, even for a minute, stop thinking about Andrew Blane?

❧

Funny how Clay had assumed he was just randomly walking. He'd started off with the idea that he needed to clear the booze from his brain—especially after that run-in with the law. It had taken maybe two hundred feet of blind walking before he'd started noticing things like the night sky above, with its wide scattering of stars, interrupted by the craggy dark peaks to the west. It shouldn't be so clear, this sky, not with the clogged feel of the air—it was hot, stiflingly heavy, although nothing like the motel walls. He had the urge to open his mouth the way you might in a rainstorm and drink it. A rainstorm. Fuck, that would be good. So good. It would clear the atmosphere, and maybe his brain too.

More steps, more distance from the lights of Main Street, his feet crunching the dry road in a gritty, lop-sided counterpoint to the moist, alive chorus of the Virginia night. *Crunch, scrape, crunch, scrape*, his limp all too apparent.

Crunch, scrape, crunch, scrape. Not a car in sight as he trudged on, stars above, bug noise all around him, almost electric in its continuity. Crickets. Goddamned crickets. Every once in a while, one of the creatures would surprise him, its voice popping out from the wall of sound, separating itself from this unholy hum.

How the hell did they know to sing that same damned note? Maybe it was the only one they could sing. One-hit wonders, all of them.

Crunch, scrape, crunch scrape.

Clay made it a game, to even out his steps against the pavement, drawing his knee as close to the other as possible, ignoring the sharper ache and shortening his stride until he made a *crunch-crunch, crunch-crunch*. Never quite perfect, but almost. Almost.

He focused on the road ahead of him, devoid of buildings and houses now, and blinked when he realized where he was, where he'd been going this whole time. Her street—the doctor's—a tunnel of wilderness on both sides, with her place at the end, the glow of her windows already there.

A light at the end of the tunnel.

He almost turned around. Almost, but not really.

The rhythm of his soles changed, faltered, as he

approached. He hesitated for a moment, nearly tripped. Should he knock? What would she do? She'd call the goddamned cops if she had any sense.

His steps stopped right across the street from her house, where the woods were thick and dark and loud as hell. As soon as he stilled there, the bugs took over, mosquitoes feasting on his skin, others buzzing around his ears. He ignored them, fixing his eyes on the lamp lit in her front window, the curtains drawn back, inviting his gaze farther inside. Didn't she know? Didn't she get how vulnerable she was alone in that house? Anyone could walk up and watch her, stalk her and—

Fuck. I'm the sick bastard doing it. I'm the person she should worry about.

But he knew that wasn't true. Because he'd seen exactly how bad the world could be—for men, certainly—but even worse for women like her. For girls like his sister, Carly, who'd trusted the wrong guys, for the club hangers-on, those women who had no choice but to align themselves with fucked-up assholes who'd end up hurting them. And even for women like George Hadley, who saw the good in people, who worked so hard to spread her special brand of warmth. The world beyond the fuzzy, golden glow she'd surrounded herself with was a treacherous, stinking, dangerous place.

Clay was the last line of resistance between her and the hell that lay out there in the wilderness of real life. He'd be damned if he'd leave her to its mercy.

At least that's what he told himself as he took raw comfort—comfort he needed more than anything right now—just knowing she was nearby.

~ನಿಲ್

Back in the living room, George made as if to go, but Jessie threw a *you've gotta be kidding me* look and held up the half-full bottle of wine. "Please don't leave me to kill this by myself. I'm pathetic enough as it is."

"You're not pathetic."

"Wanna bet?" One brow raised, Jessie poured out two full glasses and held hers up in a toast. "I just realized that I haven't gotten laid in two years. How's that for pathetic?"

George's giggle stopped short. "Oh. I…" Her eyes lost focus as she tried to latch on to a memory.

"What?"

"I've got you beat," George admitted.

"What? No way."

"Yes, way." Her eyes blurred over with tears. It was the wine. She really wasn't used to drinking. "Haven't in…" Another gulp, another swallow, a memory of the last time she'd done it. *Done it* wasn't even the right word. It had been…a good-bye. "Almost a decade."

Jessie spat out a mouthful of wine at that. "What the *effing hell*? Are you kidding me?"

George shook her head, embarrassed, teary-eyed, but laughing nonetheless.

"You, George, are a born-again virgin. You realize that?"

"What?"

"Yeah. Oh man." With a conspiratorial look over her shoulder, Jessie asked, "Should we, like, hire a pro or something? Just to get us out of our dry spells?"

After a fit of giggling that nearly ended in actual sobs,

George leaned back, wiped her eyes, and hiccupped. Her breathing was shaky, and she tried hard to get it back. It was hilarious, really. Wasn't it? Not having sex in that long and the born-again virgin thing—it was funny. But, for a few seconds, it was all too unbearably sad to laugh at. So sad that she had to fight back the tears and force a tight smile.

"We really have to do something about this, though. You do get that, right, George? Find you a man and…" She sat up straight and wiped the grin off her face. "Are you, like, a lesbian or something?" One hand out. "That's okay too. I mean—"

"No. Not a lesbian. I'm just… I was married once. To a man. A long time ago and…" George sucked in a big breath of air, forcing the tears back. Funny how the laughter and the crying were so close, so wrapped up inside her, so intertwined and interchangeable. When had she so lost control of herself that she couldn't talk about her past without opening the floodgates to an emotional deluge?

Never. She'd never talked about it. Any of it. To anyone. She couldn't start now.

Rather than go on, she cut it short, nipped it in the bud, clammed right up. "I don't like to talk about it."

"Oh." Jessie looked taken aback, and George's skin heated with embarrassment.

"I'm sorry. I'm really bad at this."

"At what?"

"Friendships. With women. With anyone, I guess." The words tripped George up, but they kept coming despite her mortification. "I'm not good at it. I always say the wrong things and don't say the right ones. I'm really—"

"Girl, do you have any idea how hard it is to have

friends when you have a kid?" Jessie shook her head ruefully. "I had Gabe young. Nobody, I mean *nobody*, could be bothered to hang out once he was born. And then, as a mother? I've always been the wrong kind of mother, you know? Couldn't do playdates 'cause I was in school and then waiting tables and then constantly working. I had a big, scary brother in prison. Not exactly conducive to developing close ties with other young moms, you know?" She paused, leaned forward, and grabbed George's hand. "You're doing fine, George. Trust me."

"Thanks."

"So." Jessie refilled their glasses and lifted hers in a toast. "Now that we've both established how bad we are at friendships... Here's to new friendships." They clinked glasses and drank. "And to better dates than the ones I've been on in the past few years."

"Here, here," said George.

"I mean how unsexy is it when dudes are like, 'May I touch your breast, please, ma'am?' and I'm like, 'Seriously? Shall I have you fill out an authorization form first?'"

"I had the opposite," George replied. "I went out with a man once, only once, who pushed me against my car, trying to make out in a parking lot after a crappy, boring date."

"D'you deck him in the balls?"

"No," replied George with regret. "I wish I had, now that you mention it. He had this cold, wet tongue, and he kept sort of swiping it over my mouth."

"Ew!"

"Oh Lord, I can't believe I'm telling you this, but...

You know what he said to me? I'd forgotten all about this." George giggled, happy to share with someone—finally. The words emerged through the laughter. "He kept saying, 'I want to lick you, George. I want to lick you.'"

"Oh gross. In that accent?"

"Yes, he was a visiting professor from Oxford or Cambridge or... I don't remember. But, it gets better. Listen to this. I said, 'You want to lick me? You *are* licking me!' because the way he did it, he had this big, flat, rough cat tongue, and he was licking my mouth and my face, but when I said that to him, you know what he said?"

"What?"

"'*I want to lick your clit, George.*'" She could barely get the words past the hilarity now, and Jessie had joined her, groaning, laughing. "I...want...to lick...your *clit*."

"Eww, oh my effing God, that is gross!" Jessie leaned back, wiped the tears from the corners of her eyes, and slapped her hand down on George's knee. "Lady, there is no doubt about it. You've got me beat. Thank you for that."

"Anytime," said George.

"So, new objective: get George laid."

With a grimace, George said, "No. Not really. I mean, yes, I wouldn't mind, I guess, but I've given up." She glanced at Jessie before letting herself talk. "I'm doing IUI." Saying the words out loud to someone who wasn't a medical professional was weirdly liberating.

"What's that?"

"Intrauterine insemination. Like in vitro, except more...natural, I guess."

Jessie's eyes opened wide. "So, turkey baster but no petri dish?"

"Kind of. Yes. I want babies." George glanced down the hall to where Gabe was fast asleep. "One. One baby. A kid like him would be great."

"Wow. Well, I'd give you mine, except…"

"Yeah. Except he's your baby, and you're crazy about him."

"I am." After a few minutes of silent sipping, Jessie spoke again, her eyes wide on George's. "You got any family?"

"No," George said, then felt guilty enough to change her answer. "Well, kind of. I'm still close with my in-laws."

"Yeah?" Jessie's expression told her just how weird that sounded, and George didn't bother to add that her husband had died and left her—left them—alone. With each other.

"I'm not very social, I suppose."

"That probably explains how we've managed to not run into each other more often." After a pause, Jessie went on. "I get it, though. All the fear and the crap I go through as a single mother. It's hard, but I know one thing for sure: I've got a family. Forever, unless something goes wrong." Her knuckles knocked on the hollow-sounding coffee table.

"God forbid."

"Yeah."

George nodded, looking away. "I want that too."

"Wow, George, I guess we really do need to get you laid, then. 'Cause that's got to be more fun than a turkey baster."

〜∾〜

A sound drew Clay's eyes to the left, where what looked like a pile of dark bushes hid another house, smaller than Doctor Hadley's. Voices, a door slamming, and he stepped deeper into the woods, his feet crunching on dry leaves and sticks. A vine or a root nearly tripped him in the process, but he wouldn't look down, couldn't, because there she was. Oh God, she was twenty feet away, fifteen, walking slowly and humming to herself in the middle of the dead-end road. His pulse went wild, working hard to drown out the night sounds.

From somewhere close by—maybe her yard—a small, dark shadow slithered out, its movements slightly off, and met her, wrapping itself around her legs; she cooed. The woman actually *cooed*, the sound high and sweet and almost as singsongy as her humming had been. She bent and grabbed the animal—a cat, he surmised, from the noises it made—and cuddled it close. They gave each other a head butt, and in the most unnatural reaction of all time, his dick hardened, just a little. The sensation was so unfamiliar he was tempted to reach down to check.

He wanted to step forward, to wrap himself around them both, or maybe to let himself be wrapped up in her, the way she'd enveloped that lucky little cat. Instead, he took a deep, painful breath and watched, eyes big and dry and incapable of blinking. If she glanced into the woods now, she'd see the dull shine of his eyeballs, fixed on her like his life depended on it. Like that creepy dude from *The Lord of the Rings*, obsessed with his

Precious. Only Clay wasn't doing it to *have* her, but rather to *save* her.

Or to save himself. It was all mixed-up inside.

She didn't look his way. She turned to the house, walking and humming again, her hips as fluid as water, and he wanted to feel the coolness of her hands on his skin again, wanted to grab those hips and change the tide of their sway. Oh, he wanted to dive into her, to sink in, to lose himself in her pale, soft efficiency.

Oh, fuck. He stumbled back, stilled awkwardly with one hand on a trunk, a fuzzy vine prickling his palm. He wanted to take his hand away, but he couldn't. She'd turned at the sound, and though her eyes were in shadow, the cat's weren't. They were two bright diamonds in the night, fixed right on him, pointing out his location like a beacon. His breath was fast and heavy in his ears, and for once, he was glad for the goddamned incessant drone of the insects.

The few seconds she searched the woods were unbearably long, but finally she turned to slip through the open gate—even *that* she didn't fucking close—up the sweet, overgrown flagstones of her walkway, then onto her porch and through the front door, without even a hint of the jingle of keys. He stood unmoving as she made her way down the hall to the back room. She didn't lock the front door behind her and still hadn't done so by the time he watched her turn off lights and disappear up the big staircase.

Guiltily, he took in the upstairs lights switching on, her shadow moving through an interior door, another light on, in the front of the house—the bathroom, wide open, like the rest of the place. He stared, hating himself, as she pulled off her skirt, too low for him to see, which was both a disappointment and a relief. She reached for the bottom hem of her shirt and paused, turned her head, and took two steps to close a set of wooden shutters, which masked the lower half of the window entirely and, therefore, his view.

Good, he thought with a sigh. Good, she'd cut him loose, absolved him of guilt by removing the element of choice, which was good, because he couldn't have looked away, even if he'd wanted to. Which he hadn't. No, he'd wanted to—

Something bumped his leg, and he almost shouted with surprise until he saw what it was: the cat. The darned thing was back outside. It had come to find him, to chase him off, or… No, not chase him, apparently, because it rubbed him in the same way it had rubbed her. Pushy figure eights around his legs, designed to influence. He bent and picked the creature up, pulling it into his chest the way she'd done just minutes before.

With a jolt of surprise, he felt the odd space where one of the animal's legs was missing. It didn't seem too hampered by the shortage as it clawed its way up to his face, embracing him with its one remaining front paw, and sniffed his mouth with its tiny, cold, wet nose.

Awkwardly, Clay stood for long minutes, holding this purring creature, waiting to see what it wanted. After a while, it settled deeper into his arms, with apparently no intention of taking off. With a sigh and a look around, Clay made his way to what appeared to be a downed log and sat, leaning against a tree, letting the animal's warmth and engine-like rumble cover up the buzzing in his brain.

It was strangely comfortable, despite the heat and humidity and the prick of mosquitoes eating at his skin. Possibly because, for once, he didn't feel quite so alone.

8

CLAY AWOKE THE NEXT DAY A HOT, SHIVERING MESS ON the motel room floor.

Immediately, he remembered what he'd done the night before: stalking Dr. Hadley. Shame weighted his gut, deep and heavy. Man, he was a creepy fucker, watching a woman in her home like that, no matter how good his excuses.

The problem was that he'd liked feeling useful. You weren't supposed to like a stakeout. You were supposed to be miserable and uncomfortable, not content, the way he'd been—not relieved to have a purpose beyond waiting around for a court date that was still months off.

And, fuck, he was a sick bastard, because he wanted to do it all over again. He wanted to be out there, watching over her. Keeping her safe in a way that he knew was wrong, wrong, wrong.

God, his head. It hurt, like he'd rammed a spike through his eye socket.

Christ, why did he do this to himself? Memories of waking up in the clubhouse, hungover, hurting, and half-clothed with some random woman next to him in his bedroom. He'd complained to his boss, who'd eventually gotten him lined up with an undercover girlfriend. Thank God. The other guys might think he was whipped, but that was nothing compared to the stress of finding ways to avoid fucking those poor women.

Women like Carly.

He screwed his eyes shut against those images.

With a rustle, his hand met paper, and memories from the day before came flooding back—Niko Breadthwaite dead, Clay drinking at the bar, then running into that cop. The man had seen right through him. He'd known something was up.

Had the sheriff *made* him? Clay wondered, the morning bringing a new perspective on that odd conversation. Fuck, maybe Clay was losing his edge and the sheriff saw right through the civilian charade.

Because that was what this was. A charade. All day, every day, Clay was playing some role, pretending to be something he wasn't... *Yeah, but you do it long enough, you become it. Whatever it is.*

Maybe it was the goddamned banner Ape had forced on him—the one that said, *Hey! I'm a fuckin' cop and I'll never work undercover again, because it's written on my face!*

After a worthless fifteen minutes of *he-made-me, he-made-me-not*, Clay stopped the internal debate firmly on the side of *not*.

In fact, he decided, he'd been so damn good at his role of stupid criminal that the man had figured he'd best take him off the streets.

Good. *Good.*

He stood, let the sweaty sheet fall to the floor, revealing his unexpectedly naked body—he didn't remember taking his clothes off after returning from his vigil at the doc's place—and moved to the A/C, pushed a few buttons, waited… Nothing. From polar ice cap, it had turned into a goddamned sauna in here, and he couldn't get a fucking wheeze of cool air.

In the bathroom, he lifted the toilet seat and vomited, made even more nauseated by the state of the porcelain rim.

Christ, he had to get out of this place. He would have spent the night in the woods if the mosquitoes hadn't eventually made it unbearable, their bites overlapping, the bumps still texturing his skin. His T-shirt was festooned with grisly smears of blood from crushing them. His blood.

Outside, his mind called again, overlaying the image of the doctor's house with another place—that mountain overlook where he'd found… What? Himself? Yeah right. His new favorite bird, the vulture? The mirror showed a cynical smile at that thought, but the notion did have an oddly true ring to it. He'd felt a weird kinship with that bird.

After a long, cold shower, a big glass of cloudy water, and his last two wrinkled apples, he made his way back into the world, only to be blinded by the sun. He was yearning for something to soak up the booze, so he headed to Main Street, on foot, avoiding the bad-news diner and going straight to the coffee shop with its hipster baristas—probably the only place in town where he almost fit in.

A pretentious pastry and two tasteless coffees later,

he felt slightly better, then caught sight of a clock only to realize it was just a few minutes before noon. He considered his options—back to the motel, where the A/C could no longer even pretend to battle the filthy, moist heat or...

Shit.

He was going to do it, wasn't he?

Clay took a quick trip to his room to change into his sweatpants, hesitating before slipping into a crappy T-shirt with the arms cut off. At the last minute, he grabbed a long-sleeved shirt to throw over himself, then headed back to the gym beside the clinic.

The clinic. Shit, he'd have to go back at some point. Or maybe he wouldn't have to. Maybe he'd just hold on to the tats, like part of his history. Hell, the kids in the coffee shop had looked at him with a sort of awe— who knew a face tattoo would get you quite so much street cred?

He knew. His fake prison tats had gotten him exactly the respect he'd needed to fit into the club.

He hesitated briefly before he pushed into the MMA school. Inside, it was exactly what he'd expected. And at the same time, it wasn't. Yes, it smelled like sweat and socks, like every other gym in the world, but there was more to it than he'd imagined. It was bigger than it looked from the outside, with mats covering the middle of the room and weight equipment along the sides, a couple of speed bags, and heavy bags in the corners. Nothing particularly high-tech or new. He liked it, which gave him a jolt. It had been a long-ass time since he'd felt *right* someplace.

Nobody manned the desk, so Clay just walked in,

ignored the stares of the two guys lifting, and scanned the room until he spotted Sheriff Mullen in the back. He stood wrapping his hands.

"Made it," said the sheriff, with a *come on back here* wave. "Get you suited up."

"For what?"

With a tilt of his head, the man indicated Clay's hands. "Wouldn't wanna ruin all that pretty ink, would we?"

Clay scoffed and unconsciously rubbed his arms. "Yeah."

"You got more under there?"

After a second, he lifted his chin in acknowledgment.

"That what you been doin' next door?"

A noncommittal sound was all Clay managed. He wasn't sure why, but after a brief hesitation, he yanked off the long-sleeved shirt, baring his tats, before wrapping his hands.

It had been a while since he'd geared up like this. The Sultans didn't believe in protection for a fight. They believed in scars and wounds. Disfigurement was a way of life for those guys—a badge of honor. The more you tainted yourself in the name of the club, the more teeth you had knocked out, the better. He had a bent finger or two to prove it, since drunken brawls were the norm in Naglestown, Maryland. Followed by drunken fucks, of course. Jesus, he missed that part of it—the brawls, not the fucks.

"You gettin' those taken off?" Sheriff Mullen interrupted Clay's reminiscing as he pulled out some boxing gloves. He threw a pair at Clay, along with headgear. "Bit late for the doctor to be workin' last night, wasn't it?"

"Just makin' sure she was okay."

"Hmm," the small man said, sounding dubious. "What kinda fightin' you done?"

"Regular kind," said Clay with a hint of a smirk.

"Yeah? Let's see what you got."

Out on the mat, the little guy hit his gloved fists to Clay's and moved back with a spring in his step. So he'd be fast. That was okay. Clay could handle fast—although maybe not today, all shaky and hungover.

And he was right. The little guy came in quick and low, arms up in a defensive position that was tough as hell to get through. He was tiny, but wiry and strong, and going up against him, Clay felt like a big, slow oaf.

But he felt good too, even as he absorbed a couple of quick, tight little jabs to the head and shoulders. The pain was right. The speed, the adrenaline. Oh, man, what a relief. He ducked and struck with an uppercut that would have stunned if he hadn't pulled back. His opponent's eyes were bright—as bright as his, probably—and his excitement ratcheted up a notch or two. Man, this was what it was about—the physical perfection of confronting a worthy opponent.

A jab, roundhouse, push, push, and the other man stumbled, but then, before he knew it, his foot snaked out, and Clay was down, with a crash that sounded loud and hollow in the room. It was quiet, besides their breathing, and he realized the other guys were watching them—*the main event*.

There was a jangle of bells at the door, and more people came in, their voices fading to nothing as they entered the space and caught sight of the two mismatched fighters in the back. Ah, hell, he'd seen enough fights, where big boxers came out looking like losers on the ground, and here he was, the smaller man's arm wrapped around his throat like an unbreakable noose. He'd hoped to just fight it straight, maybe a little dumb, but…

His body moved faster than his brain, and before he'd thought it out, his arm rammed into the crook of the guy's elbow, his hand to his shoulder. God, he loved jiujitsu. And he'd missed rolling with someone who knew what he was doing.

The sheriff's arm remained around Clay's neck. Christ, he was strong for such a lightweight, but he'd left his ankle out in the open, and Clay went for it—pushed up on his legs, threw the little guy up, up, over his shoulder.

Past the blood rushing through his ears, he heard a murmur in the room. He was providing the entertainment. *Fucking Fight Night Challenge over here. Shit.* He'd blow his cover if he wasn't careful.

But it had worked, that move, and he liked it, loved coming out on top in a fight, could see that the sheriff had enjoyed the challenge of being one-upped—and now Clay wanted more.

They shared a painful fist bump before the man pulled him straight into a clinch. "Not just a street thug after all," he said into Clay's ear in something just above a whisper. "You ex-military?"

Clay shook his head.

"Hmm. Let's see some more like that," he yelled and pushed away, going straight for the feet.

Fuck, he should stop. He had to if he didn't want the guy to know he wasn't a civilian. But civilian life was overrated, and this felt good—way too good to put an end to it.

∽

At the knock on her door, George looked up.

"You've got a visitor," said Purnima.

"Oh?"

Expressionless, as always, the nurse nevertheless managed to convey *something* with her look. "Andrew Blane."

She took a big, shaky breath in. "Oh."

"Shall I…?"

George stood, breathed out. "I'll be right… No." She sat back down. "Send him in. Please."

"All right. You want me to stay with you?"

With a frown, George considered before answering with, "No. No, I'm fine. Go on home."

Purnima hesitated but finally turned and left the room, returning shortly with Andrew Blane in tow.

"Come in," George said with what she hoped was placid concern.

He stepped inside, disheveled and sweaty and… Oh, geez. Something else. Not hot, but *heated* maybe? Intense.

"I'm sorry," he said, remaining in the doorway.

"It's okay."

"No, I mean, I'm…" He looked away. "I shouldn't have missed yesterday. I had no excuse."

"All right, well…" She swallowed hard, avoided his eyes, and then, maybe because he'd hurt her and she wanted to hurt him back, she said, "You'll have to pay for the missed time."

"Of course." He waited, just stood there breathing

hard, and she couldn't help but notice his chest beneath his sleeveless T-shirt, moving.

"Can you take me today?"

"Have you put on the cream?"

"No, but…" His smile, dry and cracked, pulled at something deep inside her. "But I can't reach most of my back anyway, so it's all the same, isn't it?"

"Oh. You don't have anyone who can—"

"No, Doc. Got nobody to rub my back for me."

"I'm sorry."

"*Are* you?" he said with a bigger smile.

"Of course I am. I've—" She stopped herself from talking. "Oh." God, why was she so dense? Was he flirting with her? And if so, why on earth would he bother flirting with someone like her? A swallow failed to wet her throat enough, and her voice, when it came out, was ragged. "I've got to finish up some…paperwork here, so…" Another throat clearing.

"Got all the time in the world."

"Good. Perfect. I'll just…apply the numbing cream, and we'll wait for it to take effect."

"Sounds good."

"All right, follow me."

He barely moved back to let her through the door, and that, even that, felt like flirtation, unfamiliar and dangerous, but so, so titillating.

In the examination room, she moved to the sink, washed her hands, and didn't watch as he settled back on the table. From a cupboard, she grabbed a new tube of cream and a roll of plastic wrap. "I'll just apply this, and you can wait about half an hour. Have you had issues with the others we've worked on?"

He shook his head, eyes steady on hers.

"Take off your shirt and lie down on your front, please. If it's not too painful." The words came out close to a whisper. Quickly, she pulled on a pair of latex gloves, waited for him to disrobe, and forced herself to breathe. Deep, slow. Okay, his chest was blistering and starting to scab, she noted before he settled onto the bench. The ink was nearly gone in some areas—the lighter applications—but others were dark. She hoped, for his sake, that they'd eventually disappear.

Although he stiffened at the contact, the first swipe of cream was easy. A thick layer of it, directly over the big, black triangle in the center of his back. If she concentrated on the cream instead of him, it was doable. But it was hard to ignore every line of his perfection—this anatomy book illustration come to life.

She watched as his skin pebbled up into goose bumps. Another swipe, over the spider web on his neck, then across a shoulder blade, and her hand couldn't help but enjoy the rigid planes, the swell of muscle, the strength. And then there was how he smelled. He'd looked sweaty when he'd come in, but it wasn't bad. No, it was...

George pulled her hand away as if stung, took a step back, and breathed through her mouth, although even that was intimate. Past the medical odor of the cream, she had smelled soap, maybe some cheap shampoo, and then...sex. He smelled the way she remembered sex smelling. Not the musky odor of genitals, but the scent of desire.

Man as animal. He smelled solid, real, warm. Right. He smelled *right*. So right, in fact, that her body did things, perking in places that hadn't perked in so long she'd thought they were dead. It was cool in the clinic, thank God, because at least she'd have an excuse for her nipples. But not for the slippery weight in her abdomen. *Lower.*

"Everything okay?" the man asked, craning his neck to look at her, and rather than face those eyes again head-on, she placed her clean hand to the back of his head and pressed. Gently. Firmly.

Oh, crap. I'm not supposed to do that, am I?

Nor was she supposed to like it.

~ço~

It was official. The doctor made Clay hard. And now…

Her hand on the back of his head… *Fuck.*

First, it made him want to fight back, pull away, get up, and take over. Because nobody pushed his head down. *Nobody.*

But it also made him want to give in—to see what she'd do. Rebel or succumb?

He went for something in between. Light resistance, up and back, into her hand, was all it took to turn things upside down.

She's not controlling me, he realized with the strangest jolt. *She's holding me. Helping me.* His mind flew back, remembering the way she'd held her cat in the dark in front of her house—and then to his embrace with the animal. He'd have held that cat all night long if it hadn't eventually heard some forest sound and sprung away, ears pricked, tail swishing, its missing limb barely noticeable in attack mode.

But right now, here, the press of her hand against the back of his head was full of something good, something like affection or desire or maybe, just maybe, tenderness. And it was the best thing he'd felt in a lifetime.

So different from recent flashes of memory—flesh smacking, hard fucks, teeth gritted, fist caught up in greasy hair. Toothy blow jobs from nameless women, victims of circumstance—collateral damage as he and Bread did whatever it took not to lose their covers.

Everything he'd taken—bottles to the face, ink, bullets, a loss of honor.

Clay stiffened.

But this—

He heard her breathe, felt the warmth on his nape, and shuddered.

That sent her away, left his back cold and him alone. When she came back, the moment of intimacy was gone. Maybe it'd been imagined anyway. He felt immune to sensation. Lost and empty and hard as nails.

He shut his eyes tight, wanting her to touch him again and so afraid of the mixed-up signals his brain kept sending.

Her gloved hands returned to his skin, warm through the cold cream. She rubbed it in, leaving a trail of goose bumps in her wake, and he wished she'd press his head again, take some of his weight, make him feel something. She walked around the table to the other side, where she stroked him with a fresh layer of cream, and something else skimmed his back when she leaned— her lab coat, maybe? In his fantasies, it was a breast. A mouth.

It was quiet in here, so quiet. He closed his eyes and breathed her in.

∽⟨Q⟩∾

He'd fallen asleep. Either that or he'd gone to that place, wherever it was, that he seemed to go on her table.

Only this time, George's hands were on him. She felt heavy and warm, and his back was big and strong and supple, but so sweet, laid out for her, waiting, needing…

Dear God, what's wrong with me?

He was numb by now. He had to be—as numb as the cream would make him, which wasn't very. Another dip, another swipe, and his flesh rippled beneath her touch. Maybe not asleep?

She wanted to put her hand on his head again and push him down, but there was nowhere to go. She wanted to lean into him and over him and maybe just stretch herself across all that muscle and bone. Desire settled into her pelvis as she stroked his shoulders, ran a hand a little too far down an arm that had absolutely no need of numbing cream. None.

What the hell is wrong with me?

But still, she couldn't quite convince her body to stop. Slowly, she kneaded her thumbs around those beautiful scapulas, felt him shudder slightly, and pulled away, hyperaware of how strange her actions were—how unethical and wrong, but maybe…maybe just…

"Don't stop," he mumbled, and honestly, that was all she needed.

His back—this solid, robust plane—was like the culmination of all of the backs she hadn't had the pleasure of touching over the years, and goodness, she wanted it. She wanted his back.

Wanted his back?

Was this how it felt to go crazy?

George stepped away, embarrassed and more than a little worried for her sanity. Was she really, truly, going to cave in and do things she might very well—no, would *definitely*—regret over some stranger's back?

He grunted—or maybe it was more of a groan—and twisted his neck so one shadowed eye peeked out at her.

"'S the best thing that's happened to me in fu…frickin' years." His voice came out low, almost on a whisper.

"This is…" George couldn't get the words out, she was breathing so fast. "This is weird. I can't… I don't—"

"No. Feels good. So damn good."

"Just…me touching you?"

"Yeah."

There was hardly any hesitation at all, and then the succubus wearing her skin stepped forward. Closer, until her belly was level with his hand. "Are you numb?" She reached out and stroked him, right on that horribly defacing burn, wondering if he could feel her. Wanting him to.

"No," he said, even breathier now. "No, the opposite. Numb when I walked in. Now. Shit. Now, it's all nerves."

The weight in George's belly turned liquid, spread out on a wave of shivery sensation that she hadn't felt since she'd been just a kid, squished in the backseat of Dylan Dean's bright-red Mustang with nothing between her legs but his hand, and nothing in her head but blind teenage lust.

"Here?" Her fingers caressed him where his skin had melted into unsightly whorls, tracing the jagged surface and wishing he'd let her do more. Although, even as she thought that, she wasn't sure if she meant *more* as in treatment for the burn, or *more* right now, to his body. To him.

"Yeah. There. Just…" He groaned, then begged, "Please."

Possessed, she caressed him, up his side, almost to his armpit and its tuft of dark hair. It looked sexual, that hair, like something she wasn't supposed to see. Then tracing along the top of his shoulder to the back of his neck and down, down, down his spine, the bumps adding texture along the way, the rocky road of his body the most enticing thing George had ever seen.

More sounds escaped him, little grunts that said he liked what she did, and those fueled her even more. Lord, she wanted to flatten herself on top of the man, to cover him, and… What? Hump him? No. Not really. Make him feel good? Touch every little bit of him? Heal him? Protect him from whatever hell he'd been through?

With a snap that surprised even her, she removed the glove that separated his skin from hers and lightly—oh so lightly—felt the reality of his flesh without the barrier of Nitrile in between. The noises were hers this time, and the contact was kinetic, burned the air, turned the heat up, ate out her brain.

His hand, right there on the edge of the table, somehow turned until his palm rested flat against her belly—not pushing, just…absorbing, fingers taking in her softness, exploring her the way she was him.

Before she knew it, she'd curled her palm around that hunk of a shoulder, leaned in until more than her lab coat pressed against the man, her breathing shaky and short. "I don't know what I'm doing," she whispered, in a dream. The bridge of her nose skimmed his hairline,

and she took him in, smelled him, got a bigger dose of
what she'd only guessed at until now. And it was good,
elementally good, unexplainably, animalistically perfect. A smell she could dive into and live off of.

She pulled back. "Got to stop. I've got to stop."

"Hang on." His hand reached for hers, grasped it,
skin to skin, and held on tight. "Don't know what the
hell you're doing to me, but it's making me crazy."

"I don't know; I don't know. I'm not… This isn't
me," George muttered, eyes clearing. She pulled hard at
her hand, blinked hazily at the man laid out before her,
and moved toward the door. "I'll be…I'll be right back."

Tea. The woman brought him tea.

She'd touched him so he'd almost cried on her table
like a goddamned baby, and after running away, she
came back in with *tea*. One for him and one for her.
And not sweet iced tea, like people here guzzled by
the gallon. No, mugs full of the hot stuff. In the middle
of July.

"Maybe we'll wait on your back" was the first thing
he actually understood after his complete and total
whatever-that-was in her office. Jesus, had he nearly
come at a medical back massage? Almost come and then
come close to passing out on the exam table.

"Yeah," he managed through a throat that was raw,
an open wound. He felt like that. Not just his throat, but
his… What? His psyche, maybe. His very being chafed.
He hurt where she'd touched him, like he'd scarred or
scabbed over, and she'd come along and opened him up
again—with nothing but tenderness. It scared the hell

out of him, the way he'd disappeared into her, made him want to grab her and fuck her. Or maybe hide beneath her lab coat.

He swung up to sitting and accepted the tea, blinking like a newborn baby, exposed, his cock semihard and heavy in his underwear.

"You okay?" she asked, sounding pretty choked up herself.

"Yeah. Thanks." He took a sip, just to give himself something to do. It tasted good, spicy.

After a couple of minutes, the fuzz cleared slightly, and he noted what he held in his fist with a strange jolt of hilarity. It was a mug, brown, with the words *Coffee makes me poop* written in big, white caps.

"Wow, that's…"

"Disgusting?" She smiled at him, and he breathed, deep and cleansing.

"Do that again."

"What?" She frowned, and he reached out to smooth the wrinkle between her brows.

"Smile."

His request had the opposite effect, of course, deepening those lines. But that only made him want to see them gone all the more. He leaned in from his perch, pressed his lips to the spot, to smooth them, to taste them, to drink her in or…or something.

The connection sent a jolt through him—just like when she'd touched him on the table. Rather than numb, he'd felt sensation: sweet and unfamiliar after so many months of nothing. And he could smell her—clean, with a hint of lady sweat, which seemed only fitting for the end of a day's work. No, not sweat on Dr. Hadley, he reminded himself, like he had that very first day—*perspiration*. He breathed in again—his nose to her forehead—weird, in theory, but in fact the most sensual thing he'd ever done. His skin crackled at the contact.

She let out a noise, long and low and full of frustration, and he knew he should pull back. He should, since he was probably freaking her out now, but instead, he slid off the table and leaned down, down to where her lips were a little bit open, poised and waiting. He put his mouth to hers and it felt…*fuck*, it felt unreal. It was a miracle that it felt like *something*.

This is a dream, he thought, and let his mouth move with the words, closing his eyes.

Her sounds grew louder, lazier, and he sipped at them, his mouth to hers, his dick at full mast now, which was another miracle, since it'd lain dormant since the shooting. Before the shooting, if he was honest with himself.

This. This was medicine. This was—

She pulled away. "I can't," she said through a gasp.

"Why not?" he asked, idiot that he was.

"You're my patient. What I already did, I should be… I could lose my license. I *should* lose my license."

"I'm your…" He blinked. *Her patient?* That was her excuse? Not "You're disgusting" or "You scare me" or "You're not my type"?

"Yes. You're my patient." She swallowed, and those big, black pupils moved to his mouth and stayed there. He watched them watch him, watched them blow up wide, her lips wet, pink, primed. "I can't get involved with patients. It's completely unethical. I… You need to go."

"Okay." She was right. He needed to go and get his

head on straight. "Okay." He rocked back a little and took her in, so serious in that lab coat. Always with that fucking lab coat—sexy, but way too much of a barrier. "You're fired," he said before he'd even thought it through.

"Oh." Her gaze was bleary and so, so cute. Innocent. Too innocent, probably, but he couldn't help wanting to taste that too. "Excuse me?"

"You're no longer my doctor, and I'm not your patient. So why don't you come back here and let me do that again?"

~⚬~

It had been ten years since George Hadley had done the sex thing. A full decade since she'd lost her husband and, with him, any chance she had of finding love. For ten long years, she'd missed sex, the contact, the skin on skin.

Oh, she'd had minor opportunities. A date here and there. Moments when a look told her there might be interest. In med school, she'd almost given in once or twice, but it had never quite caught. Never seemed worth the effort.

Until now.

But no, that wasn't quite right. It wasn't that she wanted sex right now, exactly—though her body did, for sure. It was more like the need for some deeper contact had come to the surface for the first time in a decade. She could feel the need, whereas for years, she'd pushed it back, suppressed it, let herself wallow in layers and layers of cotton wool.

A protective covering, probably. It had formed after

losing Tom. She'd put so much into that marriage and then lost him. Lost that precious connection and, with it, everything. After that, it seemed better not to have connections at all.

As to why it all came barreling back now, George wasn't entirely sure, but she accepted it in the way life often forced you to accept the inevitable. She let the need, the desire, the vulnerability take over, and following some deeper instinct, she rocked forward until her knees bumped his legs, gently pried the ridiculous mug from his hand and set it aside, and then turned back to concentrate on this man.

She took his face in her hands. *What am I doing?*

He blinked slowly, and her thumbs moved up to sweep over those poor eyelids, the scars on his face making her want to weep.

"How does it feel?"

He blinked again, confusion muddling features that were lovely, really, beneath that stupid, stupid destruction. "This?" he asked, taking her in with a flick of the eyes. "Fucking beautiful."

"Your eyelids."

"Oh." He swallowed. "They're fine."

"Healing okay?"

"I…I can't feel anything with your hands on me."

"I'm sorry," she said, although she wasn't entirely sure what she was apologizing for.

"Don't be. I can't feel anything bad. Just you, Doc."

That brought things screeching to a halt. *Doc. What am I doing?* Her brain screamed again, while her lips said, "Call me George."

"Don't be sorry, George. I'm not."

"No?"

He smirked. "Oh, I'm sorry about a lotta shit, but not this. Not coming here. Not you." He covered one of her hands with his and, with the other, reached out, around her, to circle her back and pull her tighter to him, and that, *that* set her on fire.

Nerve endings waking up like wavy little sea anemones, heads prickling painfully along skin that had gone dead from disuse.

"Give me a kiss," he demanded, and as she watched, he softened, his gaze running a tender path from her lips to her eyes and back again. "*Please* kiss me."

In a dream, nowhere near herself, she did.

It was gentle at first, despite the raging fire inside. A touch of lips, dry but soft—feverish, almost. There were smells mingled with that contact, new scents that shouldn't feel so intimate. A face, a cheek, a jaw. A confusion of sensations with just one touch. His tongue was sensual and slow. She gave in to her urge to open her eyes, and when she did, she met his, the dark brown almost gone, eaten up by his pupils despite the bright, sterile light.

Lips, teeth, tongue, the slide of chins and noses—it was the purest, cleanest, rightest thing she'd felt in her life.

How odd, in the midst of so much unfamiliar sensation, that her mind should wander again to her marriage—her first kiss with Tom. She'd been clammy back then, with desire, which was such an odd contrast, such a strange thing to recognize. But here, this man, was *heat*, scorching heat, urgency so hot it cauterized the guilt.

With a growl, he sank back, nudged and pulled until somehow she wound up in his lap on the exam table, straddling him. Closeness, new and unexpected, sent a searing flush to the surface of her skin. She remembered the last time she'd done this, the last time she'd kissed someone with intent to do more, and it brought a wave of unwanted emotions. Regret, sadness, worry that whatever this was, it was wrong—cheating on a husband long gone.

George sucked in a hiccuping breath and realized, belatedly, that he'd stopped.

"What's going on?" he asked.

"I'm…"

"You don't want this." It wasn't a question. His voice, rich and dark before, was flat now, defeated.

"I…" How to respond to that? How on earth did you tell a man that yes you wanted him, but he was too much for you? How did you let him know that his intensity, his beauty, the smell of his skin, all made you hungry for something you'd given up on entirely? Something you probably didn't deserve.

How could you say that to the tattooed criminal you'd straddled on an exam table? Not exactly first-kiss banter, was it?

She looked up to find him eyeing her, to feel a rough thumb swipe away a tear she hadn't been conscious of crying.

"You want to tell me?"

"No," she answered.

He nodded.

"You want me to go?"

This time she shook her head, and he tightened his

arm around her back, slid his hand up from her bottom to her shoulder blade. He could probably have spanned both with one of his enormous palms.

"I scare you." ·

"No, Mr...." Oh God. What was she supposed to call him now? This was so messed up, so against every ounce of decency ingrained in her, that she cringed and looked away.

"Call me..." He stopped, blinked hard, and cleared his throat. "Andrew. Call me Andrew."

"No, you don't scare me, Andrew. Although..." She looked at him askance.

"I should."

That made her smile. "Yes, you probably should."

"Not as smart as you look, I guess," he said, and that broke through whatever this was, this shell of fear or regret that had hardened around her. She laughed.

"Definitely not."

"Come here," Andrew said.

With a sigh, she leaned her head in, set it on his shoulder, and sucked in his strength. His arms stayed warm and close, and through it all, she felt the beating of his heart, steady and slow. He was comforting her, she knew, but she couldn't rid herself of the guilty evidence of arousal or the nervy need thrumming through her overheated veins. She needed to stay here, in his embrace, for just a little while longer and pretend everything was as it should be, wishing she could memorize his smell.

After a bit, George pulled back, hating herself for doing it. "I think we should go."

"Oh. Sure. Of course," he said and, after helping

her down, rose with a grimace that made her wonder, again, about his limp. "I'll wait for you and walk you to your car."

And just like that, their moment of folly was over.

9

"So, Doc," Clay said as she led him out front, "you know of a good place where I can get my tattoos removed?"

"Wh—" She turned to him, then cut herself off, and he saw, with regret, her body loosen, sink in on itself a little. "You'd have to go to Richmond."

"All right." He nodded, wondering what the shit he was doing. He had that weird sensation that he sometimes got of being just a shell, with nothing on the inside but hollow space. It was a feeling a lot like regret, except it couldn't be—not for this, not for what they'd begun in that exam room. But maybe, just possibly, he was feeling it for her. Empathic regret. Like she hadn't meant to take up with someone like him.

"I'm sorry, Andrew."

"Don't be." He looked around and saw her car, parked alone up ahead under that fucking unlit streetlamp. "I'll walk you to your car."

"Oh, you don't nee—"

His expression must have stopped her, because she

just shrugged and let him walk beside her to her door, which was—surprise—unlocked.

"Got to start locking your door, George."

"Why?"

"Don't remember what happened last weekend?"

"How would locking my door change what happened?"

He shook his head and smiled. "You people and your small-town delusions."

She ignored that and asked, "You hungry?"

"I'm…" He hesitated, taking in all the shit crowding his insides, and realized that, yes, there was, in fact, a big, yawning hole there. When had he last eaten? "Yeah," he finished with a smile. "Wanna go to the Nook?"

"Come home with me," she said, probably with more of an undertone than intended, and his pulse hitched back up a notch.

"Yeah?" he asked in something close to a whisper.

Her eyes took an age to get to his, but when they did, any misgivings he might have had dissipated. She was an adult. A woman, not a kid, and not one of the MC hangers-on who'd been coerced or forced by necessity to mingle with the bikers. To *put out* for the bikers.

"Let me make you dinner," she said, and right there, in the middle of Main Street, where anybody in the whole world could see him, Clay Navarro came dangerously close to crying his eyes out like a little boy.

"No, I… Thanks, George. Thank you, but you don't want—"

"Shut up, Andrew," she said, knocking the air out of his sails. "Get in."

"I'll meet you there," he said. "I should get my truck and a shower."

"You remember where it is?" she asked.

Oh, I know, he thought, half listening to her directions before heading back to his room at a jog, anxious and excited with a good dose of guilty.

The guilt grew as he showered and changed, taking in his grim surroundings. George Hadley was a good woman, a clean woman, and the last thing she needed in her life was Clay's brand of filth. What the hell had he been thinking?

He considered not going but went anyway, telling himself it was because he didn't like to keep a woman waiting, but underneath he knew that wasn't it—not really. He *wanted* to go, damn it. He wanted a little of her pristine existence to rub off on him, polish him up, and get rid of some of his grime. It was selfish, especially considering how dangerous his situation was, but…but he'd tell her in person. He'd tell her he couldn't, and then he'd stop by the store for another bottle of booze and come back to this shithole, where he'd drink and maybe even jerk off for the first time in months.

He'd get through this, just like he always did—and he'd do it without dragging her with him.

George put down her empty glass and looked at the clock—an hour had passed since she'd left Andrew Blane in the street in front of the clinic. An hour in which he'd no doubt gone back to his place and decided not to reemerge. She'd even stopped off on the way for beer and a bottle of wine. She'd panfried a couple of trout from up the road in Madison and steamed some green beans from the garden—then, considering his size, made the whole package of rice. Would four cups be enough?

Only now it was an hour later and he still wasn't here, which meant he wasn't coming, and all the anticipation had fizzled into something hollow and tight and much too large for her chest.

That was the problem with removing the layers and layers of protection she'd built up over the years—things hurt.

George sat in her kitchen on one of the overstuffed armchairs beside the cold wood stove and let herself tear up for about thirty seconds before nipping the self-pity in the bud. Whatever the man was, whoever he was, he was messed up in ways George wasn't equipped to handle.

She'd do best to forget about him entirely. Maybe she'd run into him in town and tell him to come back to her practice, because they were better off as doctor and patient. He needed the job done, and she was qualified, so she might as well be the one to do it.

With a satisfied nod, she moved to the front door to turn off the porch light. Just as it flicked off, she saw it again—the movement she'd seen, or rather felt, in the woods across the street last night. She narrowed her eyes at whatever it was and then, without conscious thought, pulled open the screen door, letting it slam behind her, and marched down the steps, straight across the street, and right to the man who slid out of the shadows.

"George."

"Andrew," she said without a hint of surprise. She'd known it, hadn't she? "Too scared to come in?"

"Something like that."

"I won't bite."

"No?" he asked, sounding a little disappointed.

"You change your mind, then?"

"Still thinking about it."

"Well, it's last call, so you'd better decide."

She saw the shine of his white teeth before turning back to her house and tromping back up the stairs. With a last, disappointed huff, she pulled open the screen and let it fall behind her.

Only it didn't slam as expected. Which meant... She sucked in a nervous, edgy breath at the sound of his footfalls, followed by the quiet thud of the door shutting, then the snick of the lock being turned into place. Andrew Blane and his obsession with locks.

"I hope you like fish. I made trout."

"Sounds good."

"Come on through."

Christ, it was hot in here. "No A/C?"

"In this old house?" She laughed. "No. Ceiling fans are about as good as it gets. I'm too stubborn for window units."

"Stubborn?"

"No way I'm giving up beautiful, precious natural light in exchange for recycled air, no matter how cool it is. I'd rather be hot and watch the sky out my window."

"Wow. A purist."

"Or stupid. Whatever you want to call it."

After a pause, during which she could feel him look around, taking in their surroundings, he said, "Nice place."

"Thank you. It needs work, though."

"Yeah, saw some of your clapboard needs replacing."

"You haven't seen the garden yet," she said.

Oh, but I have, Clay thought as she went on. "I can hardly keep up. The fence is a mess, and the chickens had an unwanted visitor last week. I performed emergency surgery with chicken wire, and it's ugly."

Soft music flowed from the back of the house—some kind of girlie folk music, a little high, a little light and slow for his taste, but it suited the place. He followed George through an open hall, beside a nice-sized staircase. He'd seen some of it from outside, but he took it in with a new perspective: hardwood floors, high ceilings, paint that had seen better days, and colorful, threadbare rugs scattered here and there. The farmhouse was loved—he could see that—but it sure needed work. Bits of crown molding were missing, and floorboards whined beneath his feet. She led him back to a big kitchen that spanned the entire rear of the house.

He was shamed by the plates of food waiting for them on the scarred wooden table. He'd stood out there for at least half an hour, watching the house, waiting and debating, sick with doubt at what he was starting with this woman. Starting something he wouldn't be around to finish.

"Sorry I made you wait."

"No problem." She glanced at him, caught his eye, and raised her brows in a way that said she knew more about what he'd been doing out there than she let on. "Beer or wine?"

"Beer, please."

"It's in the fridge. Help yourself."

He turned to the old-fashioned-looking appliance,

pulled out a bottle of beer—a local brand; what was it
with people around here and their locally made crap?—
and twisted it open.

"You want one?" She shook her head, and he took a
turn around the room, bypassing the open door leading
to a big screened-in porch and ending up at the wide
back window, which overlooked the yard, where green
things fought for supremacy. "Cozy."

"You think?"

He nodded, taking in the layers of stuff everywhere,
so much like the plants out back in their cheerful disarray. Not like one of those hoarder houses, not suffo-
cating. More artfully arranged. Flowers, tons of them,
some in vases, some in pots; a couple of lamps, cool-
looking marble with ornate, colorful shades; wooden
chairs, worn like the rest of the place, with cushions on
them—no two prints alike, but all somehow belonging
together. A happy chaos.

"Have a seat," she said, and he looked at his choices—
two big armchairs by a wood stove or four wooden chairs
flanking a big, scarred table by the window. He opted
for the latter, pulling out one of the chairs and nearly
screaming like a little girl at the animal who stared up at
him, one-eyed and three-legged.

George laughed at his shocked, "Oh Jesus," and
moved to shoo away the cat, who wanted absolutely
none of it.

"Go on, Leonard. We humans get to use the chairs now."

The cat dropped to the floor with a *thunk*, only to
return to his rightful spot a few seconds later, right up
under Clay's chin like he'd been the night before.

"Wow," George said with a surprised frown.

"Leonard's a bit of a recluse usually. He doesn't take to strangers quite so fast."

Little do you know.

She walked to a counter, where she grabbed a dish and stuck it into the oven. "Brownies," she said with a little smile, twisting a tomato-shaped timer and putting it on the table between them in a weird parody of some speed-dating ritual.

She sat across from him with a glass of white wine, and he could see, even in this golden, candlelit room, a rosy blush high on her cheeks.

"You're beautiful," Clay said unexpectedly with a nervous expulsion of air.

"Oh. Oh, thank you."

"Thanks for inviting me over. Haven't had a home cooked meal in…" He swallowed. *Years*, he wanted to say, although it wasn't quite true. Jayda and Tyler had invited him over before he'd taken off. Once. Only once, because he'd seen the look on Jayda's face when the kids had checked him out, limp and tats and inappropriate vocabulary and all. He'd noticed that night that he couldn't get a sentence out without an f-bomb or two, which was part of what had kept him alive these past few years. But now that he was out of the MC, well… he was just some cussing, inked-up asshole you couldn't even have over to dinner.

"It's been a while," he finished, and George nodded.

"So. Welcome." She cleared her throat, held up her glass, and knocked it gently against his bottle. "I'm happy to be able to offer you that."

He nodded and shoveled in a bite of fish, which, even cold, was delicious. "It's good."

She smiled. "Thanks."

"Why're you so nice to me, George Hadley?"

"Nice? I'm just normal."

"You shouldn't even be talking to me."

"I shouldn't?"

Clay shook his head. "No. You really shouldn't."

"Why not? You said you weren't going to hurt me."

"I'm not," he said, although for the first time he wondered if that were actually true. "But I could, you know."

"What are you talking about?"

"I mean, having me around isn't necessarily a good thing."

She shrugged, indicating the room. "As you can see, there's nobody here to complain. Except maybe Leonard, but he'd bitch at Mother Teresa. Although, apparently you pass muster."

"Oh yeah?" Clay glanced down at the cat, which, as if understanding their words, curled into a tighter ball on his lap and let out a funny, little birdlike trill. "Seems friendly enough."

"Yeah, right. You can push him off."

Clay let the cat stay, a vibrating heater. They were quiet as they ate, serenaded by the animal's engine-like rumbling and the incessant song of the crickets outside.

"What *is* that noise?"

George cocked her head. "What noise?"

"That… Like crickets, except…loud." *Unbearably fucking never-endingly loud enough to make a person go completely insane.*

"It's the cicadas. They've graced us with their presence."

"This is a good thing?"

"Every seventeen years. That's how often they get to come out of hiding. And here they are, finally. Alive again!"

"Wow. When you put it that way..."

"Come on," she said, standing up and heading for the porch, where it was overwhelming—ultra surround sound, with the added ominous rumble of distant thunder—and then down three steps into the backyard, which was bathed in pale moonlight. George took a central path, leading to the far end of the yard and the woods beyond. It was a jungle out here—plants barely held back by metal structures, poles spilling onto the walkway with abandon. The moonlight turned everything the same shade of gray or green, but alive, so damned alive with the buzzing, ticking, humming energy of unseen fauna and rampant flora that Clay had to stop, breathe, get his bearings, gather himself before following her.

Close to the back of the yard, she stopped and turned to look at him, and although the colors were washed out, he could see the excitement on her face, could feel it in currents as electrified as the far-off flash of lightning.

The noise. He couldn't take the fucking noise. The deep, constant background sounds drove him a little crazier every day. And this woman loved it? They were worlds apart, weren't they?

"This is not the end yet," she said. "They'll get louder over the next week or two. And then... Oh, this is..." She swallowed, pressed fingers to her mouth, and he wondered if she was going to cry. "And then they're gone. Seventeen years before we see these guys again." She grabbed his hand, squeezed, and he could barely even understand the level of emotion this woman felt over something so…so inconsequential. So annoying as these loud-ass insects taking over the night—and more than a little real estate inside his brain.

"Not the most pleasant sound I've ever heard. So fu—so damned loud," he said.

He hated how disappointed she looked at his words, hated even more the way she took her hand away from his, leaving him bereft. For those few seconds when she'd touched him, the noise hadn't been quite so bad. Like a Mute button, she'd staved off the panic.

He wished she would do it again.

"Loud? Yes, I suppose they are," George agreed.

Loud? It was beautiful.

He looked away from her in a way that smacked of avoidance. "How can you even sleep here? I need the A/C on just to drown out the night noises, and now this… Man. I'd go crazy."

"Oh, I…I like it." And here it was again, that moment when George realized she wasn't quite the norm. "Let's go back in."

He followed her inside, and they sat and picked up where they'd left off. Only George felt the tiniest bit crushed. She shouldn't, of course. It was stupid to think anyone would understand her excitement at such silly things.

They sat at the table, a little too close, a little awkward. Leonard hopped right back up onto Andrew's lap, and George shook her head.

"He's really into you."

Andrew shrugged, looking, if she wasn't mistaken,

a little sheepish. Was that a flush on his cheeks? He took a bite of trout, and the flush deepened. His eyes rose to hers.

"This is—oh God—this is amazing. Best thing I've had."

She laughed.

"I'm serious, what did you do to make this so…" He chewed, groaned a little, and swallowed, taking another bite and then another. "This has more…flavor than anything I've eaten in months."

She shook her head and took a bite of her own. "It's just trout, you know. It's local, from over in Madison County, but nothing special. I guess the butter's local too, so maybe that's what you like about it? Fresh ingredients, I suppose?"

"You're an amazing cook. That's what it is."

It was her turn to blush. Compliments made her feel awkward, and rather than continue to endure his, she deflected. "Sorry about going overboard outside with the cicadas. I…I get worked up about that stuff. I guess I'm just a hippy at heart." She waved her hand in the air. "It's…it's the magic of it. Of these creatures. Of the world, you know?" He didn't. She could tell, but she couldn't seem to stop herself. "They spend seventeen years underground and then, all together, they come out. *As one.* They sing their song, and they slough off their shells and journey up into the trees. A long, arduous climb. All in the service of nature. Propagation. Beautiful, lovely, natural. This is the world around us. This is beauty." Lord, how lame. But it was true. And George couldn't ignore something that moved her so very much.

"I guess I…I see what you mean."

"Yeah." She took a bite, not tasting the food anymore. "I'm sorry."

"What? What for?"

"I get excited. About things."

"No, it's fine." He took a swig of beer, his eyes on the bottle in his hand and then, suddenly, unexpectedly, on hers. "It's actually refreshing. I mean, you are. Refreshing or… I've seen a lot of pretty nasty shit."

She nodded, waiting for more.

"So you…you're like this breath of fresh air. Like this clean, perfect, sweet person."

"Um. No, that I am not."

"Whatever you are, I'm afraid I'll…" Another swig, and Leonard the antisocial cat fell from his lap as Clay stood. He towered above her, big and overwhelming. "I gotta go, George. This was—I kid you not—amazing. Best meal I've ever had. I just can't… I'm sorry."

"Oh, no. *I'm* sorry. No, don't—"

"Look, you're a… You're a real nice lady, all right? I just… I don't… You don't deserve this."

"Deserve what?"

"What I have to give."

"How can you be so sure?" *I know who you are*, she wanted to say. *I know about the Sultans. I know you've done bad things, but so have I. Maybe we both deserve a second chance.*

"I…gotta go," he said, putting down his bottle with a final *thunk*, footsteps pounding down her hall and out the front door with depressing finality.

George considered getting up, considered running after him. But she couldn't, she wouldn't, because he had to *want* to stay.

Her gaze landed on Leonard, who, offended, licked his paws on Andrew's recently evacuated seat cushion. You couldn't force an animal to stick around when he didn't want to—she knew that. Some creatures, like Leonard, you couldn't even cajole.

She knew it, but she didn't like it.

In the distance, a vehicle started up and rumbled off down the road toward town, echoed by the hum of thunder from over the mountains. Would it just *effing* storm already? George looked down at her plate, where half of an unappetizing fish sat congealed in the hardened butter sauce she'd restarted three times. On the table beside her elbow, the buzzer sounded, a perfect end to this ridiculous parody of a date she should never have embarked on to begin with.

10

BY THE TIME THE SUN CAME UP, CLAY NEEDED TO RUN, TO feel the pain in his thigh, the ache in his back, the rough burn of his knuckles and eyelids, the sharper torment of his blistering chest. Distraction was what he needed.

So, up and out, ignoring the gaudy sunrise, the moist air and dry ground, and onto Blackwood's sleepy streets, pounding the pavement, breathing, aching, wanting.

I want.

What the fuck did he want?

It wasn't about what he wanted, was it? It was about need. Necessity.

Get rid of the ink. Go to court. End of story.

He pushed himself harder as he approached the bottom of the slope he'd only driven up thus far, then cranked the pace and forced himself to jog the steep drive. Up, up, up, above all the shit, the morass of his life, the memories.

He made it to the top of the mountain, fueled by self-recrimination, and collapsed on the outcropping of rock overlooking Blackwood and the foothills beyond—all the way to Charlottesville, which was nothing but a pinkish haze on the horizon.

He should go. Find someplace else to hide out—because he couldn't even trust his own team anymore. Because this case was huge—weapons, drugs, prostitution, racketeering. With every possible state and federal agency involved now, it was so much bigger than he was. But Clay had been the one to break it wide open—mostly due to his fearlessness in the face of odds that had seemed truly impossible. He'd cared more about taking them down than his personal safety; his very existence was just that.

He closed his eyes, remembering how he'd felt the day he'd finally been patched in to the Sultans, the way Handles had thrown that heavy arm around his shoulders. It'd been so good, on so many levels. Being accepted, after so many months of groveling, brought in, loved…a fucking brother.

"One of us now, kid," Handles had said, his voice full of pride. And fuck if Clay hadn't felt it.

And how messed up was that? To be an agent, to be undercover, to believe in what you were doing in the deepest, darkest part of your soul, but in order to get there—Jesus, he'd become one of them at heart.

He'd loved those dudes. His *brothers*.

And now, Bread was dead.

Bread, who'd been somewhere on the compound the day all the shit had gone down. Bread, finally, had saved his life, once all hell broke loose. Jesus, Bread had risked it all that night when he'd bludgeoned Handles over the head and hauled Clay from the room, out the back door, and away from the firefight.

And me, a chunk of my leg shot out and two little, round scars in my back. Put there by Handles himself. Dear old Dad.

Get your goddamned story straight. He kept hearing the lawyer's words. Straight? What the hell was straight?

The confusion of rights and wrongs, friends, enemies…that was what made Hecker's directive so difficult to follow.

Stay alive was not an order he'd been given. Not directly by Hecker or McGovern or anyone else, but with Bread dead, he was all they had left. They needed him to make this case, to make the charges stick, because without him, all they had were random accusations of murder, torture, and gun and drug offenses with a few recordings to back them up.

He'd gotten into the Sultans, had managed to get a colleague in after him, and now…now Bread was gone and Clay was alone and he wasn't safe anywhere.

The only reason I'm alive is 'cause nobody knows where I am.

And that thought led right back to the memories he'd tried hardest to suppress over the last few hours: George Hadley in her perfect storybook world.

Images flew at him: her messed-up cat, purring in his lap; kissing her; his goddamned aching hard-on… He closed his eyes on the view again, the better to remember her arms around him, the solid reality of her grip, the good, clean wholesomeness of her. He didn't deserve it. Any of it. He deserved the shitty-ass motel, the pain in his body, the fucking zap of the laser. He deserved to die, even, but…

Man, she was hot.

The thought hit him unexpectedly. Out of place and weird. But up until now, she'd been…something else. Something too pristine, a little uptight. A sexy doctor, but still his *doctor*. And completely out of reach. Now, with the things that had happened, she was different. Hot and essential and *available*. So, of course, he'd gone and botched that up. Well, he kind of had to, right? When things were way too good to be true? You couldn't go around living the high life with a giant *X* on your back.

Could you?

～◈◇～

A busy workday helped George think about something other than Andrew. Except in the end, she couldn't stop thinking about him at all.

It was later than she usually got home, because like an idiot, she'd prepped a room and waited at the clinic for him to arrive. When he hadn't, the only person she'd been angry at was herself.

Irritated all over again, she slammed her car door and headed toward her house.

"Hey, neighbor," called Jessie from somewhere beyond the hedge.

"Hi, Jessie."

"Busy?"

"Oh." She paused. "No."

"Wanna come hang out?"

"Yes!" she yelled a tad too loudly. *Distraction!* "Let me get cleaned up and—"

"Oh, take your time. I've got the booze tonight," Jessie said, rattling something in what might have been a bucket of ice.

"Oh, good. I'll bring snacks."

"Match made in heaven," Jessie said.

George ran inside to feed Leonard, then back outside to put the chickens to bed, pick a bowl of salad, and, with a mournful glance at the sky, turn the sprinkler on.

Back inside, she pulled out leftovers and some of the same mini quiches she'd made for her in-laws. Just as she was headed out, her gaze fell on the pathetic, untouched tray of brownies from the night before, and with a bratty huff, she picked it up and stuck it in her basket before slamming out the front door and heading over.

"Oh my God, how are you still single?" asked Jessie when George unpacked everything in the kitchen. "What a cornucopia of delight."

"Where's Gabe?"

"At a sleepover." Jessie's smile faded. "I am such a mess. My boy goes on a sleepover, only like the third one in his entire life, and I'm putting a brave face on it. Like, I love the free time to, you know, drink alone on the porch and all, but my little boy's growing up, and *he's already deserting me!*" The last bit was moaned in an "I'm having a breakdown" kind of voice that George could appreciate, although probably not entirely relate to. Solitude was, after all, her norm.

"I'm sorry" was her inadequate response.

Jessie, though, didn't seem to mind. "Oh, whatever. I really need to get over myself. Here, have a glass and tell me about your day while I plate these amazing morsels you brought."

"We need to wash the lettuce."

"On it. Wash lettuce. That's something I can handle. Now grab yourself some vino. It's on the front porch."

A few sips into her glass, George's phone rang. The number was Uma's. "Hello?"

"George? Hey, it's Uma. Hope now's an okay time?"

"Hi! Yes, it's fine. What's up?"

"I hate to call you for work things at night, but…"

"No, please, don't be ridiculous. Are you okay? Is this an emergency?"

"Um, no," Uma said with a bit of a laugh in her voice, and George relaxed again. "Well, not *my* emergency, in any case. It's…um, somewhat delicate."

"What? Is it Ive? Are you okay?"

"No, it's fine. It's… You remember Cookie Lloyd? My neighbor? The woman I stayed with when I first got to town?" A voice rumbled in the background, and Uma responded with something about Steve having enough on his plate already. And a giggle. "Hey! I'm on the phone," she said, the smile in her voice belying the scolding words. "Anyway, Cookie's got a rash, and I'm not sure you recall this, but she won't leave her house."

"Right. Didn't I see her out on the stoop last weekend?"

"Yes. Her being out there was a big deal. Anyway, I was wondering if you'd have time at some point to come by and see her."

"Sure. Of course. I'd love to."

"I know it's a lot to ask, but…" Another mumbled male interruption. "Yes, she'll pay her, Ive; you know she's not that tight-fisted. Stop being such a—" He said something else, and again, Uma giggled. George couldn't believe this woman was giggling. *Giggling*, after everything that had happened to her.

She smiled. "Is Saturday okay?"

"Yes, great."

"Do you want to be there, or should I—"

"You need me there. Trust me," Uma said darkly.

George smiled again. "Okay. See you Saturday then."

Jessie stuck her head outside after George ended the call. "Coast clear? Figured it might be a work thing. I didn't want to interrupt."

"Yes, thank you. Come on out."

"Wow. I had no idea a dermatologist had such an active professional life."

"Oh, you would be surprised. It's…" She thought of Andrew Blane. "It's actually even surprising to me how crazy it gets sometimes."

"Well, I get crazy clients. Some of the people I see, man… I'm not allowed to talk names, but, without citing particulars, there's this…situation at work right now that I have no idea what to do with."

"Really? I'm all ears."

"I think my colleague is sleeping with one of our clients."

"And by 'client' you mean…?"

"Probationer, yes. Offender."

"Wow. That's… What are you going to do?"

"I don't know, George. I mean"—Jessie swigged her wine, leaned back, and shook her head—"I get it. I do. There's a whole series of shit that happens with these people. We're there to help them, you know? Contrary to what people might think. We're here to ensure that they don't go back inside. We want them to succeed, which sometimes drags us right into their lives—their situations. They also, sometimes, look at us like their saviors, which is one hell of a pull on its own, and… Shit. The guy is hot. I'll give her that."

Oh. My. God. A shiver of shame ran down her back.

"I have to tell you something." The words burst out of her, hard, hot, and painful in her mouth, but she just couldn't hold it in anymore.

Jessie stopped talking, blinked, and waited. A good listener, this one.

"I've… Crap, I mean, no… I mean *shit*! Just shit, shit, shit!"

"Whoa, George, gettin' all crass on me, girl?" Jessie moved her chair over to bring her right next to George. "Now I'm just dying to hear whatever it is that's turned George Hadley, Medicine Woman, into a potty mouth!"

George let out a halfhearted laugh-moan and dropped her head into her hands. "I've messed up, Jessie. I mean really, really messed up."

"I believe you mean *royally fucked up*, George. Come on, if you're going to go potty mouth on me, please go all the way."

"Yeah, so. I've fucked up. Or I *am* fucked up. Or something. I'm not sure which, or… Yes, I am. I am fucked up, because I haven't gone that far yet, but I really, really want to." One hand still covering her face, George shook her head and groaned.

"Oh. My. God. Is this a patient? Please tell me it's a patient."

"It's a patient."

"Yes! I mean, I'm so sorry, but…" Jessie sighed, sounding suddenly serious, and George finally looked up. "I want you to be happy, George. You're a good person. You deserve it."

"Oh, well, I'm fine. Happy, I mean."

Jessie raised her brows at her—just that—and George knew she wasn't tricking anyone.

"Yes, so. All right, I'm not happy. And this…situation isn't improving that. But…"

"But? But what? Please don't leave me hanging here! Okay, hold on. More wine. Here. And some for me. Now. Out with it."

"Okay. Okay." She took a swig, trying to formulate it in her head. "I have a new patient."

"New since when?"

"Um…a week, I guess." George pulled out her phone. "No, that can't be right. It must be longer, it's… Oh my God. It's been exactly one week. Today."

"Fast worker."

"I've seen a lot of him. Almost every day he comes in for his…treatment. Anyway, he's…he's interesting."

"Oh? How?"

"It's his…" George waved her hands in the air in front of her but couldn't say the words—wasn't allowed to, in fact. "Appearance. Tattoos and…scars. You know, a bad boy."

"Oh. Mmm-hmm. I've got some of those."

"He showed up last week, when I'd sent everyone home and the A/C was out, and it was just the two of us in the office."

"You saw him alone?"

"Yes. I'm an idiot, right?"

"Yes. Go on."

"So, he needed me. My help. Pretty desperately. I couldn't say no."

"A dermatological emergency. Okay, I get that… Go on."

"Anyway, there's…there's more to him than his"—she waved again—"skin issues."

"Right."

"I mean, I think he has something psychological, and I don't know how to deal with that kind of thing, but…I did something terrible last night."

"Wait. Psychological?"

"Like PTSD. Or some kind of trauma."

"And he comes in at night?"

"After we're closed."

"His choice or—"

"My suggestion. I'm seeing him off the books—pro bono. And…I don't want my other patients seeing him," she said, when really what she meant was *I want to keep him secret. All to myself.*

Jessie sat up. "Whoa. George, are you sure you know what you're doing?"

"No! Of course not! But…but more than his skin or my compulsion to help people, there's this…thing between us."

"Not *his* thing, I hope?"

"Oh, come on, pl—"

"Just kidding. Keep going, I'm…" Jessie waved her hand in front of her face, like a fan. "I'm actually kind of worked up by this. It sounds…intense."

"God, yes," George said, almost in relief, because that was it. Exactly. Intense. "*He's* intense, and between us, there's this…chemistry. I've never felt anything like it. Not even with my husband. It feels like pain and excitement and titillation, and I want to hold him and… I'm mortified. The man is unwell, and I took advantage."

"You did?"

"Yes! I'm a professional! But he needed help, and there I was, rubbing his back, and instead of doing the job he came to me for, I acted like a prostitute in a back-street massage parlor."

"Holy crap."

"I mean, I gave him everything except the stupid happy ending!"

"WHAT??!!" Jessie jumped up like a monkey, crouched on her chair, excitable as a child. "Tell me everything!"

"I don't know, but I started it. It was like I was possessed or something. Oh my God, Jessie, when he takes off his shirt, it's like—"

"He takes off his shirt? What the hell do you people do in that office?"

"I'm examining his skin! I'm treating him; it's all aboveboard!"

"I know, I know. Just kidding. Geez, I'm flustered. It's… It sounds sexy."

"Yes. Yes, it's sexy. Painfully sexy."

"Why painful?"

"He fired me. So that we could…continue to kiss, I guess."

"Kiss? So you kissed him?"

"No. Actually, he kissed me. And then I asked him over last night. And he almost didn't come, and then when he did, he…he freaked out. Or something. And he left."

"Oh, shit. Drama queen. Stay away."

George opened her mouth to protest but stopped. Stay away. Right. Good advice.

Unfortunately, no matter how dangerous the man might seem, she didn't particularly want to follow that advice.

～⚬～

After another sparring session with the sheriff, Clay left town. He headed to Norfolk, making sure he was a good three hours from Blackwood before turning on his phone and checking in with his boss, against his better judgment.

"McGovern."

"Navarro here, ma'am."

"Na—Where the hell are you, Navarro?"

"Rather not say, ma'am."

A pause. "Excuse me?"

"I heard about Breadthwaite."

"Random accident."

"You don't truly believe that, do you?"

Another pause. "It doesn't matter. I told you to lay low, not to fall off the grid entirely. I can't have you disappear—"

"I don't know who to trust. I'm sorry, it's not—"

"You can trust me. Now, goddamn it, what is your location?"

A pause while Clay decided how best to say—or not say—what he was thinking. "You heard anything about my whereabouts?"

"No, I haven't, Navarro."

"Just wanted to make sure I haven't been compromised."

"Not here, at least."

"Okay. Good." His body loosened, the burning in his gut lessened, and his headache eased off just a notch.

"I should tell you about a couple of issues we've had here, Navarro."

At the dark tone of his boss's voice, Clay waited, breath held.

"You know the assistant U.S. attorney hired to the case?"

"Hecker, yeah."

"His family's been threatened. Locals too, and… Well, everyone involved."

"What's that mean for me?"

She breathed a big, exhausted-sounding sigh before speaking to him, fast and low. "Are you safe where you are?"

"Believe so, ma'am."

"Anyone know who you are?"

"No."

"Any sign of them?"

He thought about the bikes he'd heard, all but certain they'd been in his head. "None."

Another sigh, slightly lighter this time, and he could picture her doing that weird chin raise she did when circumstances got rough.

"All right. Good. You want to tell me where you are?"

"I'm sorry, ma'am. I'm…I'm safe. I'm alive. I'll check in next week. In the meantime—"

"Don't you dare hang up on me, Navarro. We need to at least set up a—"

He hung up, cutting her off and probably destroying

what was left of his career. Somehow, he couldn't seem to muster up the energy to care.

George was tipsy.

Tipsy turvy, her face hot, her brain out of focus.

"I'm wondering," she said to Jessie, who looked as flushed and fuzzy as she felt. "Do you know anything about motorcycle gangs?"

"Motorcycle gangs?"

"Yes."

"Why?" Jessie's face crinkled up when she asked that, making her look exactly like her son.

"Curiosity," George said as nonchalantly as possible. At Jessie's narrowed eyes, she went on. "Really. Just interested in finding out more."

"Hmm. Yeah," she said slowly, doubtfully. "I'm not an expert, but I consult with a guy in DC when one of my probationers has been involved in a club. Got connections."

"Who is he?"

"ATF. High up. He's on some gang-related task force, and apparently, motorcycle clubs are right up there with the worst of them. Worse than the mafia." Jessie leaned in, her easygoing drunkenness replaced by a laser-sharp interest. "What's going on?"

Another sip of wine reinforced George's sense of purpose—her zealous need to heal—and obliterated any worries about the very fine line she was treading. "Do you know anything about the Sultans Motorcycle Club?"

"They're out of Maryland?"

"Yes. I looked them up, and they appear to be—"

"They're rough. Like insanely rough. That's what I know."

"Rough. Yes."

"Stay away. Like, if you see one, turn right the hell around. They're vicious, violent lunatics, George. These are guys who don't kill just for money or whatever. They kill for fun."

"I…I'm not involved. I just…"

"Is it that guy?" Jessie asked, proving that George had no knack for prevarication.

"Who?"

"You know who. Your patient?"

"I'm really not in a position to—"

"Okay, George, fine. I can make a couple of phone calls, but"—Jessie put down her glass and grabbed George's hand, looking her right in the eye—"don't get involved with this guy. Please."

George wanted to deny that they were talking about the same man, but it seemed pointless. And suddenly she was exhausted. "I want to help this person. That's all," George said, thinking as the words emerged that they were lies, all lies.

❧

It was that special, syncopated double thrum of a Harley that pulled Clay from his vodka-induced stupor late that night. Not once or twice as you'd expect in a town like this, but over and over again, he heard them driving by. Two bikes, it sounded like, passing one too many times in the night.

They're here.

The sound had his back tensing, his stomach burning, and his breath coming fast as he packed up his room, threw his shit in the back of the truck, and drove slowly, carefully through the otherwise quiet streets of Blackwood. He hunted them for an hour, watching, waiting, sure he'd catch sight of one of them. After long minutes of nothing, he headed straight to Jason Lane, pushed by a need to see George, to protect her. Maybe to be comforted just knowing she was close. He parked in an overgrown drive and jogged to her house. From the woods across the street, he watched, relieved, as she tripped her way over from the neighbor's house and then stumbled up her porch stairs.

After a while, the light went out, and Clay waited, wishing that ugly-ass cat would come out and keep him company.

⤟

George walked the fifty-two steps separating Jessie's place from hers more than a little tipsy—something that was apparently getting to be a habit, but one she was enjoying.

Just let me enjoy it a little longer, she thought, pulling a fresh nightgown over her head, her movements more languid than usual, her body relaxed. Starfished across her bed, she recognized, in a moment of drunken clarity, that the thought could just as easily apply to Andrew Blane. *Let me enjoy him a little longer.* She didn't want him to stop coming to her, no matter how dangerous Jessie thought he was.

She didn't want to see his skin as an organ, couldn't make herself if she tried. It wasn't just work—it was a work of art, and ashamed though she was, at least tonight she could admit to her desire.

Her hand followed the curve of her body, remembering the sensuous slide of him, the give and take of his shape—the ins and outs of him. Down to the place between her legs which had, in the past week, experienced more intense sensation than in the past decade.

Which is pathetic.

Pathetic, but true, something analytical in her mind argued, and there—there was the reasoning she'd been looking for. She allowed her hand a stroke over the clean cotton, wishing for his rougher, unfamiliar touch. It would be good with him, even if it was bad. It would be good, she knew with absolute certainty, because she *wanted* him so badly.

That was the thing about chemistry, wasn't it? It was selective. You never knew when it would hit. One woman's feast was another woman's… No. That wasn't quite it. More like cheesecake. George loved cheesecake. Loved it. But the men she'd dated had been…banana cream pie or something equally unimpressive. Not bad, per se, just *meh*.

She had a feeling—wrong, probably—that the cheesecake didn't have to be *good* to make her happy. It just had to be cheesecake, and she'd had cheesecake only once before in her life and—

"Cheesecake is bad," she moaned, removing her hand from the wetness and startling Leonard off the bed in the process. Okay, so definitely more than tipsy, if the cheesecake analogy was anything to go by.

Her side table caught her eye as she leaned over to turn off the light, and her gaze fell on the bottle lying there, along with the pack of syringes. Oh, crap. She'd forgotten today's injection, and it was…Thursday?

How could she have forgotten? And yesterday too, she realized with the strangest, guiltiest jolt. What was wrong with her? Andrew Blane popped right back up in her mind's eye, answering that question as surely as anything. Of course. She'd been *distracted*.

Well, it was time to stop. The short needle she jabbed into her bruised belly was a perfect reminder of everything she'd worked for all this time, everything she had to lose. So, no. No.

Tears rushed to her eyes, clogged her throat, and George fell back onto the bed, already regretting a love affair that was never going to be.

When she fell asleep, teary and emotional, reaching for the image of that baby she wanted so badly, for the first time in forever, she couldn't quite seem to find it.

11

"You ready?" Sheriff Mullen asked.

Clay nodded. He was ready all right. Aching, in fact, to tear some shit up. Or maybe even get his shit torn up.

Because I'm an idiot.

An idiot who messed with the doc—the only person he'd found to help him—and then took off. Not, of course, because he didn't want her, but because he had shit for brains.

Because she scares you.

"Yeah. Let's do this, Sheriff," he said, pushing memories from the past few nights before from his mind. He'd figure it out later.

"Steve," said the sheriff.

"Steve. Okay. I'm…Andrew."

Today, the gym was nearly empty, which was a relief, since he hadn't really loved having an audience.

"All right, Andrew. Ready for another challenge from the man who claims he doesn't know how to fight. You say you're not military…" He squinted at Clay, who felt suddenly naked. "That's okay. I still got some moves. Little guy like me can still kick your monster ass, don't worry."

"Oh, great," Clay said, faking annoyance but actually pretty revved.

On the mat, he let Steve get a couple of hits in: nothing big, but enough to rattle his brain in his skull and wake him up. It felt great to let loose, despite his aching leg and stiff back. He ignored those and just let his body go.

After a few rounds, though, he forgot to hold back, allowing his instincts to kick in and letting them lead, twisting into the counters rather than fighting against them. He had too much on his mind. That woman who'd torn him up and turned him inside out. The shit back in Baltimore, the goddamned bikes he heard revving outside every single night. The bikes weren't real. They were in his head. When he lived in his body like this, just moved and let go and went with the flow, he could pretend none of it was real.

At one point, Steve came at him with an uncharacteristically blunt attack, open-handed, almost too obvious, and Clay went for it. Quick slide to the side, hand over his opponent's wrist, into his body, forward propulsion, roll, then Steve's head between his thighs. All fast, lightning fast, and *oh shit*… Steve slapped out.

"No, sir. No way," the man said between tight lips before stepping out of the ring. "In the back, Blane, *now*."

Clay hesitated. *What the hell?*

"In my office," Steve ordered. He might be little, but he was bossy as shit, and Clay followed wordlessly.

By the time the door closed behind him, he knew he'd been wrong to follow the sheriff back here.

"Who the hell are you?" Steve asked, voice quiet and hard, eyes slitted on Clay's face.

"Andrew Blane."

"The hell you are, son. Ain't no goddamned bricklayer or whatever the hell Andrew Blane does for a livin'." Steve was breathing hard now, his nostrils wide. "I'm asking one more time. Where the hell'd you learn to fight like that?"

"Here and there," Clay said, forcing nonchalance as the noose tightened around his neck.

"Yeah? You show up in my peaceful town, claim you ain't never done a real fight, and then pull out that *Krav fuckin' Maga* shit?" All five foot ten of the guy stood up to Clay, in his face, finger poking his chest, and ire focused fully at him. "Who. The fuck. Are you?"

Was it so wrong, in that moment, that Clay wanted to tell him everything? Wrong, maybe, but definitely not surprising.

"I can't say. Sir."

"Why Blackwood? There somethin' goin' down here that I should know about?"

Clay shook his head, swiped a hand across his face, sighed. "Got nothing to do with Blackwood."

"Anybody here I need to take a look at?"

"Me?" Clay said with a halfhearted chuckle.

"Right you are, son. If you aren't military, then you're a cop, and I want to know what you're doing in my town." The air whooshed out of Clay, leaving him stretched out and empty. "Try to fool me? I know law enforcement when I see it, even with that crap tattooed on your skin. You are no civilian, innocent or otherwise. Spotted you a goddamned mile and a half away."

"Yeah?" Clay asked with a tight smirk. "Never happened to me before."

"What, that you got made?"

"Yeah." He cleared his throat. "Look. I'm just here to hole up till trial. I don't want any trouble."

"That makes two of us."

"You want me to leave?"

"What, Blackwood or the gym?"

"Either. Both?"

Steve stepped away from Clay, shook himself like a dog, and looked him hard in the eye.

"You swear you're on the right side of whatever it is you're running from?"

Clay stiffened and nodded, hard. "Yes, sir. I swear."

Finally, the older man sighed, running one knobby hand over his cropped, salt-and-pepper hair.

"You… This town… It's real quiet, you understand? We do accidents on the highway, break up some tussles. Nothing big if we can help it. I'm short a couple of deputies right now. I don't have the manpower to handle whatever trouble you're dragging behind you. Please tell me I'm not about to face Armageddon in my backyard. Because it's too close to my *goddamned* retirement to have you mess this up now, you got it?"

"Yessir."

"I don't care who you are, where you come from. This is a quiet town. Hear me?"

"Loud and clear."

"Good. Now get your ass back out there and walk me through those moves."

～∾

When the knocking started that evening, George knew it was him. Tamping down the swell of excitement that tried to sneak up her throat, she didn't straighten her clothing or shake out her hair as she walked to the waiting room, slow, calm, and collected, then to the clinic door.

"I'm sorry," he said as he stepped in. "Again. I'm sorry again."

"It's fine."

"I want…" She watched, fascinated, as his Adam's apple bobbed, covered in an extra day of growth. He hadn't shaved in a while. "I haven't been in this position before."

"What position?"

"Where I…where I need someone's help."

She raised her brows and waited, the hurt she'd felt the night before raising its ugly head and wanting him to suffer just a little.

"Will you be my doctor again?"

"Of course," she responded, although she'd pictured this. For two days, she'd imagined him coming in and begging. She'd wanted that, wanted the begging and pleading, and in that silly, little-girl fantasy, she'd pictured herself turning away with a tight, little smile to jot down a referral. "Let's go."

He hesitated, but rather than wait, George led him into the back, ignoring how bad his limp sounded today, set him up in a different room from last time, and avoided letting herself be too aware of his eyes on her. "What are we doing tonight?" she asked.

"Try the back again?"

"Fine."

"We'll, uh…we'll forego the numbing cream, if you—"

"Right." She nodded. "No cream."

He slid onto his front, and George ignored her body's reactions to the sight of him—the muscles: bigger, stronger, more sensual-looking than anything she'd seen on another human being. The tightening of skin over bones, the oh-so-human prickle of goose bumps in the cool office air.

George switched the machine on and watched his body tense, waiting for his reaction. She approached, non-laser-wielding hand held safely behind her back. No chance for an intimacy that hurt way too much.

"Ready?"

He nodded. "Go ahead."

George leaned in to guide the laser over his neck, and when his body jolted, she forced her sympathetic reaction down. It hurt. It burned. He'd get over it.

Out of the corner of her eye, she saw his arm tense; his hand, clasped into a fist, shook—all that strength serving nothing but panic, anxiety. Fist squeezed behind her back, she paused.

"Should I stop?"

"No. Got to get it done."

She leaned in, watching him tighten up again, and before she'd actually made up her mind to touch him, before she'd allowed herself to consider the ramifications, her free hand landed on his shoulder, his head, then back to his shoulder in a soothing caress, the shock of their chemistry buzzing harder than the laser in her hand. *Stupid. Stupid.*

This time, as she worked, she felt the stress in his body through his skin, and she tried, hard as she could, to soak it up, pull it in, take it from him. Even though he'd hurt her, she wanted him to hurt less. *Yep, stupid.*

"Okay. Neck's done. For now, of course." She stepped away. "Think you can handle the back?"

He nodded, and she focused on a shoulder blade.

"George…could you…could you put your hand on me again?" he asked, his effort audible in the gravelly strain of his voice. "Please?"

At those words, she lost every last ounce of resentment. Every stored up grain of hurt at him leaving the other night poured out of her, and with a big expulsion of breath, she put her palm on his arm, squeezed, leaned in, and finished the job.

They were done in less than half an hour, and after spreading a thick layer of petroleum jelly over his back in a sad, quick parody of the last time, George left the room to let him pull on his shirt and get himself together again.

Get *herself* together again.

When, a few minutes later, she emerged from her office, purse in hand, he stood waiting in the hall, big and beautiful and wounded. How strange, after all of it—the back thing, the dinner, the leaving, his pleading—to see him as this intimidating monster again, ugly lines and scars marring what would have been quite the canvas. This man…he was a tragedy of a human being, whose bark was so much worse than his bite, and loathe though she was to admit it, his bite was something she wouldn't have minded feeling right then.

Crap, how had this happened? How could she let herself feel so much for this person? And not with her usual clinical empathy, but…

"Walk you to your car."

"You don't need to."

Ignoring her, Andrew followed her as she turned off lights.

He opened the door, letting them out onto the sidewalk. George locked up, then turned and stopped.

It was a taut moment, that second when her eyes landed on his and she saw desire there, raw and painful.

He wants me, she thought with a sad sort of elation.

Overhead, the light buzzed with insects, their drone a comfort to her, their *tap-tap-tapping* on the glass globe a welcome sound. Somewhere, a car drove by, a shout sailed down from the direction of the Nook, a train whistle blew, and beyond all of that, the usual nighttime hum of life had expanded, bigger than usual, with the overwhelming and beautiful swell of the cicadas' song.

They moved along the sidewalk, into the street to her car. His was nowhere to be seen. "Need a ride?" she asked, ignoring his sigh at her unlocked car.

"I'm good," he said, but something didn't ring true. He didn't seem good at all. His limp, for one thing, looked like it hurt.

"You sure?"

"Guess I won't need to come in to see you for a while."

"Right," she said, saddened at the thought and relieved too. "Give me a call in a few weeks, and we'll set you up to come back in."

He nodded. "Night, George. And…thank you."

"You're welcome, Andrew," she said, letting him close the car door. She hesitated before rolling down the window and saying the thing she'd been thinking all night. "If you need anything…help or—"

"I'm fine, Doc. Thanks."

She cleared her throat again and went on, watching his face, girding herself for his response. "Your back. The uh…the tattoo. I looked it up, and the Sultans are no—"

Her car door swung back open. He ducked down, in her face, looming over her body faster than she'd imagined possible. "How do you know about that?" he demanded.

"Online," she stammered, her breath coming fast, too fast, and her throat tight with anxiety. "I looked up the image on your back."

"Don't. Ever. Say that word again. Ever. To any-body." His grip on her shoulder was tight, the urgency in his voice frightening. "You understand?"

George nodded and whispered, "Yes," before he let her go. "I'm sorry."

"That part of your job? To look me up?"

"N-no. Of course not."

"Well, don't do it again."

"I'm sorry."

"It's not safe, George. I don't want you getting hurt."

A firm nod, and still he didn't quite release her arm, not before giving her an odd stroke, as if to smooth away the pain of his hold.

"Six weeks?"

"Maybe sooner."

"A month," he said with finality before stepping away and breaking her heart just a little.

She felt him watching as she started the car and drove off at her usual sedate twenty-five miles an hour toward home, wanting so badly to go faster. Or, no, not faster. Not fast at all. She wanted to throw the car into reverse and back all the way up to where he still stood in the dark street and make him get in. Make him stay with her—although she wasn't sure if it was for his protection or hers.

She knows about the Sultans.

Of course she did. The doc was a smart woman, and he was a fool for thinking she wouldn't take an interest.

He should go. He should leave this place, hole up somewhere else.

Tomorrow. Right now, he needed to think. And when thinking didn't work, he opted for the woods across the street from the doctor's place, vodka bottle in hand.

Just enough to smooth the edges and dull the regret as he sat down, back to a tree, and watched her do her regular things. Her beautiful, healthy, perfect-life things.

Slugging back the vodka, he could watch, through narrowed eyes, and almost picture himself in there. Picture ending the other night on a different note— one where he'd stayed instead of taking off like an asshole. His belly hurt, empty of food, full of booze, and lined with acid. Up for a piss, not too far from the seat of his vigil, then back to stand guard. Empty bottle. *Fuck.*

He threw it against a tree, wanting a loud smash, hoping it would wake her up, and she'd come out to find him and take him in. But the stupid bottle thumped almost silently to the ground, and Clay slumped against the cool bark and let his eyes close.

His head was filled with popping, bright and real,

followed by screams, the screams of friends, brothers, men he'd sworn to die with—and for.

Burning flesh and hair, sweet and sickly, acrid. Adrenaline hitting him like a dose of methamphetamines, hot in his blood, a rush like nothing else—and then instinct kicked in. Only, this time it wasn't a lawman's instinct to protect the innocent. It was a Sultan's instinct to fight off the attacker—to avenge and carry out atrocities of his own. Bloodlust. Fucking overwhelming, murderous need had him picking up a beer bottle and smashing it, over and over on some fucker's head, watching the blood coating him and wanting more, more, more.

Later, on Ape's table, the buzz of the man's tattoo machine, putting letters into his side. *Sultans for Life*, those letters had said, and with that tattoo, Clay had sworn to kill for his club. And that night, he'd meant it.

On a cry that was bone-deep remorse and shame and a vestigial curl of allegiance to a cause he was supposed to abhor, Clay woke up on the forest floor, steeped in the stench of booze and blood and stinking sweat, with something tickling his back and a crick in his neck.

He didn't want to think of it. He didn't want to relive the day he'd lost his shit, his mind, and any sense of right and wrong, but in his sleep, he was powerless to stop the memory.

It was a couple of months after the lie detector test and being patched in that the Sultans were attacked by a rival club—the Raising Canes. Just a regular night at the Hangover: a bunch of guys playing pool, a crew out back kicking the shit out of each other for the fun of it, grunts from the bathroom, and Ape in back wreaking havoc with his needle on some poor fucker's skin.

Outside, there'd been a scream like something out of a horror movie, and the front door had blown in on a hazy gust of smoke and flames, surprising the fuck out of the Sultans and dragging them into a firefight of epic proportions.

The worst part had been Clay's reaction—his visceral desire to kill. The instinct to protect his brothers. It had been so strong, he'd finished off the night getting that Sultans tat inked into his side. Meaning it, deep to his core.

Months later, long after the smoke had cleared and the big players had been indicted, Clay had taken an iron to that piece of skin. And only then had he felt even the slightest bit of absolution.

But not really, he knew, staring at the doctor's quiet house in the middle of the night. Not really.

~∽∾~

"Virginia?" Ape said into the phone.

After a pause, the voice answered, "Yeah. I think so."

"If you're pullin' my chain, I swear to God, I'll kill 'em all. Every last one of your—"

"No, no, I promise. I swear on the life of…" Ape could hear the heavy breathing, could smell the nerves through the phone line. "On *my* life, I swear that's where he is."

Hanging up, Ape shoved the phone into his pocket and looked at the stars above his head. Virginia wasn't so far away that they couldn't get there tomorrow. They'd find the asshole eventually.

Ape smiled. With those fucking tats, Ape had turned Indian into a fucking bull's-eye, hadn't he? It sure did make him happy.

Goddamn, I'm smart.

12

Sore and painfully sober now, Clay spent the early morning hours scouring the town of Blackwood for Sultans and finding nothing. Nothing still.

He remembered the shrink had listed hypervigilance as one of the many possible symptoms of PTSD.

Had there even been bikes in town the other night, or had he imagined them?

Fuck, fuck, fuck. Was he losing it entirely?

Probably, he decided. Probably.

A month. Four whole fucking weeks until his next laser treatment. He should go do something while he waited. Maybe head elsewhere so as not to remain in one place too long. Four weeks. After that, there'd be just over five months until the trial date. Couldn't go by fast enough.

Rather than hole back up in the hotel, pecking out from behind the curtains, or parking himself outside of the doc's house like a messed-up guard dog, he needed distraction. Something. Anything.

A good fight would do it.

But as soon as he walked through the front door of the gym, he wondered if he hadn't made a mistake.

Something was off. The noise, first of all, was at a volume he hadn't experienced here before. Kids, it sounded like, and a quick glance around proved that to be the case.

He should have turned and walked out right then and there. He should have, but he didn't actually have anywhere else to go, so he stayed. The tickly, wrong sensation only intensified when Steve approached him, big smile on his face.

"Good to see you, Mr. Andrew Blane," the sheriff said, and on that note, Clay did turn. He didn't wait to find out what was afoot but took four strides and almost made it to the door by the time the other man caught up to him and laid a heavy hand on his shoulder. "Need a favor, son."

Clay stilled. "What?"

"Got an instructor out today. Need someone to teach the class."

"Well, then you teach it."

"Can't. Got someplace I gotta be."

"Yeah, well, me too." He shook off the older man's hand and walked outside.

He'd made it a few more steps when the man's voice rang out, too loud. Too damn loud. "Just hold it right there, young man." Clay stopped, recognizing that law enforcement tone for what it was, knowing it inside out but obeying it nonetheless. Steve drew closer and planted his body right beside him. "Told you I needed a teacher."

"I'm not a teacher."

"Yeah, well, give it a try."

"No. Kids hate me."

"You think I haven't looked into who you are?" Steve whispered. "Read about a case last night. Some big multi-agency biker club takedown up in Maryland."

"No, you can't tr—"

"Shut it." This was serious Steve now, not the jovial old man, and this guy had the kind of authority you didn't ignore. "I'm letting you camp out here because the arrangement suits me, got it? All I need is one little sign of trouble from you, and I'll make a couple phone calls to some folks I know up near Baltimore."

"You'd give me up?" Clay asked, shocked.

"Hell no, dumbass. You think I want a bunch of bikers in my town? No. But it's a threat you can't afford to ignore, 'cause I got media friends and ATF friends who might be interested in knowing where one of their own is holed up."

Clay shook his head, not looking at the man who'd figured him out way too fast. "What do you want from me?"

"Want you to take on a couple of classes this old man doesn't have the energy for anymore. Not a whole lot to ask."

"Can't you hire another teacher?"

"That's what I'm trying to do right here, son."

"Blackmail? That your recruiting technique?"

"I'm an opportunist," Steve said, smiling. "You get to be as old as me, you'll understand."

How the hell'd I get here? Clay wondered a half hour later. For the millionth time.

The gym was packed, and Clay hated, among other

things, the scrutiny. Because, once again, he was center stage, only this time it was different. This time, he was in charge.

Of a goddamned group of school kids.

"All right," he said, gritting his teeth. "Now follow through, Carter."

"What?"

"When you see the guy that close to you, it's too late. You're not gonna have time to just slap that foot away from your nut—"

"Groin!" yelled Steve. Didn't the old guy have someplace he needed to be? He hadn't budged since Clay took over the class.

Clay turned to him and stage-whispered, "Who's teaching this fu—"

A loud throat-clearing from Steve this time, and Clay thought he might just give in to the irritation. Maybe throw a little fit and go for a run or a drink or something. Nobody had checked to see how Clay felt about kids or whether this was something he wanted to waste his Saturday on.

Right, because he had so much going on.

"Look, watch. Eyes on me!" he yelled, since the whispering had started up again. "From your passive stance, let's go again."

"What's pass—"

"Neutral. *From neutral.* You know, like your basic jiu-jitsu stance or whatever it is you kids usually do here. Only, since this is self-defense, this is like…if you and your friends were hanging out on a street corner stance. Hands down at your sides, because we don't all walk around in a fighting stance all the dam—all the *darned* time. Got it?"

He glared at the kids, got a few nods, and went on. "So, first, when I come at you, you've got to get out of the way, right? We're not trying to get kicked in the nu—in the groin." A few kids snickered, and Clay threw them a look. "So, I come in slow, giving you time to sliiide to the side. Just a quick step-step. Good!" The kid finally got it.

"All right, guys. Now that you're out of immediate harm's way, you hit my heel." Clay kept his leg up in a low kick, but even that hurt like a bitch. "Yes! Smack it out of the way. Now punch me with your right fist and—yes! The best part is that you use your body movement and mine. You follow through, and I follow through 'cause I can't help it since I'm recovering from my kick—and now I'm in pain, and you can run the hell away!"

Another throat-clearing from Steve, and Clay had had about enough. "Steve's gonna come back up and run through it with you a few times," he said evilly.

Clay got a drink of water, just as an excuse to escape. He fully intended to leave before getting snagged again. On his way to the door, though, Steve's voice rang out good-naturedly. "Oh, I'm not sure that's right, Becky." He sounded old and a little frail. "I think you've just gotta use your right arm for that."

"But I'm left-handed, Master Steve."

"Oh, well, then I guess you'll just have to… I don't know, maybe you could—"

"They're interchangeable," Clay broke in. "And didn't you have somewhere to be, Sheriff?"

"What?" asked Steve, and right then, Clay understood just how much he was being played. Christ. The old guy was worse than the most manipulative bastards he'd dealt with in the line of duty.

But instead of getting annoyed, he just shook his head and smirked a *you dick* smile at the guy. With a sigh, Clay bowed himself back onto the mat. "You've gotta run these drills on both sides. Over and over. But there's a closer defense, using the outside arm, where you block and punch simultaneously. It's one I've—" He cut himself off. *One I've used numerous times in real life*, he'd almost said, but what the hell kind of message was that for a class of kids this age? Like, *You'll need these moves, kids. It's a shitty world out there.* He lifted his eyes and met Steve's and saw that the other guy knew exactly what he'd been about to say.

But the kids had already turned to him with what looked a lot like anticipation, and Clay let himself get wrapped up in the moves, running through the same sidestep and into the counter. "With this one, you punch with your left arm, while the right shoves the fu—shoves away."

Over and over, he drilled it with the kids, and by the time class was done, his stomach had lost that acid coating. The anxiety of the night before gone on a swell of… What? Accomplishment, maybe?

Which was one hell of a thing.

The parents didn't give him the friendliest looks, of course, when they came to get their children, but their cautious, mistrustful glares brought home a fact that had, up until that very moment, escaped him—the kids hadn't been afraid of him. They were treating him the way they'd treated Steve. Or, maybe not quite exactly, because Steve was an old guy and someone they were used to. With Clay, the kids had been curious, maybe a little bit awed, which was flattering and refreshing and entirely new.

When he left the gym that afternoon, Becky's voice calling out a last excited good-bye behind him, Clay felt tired but almost normal.

◦⌇◦

George cut short her usual Saturday visit to the in-laws, breathing a sigh of relief as she rushed to get out, with a promise to return the next week. She'd mentioned her upcoming doctor's appointment—the fertilization she'd be undergoing Wednesday evening—and now, as she drove to Cookie Lloyd's place, she regretted the urge that had led her to bring it up. She'd wanted to share something with Bonnie, felt compelled to give her mother-in-law something to look forward to.

During the drive to Ms. Lloyd's place, she ignored her nagging conscience, pondering instead what kind of diagnosis she might be facing. She knew from Uma that Ms. Lloyd was an agoraphobe. At least she wouldn't have to worry about sun damage.

She pulled up to see Uma awaiting her on the woman's porch steps—a porch entirely devoid of furniture.

After a quick hug, Uma turned and knocked, with a muttered, "Brace yourself."

The door swung open.

"Well, don't just stand there gawking—come inside," Cookie Lloyd snapped at George and Uma, who gave George a wry glance before leading the way in.

"As promised, Cookie, I bring you…a doctor."

The short woman squinted at George, giving her the

urge to back up a step or two. Maybe walk right back out the front door and down the porch steps.

"You going to check me or just stare?"

George forced a brief professional smile. "First of all, Ms. Lloyd, would you like Uma here, or do you want her to go?"

"Oh, I'll go. Call me if you nee—"

"You stay right here, young lady. I want you in the room. Lettin' strangers in and then takin' off to your man. My goodness, the fickle youth of today. Trusted confidante one moment, near stranger the next! What is this world coming to?"

"Fine. I'll stay." Uma moved into the living room—a claustrophobic den of doilies and dahlias that had George itching to run home and throw away every print she owned. She helped Cookie settle onto the sofa before taking an armchair and leaving George to choose her poison: armchair or sofa beside the somewhat terrifying Cookie Lloyd? George, being a masochist, perhaps, opted for the latter.

"Why don't you tell me what's going on first, Ms. Lloyd?"

"I got an itch, don't I?"

"Okay. What kind of itch?"

"It's…it's just uncomfortable." The eyes behind the woman's glasses blinked, slow and strange.

"Where is this itch?"

"It's…" The eyes flicked to Uma and back to George. She bent toward George in a waft of starchy, floral talc. "It's on my va-jay-jay."

"Okay. Okay, we can deal with that. I might not be the right doctor for this, but we can talk through it."

"It's since I started takin' that sheriff to bed. The man. I tell you, he—"

"*Whoa. Cookie!*" Uma said, standing up with a gasp. "Look, you do not need me here for this. It's—"

"Why don't you go, Uma? I'll stay and talk to Ms. Lloyd. We'll figure this out. I'll be over to see you when I'm done here," she added and waited until her friend left before speaking again.

"Now, tell me exactly where it itches. Is it on your vulva, Ms. Lloyd?"

"No. On my thighs."

"I don't understand, you said vagina and—"

The woman smiled. "I like to keep Uma on her toes."

"Ah. Make her uncomfortable, you mean?" Ms. Lloyd gave a little shrug, and George nodded. People did the strangest things for a little attention. "Okay. Is it bumpy?"

A sniff. "Yes."

"All right. It's probably not something you contracted from…anyone. Why don't I take a look at it, and I'll prescribe you something if you need it."

Another sniff before the woman rose and pulled off a pair of dark polyester trousers circa 1978.

A quick look confirmed what she'd already assumed. "It's a fungal infection, Ms. Lloyd. We'll get you set up with a cream to apply, and that should be—"

"Did I get it from him?"

"Ah…not necessarily, but it does sometimes occur. I would recommend treating both of you at once. I also would recommend more…breathable fabrics, if possible, this time of year in particular. Cotton underwear and cotton pants would be best. Would you like me to include a prescription for your, ah…partner?"

"He'll get his own."

"Fair enough. Is there someone who can pick it up for you?"

Ms. Lloyd gave her a *duh* look before answering. "Uma, of course. Don't call it in—just give it to her, will you?"

"Certainly."

"What do I owe you?"

"Nothing," said George. She'd seen the state of the house outside. This wasn't a rich woman, and there was no point charging her for what had turned out to be a pretty routine, if somewhat atypical, visit.

After taking her leave, she headed back over to Uma's house, scrip in hand.

"Knock knock," she called in through the front screen door.

"Come in! We're in the back."

George walked inside, loving this house, so similar to hers, only bigger, and in much better shape.

In the kitchen, she found Uma and Ive sitting at the table, looking at…*oh, crap*. A book of baby names.

"Oh, wow. Are you guys…?"

Uma smiled, bright and happy-looking. "Yes! We're having a baby!"

"My goodness, that's wonderful!" George said, meaning it. Really meaning it, because she couldn't imagine a more deserving couple. A more loving pair.

"We just found out, and Ive drove all the way into C'ville to buy this book."

"Yeah, didn't want the Blackwood gossips spreadin' the news."

George smiled, hard. "Any ideas so far?"

"Oh, no. I mean. I'm only nine weeks along, so…"

"Don't know if it's a boy or a girl yet, but I'm hopin' for twins," said Ive in his slow voice, and the sweet, happy look on his face made George want to cry. *With joy*, she was pretty sure. *With joy.*

Clay hurt worse than usual—probably from all the workouts. Not something the doctors back in Baltimore had recommended.

The pain, he told himself, was why he headed over to George Hadley's house that evening around dinnertime, clutching a sad bouquet of grocery-store flowers and an overpriced bottle of Virginia wine.

He stood on the doctor's front porch, wearing a neat button-down shirt and jeans, as if they had an actual date, when in reality he was just busting in on her night. The woman probably did have a date. With an entirely different kind of man.

She came to the door at his knock and greeted him with a wide-eyed "oh," which he could take as either a good omen or a bad one.

"'Oh, what a pleasant surprise'?" he asked. "Or 'Oh, get the hell outta here'?"

It took her a second to decide, apparently. Not the best of signs, but…hey, he'd take what he could get.

"Come in," she said with a friendly air, if not quite the smile he'd wished for.

He followed her into the now-familiar main hall, again bypassing the front rooms and heading straight to the kitchen—the heart of the house, he surmised.

"Those for me?" she asked.

"Oh, yeah. Here." *Gracious as always*, he thought. *Man, aren't I a prince?*

She smiled her thanks and plunked his bouquet into a vase that far outshone the flowers themselves. A look around reminded him of all the other flowers strewn about—and behind her, through the screen porch, daylight revealed the bright, happy disarray of growing blooms the moonlight had washed out the other night. Right, no flowers next time. Chocolates. Or something.

Next time. There probably wouldn't be a next time, judging by her expression—all closed up and professional like he'd never seen her. That was just what he deserved for running away before.

She set the wine on the counter, pulled a corkscrew from a drawer, and placed it beside it.

Instead of opening the bottle, she turned to him, arms folded across her chest, and he saw new, tight lines pulling her eyes down, puffiness beneath. Had she been crying? Shit. He hoped not.

"What can I do for you, Mr. Blane?"

Jesus, he hated that name. Hated it.

"I…" He wasn't sure, actually. What was he doing here, again?

"I needed to see you" was all that came out. Thank God, because in his current state, Clay could see himself spewing some of the crap rotting out his brain. And no, that wouldn't be a good thing. Not at all.

She stood there, looking…sadder? *Oh hell.*

"Why?" she asked, and fuck if her eyes didn't look a little too shiny.

He swallowed, glanced out back at the woods and the

raging cicadas there, and said the only thing he could think of: the truth.

"It's better when you're around."

～∽～

The man standing in George's kitchen was broken. Broken and alluring and, apparently, the answer to the emptiness eating up her insides.

"What's better, Andrew?"

"There's all this…*shit*, you know? My life. Crap I've done and… It's in my brain. I just want *quiet*."

"But you left the other night because of the noise."

"No, the noise drives me crazy, but that's not why I left." He turned away, and she was fairly sure he'd walk out again. He continued, though, and what he said… what he said slayed her. "You're too good for me."

"Oh." She swallowed. "And now? What's changed?"

"Nothing. Everything. I don't fucking know."

"You're still my patient."

"I still don't care." He paused. "And I'm not for another six weeks, anyway."

"Maybe sooner," George said, her voice embarrassingly breathy.

"How much sooner?"

"Depends."

"On my tats."

"Yes."

He nodded. "Come here?"

She shook her head. "We shouldn't do this."

"You're probably right. But I sure as hell want to." He looked at her—straight on. "Do you?"

Did she want to be with this man? Physically? Because

that was what they were discussing. George couldn't lie—not after spending every waking moment—and some sleeping—thinking of him. She could only nod.

"When…" He swallowed, cleared his voice, and looked around, as if for something to do. "You think I could…" He indicated the bottle of wine.

"Oh, of course. Here, I'll do it." She grabbed the wine key and the bottle, pushed it in and twisted and broke the darned cork—and almost started crying. But before she could, his hands were there, over hers, carefully pulling the bottle away, inserting the metal into the mangled cork and gently, gently prying it out. He brushed away the few remaining crumbs from the surface of the green glass and set the bottle down. George couldn't look up at him so close beside her. Too close. *Unbearably close.*

One ink-covered finger moved up to her face, where it lingered, knuckle-first, at her cheek, then stroked down to nudge her chin up. Her eyes, of course, followed, and she met his gaze and latched on, something swelling hard in her throat. So hard it came out on a big, fat sob, and rather than the kiss she'd anticipated, he pulled her into his arms. Tight and warm against the soft cotton of his shirt.

God, when was the last time she'd been held like this? Just held? She couldn't remember. She didn't *want* to remember those days when she'd been the one holding a husband who was too frail to hold her back.

She rubbed her face into the shirt and inhaled. The smell of him broke her. It wasn't her husband's smell—not even close. And how wrong was it that she wanted more of this warm, masculine scent? She wanted to suck it in and revel in this body—solid and very much alive.

George lost control. It might have been from guilt or sadness or, more likely, the hormones. Whatever it was, she fell apart in a way that should have embarrassed her.

It didn't, though.

They wound up on the sofa in the parlor, him sitting and her cradled like a baby across his lap, in tears. Weird, so weird this reversal of roles. This man coming to her for some brand of comfort and her leaching it from him instead.

"I'm sorry," she eventually choked out on a hiccup.

"'S okay," he said before hunching forward to rub one rough, sandpaper cheek against hers. That, just that, brought a sound to George's lips—a continuation of her sobbing, perhaps, but altogether different in nature— darker, warmer, and sparking deep inside.

She rubbed him back, her body taking over when her mind told her it was wrong. Her skin prickled where they touched—and not just from his five o'clock shadow. There was electricity in the air that shouldn't have been there after she'd torn through any attraction with those sobs. Yet, it was still there, a chemical, skin-to-skin reaction that even her outburst hadn't dampened.

"It's okay." The words were soft, placating, spoken as if to a child or a wayward animal. "It's okay."

"It isn't okay." She moved away, just a bit, because his pull was so darned strong. "You came here because you needed me, you needed—"

"No. I came here because I couldn't stay away." He sounded angry, but he kissed her anyway, good and firm so she could feel it deep in her bones, sharp like a chill, only searing hot.

It all happened fast then—no languid explorations for this man. No, he was rough and quick and pushy as hell, and George found herself rising to the challenge, taking it in stride. From his lap, she somehow wound up on her back on the sofa, stretched out with him above. And there was *biting*. There'd never been biting before for George, but those were distinct nips he was giving her, and instead of stopping him, she opened her mouth and did it back—nothing painful. It couldn't have hurt, since she'd barely felt the scrape of him under her teeth, but God, there was something powerful in that scrape. Wild and animalistic and perhaps just a little uncontrollable.

I'm out of control, she thought as he dipped his pelvis against hers and she recognized how vulnerable she was in her skirt, with her legs spread and this big body opening her up, grinding. The stiff seam of his jeans rubbed her inner thighs, and she wondered if there'd be burn marks in the morning.

They shouldn't be doing this. They shouldn't. George pulled her mouth from Andrew's, shocked at how out of breath she was, and, avoiding his eyes, said, "We should stop."

He stilled and watched her, his breath fast and intimate and already so familiar against her mouth. "Okay." He inhaled loudly—getting himself together, she thought. "You're right. I can't do this to you."

It was her turn to suck in a breath and look him straight in the eye. "What do you mean? Do *what* to me?"

"This. Make you…do things with me." He started to pull away, and she stopped him with a hand on his arm.

"You're not making me do anything." She moved her hand to his side, a place she knew was safe to touch without hurting him. "I...I just needed a second. I haven't felt this much..." *No, no, don't talk about feelings.* "I haven't done this in forever."

"No?" He sat back a bit on his haunches, looking down at her, at the way she writhed on the sofa beneath him, her treacherous skin nothing but a network of nerve endings, begging to be tweaked. "I don't get that. You're so...beautiful."

"I'm not—"

"You are." He lifted a hand to her jaw, not quite grazing her skin. Even that almost-touch seemed proprietary, and suddenly, George wanted him to do it for real.

"Touch me there," she whispered.

After only the briefest of hesitations, he did it, although not rough and bossy as she'd imagined, but gently—as if he were in awe—and that careful caress almost broke her.

"Do it harder," she ordered, an edge to her voice.

His eyes met hers. "Thought you wanted to stop."

"I should, but I don't."

He nodded, easily accepting her change of heart, before moving that big hand over her shoulder, to her chest. George's body liked that. It gave its undeniable response.

"God, look at you, George. Look at this." He reached a finger to nudge one painfully hard nipple and slipped his hand down between them, to where her flimsy skirt had flipped back, leaving her exposed, open, and wanting.

She made a noise deep in her throat.

"And what about this, George?" He pulled her soaked

underwear aside and ran one finger along her. "How the hell can I stay away when you're like this for me, huh?" he asked, and she truly, truly didn't know. She felt the same, after all. She wasn't just attracted to the man; she was drawn to him, inevitably, magnetized by his presence.

And he knew how turned-on she was. He had to, with her...arousal all over his hand. His fingers, for goodness sake, couldn't even find purchase. They just slid and slid until, somehow, finally, one of them worked its way slowly inside her, and George's throat let out a noise—an unsexy grunt that proved just how long it'd been since anything that exciting had breached her body.

"I'm sorry," she said, because it was true. She shouldn't be doing this with a patient, a man too messed up to know better. She should be the one to know better. "I'm not... I don't know what to do. I want to see you too, but I can't even—"

"Yeah?" At her nod, he leaned back again, removed his hand, leaving her cold, undid his belt, yanked down his zipper, and with a quick glance at her face, reached inside his underwear to pull himself out.

No ink, she thought with relief. He was big. Thick, veined, and somehow glorious—not a word she'd ever used before for a penis. Penises had always seemed like such utilitarian features. But this one... *Too big*, thought George, who'd used nothing but a crappy little AA-fueled bullet vibrator for the last decade. She wanted to touch it, feel how unyielding and stiff it was, how soft his skin, measure its weight in her palm.

Her eyes returned to his face, where the dark imprint on his lids gave him such a look of violence that she shivered, utterly certain that this was the worst mistake she'd ever make. And yet, everything in her pushed her toward this man. Everything made her yearn for this, to be with him, to taste him and touch him and remember what it felt like to be alive.

"We don't have to do anything," he whispered, no doubt mistaking her trembling for fear. But it wasn't. It was something else—excitement, perhaps? Titillation? She didn't know. How could she know?

"Oh God. I want to." Another glance showed that body she couldn't stop thinking of. She'd die if they didn't do this soon. She'd burst into flames, her skin was so scorching hot.

"Yeah?"

"Yes. Yes, I want to." She writhed against him, asking him to touch her again without words. "Do it. Make me…make me feel…" Good Lord, what was it she was going to say? *Make me feel whole again?* Those weren't the right words, she knew. But she couldn't, for the life of her, make the words come out.

Instead of talking, she let go of her doubts, sucked in a big, shaky breath, and made a decision. This was it—a letting go she hadn't realized she was capable of. She threw worry and shame and responsibility to the wind as she reached down and grasped the hot, hard sex of this man who'd taken her life and torn it into a million beautiful, little pieces.

13

Clay had stopped hurting the minute he'd touched her. *It's psychosomatic*, he understood in the only sane part of his brain—a thought he quickly tamped down. Because, whatever the reasons for the reprieve, he knew better than to look a gift horse in the mouth.

Besides, right now, with her cool, prim, white hand on his dick, there wasn't much point trying to sort out what was right or wrong, good or bad, or any of that other shit. No point at all, because he hadn't felt this good in months. *Months?* Fuck no, years. It had been years since Clay Navarro had felt anything so right.

"Tighter," he said, because she was teasing, and he wanted *real*.

She tightened her fingers, reminding him of how efficient she could be with those strong hands. Down his cock, then back up, without really hitting the head— still with the teasing—until he glanced up at her face and understood this wasn't about that at all. She looked fascinated, curious, and completely taken in. "Don't worry," he said. "You can't hurt me."

Her eyes met his at those words, which he realized with a start could be misinterpreted. The green was nearly gone from her gaze, pushed out by a gaping black pupil. Her face was flushed and she looked different in the throes of desire: kind of lost but also curious and… What was that other thing? There was something hungry there, something that made his cock even harder, while his mouth watered and his mind went to a darker place. The image he'd gotten, looking at her just now, wasn't one he'd pictured before.

Suddenly, he wanted to *wreck her* a little bit—to take her pristine, white shell and crack it.

It made him feel guilty, the image his sick mind had conjured of her. Guilty but hard, which was one hell of a fucking complication for a man who'd lived a double life for so long.

His mind went back to all those women who hung around the MC. He'd had to pretend he felt like the other guys, had to act like just another horny bastard. The guys who used them and threw them out. Women like his sister, Carly, whose suffering had just been par for the course in their fucked-up world. Not even collateral damage, since collateral had value. And he'd had to taint Carly's memory by pretending to use women just like her. The memory made him sick.

Better to stay in the moment, here, with *this* woman—this woman who made him almost feel whole again.

He thrust once into George's hand, and she got the picture, tightening and moving up, around the head of his dick, and back down. "Pull up your shirt," he said, even as a part of him insisted this wasn't the way to talk to this woman. "Let me see your tits."

The thing about Dr. George Hadley was that she was a lady. Definitely a lady, except…except the look in her eye told him she liked it when he talked to her rough.

Unable to get the fabric up, she made as if to let his cock go for a second, but he reached down and held her there.

"No. Do it one-handed," he ordered, understanding that something about this wasn't quite right. This wasn't how it was supposed to be with this woman. He was supposed to accept her tenderness; he wasn't supposed to be this way anymore.

But that made him wonder what the fuck she was doing with a guy like him.

She was into tats. She had to be. The tats and the danger of a bad boy. She was responding to his rough edges. That was it, wasn't it? He thrust into her hand again, aggressive, and jerked her bra down, hard.

"You like that?" he asked, feeling filthy, horrible, but also needing to know. *Do you like that? Do you like this side of me I may never be able to get rid of?*

He pinched George's nipple, and she moaned, deep and low, so he pinched it again, harder. Her cry jostled free memories, shame. He didn't deserve this—her. He didn't deserve to have this kind of forgiveness, acceptance. The last time he'd done this…

There'd been a woman at the club… God, he didn't want to think of her right now. Those girls who'd let the guys do anything. He shuddered, his brain fuzzy around the edges as another memory seeped in—

His face—the day he'd gotten this scar he'd wear for the rest of his life. He'd gotten sliced in service to the Sultans. An unfortunate occurrence, which had turned into the boon he needed and helped earn his status as Brother. *A scar for a Sultan patch. Not so big a price to pay.*

Another jagged scar, on his sister's body, like the one on his head. She'd been cut. They'd cut her.

Clay blinked, feeling wrong, in the wrong place, mixed up, and fuzzy. He shook his head to clear it, brushed off a hand, tried to back off, said something. Slurring, panicked, his head full of a powdery fog, clogging him, breathing impossible, the buzz inside his ears a hive of bees or—

He was on the floor, seated, his back to the sofa, and a woman was on her knees beside him.

"The fuck?" he said, squinting, his voice raw. The room was a broken kaleidoscope, his heart pumping poison.

"You need a doctor," she said.

"No."

"What's going on, Andrew?"

"*Andrew?*" he asked, trying to see past the gray honeycomb filling his vision. "Who the *fuck* is Andrew?" Her hand was on him again, and he pried it off. "*Don't.*" Why was he slurring? Had they given him something? What the hell had they given him? He couldn't think past the panic. "Where's Handles? He know I'm here?"

"I'm, um…" The woman swallowed audibly. "I'm not sure. What's your name?"

That cleared the clouds from his brain, just enough to know there was danger in this question, and he grabbed her hand, hard. Her tiny bones rubbed together in his fist. "Why—" He blinked. "George."

"Yes, you seem to be having some kind of…"

Attack. Episode. Flashback. *Something.*

But it was over now. The fog was clearing.

"I'm fine." He'd be fine when he left. He blinked, stood, tucked himself back into his clothes, and gave the place a bleary once-over before stumbling out the front door—running before he lost himself in memory again.

Because, after all the worrying and watching over her, he'd never forgive himself if he was the one to hurt her.

George blinked after him, confused and hurt and worried and a little angry.

What was going on? No. No way could she let Andrew Blane leave her behind for the second time that week, clearly in pain, clearly needing *help*. It tweaked something in her brain. No, it didn't just tweak her— it set her off, exploding in her chest and sending her running to the front door to… She didn't know what she'd do when she had him cornered—keep him here so he'd explain? Make him stay so she could take care of him? Whatever it was, she couldn't stand this feeling of impotence.

Oh, she'd felt it before, hadn't she? The inability to do a single blessed thing to help. But she could help this man, if he'd only let her. And there was no way she'd let him push her away like this.

So rather than go back to worry, to wait, to wonder in silence, George walked out her front door.

She tromped down the stairs, eyes going right to where his truck was turning around in the cul-de-sac. She stalked out into the road and waited.

The truck stopped; she walked around to the passenger door and climbed in, facing him, feeling so damned *reckless*.

Without even really thinking, she pulled back a hand and slapped his shoulder. "Don't. Ever. Walk out on me again," she said, her words more measured than her breathing.

"What are you—"

She scooted in and pushed at that shoulder again. It was a ridiculous, ineffectual move against someone so much larger than her, but she wanted to *reach* him, damn it. Wanted him to *feel* it.

"I don't want to hurt you, George."

"*You* don't get to decide how much hurt I can take. So, just…*fuck you* for thinking you get to decide. For us. For me," she spat, raising her hand in frustration. He reached out and grabbed it, drawing their eyes up together to where his inked fist held her naked one.

"Go inside, George." He let her hand go.

"You…you need help, Andrew. Why won't you trust me?"

He shook his head at her and looked away, and she wanted to scream with frustration. This was someone she could do something for. This wasn't someone being threatened by disease and—

Unless… "Are you dying? Is that it? Do you need—"

"I'm not dying. I'm fine."

"Oh, thank God," she whispered on a great big sigh of relief. She wasn't sure she could go another round with cancer as the enemy. "Why then?" She kept her eyes on that beautifully harsh face and thought, *Fuck it. Just fuck it.*

He leaned in to talk to her, eye to eye. "This isn't gonna—"

She cut him off with her mouth, hard and wet against

his, and there it was again, the zing of desire straight to her crotch.

With a grunt, he responded, one strong arm running down her body, under her bottom. He pulled her up and over the armrests, slamming her into his lap, her legs around his waist, strong arms hauling her against him, stuck tight between the wheel and his body.

An accidental tap against the horn, the sound of keys jingling, then the gearshift shoving into Park, and with a curse, Andrew tried to pull away, but she wouldn't let him. Wouldn't let go.

"This what you fuckin' want?" He tilted his hips into hers, squeezed her ass tighter, pushed against her.

"Yes."

"Doctor likes the bad boys, huh? That what you're into?"

"No," she whispered as she ground herself against him. And then stronger. "Maybe," she said before pulling away. "But you don't always get to decide. You don't get to run away when things are tough. Remember that, okay? *Remember* that."

He nodded, looking dazed, and George bit his lip before throwing open the driver's-side door and sliding out, down, and onto the asphalt. "You coming?" she asked, channeling someone who knew what they were doing. It was an odd thing, this strength that ran through her. It made her feel like a different sort of woman—one who acted because it felt good, not because it was smart or made sense.

And there was one thing she knew for sure: this decision wasn't even close to being smart, but whatever happened tonight, she would never let herself regret it.

⤜⤛⤔

Clay parked in front of George's house and followed her, chastised but turned on like crazy. And wanting her to understand.

What? What the fuck did he need her to understand?

Inside, she stood by the stairs.

He took her by the shoulders. His kiss was hard and probably hurt, but she didn't seem to mind, responding with equal ferocity, her body strong and lithe under his hands, her teeth clashing with his in what might have been anger.

"This what you want, George?" he asked. "You want me to fuck you?"

"Yes," she said. "No. I don't know."

"I'm a mess."

"Aren't we all?"

"You're not a mess. You're perfect."

"Me?" She chuckled, the sound low and sexy. "I'm worse than you are. How messed up is that? Taking advantage of people? Feeling up patients in my care."

"*Patients?* You saying I'm not the only one?"

Her green eyes got wide as she stilled and looked up at him. "You're the only one," she said. In that moment, he felt like it—the only one. The way she looked at him made him feel huge, whole, important. Like the only one ever.

He couldn't remember wanting anyone more than this woman in this moment. As messed up as he was, he couldn't run from her anymore.

"Come on," she whispered, her voice as eager and full of wanting as he felt.

His hands tightened on her, helpless against her power, and he urged her up the stairs, half walking, half crawling, tripping in their haste and then staying down, the air leaving him with an audible whoosh. Because here was as good a place as any, wasn't it?

He was stuck, on his knees on the stairs, needy and wanting and ready for whatever she'd give him. He scooted up the two steps to where she was, took in the smile on her face when she turned to look at him, and then kissed it off. Hungry, God, he was hungry for her. He covered her with his body and lost it, grinding against her with blind, animal urgency. Before he could think it through, he pushed her skirt up and shoved two fingers past her panties where they sank into her hot, hot pussy.

∽◉∼

George lay splayed on the stairs, Andrew's fingers inside of her, his tongue hot in her mouth.

Over the past decade, she'd wanted sex in a vague sort of way. She'd masturbated, but it had always felt physical—the call of hormones—rather than emotional. Even with Tom, there'd been something…practical about the way they'd made love. Here, though, with Andrew, there was more to it. Its roots were deeper. A spirituality or something that she'd never before associated with a man or a relationship. Whatever kind of relationship this was.

Doctor/patient, came the words from a guilty, dark little corner of her brain, quickly tamped down. *Lovers*, came the second, more honest label, which she chose to embrace.

"Fuck, George," he said, pulling at her hips, pressing his into her. "I can't get enough of you."

She felt the same way, but she couldn't say it, too busy breathing to talk through this intimacy.

From below, she watched his eyes rove across her body, enjoyed the admiration and fire in them. But he was fully dressed and she lay there with her skirt bunched up, and it felt unbalanced. She wanted to see him, his strength above her, his skin.

She reached a hand up to touch his chest, where even beneath his T-shirt, his nipple beckoned.

"You're so fucking wet for me."

"I've been like this for days," she breathed.

"And I'm like this," he said.

"I want to see it again," she said, shocked at her brazenness.

With a long, heavy-lidded look, he ordered, "Take me out."

Oh, that pushed a button she didn't know she had.

Quickly, she half sat, reached for him, fumbled at the belt and snap, then yanked down the zipper and pulled him out gently, her breath coming hard. Her eyes darted up to meet his before they both turned back to their bodies—his erection stiff between them, angry and red. It almost made her smile—gave her a sharp jolt of power. Here she was, beneath him, open and vulnerable and yet…she could do anything.

"Here," she said kindly. With one hand, she grasped him, stroked him up and down, watching how his eyes narrowed to slits, his cheeks flamed red. She shifted, let her bottom land on the next step down and then the next, until she could take him into her mouth, just the tip—just a taste.

Andrew groaned and touched her head. Was he seeking permission? She grasped his hand and shoved it into her hair, showing him. *This is what I want.*

Without hesitation, he tightened his fist and tilted her head back, his face going from flushed and lost to hard and animal. That change hit her low in her belly, as did the groan he let loose.

She pulled away from licking him. "I want to suck you," she forced herself to say, her voice edged with something hard and brittle but stronger than she'd have imagined. "I want you to…" *Make me.* God, she couldn't say it, couldn't even think the words. Being used by a man was masturbation material—not something she'd ever thought she'd actually try.

She must have said the words, she realized with a start, because he did it. That was all it took to release the creature caged inside him. Face hard with lust and power, he pulled at her hair—so hard it almost hurt—and lifted her up.

"You want this?" he asked, voice ragged.

"Yes. Yes, I want you to…do things to me."

"You're sure?"

"Please. I want this. Please."

A swift pinch of her nipple made her gasp and scramble slightly—only she couldn't scramble far, because his hands closed around her hips, tightened, and rolled her onto her stomach.

I couldn't move even if I wanted to, she realized with a jolt of hot shock as he put her where he wanted her, showing her how strong he was. The words *brute strength* floated through her mind, turning the shock into something more visceral, shaded with images of cavemen hunting down their prey. Her knees hurt where they ground into the step.

Good thing I don't want to move. The thought edged on shame, that ridiculous image of being bested by the caveman, but she let that go—she let it all go, the fear, the guilt, the weight of responsibility.

She felt him shift, fumble at something, then a plastic crinkle and the acrid smell of rubber.

On her hands and knees now, with Andrew Blane's bulk behind her, she waited for him to do it. For the longest time—a handful of seconds probably, but it felt like forever—he stayed there, mighty and unyielding, but also shuddering in a way that said he was close to losing control.

She turned to look at him over her shoulder, caught those wild, dark eyes, and said, "Fuck me."

The words pushed through whatever hesitation he still had, until she felt the blunt tip of his cock slowly, inexorably easing its way into her body. He was hot, stretching her, the feeling so new it was like learning how all over again.

While her mind continued to adjust, her body seemed to know exactly what it was doing, bringing out a side of herself she'd completely forgotten. The animal in her: instinctual, elemental, basic. She craned her neck to get a look at his face.

We're not civilized at all, she thought as he filled her again and again, faster with every thrust, his body enveloping hers, his testicles slapping her thighs, the slippery, sweaty smack of his hips loud in the still night air.

He was saying things, she could tell—although, being nothing but a creature of the senses now, she couldn't decipher the actual words. Only that they were guttural and raw, probably too harsh for her soft insides.

George jolted at the sound of him smacking her bottom before she even felt the sting of it, but she involuntarily tightened around him, and he groaned louder, thrust harder—hitting her high, on the cervix, before leaning forward, truly bestial now, to bite her neck, hard and marking. *Mating*.

George had never done sex quite like this. Never. Not as a horny teen, nor as a loving spouse. And as her body reacted with intrinsic knowledge, it wasn't a memory so much as *instinct*. Deep and ancient and rooted in her genetic code.

Hands on her hips, lifting her to meet him, holding her buttocks apart, spreading her wide so he could get in deep… And that bite, that brand of ownership, made George grunt long and low—the kind of sound she'd never uttered in her thirty-three years on earth—and climax hard, the sensation new and unexpectedly moving.

~∾~

Clay's orgasm came too fast, too hard, an uncontrollable blast that left him gasping and immobile, collapsed over George's back.

He didn't want to move, wanted to stay in this blissful limbo, wrapped around this woman who'd thrown him for such a loop.

Slowly, things began to refocus. She shifted, and he woke up to her position on the steps—splayed out on hands and knees with nothing but wood to cushion her. With a final squeeze, he pulled back, gave himself a moment to take her in from top to bottom…and froze when his eyes landed on her neck.

Tooth marks. Deep and red and painful-looking.

I did that. I hurt her.

And there, on the stairs, it came hurtling at him—the guilt, the fucking sea of guilt. For everything, for all of it. For sitting there, just listening *and pretending to agree* while Ape and Handles and Boom-Boom planned the murder of a local sheriff's deputy who'd gotten too curious. For drinking and fighting and joining them in their vicious, raucous partying. For flirting and fucking when he had to. And worst of all—Jesus Christ, far worse than anything else—for feeling it, wanting it, actually becoming a part of it all.

Now, here, he'd brought that to *her.*

"I'm sorry, George," he croaked out, body already far removed from hers.

"What? Why?"

"Your neck. I hurt you."

Avoiding her gaze, he focused instead on her hand as it flew to examine the place where he'd marked her. He quickly pulled his jeans back up, yanked at the zipper, and worked to close the belt, shaking, shaking with shame.

"I'm sorry. You won't ever—"

"Stop that and come here," she interrupted, grabbing his hand and tugging him down. She covered his mouth with hers, giving him another dose of that medicine he couldn't seem to get enough of—tenderness, understanding, feeling, or whatever it was. He had no idea what he'd call it. All he knew was it made him raw and open, its newness blinding. "Come upstairs, Andrew. Come to bed and hold me."

"Okay," he said, helpless before her, and let her drag him up the steps.

They did the normal nighttime things that he usually took care of blind drunk nowadays. She brushed her teeth and loaned him her toothbrush, which should have been gross, but instead felt like a tiny slice of trust. Intimacy that was painfully real.

After, he followed the light to her room, where she waited for him in one of those antique-looking wooden beds. Jesus, he'd never slept on anything this fancy before. Bright-white sheets, a faded quilt folded down at the feet, the window wide open, and nothing but the ceiling fan to press out the heat.

He didn't care, though, as he lay down naked beside her, switched off the lamp, and let her scoot right up into his side.

Enveloped by the heavy air, he wound his arm tightly around her and enjoyed knowing he could watch over her here, tonight, even if he didn't deserve this unexpected sense of security.

Within minutes, he felt heavy, sleep nearly shocking him at how easily it deigned to come, the woman beside him something solid to latch on to as his heart slowly began to unfold.

Hot, can't breathe. Hot, hurts.

He was caught, trapped on the bed. They'd found him. How'd they find him? Fuck, it was hot, searing pain through his back, his leg paralyzed. Holes in his skin. The noise, the fucking *roar* of fire.

Clay pushed and hit and somehow worked his way

out of the bed, as he'd done so many times before. The fall to the ground was harder than he remembered, the bed higher. Shooting him in the back hadn't been enough to kill him apparently, because he was here, here, alive, hurting. And yet...

They know. They know, his brain told him over and over. *How the fuck do they know? Who the fuck told them? And where the fuck's the team when I need them?*

He was screaming, he thought, although he couldn't hear his voice through the sawing in his brain, the acid in his sinuses. Something was on him, then, cold and wet, and he reached out to whack it off, but it came back, and with it, a thread of a voice—clean and clear and *magic*. It pierced the fog, the mush in his brain, and he opened his eyes to see a shadow of her there in the dark.

"George," he croaked, and she curled into him. "George."

It was a whisper this time. A whisper of relief as his arms found her, her body already sturdy and familiar in the dark, hot night.

CLAY WOKE REFRESHED, ON AN UNFAMILIAR FLOOR, ALONE. Or actually, not quite: a hot, little rumbling radiator of an animal lay curled up against his belly. Quietly, he sat up to find the bed empty; he wasn't sure if he was relieved or disappointed.

Last night had been completely different from any other experience he'd had with a woman. Nothing stilted or awkward after they'd fucked. No hard or hurt feelings—just that peaceful feeling of comfort, until he'd finally fallen asleep with her wrapped in his arms.

And then the Dumpster dream. The one where he found Kathy, thrown out behind the clubhouse like somebody's garbage. And as if that weren't bad enough on its own, in that particular nightmare, Kathy always turned into Carly for the usual epic grand finale where their deaths and his tangled into a single, soul-destroying moment. He wasn't sure his heart could take many more dreams like that. You only had so many heartbeats in a lifetime, right? If that was the case, he'd use up his quota in his sleep.

He rose, threw on his clothes, and made his way downstairs. The smell of coffee led him to the kitchen, and then to the screened-in porch, where George sat sipping from a steaming cup and staring out at the yard, looking so young and innocent, her face puffy and creased with sleep. *A face I shoved into a stair tread.*

"Morning," he said, cutting through his inner voice, stepping down onto the porch and taking a moment too long to decide between the sofa next to her and the armchair on the other side of a low table. The air outside was filled with the sound of those fucking bugs, holding their once-in-a-lifetime megaconference.

Her smile was soft, sweet, her eyes sleepy when they met his.

Her shy "Hi" gave him all the impetus he needed to go sit beside her and follow stunted romantic instincts that told him to plant a soft kiss on that warm, fragrant neck.

"Sorry about last night. I—"

"It's fine, Andrew." His insides clenched at that name. Fuck, he wanted to tell her.

"It's not fine. I… We… First, the stairs and, after passing out like a goddamn—"

"It was good," she said, the smile still there, her eyes even warmer, her side snugged tighter into his. "It was really, really good."

"Yeah?"

Another smile, hidden behind her mug. "Yes."

Not bothering to suppress a grin, he nodded, looking out at the yard. Jesus, was this how normal people felt after sex? Like singing? Howling? Grabbing her and hauling her right back to those stairs?

But then there'd been the night, where, Jesus, he really could have hurt her—completely beyond his control.

"Are you okay?" he asked, suddenly sure that the softness around her eyes was from crying, not sleep. He was quiet, already defeated, when he said, "I scared you."

"Scared me?" she asked, blinking.

"Last night. My…" Christ, what would you call them? *Episodes?* "Nightmares."

"You didn't scare me, Andrew; you…worried me. There was nothing I could do." Her hand squeezed his, and they lapsed into silence.

"No, no, you helped."

"You remember?"

"I remember feeling you around me." Why was it so hard to admit that?

"I'm glad," she said with a gentle smile, and Christ, he'd get lost in those eyes if he let himself.

With a yawn, she turned back to look at her yard and seemed to disappear into her head.

"Got plans for today?"

She shrugged. "Work on the garden."

"Want some help?"

"Yeah? That would be lovely."

"Thought maybe I'd go into town for some supplies. Then I'll come back and help."

"I'd like that," she said. And then she kissed him, her openness and joy crumbling yet another brick in his wall. It should have worried him, the way she pulled him apart, because without that wall, he'd have no defenses against all the shit he knew lurked in the world.

It *should* have worried him, but right now, with her… it didn't.

∽⧟∾

George had spent the hour or so before Andrew had gotten up going over the things that had happened in the night. He'd screamed. Screamed and freaked out, pushed her away when she'd tried to hold him, and then flung himself onto the floor. She'd followed him down, had taken forever to calm him, and finally wrapped her body around his and held him as he'd fallen into a hot, fitful sleep. It wasn't until much later that she'd recognized the danger of the situation—this big, powerful man out of control in his sleep. He could have hurt her—badly.

And yet, she couldn't seem to get worked up about her safety. What worried her, truly, was him. How powerless was she, here all alone, with no weapons against whatever was haunting him?

She'd wanted to help him. She still did, but now… After sleeping with him, after seeing his body wracked with fear and pain, and now, after toast and coffee and normal talk, something had changed. The do-gooder in her didn't feel quite so good anymore, and after he'd left for whatever it was he wanted to do in town, the feeling overwhelming her was the shame of betrayal.

Fueled by a sick sense of responsibility, she stomped over to Jessie's house and knocked on the door. It was still early, but her neighbor must be up. Didn't people with kids rise at the crack of dawn?

"Hey," Jessie said, looking only half-awake. "Come on in." Jessie led her into the kitchen. "Geez, girl. Look at that thing," she said, indicating George's enormous mug. Across the front, BEER was spelled out in tall letters. "Bit early for that, isn't it?"

"I have a thing about mugs."

"Mugs? That doesn't seem like you."

George frowned. "It was Tom, my husband. I always liked delicate china cups. The civilized, tea-drinking kind. I had a couple in my dorm room when I first went to school, drank my tea in them while everyone else guzzled coffee from those thick college mugs. Anyway, Tom made fun of me and started buying me these; he said it was a better investment." She held up the mug, remembering his ribbing with a brief, almost painful, nostalgic pang. "He was right."

"Did he buy you that one?"

"Yes. This and about twenty others. But it's gotten out of hand—even today. Every Christmas, my nurse and receptionist buy me ridiculous mugs. I've got…many."

"Hmm. Want a refill?" Jessie asked, and George held out the vessel in question. "So, what's goin' on?"

"Don't call them," George said.

"What?"

"Don't ask about the Sultans."

"Don't—Oh. Why not?"

"It's…it's a betrayal, what I did. Not just unethical, but…" George swallowed. Closed her eyes. Opened them again. "I betrayed him. I wanted to help him, but… whatever's got him running, it's not good. He trusted me, and I betrayed him."

Jessie put her cup down. "Can I help?"

George shook her head no.

"Crap. I made a call already. I'm sorry."

"Oh." George deflated, closing her eyes as she sank into the chair.

"Hey. Hey, don't worry about it. It's fine. It'll be fine.

Left a message, which'll probably never get returned. Some bigwig in Baltimore."

"He's…he told me never to discuss the Sultans. He said it was too dangerous. For me. Probably for him too."

"Look, I'll be subtle if they get back in touch, okay? Besides, the guy I called was ATF. It's not like I called Sultan headquarters or anything, right?"

George nodded. "Right. That's true."

"And if he's trying to get away, to get out of that life, then there's no reason for them to look here. There's nothing to draw them here."

"Okay. That's true too."

"So, you're involved. With him."

George nodded.

"George." Jessie grabbed her hand, waiting until she looked her right in the eye. "Don't feel guilty. You've only been good to him. If the man is in trouble like you say, then he couldn't have picked a better person to ask for help. You get that, right? You've got this heart of gold, and he's lucky to have found you. Stop worrying about the Sultans and enjoy this…thing for whatever time you've got it. Just don't get too invested. Please?"

George nodded, picturing him on her floor, his flesh hot, his body taut beneath hers. She pictured his face: the pain stretched over his features, the skin pulled too tight over high cheekbones. She remembered the way her chest had felt when he'd groaned, like she'd been hit with a sledge-hammer, her throat clogged with the need to love him.

Not too invested. Right.

❧

Clay was happy when he set out to find a hardware store. Jittery happy. First-crush happy. *New-life happy.*

Unfortunately, Sunday morning in Blackwood, he remembered belatedly, was a retail wasteland.

You couldn't fix sagging steps and rotting clapboard without the proper tools, but nothing was open. Nothing but churches, that was. The churches were doing one hell of a brisk business.

It wasn't till he hit Charlottesville and found a big chain store with a hardware section that he could stock up, without knowing exactly what he needed. The half hour into town and the half hour back gave him plenty of time to wonder if he'd fucked everything up last night—between the brutal stairs sex and the night terrors. *Christ.*

By the time he got back to George's, the sun was high overhead, and those fuckin' bugs were hissing their whirligig song. He was exhausted and nervous at what kind of reception he'd get.

Getting no answer to his knock, he peered through her screen door. The inside of her house looked dark and cool compared to the sweltering heat out here. Over a hundred today, the cashier at the store had warned him, and Clay had nodded. Of course. And the woman had no A/C.

He pulled open the door—unlatched, as usual—and walked inside, calling her name.

Quiet, still, relatively cool. With the windows shut, the busy drone from outside was held somewhat at bay, and it smelled like... What was that? Not flowers, exactly. Not so girly as that, but close. It smelled cozy and clean, like herbs or cinnamon or something.

A place to rest, to heal and restore not just your body, but your soul.

He eyed the couch, considering a quick nap in this oasis while he waited for her but pretty sure that wouldn't happen, since he could almost feel her presence out back. Setting his purchases down, he went through to the kitchen to the screened-in porch, where he finally caught sight of her, toward the rear of her yard, struggling with some huge wire structure wrapped in what looked like vines.

Watching her, Clay smiled. There was something epic about this small woman and her big house, her massive garden, her funky animals. She yanked at the metal again, attempting to pry it up from the ground and replant it in the soil. She might have cussed, but he doubted it. Knowing her, she was probably whispering sweet nothings to the stupid object. He should go out there and help her. He should, but she was so perfect like this, pissed, but civilized in a way he admired but could hardly comprehend.

Anyway, he must have made some noise, because suddenly her eyes were on him, wide and cautious before creasing at the corners into a welcoming smile. Clay folded up a little bit inside at the sight. Or maybe he unfolded. It hurt, even that little unbending. Like a cramp or a growing pain, it touched a part of him he wasn't used to feeling. All he could do was smile back.

"Think you could lend me a hand?" she called. "Or you going to just stand there and watch me make a fool of myself?"

Clay's smile widened, and he stepped outside, letting

the door slam behind him. "I'm all yours, ma'am," he said, breathing in the cracked-earth smell.

"Help me with this tomato plant."

"That's a tomato?"

"Yes. The cucumbers seem to have attacked it, and they've all gone kind of crazy, and I've been so distracted by—"

She stopped midsentence, and Clay wondered what she'd been about to say. "By me?" he finally asked, almost at her side now.

After a quick second, where he figured she'd opened her mouth to protest, she closed it and nodded, one side of her mouth quirked up. And that, right there, was what was so absolutely appealing about this woman. No games. No bullshit, no hiding or embarrassment— although that last might not be entirely true, if the blush working its way up her face was any indication.

He wanted to touch his fingers to that blush, wanted to greet her with a kiss but held back, uncomfortable with the impulse. Instead, he reached out, took the wire frame from her hands, and went to work.

Clay's stomach had been growling for a good hour at least by the time he raised his head and noticed how far the sun had dipped in the sky. A look around showed the garden relatively still, aside from a bird or two—even the chickens knew better than to stir up trouble in this heat—and George nowhere to be found.

Things were looking pretty good after what had to be at least five hours of hard labor, and Clay felt deep satisfaction at the part he'd played. He flexed his shoulders, stretched, and swallowed a yawn. He hadn't had the best sleep last night. He slapped at a mosquito lazily sipping from one more pinprick in his skin and came away with a smear of blood. The bug bites itched like crazy, and he was hungry enough to eat a cow. Time to head in.

Clay let his dirt-encrusted boots fall to the porch floor with a *clunk* before heading inside to find George exactly where he'd pictured her—in the kitchen. She'd changed into something white and flowing, loose and fresh-looking. He wanted to go up and put his hands on her waist, feel her flesh through the cool cotton, burn his mouth on her neck.

"You hungry?" she asked, throwing a lazy smile over her shoulder. *Fuck*, she was pretty. His stomach tightened with something that felt strangely like fear.

"Starving."

"You're a mess. Want to go upstairs and grab a shower?"

Only if you come with me, he thought, although nothing she'd done made him think she'd feel that way about him in broad daylight. "Sure. Didn't bring anything to change into, but…"

She eyed him dubiously. "I might have something that'll fit you."

"'S okay. I'll just put these back on."

"Come on," she said, leading him up a staircase that was wide but creaky, to a bright landing, a cozy nook with a little desk and an armchair, and past her open bedroom door to the bathroom—the only one in the house. He hadn't been surprised at the claw-foot tub or the old-school enamel sink, but the whiteness of everything still shocked him a little, after the Technicolor chaos of the rest of the house.

"White," he said.

"Hmm?"

"Your bathroom, it's so…different. It's nice."

"Oh." She looked around, big green eyes blinking as if she'd never been here before. "Thank you. Here, towels and…I'll find you something to put on."

She disappeared, closing the door behind her, and he stood for a few seconds, alone in her pristine bathroom, before reaching down to pull off his filthy T-shirt—one of the dozen he'd bought at her suggestion. He caught sight of himself in the hazy mirror over the sink, and the air blew raw through his throat. *Fuck me.* He took in the scabs and redness, the scar, and the mean face. There'd been moments, as a kid or even in college, when he'd seen himself and stared into his eyes and failed to recognize the link between inside and out. But here, now, in this perfect, calm, white place, he saw with utter clarity the rightness of his skin. Ugly. Inside and out. Ugly like the tight knot of pain in his gut.

With a scowl and a sniff, Clay stepped into the shower, wanting it cold but getting only lukewarm. The water ran over his skin, highlighting his faults rather than washing them away.

This is what I am now, he thought defiantly. *Condemned. Past renovation.* It worked—the water and the defiance—hardened his mind to the warmth of the woman who seemed to think he was worth saving.

There was a quick knock on the door, followed by her voice. "Found something."

"Thanks," he responded, knowing he wouldn't use it, whatever it was. This had dragged on long enough. He'd kept letting her think he was salvageable, but he *wasn't*, and spending time with her now was just giving her mixed messages. The wrong message. He had to go, had to—

With a metallic whistle, the shower curtain flew back, and she was there, completely naked, and, in one fell swoop, he lost his breath, his decisiveness, *his fucking mind*.

She stepped in, shrieked, and moved to turn the temperature dial. "You're crazy! This is freezing!"

"I'd have told you if you'd given me some warning," Clay said as his hands found the wet, goose-bumped indentation of her waist—all misgivings forgotten in the face of her nudity—and pulled her in, fitting their bodies neatly together. "It's what you deserve, though, for busting in on me like this."

She sighed when he kissed her—a soft touching of lips overlaid with warm, sluicing water—and Clay's shoulders relaxed, doubts and worries flushed down the drain like the dirt from her garden.

It was fast and slow after that. Too slow for his taste, because what he wanted was to press her up against the wall and shove into her, but that wasn't going to happen, or they'd fall in the slippery tub. Everything was quick too, though: the way their kiss heated him from the inside out, the way it burned him hard and violent, the way she ate him up. Pulling at his hair until he lowered his head, bit her nipple, and got harder at the low moan she let loose.

Another tug at his hair, and she muttered into his mouth, "I went and bought a box of condoms while you were out today. Just in case." The words, so utilitarian, so practical, just like his little doctor, inflamed him, so he dropped thoughtlessly to his knees, wanting—no, needing—to taste her. His groan, when he hit the porcelain, wasn't of enjoyment, and if she hadn't been so open and pink and beautiful in front of him, he'd probably have rolled up into a little ball of pain.

"Me too," he said with a chuckle, sucking in her smell, the trembling of her legs, the unfamiliar sight of a woman with hair on her. Weird, wasn't it, how shaving had become the norm? Well, he liked this; it was a womanly sight, rather than an ambiguously girly one, and he appreciated that.

Unable to resist any longer, he leaned in and nuzzled her. Right there, where her hair curled up thick, soft, and wet, and she smelled like fucking heaven. Never one for useless teasing, he dove right in, tongue and teeth and his entire being focused on consuming this woman.

Despite loving Tom, George could finally admit that he'd never gotten her quite this carried away. She remembered one time when they'd had oral sex. They'd watched a movie—*Secretary*, maybe. The spanking scenes had gotten her totally riled, and they'd ended up, somehow, half-dressed on the sofa in a head-to-tail position. George had tried to enjoy it. She'd closed her eyes to the sight of her husband's testicles in her face and licked him while he'd performed his hallmark, swirly tongue thing down below. She could remember, to this day, lying precariously side-by-side on the sofa, the smell of him in her nose, and the way he'd shoved his tongue deep inside her, neatly missing her clit with each rare pass to the north.

She'd loved Tom, she had, but she'd never until now

known real hunger, never wanted with such desperation, never felt every breath a man expelled with an awareness like pain, a connection too kinetic to understand. This man didn't need to touch her to make her feel. He just needed to breathe. And in this brief, wistful moment of comparison, she knew with certainty that she'd never feel this way with another person again. How could you when you'd gotten this far and there was one man—only one—who did this to you?

Stop it, her brain ordered. *If this is your only chance, you've got to enjoy it, not regret it before it's gone.*

And so she did. With a long, low *ooh*, she let her head fall forward, squinting at his dark hair, sleek under the pelting water, and felt each pull of his lips, every scrape of his teeth and slick slide of his tongue.

It was when he looked up at her, his warm, brown eyes, blinking and lashes gathered into wet, little commas, that she came, hard and debilitating, in his mouth. Muscles like Jell-O, she sank to the bottom of the tub beside him and let his mouth take hers, explicit and musky, but gentle in a way he hadn't been before. Sweet slide of nose to nose, scrape of cheek to cheek, his hands on her breasts. They were too sensitive for it now, but she let him anyway. He could do whatever he wanted after the orgasm he'd just given her—the pulse in her clit completely unfamiliar.

"You're so fucking beautiful," he said, gathering her to him. His voice was rough, raw, and she believed him. He was under her now, his legs straight and his hot, hard erection against her sex, her thighs around his waist. He took himself in hand, lifted her up a little, and angled himself down, giving her the brief notion that he'd penetrate her, just like this, but instead sliding beneath her, leaving her empty, with nothing but an illicit shiver of disappointment.

But the disappointment fled as he started to move, all business, his eyes locked on where their bodies came together. His shoulders flexed, and he moved her, forward and back, her wet heat lubricating him.

"This is good," he breathed into her ear, and it *was*. It was *perfect*. Dirty and rough, but somehow sweet beneath it all. He looked so needy, the way his brows sank and those stark lines etched deeper into his skin, his scar taut and white. Scrawled across his lowered lid, in stark contrast to that sweet sweep of lashes, the scabbed-up ink tried hard to look like fighting words but came out empty and weak in comparison to the true beauty of the man.

A good man, she knew, could feel it in her bones, certain in a way that should have worried her, but instead only made her want to give him things: her body and food and love.

The water ran cold by the time he got close to finishing, pulling her quickly away to yank his erection up between them and give her a chance to help. She grasped him, hard, the press of his skin beneath hers igniting her as it had since the first time she'd grazed him wearing a thin Nitrile glove. Something snapped in her brain. Synapses connected; fuses blew.

He clasped a big hand over hers, tightening even more, and showing her the rhythm he needed, his eyes skipping over her body until, for one frantic moment, they landed hard on hers, vague and young-looking, before closing, and he spilled all over their joined fists—his come emerging in hot, short bursts, too quickly washed away by the water.

∽ح

After drying off, Clay moved to put his nasty clothes back on, but George stopped him by throwing a worn, brown terry-cloth robe in his face and racing off with his dirty stuff, giggling.

He got her back in the kitchen a short while later when he snuck up on her doing dishes, pinching her under the ribs and sending her into a squealing, vertical leap. Her reaction was so adorable that he had to kiss her, right there against the sink, and before he knew it, her hands were on him, under the robe, and they would have gone at it again on the kitchen floor if some timer hadn't gone off, sending them apart like guilty teenagers.

He liked her like this, flirty and light. He liked *himself* like this, which was rare enough to shock him into silence for the few minutes it took her to get their food plated. They wound up eating on the porch, with front-row seats to a fucking cicada symphony, and Clay was only minimally bothered by it. It was George, he figured, watching her eat out of the corner of his eye. Her presence muffled the buzzing, dulled the agony. It felt good not to hurt quite so much.

They talked about her plans for the garden. He asked what needed work in the house, and all of it was done with a blind eye to reality—to the weirdness of the two of them, such an ill-suited pair, discussing normal things. He couldn't just hang out here with this woman for the rest of his life. He couldn't, because he had a job to do—or he would eventually. He had a life to get back to. Duties. It was all he knew, and he couldn't imagine doing anything else... Although, at this point, he couldn't imagine going back, either.

So, maybe I can do this right now. He tried out the thought, and no bells went off in his brain. For once. *Just for now.*

She got up, cleared their dishes, and disappeared inside, leaving him with the precarious happiness he'd allowed himself. "Leave the dishes," he called after her. "I'll do them."

"I should hope so" was her sassy reply, and he liked it. *I like her*, he thought in this rare moment of clarity—no vengeance, no violence, no bitterness to cloud him. *I really like her.*

Although *like* had never ached so much before.

15

THERE WERE PRACTICAL THINGS TO DEAL WITH: DISHES TO
wash and lights to turn out, but none of that mattered.
How could it matter when George's life had just shifted
so drastically? She tugged Andrew's hand, brought him
up the stairs to her room, to her bed.

He shut the door, which she found sweet, and walked
toward her in the dark, dropping the bathrobe as he
went. Her husband's bathrobe—the one that had finally
lost his smell. It should have bothered her. It would have
on any other man, but not this one, not *this man*, whose
arrival in her life had been brutally unexpected, but
whose presence was now so very right.

Andrew's hands on her face were gentle, his fingers rough against her mouth, his thumb firm on her
tongue. She sucked it in, let him paint her lips with her
saliva, and shuddered when he closed in with a kiss. She
couldn't see him in the dark, his ink and his scars and
the life story he wore like a sordid badge, but she knew
him in ways she couldn't quite fathom. And this kiss,
this moment, twisted something inside her.

She let him peel off her clothes, helping him with the buttons on her dress. Her breathing picked up as his hand made its way down her side, curving along her waist and hip, to squeeze her bottom and pull her in against him.

"You got those condoms somewhere close by? Left mine out in the truck."

"Bedside table," she said in a rush, and things went fast. On the bed now, with his heavy body sprawled across her, and all she wanted to do was stroke him—like a woman, not a doctor. Straight to those hard, little nipples that had given him away in her office, down over his belly, where she could picture the ink but couldn't feel it. His shoulders. God they were thick. The heft of them surprised her, affected her in a visceral way.

"Please don't." He interrupted her progress, one hand clamped on her wrist.

"Don't what?"

"Touch me like that."

"Like wh—"

"All soft and sweet and like you care."

"But I do ca—" She stopped herself. "Why don't you want me to touch you?"

"You touch me like that, George, I'm gonna blow in two seconds."

"Really?"

"Got no idea how close you get me when you touch me like that. Fuck, in your office, even."

"Really?" she breathed, remembering how there'd been no tenderness on the stairs the night before. Only heat and passion.

"You're so…soft," he said.

"I want to make you feel better."

"Here," he said, putting her hand on his erection, tight.

"Hang on. You're afraid tenderness will make you…"

He let out a dry, little half laugh. "Yeah. Freaky, huh? I'll come too soon if you're nice to me, but you can jack me as hard as you want. How fucked up is that?"

"I *want* to touch you."

"Later. I can't take it now. Please."

A quick slide of her palm over his erection brought a grunt to his lips. It lit her on fire.

"You like that?" she asked. Teasing, actually *teasing* a man for what might have been the first time in her life.

"Yes, fuck yes," he groaned. "Do it again. Squeeze my cock."

His cock, she thought, pulling at him hard, wanting to leave an imprint of herself, a mark as indelible as the others on his body. More indelible because she'd get rid of the tattoos. But this… She squeezed him, letting her hand take in the contours of his…his cock. *This* she wanted him to remember.

"Your cock."

"Mmm?"

"What do you call *this*?" she asked, running a hand lightly over her sex.

"Your pussy," he said.

She grimaced. "I don't like that."

His eyes roamed her face and narrowed with dawning understanding. "All right. Your *cunt*."

Pleasure sparked deep and low in her body. "That's a bad word," she said, half teasing.

"But not a bad thing."

"My…cunt?" She ran a hand over herself again, dipping in to show him her explorations.

"Fuck, George. You're killin' me."

"I'm sorry," she whispered, not meaning it one bit.

"Get a condom." Andrew's words came out as an order. She let him go just long enough to obey. "Put it on me," he said, and she got wetter from the roughness of his words, the ragged quality of his voice.

It took too long to open the drawer, pull out the box, and struggle with the cardboard. Too long for Andrew, apparently, because in a flash, he was up and on her, grabbing it from her hands and tearing it open, sending little packets everywhere. A giggle formed in George's throat when he finished rolling it on and pulled her onto his lap, but it caught there as the blunt head of him sought her out, rubbing once, twice against her, until it found her opening and sank in, one inexorable inch at a time. Slow, slow, painfully slow, but good, better than anything she'd felt in a lifetime. A million lifetimes. Better than the night before—more explicit and real, less of a dream.

He'd gotten inside her, all the way, with her on his lap, stretched around him, too full to move. Not just her...cunt, but her throat and her chest, where emotion swelled. A tear rolled down George's face—a rogue bit of love or something equally mushy. She wiped it, fast, so he couldn't see it, and went to lift herself up, but he grasped her hips and held her still.

"Don't. *Don't*, baby. I can't…" He finished on a groan, an uncontrollable, dark, desperate sound that made her want to move even more, swallowed up by desire.

She lifted up, her thighs trembling with the effort, but it was so worth it when his hands bit into her hips, fingers hard points seared into her body. Every slide up, every inch back down was a slow, smooth glide, gorged with sensation.

"You…you don't fucking know, do you?" he asked, and indeed, she had no idea.

Another slide up, and one of his hands shifted to her butt and slammed her back down too hard, wrenching a gasp from her lungs. Again he brought her up, fast and furious, and down, leading the dance, his rhythm so much more vigorous than hers, a piston to counter her caresses. And that speed, that power, pushed her toward climax unexpectedly, brought her close, so close she almost wanted to stop him—almost, but not quite. Because who in their right mind would say no to an orgasm like the one his body promised?

It was the slap on her ass, though, that pushed her, groaning, over the edge. Sharp and stinging and reminiscent of that long-ago screening of *Secretary*, it sent her mind elsewhere, while her body convulsed and pulsed around his cock, the orgasm inescapable.

Andrew's hard gasps warmed George's face before he kissed her, ate at her, consumed her again, and left her nothing, nothing but the quivering shell of a woman satisfied.

It wasn't until she came back down, collapsed over Andrew's lap, that she realized he was still inside her and very much not finished.

Do whatever you want, she thought, and then she said the words, which led to a breathless, eager-sounding, "Yeah?"

"Within reason." She laughed, and he joined in weakly.

"I wanna do *everything* to you right now, George. I

mean *everything*. I want to fuck you everywhere and…
shit. I'm not usually out of control like this."

"No?" George answered, feeling light-headed from
the possibilities. Lust. The man *lusted* after her. How
crazy was that? "Well, pick one."

His laughter moved him in her, and she tightened
unconsciously around him, drawing a helpless, crazed-
sounding moan from his lips. She'd move again, she'd
just decided, when he pulled out and tapped her hip. "Lie
down. I wanna…" He didn't finish, but she knew what
she wanted right now. She wanted to see his face while he
came. She wanted to see how lost he'd look, and thankfully, there was just enough moonlight to give her that.

George lay pale and ghostlike against her sheets, her
body strong and very much alive. He settled between
her thighs, wanting—no *needing*—to get back inside her,
where everything was right in the world.

Quickly, faster than he'd meant to, he shoved back
in, the smell of sex and latex coming at him in a sultry
whoosh and dragging him back, against his will, to
another place, another time—a world he wanted more
than anything to forget.

Fuck no, he was here with this woman now, and he
wouldn't let his mind take him back to that hell.

She must have felt something, because her arms were
around him, comforting and tender, tight and firm, her
thighs encircling his hips, and he wanted this—not just
the sex, but the rest of what she had to offer—in a way
he'd wanted little else in his life.

But first, he wanted to come. He thrust into her a few

times. Not deep enough, not as far as he wanted to go. One hand beneath her ass, he dragged her up, pushed one of her legs to her chest with his other hand, and there…there, he pounded, as hard as he could, forgetting who she was, the delicate sweetness. He didn't think he'd ever fucked so hard, so wild, so out of control. He heard her scream—a strange sound, soft and muted— and when he pulled back into his brain, truly focused, he saw his ugly, scarred hands pressing tightly into her perfect, white throat.

"Fuck," he grunted, pulling out and shooting up off the bed, breath gone wild, head buzzing, eyes impossible to clear. "I hurt you."

"I'm fine," she said, the hand at her throat proving the lie.

"I don't hurt women."

"I'm not a victim, Andrew. I want to be here. I *want* to be with you."

"Even if I hurt you?" he said, hating the reedy sound of his voice.

"I'm not afraid of you."

"You should be, damn it. Look at me, for God's sake!"

"I…I liked the spanking," she said, head turning away. "Are you planning on hurting me more than that?"

"Who the hell knows! I mean, your throat…" He stalked to the closed door and rammed his fist into the hard wood with a quiet, "Fuck!" And oh, the pain was good. Letting go was good, so good. "I go into my head sometimes, and then I…I can't control it, the shit I do. You've seen me. I could hurt you, and I wouldn't even know it till it's too late. Too fucking late, George!"

His mind slipped back to Kathy with a *K*, against the

clubhouse wall. He pictured fucking her there, above and beyond the call of duty, but so very in character for Indian Greer. He remembered pulling out, loosening the fist he'd had wrapped tightly in her hair, stroking her face and then her shoulder in an odd, platonic, placating gesture, and then waiting a half second before muttering a quiet, "Sorry," and walking away.

Those memories were fine, though, compared to the image of Kathy's dead, blank eyes staring at him from beside him at the bottom of the well only a couple of weeks later. She'd just been more collateral damage, killed because of her link to the club. The murder of Kathy with a *K* had been the last straw, and even that had been rife with shame. He could have saved her.

He'd torn himself up about Kathy—for not getting her out in time, for using her—but the worst part, the very worst thing of all, the thing that ate him up inside, made him worthless, soulless, and ready for hell, was that even in death, she hadn't meant enough to mark him. Because the face he'd seen attached to her body, bruised and battered and thrown down there like unwanted trash, hadn't even been hers. It had been Carly's. And no matter how hard he tried, he couldn't for the life of him remember what Kathy with a *K* looked like.

Andrew stood rigid at the foot of her bed, doing a strange heavy breathing that scared her as nothing else would. He could have yelled and screamed and threatened her physically, and she wouldn't have felt half as helpless as she did right then.

Because she wanted to love him, she realized, with a

tragic dose of reality. Tragic because you couldn't love a man like this and not get hurt. She shouldn't love him at all— not after so little time, not after all the strife. But she wanted to; she wanted to give him that. Maybe even give it to herself.

Across the room, the moon highlighted wet streaks on his face. Crying. He was crying, and George wanted to fix it—fix everything. She'd do whatever it took to take him in, to protect him, to make him better.

And not just his skin, but every beautiful, scarred inch of his psyche.

She stood up and walked to him, put a hand out, let it rest on his chest, and when he opened his arms just a little, she moved in, settled against him.

"It's okay, Andrew," she whispered into his neck. "I'm here. I'm here."

After a while, he let out a shuddering breath and pushed gently away from her to walk out into the hall and then the bathroom. She heard the water run and wondered if this was it. This man wouldn't stick around to discuss it, whatever it was. He couldn't. He had too much pride. He couldn't let her take care of him and still keep his man card or whatever the hell they carried around besides their big cars and penises.

With a sigh, she followed him to the bathroom, hesitating outside the closed door.

"Andrew?"

Nothing except the turning of the faucet and the water stopping.

"Please stay."

She could hear him sigh, even through the door, and could only picture how heartfelt it was.

"You don't want my brand of crazy, George. I'll only drag you down."

"I thought we discussed this, Andrew. I thought we established that I could decide these things for myself."

A weird, choked-sounding chuckle came through the wood, and George relaxed slightly against the door.

"I…" George swallowed, not entirely sure she should reveal this much, but too honest to lie. "I don't want to give this up. I don't care how hard it is. I…I like you. And I don't want to lose whatever we're doing. Okay, Andrew?"

Another sigh, and the door swung unexpectedly back. Good thing he was there to catch her. He kissed her, hard, and she didn't care. She wanted it. She liked it like that.

"It's not Andrew."

"Hmm?" It was hard to pull back and focus after a kiss like that, but she managed, bleary-eyed, her pulse going a million miles an hour.

"My name. It's not Andrew."

She blinked. "Oh."

"My name's Clay."

"I see," she said, stepping cautiously out of his arms.

"No, baby. No, you really don't see."

"Why don't you tell me, then?"

"How much time you got?"

"For this? As much time as it takes." George swallowed. "*Clay.*"

❧

"What's your last name?" she asked a few seconds later.

He nodded, resigned. "Navarro."

"Oh." She looked confused and took another step back, eyeing him. After another beat, she seemed to come to some decision. "It suits you."

"Yeah?"

"To a T. It's sexy."

That surprised a chuckle out of him.

"You... Would you like a drink or something... Clay? I—"

"No. Thank you. I want to come clean."

"Oh, right, well...do you mind if I...?" She led him back to her room, sat in the rocking chair, hands in her lap, face strong and set, and waited for whatever news he had to give.

Christ, he liked this woman. Like, really, *really* liked her.

Pushing back a wave of emotion, Clay sucked in a breath and settled into the armchair, needing to tell the truth.

"I'm an... *Was* an undercover agent with the ATF."

George's eyes were huge, her face unnaturally pale.

"Still an agent, but... Actually, I'm not entirely sure I still have a job. Coming here, I mean. Boss wanted me to take a break, but I'm keeping my location quiet, and she's pretty pissed."

"Oh, thank God."

"Thank God?"

"I...I wanted you to be a good guy," George said, looking like a weight had been lifted from her shoulders. "So badly."

"Yeah? I get that."

"So, you were...undercover?"

"Yeah. Can't talk about my last case too much—still

hasn't gone to trial—but I wanted you to know. I…I guess I'm tired of looking like a bad guy all the time. Although…I've done some pretty horrible things."

"In the line of duty?"

He grimaced. "Yeah. Didn't always feel like it, though."

"Why not?"

"I don't know how to explain." He took a breath and rubbed a hand over his face, wishing everything were more like the movies—all black or white, good or bad. How could he explain this in-between shit to a civilian?

"Going undercover's like…like a blood transfusion or something. Like you've got to make room for the soulless bastard you'll be pretending to be for the foreseeable future. And to do that, you've got to willingly rip out essential parts of yourself—parts like honor and humanity. The shit that made you want to do your job in the first place. That shit's got to go, 'cause it's what'll get you made, right? So, by the time I'd finished with the Sultans, I was one of them. A full-fledged, motherfucking asshole of a murderous Sultan."

George gasped and started to speak. "Wha… Wait, I don't… Did you—"

"No. No, but there were moments where I got pretty fucking close, times when I'd be egging one of my brothers on and—" He stood, clearly startling George, and pulled his shirt up to reveal the severe burn on his side. "Remember you asked me about this? Who did this to me? *I* did, George. Me. I took a hot-ass iron, dialed it up high as it would go, and pressed it right over the tat there. You wanna know why?"

No! Stop it! George wanted to scream. *Don't say another word. I don't want to know.* But the desperation on Clay's face was enough to make her stop and shove back the tears surging into her eyes and stinging her sinuses.

"Tell me."

"'Cause I *asked* for that tat. Not like these." He pointed to his eyes. "Or the ones on my hands. Those were forced on me, but this one…this one was my Sultan self *feeling* it. Feeling like one of the brothers."

"What about the one on your back?"

"No, no. I got that when I became a full-fledged member. That one's standard issue. If I wanted into the club, I had to get the colors on the back. This one? This was me—not me Clay, but me *Indian Greer*, telling those assholes that I'd die for them. Wanting to die for them." He looked down at her defiantly and George wasn't at all sure how he expected her to react. "How messed up is that, huh, George?"

The tears overflowed—the feelings too—and George stood up, went to where he sat in that old wingback chair, and ducked to wrap her arms around him. She didn't say a thing.

"The worst part," he went on, his voice floating into the air above her head as she squeezed into the tiny bit of leftover space, "the worst part is that those fuckers killed my sister."

George stilled, shifted back, and waited, her breath audible in her ears.

"It was personal, me joining the Sultans. Always personal." He sat watching her, defiantly. Waiting, if George wasn't mistaken, for her to throw him out or something.

Instead, she took his hand and nudged him until he sat back and made more room for her beside him.

"Tell me the story," she said, sliding in close.

"You don't want to hear about—"

"I want to hear your story, Clay. Tell me your story."

"My story?"

"Who are you? Where are you from? I don't know anything."

"It's not very—"

"Tell me about you. And your sister. Please."

Forehead resting on his fists, tension palpable, he shook his head.

"Okay. You don't have to." She ran a finger over one of those fists, felt it loosen, took it in her hand, and waited him out.

"I don't know where to start," he finally said.

"How old are you?"

"Thirty-four."

"Where are you from?"

"Baltimore." He paused, head tilted to the side, and focused on her. "How old are you, Doc?"

"Thirty-three."

He gave a satisfied harrumph and wrapped one of those solid arms around her. "So, the Clay Navarro story. Short version."

"Long version's fine too."

"How about the medium version?"

"Okay."

"I grew up kinda lower middle class, I guess you could say."

"Working class," she corrected in her know-it-all way, before tamping that down.

"Right. Blue collar, or whatever."

"I'll stop interrupting. Sorry."

"Don't be," said Clay with a small smile in her direction. He squeezed her hand. "So, we did okay, with both my parents working. Then my mom died when we were little."

"Who's we?"

"Oh. Sorry, I thought I'd told you. Carly." There was a moment of silence, and George could feel the importance of the name.

"Your sister."

He nodded. "My little sister."

"Okay. Go on."

"So, anyway, Mom got breast cancer, and…well, she died, and without health insurance, we ended up living in the projects." George swallowed past the lump swelling in her throat. "Christ. I didn't mean to go back this far." Clay swiped a hand over his eyes, pinched the bridge of his nose, and went on. "I was pretty close with her." He paused before saying the name again. It came out strangely slow and foreign-sounding. "Carly. After Mom died, we got pretty close. The place where we lived sucked, and Dad…Dad didn't do so well. You know, Baltimore. Not the easiest place in the world, especially for a Latin American whose English was still rough. So, anyway, Dad died when—"

"Your father too? What of?"

"Untreated pneumonia."

"I'm so sorry."

"Shitty job, no savings, no insurance. And he wasn't all that fond of hospitals, so… Yeah. Anyway, I wanted to…I wanted to be a history teacher, of all things. I'd had a good one in high school. Inspiring, you know? And so the plan was, community college first and then… Too much detail." He urged her to shift to one side and stood up, running his hands through his hair, and George watched him cross the room, flick aside her bedroom curtain, which she didn't remember closing, and look outside. Paranoid or just cautious—she suddenly wasn't so sure.

He told the next part from his spot by the window, voice muffled. "Carly was a wild child. She was impatient and needy and… Man, she was a handful. I tried to help her, tried to keep her in line, but I had my own things I wanted to do, so by the time I realized shit wasn't what it was supposed to be, she was…" He turned, met her eyes, and she thought she'd never seen a face so filled with pain—so marked by regret. "She was too far gone. Hooked on smack, crank, whatever the hell she could get her hands on. And she'd gotten into this Aryan brotherhood thing, which was fucking ironic, considering our dad was South American, so… I tried to get her out. I swear I tried, George." He was pleading with her now, and George's eyes burned with a new veil of unshed tears. "I tried, but it was too late. Too late for my baby sister and…" The hand that ran through his hair shook with emotion, and she wanted to get up and hold him. "Carly got involved with those fucking creeps, and eventually—or actually, pretty fucking quickly—she died."

His eyes when they met George's were naked, raw, open, sad…but not dead at least. No, so alive with pain that she could feel it, a gaping wound in the middle of her bedroom. She did get up then, crossed to him, and

wrapped her arms around him, trying her best to hold his
broken pieces together.

"And you joined the ATF after that?"

"My mission in life's been to take those fuckers
down."

"I'm sorry, Clay. I'm so sorry."

"You know, I haven't told this story since…since
right after it happened. The cops didn't give a shit. They
had bigger fish to fry than some poor little smackhead
like Carly, but I knew…I knew exactly who'd done it.
It was the fucker she'd been hanging out with. A racist
MC son of a bitch. Those bastards killed her. The official line was that it was an OD, but I'd seen her body.
I'd seen what those motherfuckers had done to her, and
I *knew*." He stopped talking, and she tightened her hold
before stepping back.

"Jesus, how did I end up here? With you? The most
amazing woman I've ever met. I…I'm not sure I deserve
this. Whatever *this* is."

"Whatever it is," she echoed, and looking at this man,
she knew it was more than sex. She wanted to show him
with her body, her embrace.

"Come on," she whispered. "Come to bed with me."
She urged him. "Please."

"There's more. I want to tell you everything."

"I know. Let's go to bed, and you can tell me."

They settled in, Clay on his back and George on her
side, facing him. She wanted to touch him everywhere,
to wrap him up and never let him back out. She wanted
to *save* him. Instead, she put her head on his shoulder,
curled one arm over his chest, and waited.

"I don't know where to start."

She pictured Clay the first time she'd seem him. "Your eyelids," she said with a long caress. "Start with your eyelids."

"That was Ape, a.k.a. Harold Herndon. But he'd beat the crap out of anyone who used his real name."

"So, Harold." She forced a smile. "He did your lids?"

"Yeah."

When he didn't go on, she prodded. "Against your will?"

"With a tattoo needle against my eyeball." He paused, shuddered, and then turned to her. "Same night I was shot. The whole damned operation was coming together that night. Ape and I were supposed to go with Handles for the final exchange, but he surprised us all by leaving alone. He must have known, even then, about me. Or had his doubts. And while he was gone, somebody ratted me out to Ape."

"Who was it? How did they know?"

"Still got no idea. But it was someone close."

"You mean—"

"I mean somebody on the inside. Someone who's supposed to be on my team."

"Oh no."

"They shut me up in my room, waiting for Handles to come and…I don't know, deliver the fatal blow or whatever. That's when the shit really hit the fan. I wound up on a bed, with a couple of bullet holes in my back…one in my thigh."

George's pulse took off fast, too fast. He had to see he was killing her.

"Your thigh?" She reached down and ran a hand down one leg, then the other, until she found it—a chunk taken out of the side of his thigh. "This is why you limp."

"Yeah."

"Clay, I'm—"

"It wasn't the worst thing that ever happened to me. Another time, I got stuck at the bottom of a well shaft with a dead woman and another biker."

"*Another* biker? You thought of yourself as one of them?"

"Yeah. Yeah, I was one of them."

She took that in, understood it for what it was. A warning? An admission of guilt?

"Had to be in order to get them to believe." He hesitated.

"And the woman." George tilted her head back to get a good look at him. "Was she someone you loved?"

"*Jesus*," he said. "No. No, I didn't love her, which is so much worse. She was…" He turned his face away. "She was *nobody*."

"What were you doing at the bot—"

"Rival club attacked us." He leaned away from her. "Why am I doing this, George? Telling you this shit? I'm looking back at my life, and it's like this big hunk of swiss cheese, you know? Only instead of air, it's full of huge, black holes. And no matter how hard I try, no matter how much I work to push those holes away, I get sucked back in, over and over again, every single goddamned night." Clay rolled slightly, trying to rid himself of George's weight; she let him. "I shouldn't have brought it up. You're just too… I'm just this big black hole, and you're so full of sunshine. What if all this shit rubs off on you?"

She opened her mouth to respond, but he stopped her, shook his head as if to clear it, and went on through tightly clenched teeth.

"Something I need to tell you, George."

She stilled. After everything he'd just laid at her feet, his tone of voice said this was worse. "Okay," she said reluctantly.

"I watched you. Before."

"What?"

"Stood out there in the woods across the street. Watched over you." He laughed, a hard, regretful sound, and something uncomfortable shimmered down George's back.

"You *watched* me?"

"God, it's even worse out loud, isn't it? It was... It's such a bad world, you know? And after you got attacked by those little thugs, I...I couldn't stand the idea of you being on your own, with no idea of all the shit out there. So I came here and made sure you didn't get hurt again."

"Have you done this before? With other women?"

He let out another harsh laugh. "No. Apparently, I've only recently turned to the dark side."

As understanding dawned, everything inside of George softened, opened up. What must it be like to be this man, walking around with the weight of the world on his shoulders?

"Every night, George. It's wrong, and I'm sorry. I'm so sorry. But I just wanted to make sure you were safe. I couldn't stand to see you get hurt again."

George swallowed back that image of this man standing sentinel in front of her house, doing the only thing he apparently knew how to do—taking care of people,

saving them. Just not himself, it turned out. He needed
someone else to do that for him.

He looked devastated when she took his cheeks
between her hands. "It's okay," she said, granting him
the absolution he couldn't give himself. "Let me take
care of you, Clay. Let me…let me hold you. Will you do
that? Will you just let me hold you tonight?"

He nodded—this big, hard, uncompromising man—
and once the incomprehension left his face, the hope she
saw there was so bright, so new, so clearly against the
grain that it nearly broke her heart.

16

GEORGE AWOKE ON HER BEDROOM FLOOR AND UNWOUND herself carefully from An—No, *Clay's* arms. *ATF Agent Clay Navarro.*

She considered trying to rouse him and get him to move to the bed but decided against it. Best to leave him there, where he seemed to be getting actual rest, as opposed to whatever he'd suffered through while they'd lain on the mattress.

Quietly, she moved around, gathered the things she'd need for work, took a quick shower, fed and released the animals, and left, feeling…

Lord, what would you call this sensation? Giddy, certainly. Fulfilled, yes. But not quite happy. Satisfied but not content. Something was missing, something she'd forgotten about, and she couldn't quite put her finger on it.

She was the first to arrive at the clinic, her brain fully occupied with thoughts of Clay as she set up for her patients and shifted gears in her mind—preparing to face a day of work when all she really wanted to do was help him tackle his demons.

The day dragged by, the usual medical conundrums failing to fascinate her the way they normally did— the way they should—and all she wanted was to get back home.

To him.

If he was still there.

Her mood, giddy one moment, swung drastically at the knowledge that he'd probably run as far and fast as possible after last night's intimacy. He wasn't the type of man who could handle closeness like that. And yet…she thought of the way he'd accepted her late-night comfort, and a wave of affection ran through her. Yes, she wanted to help him, but it was more than that. So much more.

She finally drove home, wondering, unsure, excited, worried. And then she was there, and his truck wasn't. It wasn't until she caught sight of the bare, new boards in her front steps that she let herself hope he might have decided to stay.

~◦~

It was Clay's third trip to Blackwood BigValue Hardware, and the clerk—probably the owner, judging from his age and attitude—laughed right in his face as he pushed through the door.

"Just closin' up for the night, son," the man said. "You forget somethin' else?"

"No, sir. Just switching projects."

"Done with those steps?"

"Everything but the paint."

That elicited an impressed pursing of the man's lips, which gave Clay a burst of pride.

"Smart to let it cure first. What you got goin' now?"

"Thought I'd start on the clapboard."

"Whoa. You takin' the whole thing down?"

"No, just a bit. Here." He placed a rotten board on the guy's counter.

"Gettin' smarter, ain't we?"

"Yep. Slow learner. But it sinks in eventually."

"Got some of this out back in the lumberyard. How much you need?"

"'Bout a dozen."

"Where'd you say this house is?"

"Didn't."

"Wouldn't be Dr. Hadley's place, would it? Over on Jason Lane?"

Before Clay could answer, the man went on. "Nice woman, the doc. Down at the IGA one day, and she come up to me at the register and tole me I needed to go and see someone, what with the spot I had right here." He pointed at the top of his shiny, bald head. "Saw me that day. Cut the dang thing out and all. Turned out to be a melanoma, and we caught it good and quick. Darn good woman, that doc."

He eyed Clay in a way that wasn't quite as benevolent as it had been before, the big wad of snuff in his cheek making him look like an angry chipmunk. An angry, *old* chipmunk. "You take good care of that house, now," he said, but the subtext was obvious. Replace *house* with *woman* and the man was warning him clear as day.

After he'd loaded everything into the back of his truck, Clay went back inside to pay. Halfway to the register, his eyes landed on a bag of heavy-duty zip ties. He threw those onto the counter and waited as the man rang him up.

As he reemerged onto the sidewalk with the old man, Clay let his eyes take in the town around him. Closing time. The people of Blackwood were headed home for the day—like Whos in Whoville. The poor fuckers had no idea. No idea.

A few feet farther up the walk, a door opened, and three figures emerged. Clay recognized two of them instantly as the little shits who'd attacked George his first weekend here, but it took them a bit longer to notice him standing there. Beside him, Clay felt the energy from the hardware store guy—nervous, edgy, and clearly unhappy. Everything shifted when the punks caught sight of him and stilled, frozen like deer in the headlights.

"Going somewhere?" he asked, almost smiling at their reactions—the fear, the hatred, the childish bravado.

"No, sir" came the reply, finally, and the three kids turned to walk away, fast.

"Great day," said the man beside him. "You wouldn't be the one who beat the crap outta those two the other night, would you?" When he didn't answer, the hardware store man spat a long, brown stream of saliva into the gutter before going on, looking Clay up and down through eyes that had grown distinctly friendlier. "Git on now, son. See you tomorrow."

The man's words followed Clay to his truck, and he whistled—actually whistled aloud—on the short trip home. It wasn't until he was about halfway there that he realized he'd started thinking of George's place as home. Christ, he was in trouble.

When Clay pulled up to George's, her car was there, and the house was open.

The screen door squeaked as he let himself inside, and he heard the scrape of one of her kitchen chairs before she appeared at the end of the hall.

Christ, her *face*. So beautiful, this woman. Radiant. Everything loosened in his body.

In the kitchen, he kissed her, sucked in the warm tomato-and-garlic air, and accepted the plate she pushed at him. He loved the way she made him sit across from her, their feet entwined beneath the table.

Afterward, they went out to the porch, where she lit a ton of candles, and he settled onto the wicker sofa they'd shared yesterday morning. George disappeared, and a minute later, guitar music curled from a speaker in the kitchen. She came back onto the porch on quiet bare feet, a tin of cookies in hand. She took one, handed him the rest with a smile, and curled up on the armchair across from him.

"What you doing all the way over there?" he asked, all heavy and warm.

She shrugged. "You looked content on your own. I didn't want to disturb that."

They sat for a while, taking in the fading light apart, but together.

George finally spoke. "Thank you for all the work you've been doing."

"Sure."

"You're a miracle worker," she said, facing the darkening yard. "The garden has never looked so pruned. And the steps... Usually, I feel like I'm channeling those women from *Grey Gardens*."

"What's that?"

"It's a movie, based on a true story. Actually, a

documentary originally. These women live in their massive old mansion while it falls to pieces around them. They have mental health issues, and it's tragic," she finished with a big breath and a forced smile. "Anyway, I've got too many projects."

"What? You? Nah."

"Yes. And don't lie to make me feel better."

"Am I one of those projects?" he asked, going for nonchalant but feeling anything but.

She looked him straight in the eye. "No."

He didn't believe her but decided to let it go. Sometimes it was better not to delve too deeply into a person's reasons. He, of all people, with his experience of the darker side of humanity, should know that.

He changed the subject. "Who is this?"

"The music? David Gray."

"This is old, isn't it? From the nineties, right? Your musical taste is stuck like twenty years ago."

"Really? Usually it's more like forty."

"Well, whatever decade you're from," he said, squinting at her, "you, Dr. Hadley, are an old soul."

"Practical, stoic Clay Navarro believes in souls? Intriguing."

"I'm *perceptive*." He put on a defensive voice but softened it with a grin. "Sometimes."

"I know that" was her only response before they disappeared back into their heads, soaking in the earthy smells of the garden and the sad strains of the music against the night's never-ending soundtrack, all of it bathed in candlelight.

After a bit, another song came on, one he kind of recognized from back in his young and sentimental days—high, soft guitar chords, intense but quiet. He closed his eyes and let it affect him. Let the music work its way under his skin, pricking through his eyeballs and somewhere inside his chest.

It got more rhythmic, swingy like a lullaby. His skin burned with recognition, and then the words slid out, warm and sad and sweet and straight from the memory of his sister's CD player.

His skin pebbled over.

So much noise in life, Clay thought. *So much, so fucking much. In stereo, all over, everywhere, layers upon layers of it, enough to smother you.*

He tuned back into the music, listened to the words, which didn't make sense alone, but with the strumming guitar, this woman, this ache… He was in a bubble that only a soothing voice, a practical white hand, a warm pair of sparkling green eyes could pierce, and then…and then he was a balloon losing air, wheezing until there was nothing left. Empty. He kept his eyes closed tight, not wanting to listen, but needing the rest of the song, the high, plaintive call to God, over and over until…

Clay's eyes opened.

George was there, strong and soft and decent and the only person he'd ever wanted with such intensity.

"Come here," he scraped out, *needing* her.

"I think you should be the one to get up," she said, although she had to see how mixed up he was right now—she *had* to.

But he did it anyway. He stood, his leg miraculously holding him, and limped the few steps to where she sat, enveloped in her bewitching brand of night music.

"Why'd you put this song on?" he asked.

Her brows lifted. "'Hallelujah'?"

"Yeah."

"I love this song."

"You love a lot of songs."

Her smile looked confused. "I do."

"You seem to…" He cleared his throat, started over again. "To love a lot of things."

"Love?" She shrugged. "There's no reason not to. It's not like we're given a finite amount of love at birth."

"Oh yeah? You got enough to spare?" Clay didn't realize until he'd said the words quite how they'd sound, but once they were out, their meaning spun dangerously in the air between them.

"You just going to stand there?" George asked, looking up at him through her lashes. It occurred to him that she was toying with him. He was dying inside, or coming awake, or something equally painful, and this woman was *flirting*.

"May I have this dance?" he asked, holding out his hand to the strains of heavenly guitar.

George stood. "Are you sure this is a good idea?"

"What?" Clay asked. "You think this is more dangerous than what we did on the steps? In the shower? Your bed? Your goddamn office? It's just a dance," he lied.

She looked at him, her eyes big and liquid. "It's never just anything with us, Clay, is it?"

God, he loved the sound of his name on her lips.

He pulled her into his arms, probably too warm for this heat, but so elemental that temperature didn't matter. *Your own skin is always just right, after all.* Slowly, he moved, and their bodies shifted together to the sad, sad music, with nobody but a cat and bats and a million little insects to witness them.

Her head felt perfect on his chest, over his collarbone, and he danced—something he'd never thought to do again.

Finally, *finally*, the song came to its mournful end, and they stilled, standing together, breathing—just breathing. And, through the deafening white noise, he could feel one thing perfectly: the beating of this woman's heart against his.

"*Jesus,* lady," Clay whispered into the top of her head. "What the hell are you doing to me?"

Clay kissed her on the porch, in the kitchen, and by the front door, leaving her waiting, dazed, when he ran out to his truck for something. Then, again on the stairs, a shivering flashback to two nights before. He filled her with wonder, this big man with his rough hands and hard eyes, whose lips were plush and tender, too soft to make sense, but perfect, perfect against hers.

He urged her up the last few steps, then into her room, where clothes started coming off, and they landed on her bed in a messy, moaning heap, nothing but underwear separating them.

"I can't…" his gruff voice started, and she knew, she knew exactly what he meant, but she couldn't either. She couldn't get enough, wanted to consume him, eat him, pour him inside her, meld and melt and come apart with him. Her hands on him made him groan until he moved them off.

"You know I can't. Can't last if you touch me like that."

"Like what?"

"Like you mean it."

George stilled, eyes hurting, lungs tight, breath scraping roughly against her throat.

"I do mean it, Clay."

"Fuck." His eyes slid back and forth over hers, and something passed between them. He dipped his hips, letting his erection slide against her panties; even through the cotton, she was wet.

Kissing again, crazed, her hands all over him, despite his protests, stroking taut shoulders, enjoying the thick muscles of his arms, and somehow managing to avoid the places where his skin was chafed and burned from the laser.

"Good. So fucking good," he muttered hotly against the side of her face as their sexes came together, the rhythm perfect, the feel utterly explicit.

And then, his underwear was shoved down and hers pushed aside, and George groaned at the feel of *him*, *there*. Slick and sliding and swollen and, Jesus, her breasts were sensitive, tight and painful and absolutely dying for his touch.

It'd never been like this. Never. Not in high school with Dylan Dean, not in her marriage bed. Never.

He leaned back, his eyes glittering in the lamplight. Clay grasped one of her legs and lifted it, bit the calf, and let his eyes travel from her face to her sex, where they stayed to watch him work and work and work through all that wetness her body had created.

Never before, she thought, drinking in the sight of him, her body dying for more of a taste.

"Fuck me, Clay," she said and, with satisfaction, watched as the intense focus in his features fell apart.

17

"STAY THERE," CLAY SAID AND WATCHED WITH satisfaction as she complied. He got up, eager as a goddamn kid, yanked his shorts all the way off, and reached for the plastic bag he'd brought in from his truck. And Christ, her eyes on him made him thicker, harder. He ripped the bag open and pulled a zip tie from it, then stilled when he saw her eyes change. From lust to curiosity but, he was gratified to note, no fear.

"What are you doing?" She sat up.

"I have to stop hurting you."

"What? You're not—"

"I almost fucking choked you last night, George. Not gonna do that again. It's the only way I can make sure." The tightness in his belly felt like guilt, shame, excitement. He wanted her, but he couldn't risk disappearing into his head again, coming to only to find he'd hurt her. The bite mark still visible on her neck was proof enough of the damage he could do.

She caught his eyes, and for a few seconds, he could see her decide.

"So, if you're all trussed up…" she said, an evil glint in her eye.

He pulled the tie on, hard, and tightened it with his teeth. "Get a condom. Put it on me."

Without a word, she leaned back to grab one, but she just held it in her hand and waited.

"How's your back?"

"Fine."

"Can you lie on it?"

"Come on. Please just—"

"I'm in charge?"

Oh fuck. Those words. "Yeah." He swallowed the instinct that didn't want to let him give up power and settled onto the bed, allowing the excitement to take over.

"Whatever I want?" she asked, clearly into this, whatever it was.

"Yeah. Like when we're in your office. I'm up on one of those tables."

All traces of indecision left her face, and she looked purely turned on—that bright-red flush she got high and dark on her cheeks. "Oh, kinky," she whispered. "I'll have my wicked way with you."

"Doesn't feel quite right without the fluorescent lighting," Clay said. He was actually joking, which was a miracle, considering he was fucking tied up—which maybe hadn't been the best idea after all, considering the way he responded to feeling trapped. He went on, "And that sexy paper sticking to my back."

"Okay, so what do you want me to—"

"You could open up that package for starters."

With a nod, she knelt above him, grasped the condom, fumbled it, dropped it on the bedspread, and reached for it again before letting her head fall forward through a couple of deep breaths. Then she lifted up to look him straight in the eye. "*I'm* in charge."

Clay hesitated, then gave a quick nod. "You're the boss."

"I want to touch you."

Feeling like he'd already crossed over to that place he'd gone when she'd touched him in her office, he said, "Do it."

"What happens when I touch you, Clay? What do you feel? Does it hurt?"

A flash: leaning over the back of the chair at the Sultans' clubhouse, the medicinal ink stink strong in his nostrils, thankfully beating out the usual smells of beer and puke and piss. The wild beat of thrash metal hot in his ears, overlaid by the buzzing of the tattoo machine. It was the moment he'd waited for, the milestone he'd worked so hard toward—he was in. And he was proving it by letting that fucker ink their goddamned blazon on his back. Around him, guys laughed and went about their business, but inside, Clay had felt every prick of the filthy needle like splinters in his soul, the ink a poison he'd never get rid of. This was it. This hellfire and damnation spread across his skin, thinner than body armor, but ten times more effective.

Somewhere close by, a softer touch, incongruously layered onto the ugly memory. Caresses along his arms, his shoulders, and he struggled, the memory slipping into another one—the stink of decay, the buzz of flies, Kathy's dead eyes and—

"Clay," said a voice in his ear, clear and strong and clean. There came a press of warm lips to his face, his neck, his shoulder and chest. A tongue painting a stripe along his abdomen, warm breath on his cock. Fuck, one of the club hangers-on. He didn't want to, because Carly, Carly had been like this, and her memory—

"It's okay, Clay." A soft, soft cheek close to his, lips tender and hot against his ear, a whisper. "It's okay, love."

Feminine flesh against him, beside him. Nothing weighing him down. His breath came easier. Humming, fingers trailing. "This is for Carly, isn't it? *Mercy*," the voice asked as perfectly cool palms trailed lightly over his stubbled, scabbed-up chest. *Her* palms. George, who had the softest touch he'd ever felt. The only woman who'd ever gotten this far under his skin. He wanted her there.

He wanted her *here* and wanted to be here with her.

A light tweak to his nipple drove goose bumps skittering along his body and brought him back to the room. He could feel it in his balls and all the way to his toes.

"And this. It's about vengeance. I've seen these before," she said as her breast slid along his side, her nails running a trail down his arm, over the plastic at his wrists, to grasp his hand. She was so small, her fingers fragile, bones so easy to break. So *fucking* vulnerable.

A groan escaped Clay's mouth, and he recognized it for pleasure rather than the pain he'd been channeling from memories long gone.

His hips lifted unconsciously, showing her how hard he was.

"Hurts," he muttered.

She stilled. "Should I stop?"

"God no. Just…go lower. Please."

Her voice was sultry when she chuckled and slid

down his body, let her breath heat his dick even more, made him feel like he'd bust something if she didn't take him in—her mouth, her body, her palm; he didn't care.

"Fuck me, George. Please," he begged, and this time, she gave him something—her hand—a crumb. Just barely enough to tide him over.

Clay's body was a war zone. She knew that. She'd known it the first time he'd come to see her, but…seeing him like this, arms tied together in front of him, the rest of him splayed out, open and exposed, George felt so many things for him. He was beautiful in his pain, his vulnerability, and she wanted to hold that, to savor it, to protect it. Such a strange notion from someone who was half the man's size.

She caught his mouth in a kiss, deep, obscene, and openmouthed. The kind of kiss she remembered from high school, the kind fueled by hormones and youthful excitement, illicit desires she hadn't even begun to understand.

Clay augmented her frenzy with his own, punctuated with dirty, little, helpless sounds that made her even hotter.

"Put the condom on me, Georgette," he said. Her blood grew thick, heavy, and she was wet with wanting the man. She ignored him, enjoying the power, liking how in charge she felt, and wanting to abuse her position, just a little. Just to help him forget.

With a nudge, she bent his arms up, hands clasped as if in prayer. She lifted a leg and straddled his long, thick body, the condom crinkling loudly beneath her knee. Wasn't this what being in charge was about? Making it last, relishing the feel of him? Torturing him in the best possible way? Letting her eyes take in his tragic beauty, one follicle, one pore at a time?

And so she did. His breathless *aahs* feeding her, she explored, took him in, ate him up. There was nothing clinical about the way she touched him, although she couldn't help the occasional diagnosis. Under her tender ministrations, the big, cagey man started to let go, his body loosening and tightening not out of fear, she hoped, or anxiety, but with pleasure.

And she didn't just use her hands, which was a revelation all of its own. She touched him with her mouth and her nose; she ran her whole body up his, climbing him, luxuriating in the rasp of his skin against hers. Her breasts were tools too, softer and sensitive in a wholly different way. And he liked that. She could tell, because his breathing got asthmatic, and he bit her ear when she got too close. Nipples, lightly run across his chest, then fed to him, one at a time. He devoured her until it hurt, and still, she was loathe to pull away.

But when she did, it was worth it, because he got mad, truly pissed off. Threatening her with awful, little things like "Don't you move away from me" and "I'll fucking get you, George. Just wait. Wait till I get my hands on you." And contrary to everything Georgette Hadley had ever believed about healthy, well-balanced relationships, those dire threats made her hotter, stronger, more turned on. Especially when he added a helpless "Please" at the end.

Lord, that dialed everything up another notch, and she glanced down to see the wetness left behind on his chest, the way her spread thighs pulled her open to his view, crushing her vulva to his body. No, no, not her vulva. Too medical for what was likely the least medical moment of her life. And oh, the terribly *explicit* way his eyes took it all in—her bottom and her...her *cunt* pressed against his chest, right over that dark ink. And she was open, wide open to him. With his arms bound, he couldn't move, couldn't budge, and she had him. Slowly rocking above him, rubbing herself so she could actually feel his nipple against her clit, she took every little poisonous word, every little threat, every frustrated bump of his cock against her bottom, and soaked it up.

And his eyes, oh... *Look at them.* No longer crushed brown marbles, they were all black pupil, with a crazy lining—some undiscovered planet, its rings peeking around the edge. Like sunrise, like discovery. Fresh and beautiful and completely unexplored—and suddenly, she felt a bright, frightening swell of emotion so overwhelming that she kissed him to hide it. Not that a kiss could cover up something this deep and shattering. Although wasn't there a certain satisfying irony in trying to hide something as big as love behind a kiss?

∽⦿∼

Clay had never believed in the term "making love." He'd always figured it was an invention by people who didn't know how good a hard fuck could be. But this wasn't even a fuck. This was touching, just touching.

And now that he was living it—the quiet, soft touches, the tenderness of her face, mixed with the obscene way she rubbed herself against him. Goddamn, the tenderness was un-fucking-bearable—he loved it, wanted more, needed it to end. And so he threatened, told her all the nasty things he'd do to get back at her. He lifted his hips as she finally slid down and brought her mouth close to his dick.

"Suck it," he said, chopping the romance in half.

"Mmm" was her only response—the only thing she'd said for the past half hour or three hours or however long she'd been taunting him.

"It's fucking torture, George. Suck me or put the condom on or—"

"Or what?" she asked with a hard, feminine edge to her voice. Shit. Shit, that wasn't George. That wasn't how she talked to him. She was kind and patient and—

The crinkle of foil stilled him—everything but his heaving chest, his lungs pumping behind his too-small rib cage—and slowly, excruciating slowly, she rolled the rubber over his erection. It hurt, his skin protesting the pressure of latex, his balls already tight with anticipation. He glanced down and almost came at the stark, filthy contrast of her fingers against the angry red of his too-hard cock.

"Does it hurt, Clay?" she asked in that new voice of hers. "It looks almost like it hurts."

"Yes," he rasped out with a thrust of his hips—up into nothing. "Please, George. Please."

Her eyes caught his, and she shook her head slowly, teasing again and almost pissing him off for making him want her like this and then, just—

George rose above him, lifted high onto her knees, and looked down at him through narrowed eyes. She grabbed him in her fist and slowly, slowly impaled herself. She was wet—the evidence of how absolutely soaking she was glistened on his chest—but still, the fit was tight. Good tight. Too good.

"Fuck, fuck, *fuck*," he said. "Too fast, too fast, I'm gonna…" He finished on a groan as she lifted up again, the strain visible in those tender, lush thighs. Clay raised his joined hands to her chest, used his left one to lift a breast, to enjoy its weight before focusing on the nipple. Shit, he wanted to bite her, mark her skin. Like a tattoo, only real. *Mine.*

Another slide down, and he couldn't stop the sounds that escaped his mouth, all pathetic, little whimpers, uncontrollable and weak. Goddamn, she was killing him. Another slide up, another down, and all he could do was hold on to one of her breasts and lift his hips up, trying to get himself deeper. *Fuck it, fuck this.*

George said, "I want your hands all over me." He couldn't respond, just watched her move up and down, so steady, sweet, and slow. She tore his heart out every time he got caught up in her eyes. "Let me cut off the tie. Let me do it."

"I can't, George. I'm not—"

She stopped moving, put a hand on his chin, and forced him to face her head-on. "You're a good man, Clay. The best man I've ever known. I trust you." She moved in for a long, deep kiss and then leaned back. "I'm asking you to trust yourself."

Christ, she was killing him. He felt her words—her trust—like a direct shot to the chest. *The heart, you ass-hole. You feel it in your fucking heart.*

"Will you do that, baby?" she whispered, so much emotion in her eyes he could feel it on his skin, under his skin, piercing his heart. "Will you trust yourself?"

He started to shake his head and then stopped. "What if I hurt you?"

It was her smile that convinced him—serene and honest. "You won't hurt me. You don't know how."

Everything inside him loosened: a release, a torrential downpour, epic and uncontrollable. There was no time to find the scissors. Instead, he let out a roar—it felt good, like busting through a dam—and wrenched his wrists straight into his chest, hard enough to hurt, hard enough to snap the zip tie in two and send her back off of him.

He followed her up, one hand on the back of her neck, easing her down, rolling over her. He needed to surround her. To own her and be owned. To undo her the way she'd undone him, from the inside out.

He pulled her open with his palms, feeling how rough he was against her perfect skin. The sight of her— giving, trusting, wanting as much as he wanted her— made his cock pulse of its own accord, and then, before he could come in the goddamned condom, he grasped himself and thrust back into her warmth. Right where he belonged.

At her long, low groan, he used every ounce of control to stop, pause, suspended, breathless, waiting, waiting. Her body backed into him; calm, clean, pristine George Hadley *backed her ass up*, taking him into her faster, harder than he would have done, and it was exactly what he needed. What he'd been waiting for.

A fucking animal. A beast. He pumped, driving, driving, letting go in a way he didn't remember doing ever. Smacking sounds, wet and obscene as her body accepted every one of his thrusts. Their slick sweat and excitement making it an exercise in precision when, with the strength of his hips, he lost her a time or two, slid off, fell to the side. *No more of that shit*, his mind decided. Clay leaned forward and grabbed her, one hand snaking beneath to clasp that same perfect left breast, and the other winding through her too-goddamned-short hair to finally settle at the nape of her neck, where it met her shoulder. His fingers sank into the muscle there, urging her to stay.

"Don't move, baby." The words escaped his fucked-up brain, and rather than offend her, they seemed to turn her on. She disobeyed, ramming her ass harder into him. "You don't ever listen, do you, George? Too nice. Always trusting. Never fucking—"

Her lost, little moan cut him off, and all he could do was hold on as she tightened around him. He held on for a minute as she came with a long, low *ooh*. His body wanted to go with her, but he couldn't yet. He needed what little control he still held on to. To show her, maybe, that he could do it. Or maybe to prove it to himself.

Breaths tight, he waited until she was done before leaning over her and whispering into her ear, "You okay?"

With a slow nod, she lowered her upper body from her hands to her elbows, her shoulders sagging into the mattress, her ass lifting higher, pulling him in deeper.

"You sure? D'I hurt you?"

"You didn't hurt me, Clay," she said, and he shivered at the sound of his name on that raspy, sex-colored voice. "It was…so…good." Was she smiling? It sounded like she was smiling.

"I'm not done," he whispered, manic, urgent.

She chuckled at the panicky sound of his voice and shifted lazily back in invitation. "Do whatever you want. I'm…I'm spent."

"Are you sure? I—"

"Shut up and take me," she said, and he hesitated only briefly before deciding she meant it.

After that, it was easy to let himself go in her body. No memories, no flashbacks, no phantoms from his past. It took only a couple dozen thrusts before his balls tightened and his world narrowed to her body clasping his cock, and his hands pressing into her hips, his tight shout as he let go, deeply, inexorably, coming harder than he ever had in his life.

Face pressed into the bed, George couldn't even care that she was mouth-breathing, drooling a big, dark stain onto the sheets.

Behind her, Clay's hands spasmed a couple of times against her hips, and all George could think was how alive she felt. Her body was vital, awake like she couldn't remember since those rebellious high school years, and even then, she'd been in an adolescent daze, not…aware like this. *In* her skin.

This is me. The realization hit with a frightening jolt of clarity that stung her sinuses and blurred her vision. It had never been like this with Tom. Tom, ostensibly the love of her life, had never touched her this deeply, never roused this elemental beast inside of her. It made her sad. For him. He'd never gotten to have this.

Behind her, Clay pulled out, and she reached back to hold him inside her, his hips tight to hers.

"Don't go yet."

"Gotta get rid of the condom."

"Okay, just…" What? What did she want from him? She finally settled for "Kiss me."

The kiss was long and slow and deep. After a long time, Clay pulled away. "I want…" She waited for him to finish, and when he couldn't seem to manage more, she nodded.

"I know, baby. I know."

He sighed against her, relaxing into her body for a bit before finally pulling out and padding off to the bathroom.

She flopped down, encountering the sharply broken edges of the zip tie, and a shiver ran through her, a sense memory of that precise moment, when he'd busted out of his bindings, his muscles huge, his neck thick and veined with strain, his strength superhuman.

But his face… She didn't think she'd seen anyone look so lost. The contrast between all that physical strength, so certain and solid, and that face, so unsure, but hopeful and innocent…

She'd never seen anything like it, and the image brought a new contraction to her belly, hard and unexpected, but nowhere near as powerful as the ache she felt in her chest. Good Lord, would she ever get rid of this ache in her chest?

❧

Jam asked, "Where we headed, Boss?" and Ape got a shiver down his back at the sound of that word. *Boss.* Yeah, that felt right.

He stood up from the diner table with a belch and patted his belly.

"Virginia Beach." *And this had better be it*, he thought, *or heads are gonna roll.*

Because he was tired of hauling ass every day, tired

of sleeping in shitty motel rooms, tired of running from one dead end to another.

It was time to find that traitor asshole. "And if this ain't for real, we're gonna have to pay some friendly visits."

There was no reaction from Jam, who took everything in stride. A perfect right-hand man. They were close; he could feel it. They just needed to tie up this loose end, and then he could move on running this club as it was meant to be run. Like a goddamned efficient business.

He popped a couple of antacids and burped again. Fuck, what he wouldn't do for a home-cooked meal, though. The injustice of having to suffer through another greasy spoon was one more thing he heaped onto the back of that Navarro fuck.

He itched to get his hands on him. Him and everything he cared about, because goddamn, he couldn't wait to see that cocksucker suffer.

18

It was easy to pretend that everything was fine with George on his side. She spread Vaseline over his back before leaving for work, and he sank into the experience, soaked up the tenderness, lost himself in the novelty of being… What? Loved?

According to her, his body was crusting over right on schedule. First blisters, she'd said, then scabs. His fingers weren't doing quite as well, since he spent so much time working, moving them, washing his hands.

He didn't care about the scars, he realized. It was the ink that bothered him the most—like a poison deep inside. He just wanted it out.

Clay worked on the house, telling himself he was paying her back, giving him an excuse to stick around, but it felt more like staking some kind of visible claim on her.

After a good few hours, the clapboard was coming along nicely, and he decided to head into town, get some clean clothes, and stock up on a few things he'd need the next day. It almost seemed normal when Sheriff Mullen caught sight of him coming out of the hardware store and called him over to his cruiser. He mentioned how much the kids had loved having him teach class the weekend before and told him he'd be needing him for the next few weeks. It felt natural to let himself get roped into it. And somehow, as he made his way across the street to the supermarket for a six-pack of beer and a bottle of wine, nodding to one of the coffee shop kids and helping an old lady unwind her leash from around one of the trees on Main Street, Blackwood felt a little bit like home.

But it wasn't until he parked in front of George's house, walked up the steps, and saw her working away in the kitchen, saw her expression when she caught sight of him through the glass, that Clay realized he was dangerously close to wanting this life—for real.

～❧～

Again, Clay held George after dinner in a slow, candlelit dance. Then they washed the dishes before heading upstairs for a cooling shower and finally her bed, where his body enveloped hers and his lips trailed hot and hungry across her skin.

The room was dark, the only light streaming in from the hall. He was intimidating above her, his beauty all the greater for being slightly off, ragged with skin that had seen better days, hair starting to grow out from that short, almost military cut he'd sported when he arrived.

George let her eyes rove across the landscape of his skin—a map of his past. From his crushingly lovely face to where his feet hung off the foot of her bed. If only she understood what he'd been through, then maybe she could help him, maybe she could make him forget.

"What does this mean?" she asked, letting her fingers ghost over the face on his shoulder.

"It's an Inca death mask. From Peru. Like my father. Me and my sister."

George stilled.

"Why do you have that on your body?"

"For the same reason I have all the others."

She raised her brows but didn't ask, waiting him out instead.

"The other side's the Gosforth Cross, and inside, it's Víðarr slaying Fenrir, taking vengeance for his father's death."

"And this one?" George asked, touching the skull but fairly sure of the answer now.

"Santa Muerte. Safe delivery in the afterlife."

"For Carly." She leaned back to take in his body in its entirety. "Every single drop of ink is for her, isn't it?"

Another slide of her eyes stopped halfway up, on the patchy, red burn scar on his side, the melted swirl of skin and ink. With some fractional ablative laser resurfacing, she could help him. Laser scar therapy could make it—

No. He wouldn't want that, would he? This man would want to keep it. To remember.

"But the worst is this," she said, letting her fingers linger. When he didn't answer immediately, she realized he couldn't possibly feel with that level of damage. She remembered the story he'd told her and winced. "You did this one."

His eyes opened. They were hard, almost black tonight as they focused on her face. The air sparked with their connection. "I did."

She pictured him doing it and her body jolted. All

thoughts of lasers and therapy obliterated by the harsh image. There was nothing pretty about this man's existence.

Leaving one hand on his side, George nudged up closer to his body, letting the other palm rest over his heart, which beat fast and strong.

"Is that where you go?"

"What?"

Her trailing fingers explored the topography of that traumatic scar, this time as a woman, not a doctor. "When you have your…attacks. Do you go back to that moment?"

He jerked once with what might have been a snort of laughter. "Hell no. The burn was nothing."

"Oh." She continued to touch him, stroke him—so, so very gentle. He seemed to sink into it, vibrating on a different level, a different plane almost. She wet her lips. "And what about when I touch you? Where do you go?" she asked.

"Go? Dunno," he responded, already dreamy, already gone.

"But it's good, right?"

"Told you, baby. Best thing. Ever. But I can't hold my shit together." He shook his head, stopped, and pulled her to him, her face tucked into the soft part of his neck. It felt intimate, but George suspected he'd moved to hide, rather than to bring her closer. "And it kinda hurts."

George tried to pull away, to look at him, but he held her close. Her words were muffled. "It still hurts? Your skin's—"

"No, baby. It hurts other things. If that makes sense." His mouth opened against her temple, the wet heat of his breath oddly arousing. "Of all the shit I've gone through, the worst part's when you touch me. The pain, I can handle; the other shit's fine. It's the…the soft stuff I'm not built for. You know, the feeling that something could be better. Something like hope, I guess, which everybody knows is, well, hopeless."

George opened her mouth in protest, but he cut her off, his voice hard. "Can you honestly look at me and say you see someone with a future?"

"You don't think you deserve a life?"

He lay flat back on his pillow, pulling her even tighter to his side. "I think we're all allowed a certain number of mistakes. I'm pretty sure I've reached my quota."

She let that sink in, wondering just what he'd gotten up to that made him feel like he didn't deserve another chance.

"Who were you before?"

"What?" He blinked at her, not understanding.

"Before your…before Carly died?"

"Doesn't matter, babe. That kid's gone."

"But maybe it does matter. It does! If you want to have a life again," George said, her voice a little too close to pleading for comfort. "Like, maybe you're supposed to forgive your young self for his stupid mistakes."

"Have you?"

"What?"

"Forgiven your young self?"

George stilled. "Sure."

"Yeah?" he said, his breath moving the hair close to her ear. "You all good with your past mistakes?"

It took a minute for George to realize she wasn't actually breathing. Another second to force her body to start up again, to take in air.

"You must've been perfect, though, right? An angel."
He shifted back and caught her eyes with his. "Perfect
little Georgette Hadley."

"Jones."

"Huh?"

"Georgette Jones. Hadley's my married name."

"Oh."

"No, she wasn't perfect. I wasn't perfect."

"You're damn near perfect now."

She snorted. "Right."

"Can't imagine you being bad." He settled back,
maybe seeing the walls she'd thrown up between them.

"Yeah, well… Would you change who you were?"

"Me?" he asked. "Hell yes."

"What about now?"

"What do you mean?"

George asked, "Today. Right now. Are you who you
want to be?"

"You want the truth, George?" With a creak of
springs, he rolled into her, pulled her body toward his,
forced her to meet him head-on. "I'd want to be somebody *you'd* like."

"I already like you," George said in a voice she'd
never heard herself use: husky and warm and clearly
from the lungs of a far sexier woman.

"Yeah? Not sure I'm worthy of that." His lips curled
down, and he rolled back again, his hands covering his
face, his voice coming out hollow. "But then, who the
fuck am I to think I'm allowed to be happy? Huh? To
be normal when my little sister's all alone, rotting six
feet underground?"

That sentiment was so close to what George felt that

she could hardly breathe. *Yes*, she thought. *Who the fuck am I to be happy again with Tom dead and buried? And what about my baby?*

Rather than talk again, rather than try to convince him with words that he was worthy of happiness and other good things, she leaned over and grabbed one of the hard, plastic zip ties from her bedside table. Slowly, affectionately, she wrapped it around his wrists, met his devastated eyes, and tightened it so he couldn't move. In theory, because they both knew how flimsy the ties were in the face of his strength.

After that, it was easy to put her arms around him, to take a little of his weight. It was simple to press him onto his back. Slowly, she crawled down his body, ignoring the way he tightened up, ignoring his protests and soaking up his sighs.

"Let me, let me," she said, nosing around his compliant hands to kiss his flat, lightly furred belly, nuzzling him there. "Please. Let me." She shushed him, and he shut his eyes on a sigh.

God, his body. The warmth and the energy of him, pliable flesh and compact bone, then the in-between firmness of muscle. She loved it all—every little bit of him, every scar, every tiny indentation was licked and suckled and made love to. At first, he shut his eyes and bore it, like torture, but eventually, he joined her there, in her room, on her bed, in his body. His protests turned to pleasured moans and begging.

"Untie me," he finally said in a hoarse voice.

Their eyes met over the landscape of his body, and she shivered at the lust she saw there—and something else. Something like fear.

"You going to behave?" George asked.

"No," he said with a smirk.

She shivered. "Then I guess not."

Back to the table for a condom, which she rolled down his erection, watching the way his mouth opened and his eyes burned, his cheeks hot to the touch.

Slowly, so deliberately, George straddled him, taking care to keep her weight on her knees, her eyes never leaving his face.

His penis was hot in her fist, searing at the entrance to her body, but his expression was hotter. It burned a hole in her soul, ate her up, and she wanted that, wanted to help shoulder his pain. She sank onto him, slow enough to enjoy it, to recognize the fit, the way their bodies came together then slid apart, that first friction unbearably sweet.

"So good," he muttered, his eyes up, on her face. "How d'you do that? Slays me every time."

All George could do was nod as she worked her thighs, clenched and rose, up and down, watching Clay strain at the zip tie, wondering if he'd decide to bust out of it. It was almost a game now, unlike before. She knew he could get out, but maybe he didn't want to. Maybe he liked her foisting tenderness on him.

Eventually, when her legs started to give out and his face lost its clarity, George reached down and rubbed herself to completion, the climax so languorous and full of love that she leaned down and kissed him, enjoying the clench of his jaw and the guttural noises he made as he came.

It took forever to come down from whatever transcendental cloud they'd disappeared on, but Clay's voice finally broke through.

"Got scissors up here, or am I gonna have to dislocate my shoulder to get outta this thing?"

She cut him out, and they lay together for a bit, this new thing between them. Fresh and raw, unfinished, but gleaming with potential.

After a bit, Clay got up and went to the bathroom. He was quiet when he came back in, and it took her a while to notice him standing stiffly in the doorway, looking... regretful? Sheepish? Oh, no. No, no, no, this wasn't how it was supposed to be. Not anymore.

"Condom broke," he said, his voice tight.

She swallowed, not quite getting it at first. That wasn't what she'd been bracing for. "What?" She ran a hand down between her legs to where she was, admittedly, soaking.

"Didn't just break. The damned thing tore in half."

"Oh" was all George said as her fingers ran through the wetness, lifted it to her nose, sniffed, and... Yes. It certainly did appear to be... "Oh no," she gasped, her throat too small for air, much less words. It was Tuesday. Tuesday, which made tomorrow...

He was talking, words floating to her, saying things like "safe" and "tested" and "screening." But it didn't matter. None of it mattered, because here she was, her ovaries rife with eggs, flourishing like the weeds in her garden, and she'd gotten herself possibly impregnated by this man.

This man, instead of the man she'd been married to. The man whose baby she was supposed to have.

"Are you on birth control?" His words sank in, and George lifted her head, blinking, still fuzzy.

"No," she said on a giddy burble of laughter. "No,

I'm definitely not on birth control. Definitely, definitely not." The laughter morphed into something less pleasant, and she considered rolling up into a ball on her bed but realized she'd do better to get up, walk around, run to the bathroom, where she peed and then got into the bathtub, ignoring the big, sweaty, crushed-looking man standing in the doorway as she ran the shower. She'd clean herself. She'd clean it, and then tomorrow, she could go to her IUI appointment and—

George stood in the shower, staring dully at the tiles, her eyes dry in their sockets, despite the water running over her and the tears throbbing to get out, knowing how badly she'd messed up. She'd let her libido rule her, allowed the momentary madness with this wholly inappropriate man to decide her future and that of the baby Tom Hadley would never, ever have. The baby she'd promised to his parents, the baby she'd prepared for in every way—her job, her house, the garden, the spare bedroom, painted pale yellow and ready to furnish. Somewhere in the craziness, Clay got in with her, said words that she couldn't hear through the throbbing guilt and shame, and held her in his strong arms.

~ও~

Clay turned off the water, wrapped George up in a towel, and led her back to her room, leaving a trail of wet footprints behind them as they went.

"You wanna talk about what just happened?" he asked.

She shook her head and walked into her closet to get dressed. She was hiding from him. *Hiding*, after everything they'd done.

"We done sharing for tonight?" he asked, going for cavalier but sounding silly instead.

"Yes." The closet was big, one of those old ones with the slanted roof, and George's words echoed from within. "No."

Standing by her bed, in her perfect, ladylike room, tainted now with the smell of sex, he voiced his main concern. "Was it something I did? Did I hurt you?"

"What?" There was a pause before she emerged from her closet, in a stained UVA Cavs T-shirt and a threadbare pair of plaid boxer shorts, to give him a hug—sorely needed, he realized—with her arms finally around him. "Oh, no, Clay. No. No."

"Good" was all he said, but that one word was just the tip of the iceberg of relief that swept through him. Not only because he hadn't hurt her, but also thanks to the hug. The hug felt damn good after everything that had gone down between them tonight.

Her head pressed to his chest, she asked, "Is there any wine left?"

"About half the bottle."

"Good. I could use a glass right now."

"I'll go get—"

"No." She stopped him. "You get dressed. Come find me when you're done."

Clay let her go, pulling on his clothes with a sort of finality he hadn't thought he'd experience anytime soon, like he'd better not leave a sock behind, because he wouldn't be seeing it again if he did. The way she was acting didn't feel right. It felt like he'd fucked up, with that condom breaking. Which made sense. And it was fine, of course, because who the fuck would want his baby anyway, right?

She'd told him to get dressed, which sounded an awful lot like good-bye.

He padded downstairs in his socks, saw his filthy work boots where he'd left them beside the front door, and considered slipping them back on and just taking off. That was probably what would happen anyway, he reasoned. Why sit through the painful conversation they were bound to have if the endgame would be the same regardless?

"I'm going out back. I've got your wine," her voice called from the kitchen, and instead of taking the cowardly route and leaving—which she'd no doubt ream him for anyway—he moved toward the kitchen. He'd miss this place, he realized with a twist of something new in his gut, something sharper than the churning that had been his constant companion.

The screened porch was empty, but beyond it, at the far end of the garden, came the bright flare of a match, followed by the glow of lanterns being lit. By the time he'd crunched his way over the flagstones and past the chicken coop to the back of the yard, she had a few of those tiki things going, the flames mesmerizing in the night.

"Never been this far back," he said, checking out the seating situation. "Smells like lemon."

"Citronella. Against the mosquitoes."

"That shit actually work?"

She shrugged, the movement barely visible in that enormous T-shirt she hid beneath like a tent, but he could see her lips, plush and sweet, turn up in a smile. "Even if it doesn't, I like the smell. And the idea."

He nodded, leaned forward to take his wineglass off

the low metal table between them, and peered around. "Nice out here."

"It's where I come to think," she said, sounding dry and sad.

"Is that a fountain?" he asked, latching on to anything besides the pain in her voice.

"Yes."

"Hardly hear it with that ruckus."

"The cicadas, you mean? Do they still upset you?"

Clay considered her question. Did the bugs upset him? He hated them and their constant racket, but he wouldn't say they upset him. And then he remembered the night he'd come out here with her, the overwhelming swimming-in-it shrieking in his ears, so shrill it had rattled his veins; how happy the stupid things had seemed to make her—how completely overwhelmed he'd felt by it all. By her, more than the bugs.

And now, today… "No," he answered in surprise. "Guess I've gotten used to the little bastards." Something sparked in the air above him, and Clay blinked. "Whoa."

At George's raised brow, he asked, "You didn't see that?"

Her head turned in the dark, seeking out whatever it was, and finally came back to him. "Fireflies?"

"That was a firefly?"

"You've never seen one?"

"Guess not," Clay said, taking a gulp of wine and sitting back. *I don't belong here*, he thought with an unexpected jolt of pain. "Look, I'm sorry about the condom. I…I didn't know. It wasn't like I—"

"It's not about you, Clay." George took a deep, audible breath, then leaned back to look at the sky. Above her head, stars—actual stars—twinkled, and something swooped by. "I've been on hormones for a couple of weeks now." She did a weird laugh that came out small and choked. "So I could have my dead husband's baby."

Clay almost dropped his glass. He almost stood up, almost stalked right out into the woods behind the house, away. But he didn't. He held on; he listened.

"Tomorrow, I'm supposed to have IUI. Intrauterine insemination. A very expensive procedure during which they insert the semen right into your cervix. It...ups the chances." He watched her swig back her wine and fill her glass again. "He died ten years ago, and this month, his semen reaches its sell-by date. Labs won't keep it longer than ten years. Well, some will, but we took the cut-rate option back then, assuming he'd survive the cancer, but now..."

Another sigh, another long, deep look at the stars, and Clay followed an unexpected instinct—he stood, dragging his chair along the flagstones to where she sat, settling in beside her, giving her his warmth or presence or something. He hesitated before putting an arm around her, but once he did, her head settled into the crook of his armpit, and he didn't regret it. How could he regret this feeling?

"Now, I'm supposed to get...fertilized." *Christ.* Clay stiffened and swallowed. "Like a barren piece of land or something. I've been prepping for it, so my body's this hormonal, egg-making machine, my ovaries are like grapefruits inside me, I feel bruised, and here I am, such an *idiot*, having...having intercourse with you. At first, I thought my attraction to you was from the...the treatment. But I didn't start ovulating until today. Right on schedule."

"We did use—"

"That's not the point, is it, Clay? I mean, yes, we used a condom. The fact that it broke is…" She stopped, eyes shut tight, and sucked in a shaky, painful-sounding breath before going on. "I loved Tom. He was the funniest, most sarcastic…" She sighed again, and this time, he could feel the weight of everything she carried with her. But he was jealous too, which made him feel like a complete ass.

He tightened his arm, and she went on. "We froze his sperm right after we found out about the…cancer. We figured we'd have it. For later, you know, depending on how treatment affected his body? He signed the papers, and we went on, dealing with things. But…he didn't. Get better. Well, he did, and then it got worse, and then…" She swallowed, hard. "Then suddenly, one day, he's gone. And he's left me all alone. *All by myself.*" Those last words, the way she said them, came out quiet but angry.

"I'm sorry, George," said Clay, feeling completely inadequate.

"Oh, you don't have to be. I mean, thank you. But…" She opened her eyes and turned her sad smile at him. It looked thin around the edges, but even sad, she was so fucking gorgeous it hurt. He cleared his throat but couldn't seem to dislodge whatever stayed stuck in there. "I've spent the last ten years being sorry enough for both of us. Anyway, I forgot about Tom's…Tom's semen, until… Maybe a year or so later, I got this letter in the mail, addressed to him. That happened sometimes. I mean, it wasn't like I'd sent out a notice to all the companies that send you junk mail, you know? Like,

'My husband's dead, so please don't send him anything because it Breaks. My. Heart.'"

Her voice reverberated through his chest, and Clay expected her to cry or something. But she didn't. Despite the wet heat of the air around them, she sounded dry, her throat clicking as she swallowed. "Not to mention, we… I… God, I got so many bills. Medical bills, every month. Constantly. I paid what I could, selectively, you know? I threw them into the pile and didn't look at the bills until they were yellow or red with these big *Overdue* stamps on the outside. So, at some point, I finally opened the one from the lab, thinking it was just another stupid company asking me to pay for something that hadn't saved my husband's life…but it wasn't. It wasn't. It took a while for it to sink in when I saw it, but I…I'll never forget that. That moment of hope. I'd been such an idiot as a kid. Gotten pregnant, had an abortion. Then, Tom and I never got the chance, and I thought… I was sure it was my just deserts."

"How so?"

"Punishment, you know? For ruining the one opportunity I'd had."

"How old were you?"

"When I had the abortion?" He nodded. "Fifteen."

"Jesus, George. You still beating yourself up over that?"

Even in the dark, Clay could see how big her eyes were when she turned them on him, how unnaturally bright and hollow. She didn't answer.

"Anyway, when that bill came, from the lab, I paid it right away, and then I…I slept with it." She laughed, the sound a little bitter. "Under my pillow. For days, I think.

Maybe longer. Okay, definitely longer. I talked to the lab and read the fine print, and apparently, he'd checked the box that said his sperm could be used posthumously." After another pause, she went on. "This was for him. And for his parents. And me too, because I wanted a baby. I want a baby. I couldn't afford it, with all the bills and then med school and…things kept getting in the way, and the time was never right. I kept putting it off. Career, house…chickens. I never felt ready, and then, a few months ago, the lab called and told me time was up, and I went right into treatment. I didn't think about it. I just did it. You can't take these things for granted, right?"

"Could you still go in? For your IUI thing?"

She seemed to consider. "I could. I could, but it might not be his baby. My body might already be… The baby could be…" The words spun between them. *Yours. It could be yours.*

"Oh," said Clay, his skin prickling. "Do you miss him?"

"Miss him?" She seemed to consider. "Not anymore. Not really. I mean, I think about him, but I don't like… talk to him or anything."

"Did you? Before?"

"I might have. A time or two."

A dark shape flew by overhead, and Clay asked, breaking the intensity of the moment, "What *are* those things?"

"What?"

"The crazy dive-bombers."

"What? Oh…bats."

"*Bats?*"

"Bats are good. They eat the bugs."

He watched the creatures swoop for a while,

crisscrossing the night sky. He took in the tiny insects, flashing like scattered Christmas lights. It was weird how calm he felt in the face of all the sights and sounds. In the face of her news. Of *her*.

"You're the first one," George said, lifting her head from the hollow of his arm.

"Hmm?"

"You're the first man I've been with. Since Tom."

He managed a calm, "Oh," but inside, things weren't so smooth. *Ten fucking years?* he thought. And then other questions he couldn't ask because he'd come off as a supreme asshole, but fuck if he didn't want to know. *How was I? How did I measure up?*

Instead, he sat there, let her lead.

"And I feel, on so many levels, that I've betrayed him." Her face, that perfect, calm, beautiful face was tortured when she met his eyes. "I've betrayed him."

"Should we…?" Clay swallowed, shame and nerves roiling in his gut like a hangover from the best sex of his life. "What do you want to do?"

"I want to finish this bottle of wine and go to bed." Her neck convulsed, pale and delicate against the dark, wooded backdrop. "Alone," she finished, turning away. "I'm sorry."

Clay rose, slugged back the contents of his glass to cover the prick of actual tears. He stood there, towering above her but about as low and inconsequential as one of those empty bug shells he crunched with every footfall.

Without a word, he turned and went back up to the house in just his socks. Weird how he hadn't noticed those fucking shells on his way out here. He'd have to pick them off the cotton before putting on his boots.

Every step, each crunch was like walking over his dead, hollow soul. Over and over again.

After putting on his shoes, he waited for a while, inside this house that smelled so strongly of home now. Fifteen minutes passed, and he understood. She was done with him.

They were done.

Footsteps heavy, Clay made his way outside to his truck, which was still full of shit from the hardware store—materials for her house. He should unload it all, leave it here for whoever she found to finish the job, but he didn't have the courage.

He drove, blindly, winding up outside the ABC store, where he bought a bottle of vodka, taking his first swig before he'd left the parking lot. His course had been set for the motel, or maybe just to leave town or something, but instead he found his truck climbing—up, up, to that overlook that kept drawing him back.

At the top, he backed up almost to the edge and sat on the tailgate, looking out over everything—over nothing.

It was dark, bats swooping above, fireflies sparking up the night. Those things that had been magic not so long ago were ugly now.

He pulled back more vodka, three or four big, long sips. The way he used to drink juice as a kid, racing his sister to the bottoms of their glasses. He'd always won those stupid contests.

He tried his best to feel betrayed, but... Who the hell could blame her? He couldn't, no matter how hard he tried.

It wasn't like she'd taken advantage of him. She'd been as messed up through the whole thing as he. Her perfect house, her homey life not a reflection of who she was, but of her absolution. Christ, they were screwed.

The bugs and bats and even the twinkling lights of Blackwood below made him think of her face, her voice so clogged with pain, the way she'd sat in that big T-shirt…how she'd hunched into his body and made him think he could protect her, make it better. He couldn't help picturing her pain.

She'd had a lot to lose by taking up with him, from the beginning. It had been a huge risk for her, being with a patient. Being with someone like him.

Jesus, he wondered, *when was the last time someone took a risk for me?*

I'm the one who risks. I risked everything.

For *revenge*.

The word should have felt noble. Instead, it felt small.

Sleep didn't come easily to George. She wished, more than anything, that she could have a long, hard cry, but tears remained elusive. Though she managed to close her eyes and lose herself in slumber, she awoke after less than an hour, almost expecting Clay to be there, waiting for her, needing her. Instead, she slept and woke, slept and woke, finally escaping to the bathroom only to face a puffy, sallow version of herself in the mirror—one she didn't have much respect for.

Being alone hadn't been what she'd really wanted. But how could you ask a man to stay and hold you after you'd talked about the other man in your life? The one whose baby you planned on having? She couldn't do that to Clay. She couldn't lead him on when everything else in her life was focused on Tom and the guilt of what she'd so easily given up. Losing Tom and trying to get him back. Sleeping with that stupid bill under her pillow for all those months, like a lost piece of him, suddenly found. A second chance. No—a third.

Rather than go back to bed, she decided to get up, call it a night, maybe head into the office early. Under the shower, she took inventory of the aches and pains she'd acquired in unfamiliar places—her lower back, her neck, her thighs...between her legs. With those reminders, it was impossible not to think about Clay and what they'd done together.

The way he'd made her feel.

And how do you think you made him feel, sending him away like that?

Horrible, she imagined, her words a harrowing echo come to haunt her over and over as she tried to sleep.

Alone, she'd said. *I'm sorry. Alone... I'm sorry.* Too bad it wasn't what she wanted at all.

19

By the time George's staff arrived at the clinic, she'd been there for hours, catching up on paperwork, reorganizing her office, and making pot after pot of fresh coffee until her hands shook like palsied leaves.

Finally, with the beginning of the official workday, she could lose herself in patient visits and forget about the mistakes she'd made last night. Mistakes and bad decisions. No wonder George kept away from people. As soon as she got involved, everything went to crap.

Self-sabotage?

At about lunchtime, she decided to stop feeling sorry for herself, to quit regretting things it was too late to change.

She'd just sat down with a box of rye crackers—the only edible thing left in her desk—when her office phone rang.

"Yes, Cindy?"

"I've got your mother-in-law on the line for you," her receptionist said.

George nearly slammed the phone down. *No, no, no. Not today. Not now.*

With a deep, shaky breath, she answered, "Thanks, Cindy. Put her through."

"Georgette?" came Bonnie's shaky voice.

"Hi there, Bonnie."

"Just calling to check in, make sure all's well."

"Yes. Yes, fine. Fine, fine," she said, sounding ridiculous.

"So, you've got the uh…procedure tonight. This evening, you said."

George swallowed, shut her eyes hard, wished for tears to wash the pain away. No, not the pain. The *guilt*.

"Yes," she said. "Tonight's the night."

A few seconds of silence passed before Bonnie went on. "Well, I'm thinking of you. I'm sure you'll… I'm certain that… Lord, what on earth is the right thing to say?"

George let out a dry, huffed laugh. "Good question. I have no idea."

Another pause before Bonnie went on. "You don't sound great, Georgette."

No response was possible. Breathing was about all she could manage.

"I… Whatever happens, dear, whatever happens is fine with me. With us. It's fine."

A lone tear dropped from George's eye and ran along her nose to her mouth.

She opened her mouth to talk, couldn't find a sound, swallowed, and then tried again. Nothing.

"All right, well, I hear they're callin' for rain tonight, George, so you're—"

She interrupted. "Thank you, Bonnie." A big breath in, and then she went on. "Thank you."

George hung up, sat in her desk chair, stared at

the framed mandala on her wall—a kaleidoscope of images—and waited for the rest of the tears to come. Nothing. Nothing at all.

Her phone buzzed, and she picked it up. After a brief pause where she knew she was supposed to say something, her receptionist said, "Mrs. Johnson's here for her annual."

"Yes" was all she could manage to say before hanging up, hand heavy on the phone.

Whatever happens is fine with me. Bonnie's words had sounded like platitudes, but were they? Were they really? George wasn't sure anymore. She wasn't sure of anything in life.

My life.

Those two words hit her like hard, little pebbles, right in the chest—in that hollowed-out place where she'd held on to Tom for all those years. When had it gotten so full?

She scrabbled through the papers on her desk until she found the sticky note with the clinic's number on it, sucked in a big breath, and dialed.

"Charlottesville Regional Reproductive Medicine Clinic, this is Sherry."

"Sherry." She cleared her throat. "Sherry, hello. Dr. George Hadley here." Hard breaths, no doubt audible to the woman on the other side. "I've got an appointment tonight, and I'm afraid I need to cancel."

"Okay. When would you like to get back in to see us?"

"I, uh…" Another audible swallow. "I'll be in touch. You can go ahead and cancel the procedure."

"You got it, Doctor. Thanks for calling in! Have a great—"

George hung up and sat back in her chair, wishing for something to drink, something strong, with some bite. Or some other pain, maybe. A slap. With fingers that were thick and awkward, she pinched her arm, needing sensation, anything, to bring her back to reality. A flash of Clay smacking her bottom had her nerve endings flaring. Shame and pain, it turned out, might just be her aphrodisiacs.

And then it sank in: the importance of what she'd just done. For a while—too long, considering the patients sitting in the waiting room—George sat and let the pain and the sorrow and the regret wash over her.

Over and over, Thomas Hadley had broken George's heart. By getting sick and then better and then worse again. By treating her so carefully as he'd wasted away. And then, one day, she'd been dozing in the chair in his room when the infernal beeping had started…and he'd left her. Swift and easy. Gone.

No, not just gone, because missing him hadn't just been about losing something good in her life. From the day he'd shown up senior year, Tom had been her hero, her friend. He'd absolved her of the choices she'd made; he'd been her *life*.

How much of this desire to have a baby, she wondered, was about Tom, and how much was regretting the abortion? How was it that, after all these years, last night, her face curved into Clay Navarro's chest, had been the first time she'd admitted the correlation.

I was too young to have a baby, too alone. She knew that, could admit today that she'd have been a horrible mother back then, but even so, the guilt hurt. It hurt to know that she could have had an eighteen-year-old today. Seeing Jessie with Gabe, a woman who'd managed somehow to survive teenage pregnancy, had brought home her shortcomings, compounded them, made it worse.

After the guilt and the shame and the regret, Tom had come in and taught her to want to make the right decisions instead of always rebelling—he'd been the one who'd made sure she went to college, pushed her toward med school.

Tom had taken her young, shattered heart, beaten raw by one tragedy after another, and he'd added to her. He'd made her whole, so when he died, it had been so much worse than if he'd never been there at all. He'd gone and taken it all away. At least that was how it had felt. Like he'd grafted a new heart onto hers and then ripped it out again.

She owed him her life. Her confidence, her desire to be a good person. Everything. And she'd wanted to make it up to him somehow. To carry on the goodness he'd given her, while maybe giving a tiny life back to the world.

And now, sitting in her office all alone, George closed her eyes and said good-bye to the baby Tom Hadley would never have.

This is my life. With her next breath, the words echoed through her, full of an unexpected hope, and she let herself wonder, for the first time in forever, just what it would be like to live life for herself.

≈

Clay was getting too old to sleep in the back of a truck. Not only that, but for the first time in weeks, the air felt cool, and he was freezing, pressed up against his new toolbox.

He shifted, with barely enough room to move, and hit something hard with his foot. The vodka bottle—empty, judging from the throbbing of his skull and the sound of hollow glass rolling before it thumped onto the ground behind the tailgate. After a good long, unhealthy cough, he sat up to spit over the side and felt the landscape in front of him like a physical blow.

Whoa.

Beautiful. Breathtaking. And so fucking *real*.

Rolling, lush green, tufted here and there with soft hills. The scattered buildings he assumed to be Blackwood, and if he looked to the right… There. Right there was her house with its bright-red roof. From here, he couldn't tell that it needed repainting. It was a perfect, miniscule train set model.

His chest hurt, right where his heart was supposed to be, and he curved into himself, hating the emptiness inside. Hating the hurt and self-loathing.

For a minute or two, he pictured himself staying in Blackwood, coming back here after the trial.

Which was stupid, since there wasn't anything for him to do in this lost corner of the world.

Fixing up George's place, if she'd let him, was all well and good, but what would he possibly do after the work was done?

Nothing. Because his life was in Baltimore, where he had a job waiting for him and friends, like Tyler Olson. The thought of Tyler hurt a little bit too. Tyler and Jayda and their kids, inviting him out on their boat in the summers. He'd gone only that one time, despite their numerous invitations, because the close quarters and the family atmosphere had been overwhelming to a man who did best on his own.

He pictured George on the boat, her hair blowing into her face, the tips of her shoulders red from the sun. He pictured the way she smiled, full of humor, but just a little restrained. Then he imagined her secret laugh, the warm one he'd heard only once or twice. That made him feel special, he realized in that moment—how private she was, how she'd let him inside.

It's time to go, he thought, looking out over this place he'd actually come to... What? To love? No. Absolutely no way.

And because it was time to go, he got down, picked up the empty vodka bottle, and chucked it into the back, then made his way around the truck, took a piss, and dragged himself into the cab.

His eyes caught on his rearview mirror. It took the breathtaking vista and transformed it into a diorama—a tiny, inconsequential window that was no more real than those scenes of cavemen in natural history exhibits.

He shut his eyes on the view, tightened them, straining to think through the throbbing pain in the back of his head, but nothing worked, nothing straightened out the pieces. Nothing made sense of the clusterfuck his life had turned him into.

❧

Clay's head was full as he finally descended the mountain. Weird stuff, like the silhouette of a vulture high in a dead tree, overlooking the hazy foothills beyond, or the dark eyes of the sheriff, taking stock and unexpectedly *getting* Clay. Other things, like the smell in the crook of George's neck—a potent blend that hit him right in the gut every time. Her sweat after an evening in the garden. Way too complex to be distilled into a single scent. Overly complicated. Just like the woman herself.

She'd asked him to leave. She wanted to be alone.

And yet...he needed to stay, he realized with an uncharacteristic sense of certainty. Had to tell her the truth. About how he felt.

Tell her that maybe she was the kind of woman he could see himself with. That she was worth fighting for and that he'd fight, even if she wasn't willing to. That she was the type of mother he could only dream of for his babies. Because—

Babies? Fucking babies? No. No babies. The last thing he wanted was to bring children into this unbelievably messed-up world. No, he'd always said he wasn't fit to be a father, and obviously, she'd recognized that, so... So what? Was he going to leave her alone to deal with the fallout of what had been the best... No, the deepest sexua—

No more lies. She had been the most meaningful *relationship* of his life. Period. While it lasted, before she'd told him to go, what they'd had was the best thing he'd ever experienced. And, he decided, eyes lingering on the dark-purple mountain crests in the rearview mirror, nothing in his life, before or after, would ruin what they'd done together, what they'd had. Nothing.

You don't get to decide, she'd said. And yet she was the one who'd kicked him to the curb last night. Well, that wasn't any fucking fair, was it?

So maybe this time she needed to be told those words. Maybe *George* didn't get to decide.

He'd go, and he'd tell her that.

And on that note, Clay headed to the hardware store and spent a small fortune on supplies for her house. A new henhouse, he decided. She wanted time to think? Fine. But no way in hell was he leaving her alone.

In fact, he pulled up in front of the clinic, parked, and got out, wanting the confrontation out of the way, needing to tell her how he felt, how this was more than just—

"Mr. Blane!"

Clay stopped.

"Mr. Blane, we need your help!" called a little voice from in front of the MMA school. He recognized one of the kids he'd taught that weekend.

"Don't bother the man, Carter," the mom said. "He's obviously busy. Sorry to bug you, Mr. Blane—the kids are just a little worked up."

"What's up?" Clay asked.

"Camp's canceled!" the kid yelled, looking like he was about to break down. Behind him, a bunch of children had gathered at the window of the MMA school, faces and hands smashed against the glass, staring at the scene.

"Yeah?" asked Clay, wary of whatever new mess he was getting into.

"Yeah. Sheriff Mullen ain't gonna do it. One of his deputies broke his leg and he's three guys short and now he can't teach our classes. So we got no camp."

"What was this, karate camp?"

"Yeah. Tae kwon do too. You know tae kwon do, right, Mr. Blane?"

"I…" Clay's eyes trailed up over Carter's head to where another dozen eyes tracked his every movement. "Sheriff in there?" he asked. The kid nodded, and Clay sighed before heading inside. "All right. Hang on."

Inside, the gym was abuzz with young voices. "He in back?"

"Right here," came Steve Mullen's voice from the side of the room, where he stood amid a cluster of tired-looking parents.

They met in the middle of the room.

"You put him up to that?"

"Hmm?"

"Carter? You tell him to drag me in?"

"'Course not," said Steve with a look that was probably supposed to be innocent but held sharp undertones of deviousness. "What, you offering up your services?"

"You seriously canceling camp?"

"Unless someone steps up and—"

On a long, hard sigh, Clay interrupted. "Just cut through the fu—" He stopped himself, glanced over his shoulder to catch the kids watching every move, and went on. "Cut the crap, Sheriff. What's the plan? I mean, you got some kind of syllabus or something?"

"Could work on that. Been doing the camp for about twelve years now, so I don't need one, but I could put one together for you."

Running a hand through his hair, Clay ignored the imploring looks focused on his back and closed his eyes. Jesus, what the hell was he getting himself into?

"Starts now?"

"Yes indeed," said the older man, the twinkle in his eyes no doubt visible from outer space.

"How'd you manage this and your job for twelve years?"

"Always found somebody willing to pick up the slack."

"Some poor asshole like me, huh? Pay better be damn good," he said before heading out to his truck for a change of clothes, to the cheers of a dozen rabid children.

~∞~

After her last patient was gone, George let Cindy and Purnima go and had just closed up when the phone rang. She let it go to voice mail the first time but decided to answer when it started up again. As she waited, she thought she heard thunder rumbling outside. Every single patient had mentioned the weather today. The weatherman had apparently called for rain, and George could feel it in the way her body hummed with energy, despite the exhaustion.

"Clear Skin Blackwood," she answered.

"Oh, good. I'm glad I caught you. This is Jessie. Listen. Something happened."

George's pulse spiked. "Okay."

"My guy finally got back to me."

"Your guy?"

"Remember, the call you wanted me to cancel? Too late."

A lump formed in George's throat, but she swallowed past it. "Go ahead."

"My contact says that your guy is a wanted man."

George shook her head, over and over and over, like a windup doll that couldn't stop. "Not possible."

"Why not?"

"He's not… I can't tell you why I know this, but he's just not."

"It was a weird call," Jessie said. "He phoned a couple hours ago, but I had to rush to court and…he sounded wired."

"What do you mean?"

"He asked me where I was. Like, right then." She shook her head. "And that's a weird thing to do, right?"

"What do you mean?"

"I…I had mentioned that a contact was asking about a Sultans tat, said it might have been spotted in the area, wanted to know what info he could give me about anyone with that kind of ink, and he freaked the hell out. I mean freaked, asking me all sorts of shit that I just couldn't answer. He then…" Jessie swallowed, sounding flat-out worried. "He said he'd get someone to see me ASAP, and the problem, George, is that I'm not supposed to hide information about any cases. I mean, I work with the courts and the police and…it's my job. I can't just make up some probationer because they'll want to interview him."

"What did you tell him?"

"Nothing. But wait, it gets worse. I'm driving home, and he just called me back and said they were following a lead. He mentioned tattoo removal and asked me about doctors in the area. He was aggressive in a way I didn't like."

"Oh God."

"What's going on, George? Is that man at your house right now?"

"No. No, he's gone," she said, hoping it was true.

"Look, I'm headed home, but I'm still an hour out. Don't go anywhere. Don't talk to anyone, okay?"

"Okay," George said, glancing at the clinic door. "But, Jessie, I want you to know that the man I told you about, my patient? I trust him. I'd trust him with my life."

"All right, well, I'd suggest you warn him. 'Cause I've got a feeling things are about to blow."

Just as she hung up, the bell rang above the front door. George looked up, hoping, almost expecting it to be Clay, relieved that it might be.

The man who filled her waiting room gave her a disquieting sense of déjà vu. She stopped breathing.

His sleeveless leather vest, along with the tattoos covering both of his arms, told her he was probably a biker—but his expression, visible behind a layer of piercings so thick you could almost hear a metallic jingle, gave her the chills. This wasn't Clay, or anyone even remotely like him. This man was a predator. *The eyes*, she thought. Where Clay's were warm, this man's gaze was dead. Calculating, but dead.

Clearing her throat, George stood up straight and asked, "Can I help you?"

The man's eyes raked her body from head to toe and back. "Nope."

"Well, we're closing up for the night." Her response came out on a shaky breath, sounding, to her ears, exactly like an excuse.

The man looked her over again. "You all get rid of tattoos in here, right?"

"Yes, sir."

"You had a biker come in to see the doctor recently? Big guy like me? Only real ugly?" His smile was the creepiest thing she'd ever seen.

"I can't discuss patients, sir," she stammered. "The doctor wouldn't like it."

His eyes slid to meet hers, and his expression, if possible, hardened even further. "Yeah? You might want to reconsider." He stood up taller, took up too much space in her tiny reception area.

"No. No, I have no patients that fit that description."

After a breathless few seconds, the man grunted, slimed her with a narrow-eyed look, and turned to go. He pulled the door open so hard the bells came out angry rather than festive and then slammed it behind him.

George rushed to lock the door. The image of the back of that man's jacket burned a hole in her mind—*Sultans*, it said, in its pretentious, curlicue writing, with an eagle, a triangle, arrows, and a river all topped by a laughing skull, the orbs of the eyes not half as empty as that man's.

I have to warn Clay. Now. She raced for her cell phone, picked it up, and stared at it for a few, slow seconds. No number. They'd never exchanged them. When would they?

Desperate, she scrolled through her short list of numbers and saw none that made sense. She couldn't call the cops—not unless her hand was forced—when Clay was doing so much to stay hidden. And rightly so, based on what Jessie had just told her.

Oh God, oh God, oh God. She had to find him. Was he at her house? Or at the motel? Maybe he'd gone back there. Fast, fast, before they found him. Outside, she fumbled the clinic key in the lock, then took a quick look around and started toward her car. Halfway there, she saw Clay's truck, half a block down—old and rusty and shining under the streetlights like a beacon of hope. She ran in that direction as fast as she could.

She barely noticed the thunder that rumbled overhead or the flashes of lightning over the mountains. It was the motorcycles—two of them—parked in the road that stopped her in her tracks and had her moving to dial 911 as fast as she could.

But it was already too late.

A thick pair of arms circled her from behind and shoved her hard against the metal of the truck, glasses spinning off into the darkening evening. *No. Oh no, please no.* The words stumbled through her mind, over and over and over again like a mantra of denial. Like, if she'd just think it hard enough, she could wish herself back to five minutes ago. Or one. Even one.

"What's the big hurry, huh?"

How strange the things she noticed, the details her brain took in. The way this man's hand hurt around her neck, the bite of his forearm on her chest. Body odor, stale and unhealthy, the gritty grind of dirt on the pavement under their feet.

But clearest of all was the strange, choked-off silence of not being able to breathe or talk or scream. This was true impotence. Not being able to do anything as the world around you fell apart.

She lost her keys and purse somewhere in the scuffle, and her phone was wrenched from her hand. After that, the man who held her—the one from her waiting room—handed her off to another man. She could do nothing but fight for breath while the first big man picked up her purse and rifled through it for her wallet, letting it fall to the ground once he'd found what he was looking for.

"So, you're the doctor." He looked her over, then glanced back at her license. "Jason Lane," he muttered to the other man. "Same street as the probation officer. Which one you think he's stickin' it to? Doesn't matter. We'll get 'em both. Leave your bike here and take her car." He examined her keys and scanned the road. "There. Subaru. I'll find her place on the GPS. You take her in that and follow me there."

Like a useless sack of flour, she was shoved into the front seat of her car, a gun trained on her once she'd settled in. Halfway down Main Street, she made a bid for freedom. It was desperate and foolhardy, but you didn't get second chances in moments like this, did you? If they took you, you were dead.

She tried to slow her breathing, made an effort to count to three, forcing the numbers out through the frantic beat of her heart.

One...two... On three, she pulled back her elbow and thrust it, as hard as she could, to connect with the man's chin. Cursing, he swerved, almost—God, *almost*—losing control. But then he got it back, pulled over to the side, and lifted a hard hand to her throat, pressing until stars obliterated her vision, and she knew this was it.

"You think we need you to get to him? Try that again, and you're dead, bitch."

And, oh God, she believed it.

At her house, a couple of other men showed up, one peeling off to check Jessie's house, and all George could do was hope she wasn't there. The fourth man was different from the others. Rather than biker gear, he wore a shirt and slacks. He wouldn't look her in the eye.

The big man—obviously the leader—opened her front door with her key. He laughed as the other one shoved her inside, and she fell painfully to her knees. They turned on lamps in every room.

"Not a single, fucking normal light in this place. Just lamps everywhere," the man who held her complained.

"What, you don't do cozy, Jam?" The big man turned and looked—hard—at George. "Doesn't matter if you like it. 'Cause I got the feeling Agent Clayton Navarro likes it just fine. I'n't that right, Doc?"

A few minutes later, the other men returned. They spoke quietly and then went back out. The big man disappeared upstairs, returning with the bag of zip ties in one hand.

"Let's get you taken care of, Doc. And then we'll worry about Special fucking Agent Clay Navarro."

As the man tightened the tie around her wrists, something about those sharp plastic edges felt so familiar. Their feel was oddly grounding, but it wasn't just that. It was…sentimental, maybe? It trapped her hands, yes, making escape almost entirely impossible, but it also served to link her to Clay, who was out there somewhere, still safe. Still alive.

In this moment, George didn't mind the idea of dying. She would have let go, giving in to something that seemed inevitable, if it weren't for Jessie and Gabe, who could quite possibly run straight into the trap.

And then another idea occurred to her—the memory or realization, or maybe a hope, that she could, right at this very moment, be pregnant. And if she gave up, that baby would never see the light of day. Suddenly, more than anything in the world, George wanted the chance to have something real with Clay—a baby, if that were in the cards, but at the very least, a future.

And in that moment, she knew she would do whatever it took to survive.

Steve had left Clay a set of keys to his place before taking off, giving him full responsibility for cleaning up, turning off lights, and locking the gym. It took forever. The bastard.

Although, Clay decided, it didn't actually feel half-bad, having this type of responsibility. The kids were… Christ, they were awesome.

On his way to the door, he caught sight of one of Jessie's self-defense training brochures—more of a card, really—offering private classes, as well as the weekly group sessions. He picked it up with some notion that he'd take it to George, maybe convince her to give it a try.

Walking out of the school, he glanced around the street, taking in details by rote—what cop didn't?—and then stopped dead at what he saw.

A Harley. A fucking chopper, parked behind the Dumpster at the end of the building. Pulse picking up, he took another glance around, slowed his pace, and walked carefully, carefully, to the bike. He knew this bike. Like the back of his hand. Jam's bike. Here, in Blackwood.

He'd ignored the sound earlier, sure he was imagining it yet again. He'd felt so in control when his heart hadn't taken off like it used to, only now… Christ, this time, he'd been wrong. So fucking wrong and…there, a few feet away, was a purse. George's massive purse, in a pile on the road.

After that, things moved too fast, Clay's brain set to autopilot as he sprinted to his truck, noting that her car was nowhere to be seen, and turned the key once, twice, almost flooding the fucking engine.

Calm down. Calm down. He put the truck into gear and pulled out into the road, with no idea where he was headed. Wait. He screeched to a halt. His phone. He reached for it and powered it up. He'd call George. He had her number somewhere. Where was that card? It took a few seconds to find it and type in the number. It rang twice before someone picked up.

"George?" he gasped, his breathing ragged, like he'd just run a marathon. "George, where are you?"

"Oh, hey! Indian? That you, man?"

The voice gave Clay the shakes. He'd recognize that voice anywhere.

"Ape."

"Hey, man," Ape went on, sounding frighteningly chipper. "Got somethin' that belongs to you."

"Oh, yeah?" Clay forced out, trying his damnedest to sound calm.

A muffled sound on the phone, and then George's voice, thin and scared. "Clay? They're at my house, but I'm fine. *Fine.* Don't you dare come here. I'm—"

"Don't listen to her, man. I'm about to—"

"You touch a hair on her body, and you're a dead man, Ape. *Dead,*" he said, only to be met with Ape's cheerfully sordid laugh.

"Trade you. Your life for hers," the fucker said before hanging up.

An image of Carly's corpse flashed through Clay's mind. Only this time, it had George's face.

He accelerated hard, ignoring the irate honk from the car he'd almost sideswiped, and took off toward her house.

He'd kill them. Ape and Jam and whoever else was with them. He'd use his hands and his knife, and he'd mess them up so bad they'd be unidentifiable.

That animal part of him, the part that wanted to take over, was roaring, a deep, dangerous primal scream like he'd never experienced in his entire fucking life, and he knew he'd tear them apart. Fuck, he'd—

From out of nowhere came an image of George, touching him, healing him, maybe just a little bit loving him, and everything stopped. He couldn't do any of those things. She wouldn't want him to. And was that truly who he was?

He'd be no better than them if he murdered them, would he? He was supposed to be one of the good guys. No matter how many times the job had forced him to cross over to the other side, he'd always been a cop.

You are one of the good guys, he told himself, only it didn't sound like his voice. It sounded like George's.

He worked hard to think like an agent instead of one of those monsters. He needed to think, to make a plan. What would he do if George wasn't part of this equation?

Steve. He'd call Steve Mullen. No calling 911, which would put up red flags everywhere, notify the ATF and anybody linked to DOJ. Steve was the only person who had no skin in this game, the only one he could trust.

Working hard at faking a calm he didn't feel, he

reached for his phone, kept his eye on the road while he dug out the guy's business card, and dialed.

It went to voice mail after too many rings, and Clay came close to losing it again.

Almost to Jason Lane, after trying the number a million times, Clay finally broke down and dialed 911. He had no choice, did he?

When the woman asked him to state his emergency, he hesitated. Kidnapping, attempted murder. Those words would raise a red flag so big that half the fucking state would be here in no time at all. There had to be a way he could save George *and* keep himself out of sight long enough to see those fuckers in court.

Instead, he told the woman it was a personal matter and asked her to relay him to the sheriff. When he finally came on the line, Steve Mullen sounded irritated.

"What's the problem, Blane? I got a four-car pile-up on the interstate here."

"I've got an emergency, sir."

"What's going on, son?"

"This is being recorded, right?"

A pause. "Yep."

"Need to talk to you offline. Please." He gave the man his number and waited for the call to come through.

"Why all the cloak and dagger, Blane?"

"They've got Dr. Hadley."

"Who has her?"

"Sultans MC," he spat out. "I'm headed to her place now. They're gonna—"

"Slow down, son, I can't hear you. Where they at?"

"Her place, Jason Lane."

"Why you calling me on the down low like this?"

"Sultans have someone on the inside. I got no idea who."

"*Hell.*"

"At least one person, maybe a couple."

"Trust no one."

"I trust you, Sheriff. I'm going in there. I've got to, before they hurt her. I can take care of this, but I need your backup. And I need you to keep this quiet."

"Go." The sheriff paused. "I'm about twenty minutes behind you." Another pause. "And don't do anything stupid, son, got me?"

A few blocks away, he caught sight of Jessie's self-defense card on the seat beside him. George had told him all about her neighbor and her cute kid. He hadn't paid it much mind at the time, but now his head was ringing. If the woman and her kid were home, they could get caught in the crossfire. He dialed the number on the card, and she picked up.

"Ms. Shifflett, this is Clay Navarro."

"Who?"

Fuck, he was losing it. "My name is Andrew Blane. I'm…I'm undercover ATF. I'm a friend of George Hadley's. Your neighbor? Look, it's too much to explain. There's shit going down at George's place. I need you to grab your kid and get out of there."

"What are you—"

"Do it. Go. Now. Call the sheriff if you have to, but go. I don't want to have to worry about two more people getting caught up in this."

"Christ," she muttered under her breath, then paused for an excruciating few seconds and asked, "Are you there, right now, at George's place?"

"I'm on my way. I'll get her out."

She let out a little distressed noise at that. "You mean they've got her? George is in there with somebody?"

"Yeah."

"All right. Go. We'll be fine. Just go."

Clay hung up, took the last turn onto Jason Lane too fast, and parked down the street from George's house. He thought his approach was quiet, although he couldn't tell through the pounding in his ears. *Don't hurt her. Please don't let her be hurt.*

He set off into the woods, giving the house a wide berth in case they'd set up a perimeter. The woods felt familiar as he crept toward her place, the night sounds no longer an enemy but a friend, covering up his approach.

Close enough to see the house now, he waited, working hard to keep his breathing normal and force his adrenaline down to where it wouldn't impede him.

It took a good minute for his eyes to find the person waiting in the night. Just a shadow from here, but so familiar that his heart took a bright leap toward hope. Backup! Help. Someone on his side!

The shadow moved slightly away from the shed, and Clay's conscious mind recognized the man. That feeling of safety and friendship and relief exploded into a million tiny splinters of betrayal, each one sharp enough to gouge out his soul.

Tyler. Tyler fucking Olson, his best friend in the whole world. The man who'd always had his back since they were kids. Clay was godfather to two of the man's children, for Christ's sake. And *Tyler* was the inside man who'd betrayed him.

Nearly doubled over, it took him a while to push past

the agony of it, to stand back up and recognize how obvious it should have been. That night at the club, his call for help. Tyler'd done nothing to help him. Nothing. And later, he'd been so goddamned interested in where Clay was hiding out, hadn't he?

He'd been meaning to sell his location to Ape all along.

Quietly, without a clear plan, he made his way toward the silhouette, acid roiling like hate in his belly.

"Tyler."

"Fuck!" Tyler turned, fast, with one hand flying to his gun, and then stopped when he saw who it was. His expression went through a quick, complicated change, shock morphing into guilt morphing into a smooth liar's smile. "Jesus, don't do that, man. You'll give me a god-damned heart attack."

Clay couldn't say a word for the first few seconds, but he kept moving closer, this face-off feeling inevitable.

"Wow, bro," Tyler said, nervously stepping back and filling the tense silence. "I forgot how fucked up you look with that shit on your face."

"My tats?" Clay growled. "You're just standing out here in my woman's yard while she's being held by those *murderers*, and you want to have a conversation about my *tats*?" Oh, the rage was coming back now, cleaning out the shock and the hurt in a way that felt righteous and strong. "Why don't you tell me more about these tats, you fucking asshole? Maybe tell me how you could possibly have stopped some of this from happening?"

"Christ, man. What are you talkin' about?"

"That's how you're gonna play it, then?" He indicated the house, glowing with an ironic warmth beyond them.

"Just stand here and pretend like you didn't sell me to the highest bidder? I don't have time for you." Clay looked away and swallowed before letting the rage take wing and hauling back to send his fist flying, right at the fucker's face. It connected with a satisfying crunch.

He didn't feel a thing, though. Nothing except rage and the need to destroy, but all the while the clock was ticking. He had to go. Fuck Tyler.

"What the hell, man? Clay, Clay…" Tyler staggered and wiped his mouth, coming away with blood.

"She inside, you motherfucker? You set her up?"

"She's in there."

"You gave her to 'em?"

"Nah, man, I—"

There was no time for more of his lies. "Shut the fuck up."

Tyler's expression changed before he shifted and started to reach for his gun, but he was no match for Clay. Tyler, who sat behind a desk and pretended to be a good man, versus Clay, who'd spent so many years out there, working hard to pass as filth. He put a hand around the man's neck and pinned him to the side of the shed, disarming him easily. So fucking easily. "What the hell do you get out of this, huh?"

Tyler opened his mouth, as if to defend himself, then closed it.

"You not even gonna give me that?" Every one of Clay's words was a whispered arrow, flying at his target, wanting, needing to hurt him. "When'd you start working with them?"

"When?" Tyler asked. "When they showed up at my goddamned door is when."

"I was under?"

"Yeah. Just toward the end."

"Before I got shot?"

A pause. "Yeah."

"So, the night you were supposed to send the team in to get me out? The delay? That was—"

"You don't fucking get it, do you, Clay? One Saturday, those fucking bastards just show up at my *house*, with Jayda and the kids in the backyard, and… fuck, man. I didn't have a choice."

There was always a choice.

"You set me up to get shot in the back." Something about his voice must have gotten through to Tyler, because he went still.

"'Course not, man. 'Course not," Tyler whined, sounding defeated, and Clay backed away. He couldn't let this go. Would never let this go.

"You the one who killed Bread, Ty? Was that you?" He moved his hand away from Tyler's neck, blinking at the pain of all this deception.

"What? Fuck no, man."

"They get his location from you?"

Tyler didn't answer, but the truth was visible in the slope of his shoulders, the way his lips turned down at the edges, and even under cover of darkness, he couldn't look Clay in the eye.

"And here?" Through the barrage of pain, a slice of anger came back. Clay was *furious*. "You sicced them on George? You—"

"It's not my fault, man. I—"

Clay hauled back and punched Tyler again, the fury taking over, the fear for her life pushing through the

bullshit excuses. He punched him again, fending off
Tyler's counters. And again. Another time on the chin,
and the man was down, cowering in the dry grass like
the fucking coward he was. The urge to kill him was
strong, so strong, pulsing inside him like a caged beast,
dying to be let out.

Don't do it. You're better than that, came that reason-
able voice that he thought of as George's.

A look toward the front of the house showed no sign
of the sheriff, but it didn't matter. It was time. Time to
go in and get his woman out.

"You fucking coward," he spat, grabbing Tyler's gun
and holding it on him, steady. "I should fucking kill you
right now. That's the best you deserve."

"I know, man. I know." His hand tightened on
Tyler's handgun, the urge so strong it hurt. "Do it. Kill
me. Christ, kill me 'cause I can't take it anymore."

Clay stilled. That instinct to hurt and kill, it wasn't
his, was it? It belonged to the men he pretended to be,
but not to him. Not now and not ever.

With something like pity, he shook his head at the
man he'd once considered his best friend and, almost
tenderly, hauled off, punching him with a final blow to
the temple that knocked Tyler unconscious.

Then he stalked off to save the woman he loved.

Being terrified did strange things to George. Unexpected
things. Her body was tired, inappropriately heavy with
exhaustion where she lay on the sofa in her front room.
But there was a strength to it too, a *you just go ahead
and touch me* thing whenever one of the men came close

to her. She was convinced she'd fight like crazy if they tried anything on her.

Which seemed increasingly inevitable as the minutes passed. The off-color remarks—things about her tits, as they called them—were growing filthier, their words slurred, their footsteps heavier. Her kitchen must be a wreck by now, judging from the sounds. She didn't know how many there were in her house. Two? Maybe three?

George lay low, being as quiet as possible, unsure if that was the right thing to do or if she would be better off attracting their attention. Wishing she'd made it to Jessie's self-defense class—but then, two against one seemed like unbeatable odds, even if she knew what she was doing. They were huge. And mean. The thought of Jessie, right next door with Gabe, their place so close, nearly threw her into a panic.

Something from the back of the house crashed, and she wiggled her arms again, trying to loosen them from the zip tie that bound her.

God, how much longer could she wait like this? A useless sitting duck, nothing but a decoy to get Clay here. She had to do something.

"Excuse me," she finally called. "I need to use the restroom."

"Fucking chicks," said one of the men in the kitchen.

"Let her piss herself," said the boss guy in his nasally voice.

"I'll take her," a third voice responded. Jam, the man who'd nearly strangled her in the car.

"Jesus Christ, man, you gonna let her piss on you too?"

"She can piss in the toilet. We're here for Indian, not to—"

"Shut the fuck up and take her if that's what you want, bro. So fuckin' pussy-whipped. I wonder about you…"

Boots clomped down the hall, and George looked up to see that biker, covered in ink, wearing the same sleeveless leather vest as the first one, unshaven and just as scary.

"Where's the head?" he asked, not quite meeting her eye, and it took her a second to realize he meant the bathroom.

"Upstairs."

He approached, pulling out a knife, and George tightened her body in anticipation, only to loosen again—too loose—as he sliced through the tie at her ankles. She stood, her legs like jelly, wobbly and barely able to hold her up.

"Let's go."

She led him upstairs, could feel his eyes on her backside. When she made it to the bathroom, she held up her wrists and said, "Could you cut this please?"

"Can't. You'll manage."

Without argument, George went inside, started to push the door closed, and was stopped by the man. "Leave it open."

"I'm not going to—"

He got close to her, too close. "Don't fuck with us… especially not him. The big one." His eyes flicked back toward the stairs. "Just do what I say."

She met the man's eyes in the mirror. In the split second before she blinked, she could have sworn she saw something reticent in his light gaze, as if perhaps he didn't want to be in this situation any more than she did.

He wore a big beard, but beneath it, he looked young. The look was gone as fast as it had appeared, replaced by that hard-jawed, mean-eyed glare.

"Why?"

"You wanna stay alive?"

She nodded, and he nudged her, left the door open, and stepped back into the hall, giving her visual privacy, if not aural. There was no way she could make a break for it with him standing guard like that.

Breathing hard, her throat raw from bile, George made it to the sink where she washed her face. A glimpse of her bathroom showed a place that looked unfamiliar, new in the worst possible way. That thought brought with it a wave of fear far stronger than what she'd felt before, prickling her skin. This was her house, dammit. Her sanctuary. They'd defiled it with their presence, and she wanted them out.

Get them out became her mantra as they descended into the main hall. *Before Clay gets here and they kill him. Get them out, get them out, get them out.*

She turned to the man and said, "Let me make you and your friends dinner."

"What?"

"Please, let me do something. I'll go crazy otherwise."

He seemed to consider, eyes narrowed on hers. "Ape," he called, his voice loud and gruff. "She wants to make us dinner."

Ape ambled into the room, brows raised. "What dinner? It's a fuckin' wasteland in this bitch's kitchen. No chips, nothing."

"I can make you something," she said, bargaining. If she was alive, she could bargain.

"Yeah? Well, come on then. I could use a fuckin' home-cooked meal. You make us dinner, and then I got somethin' to feed you," he said, his expression dirty, the insinuation disgusting. His face was... Lord, it was weird. *Unfinished* was the only word she could find to describe it. His features were lumpy, soft in a way that should have been unthreatening but made her instead wonder if perhaps he was incomplete. As if he wasn't entirely human.

Overlaying those pale mounds of flesh, this man had covered himself in tattoos. His brows, not particularly prominent, were lined with piercings, which created structure. Pasty, waxy, a skull without definition, his arms nearly black with ink, and all of it bloody, vulgar, murderous.

George nodded, forcing her breathing to slow, and looked around, her kitchen different with these big, unfamiliar bodies in it, the smell of unwashed hair and cigarettes thick in the humid night air.

What could she make these men? Her mind blanked. She pictured them tearing at joints of meat and thick loaves of dark bread, like medieval villains, nothing remotely like what she had to offer, only... *Boiling cauldrons*, she thought. Hot, hot oil, poured over castle walls. *A possibility. A weapon.*

Whatever she was making, she'd boil it first, she decided then.

"Get cooking, then, bitch," the mean one said—the unfinished one they called Ape—dull shark eyes focused hard on her as she brushed too close by him.

I'll cook for you, she thought, the fear fizzing high in her throat. *And then I'll burn your damned face off.*

She put a pot full of water on the stove, took out a couple of steaks, and moved to reheat some greens.

They were impatient, asking her every three minutes if she'd finished yet. If she hadn't been so frightened, she'd have glared.

"You almost done?" Ape asked George from that spot too close beside her.

"Yes," she lied.

"Girl's good in the kitchen, ain't she, Jam?" the man said in a way that didn't feel like a compliment, but like he'd started to undress her already. "Might should take her back home with us. Let her serve us." He grinned his gapped-tooth smile. "Service us." A meaty hand reached out as if to cup her crotch from behind, and she jumped.

Nauseated, sweaty, shaking. Scared as can be, but also mad as hell.

"Where the fuck's your boyfriend?" he asked, that hand close to touching her, and she pictured Clay's face. Imagined the way he felt. Wishing he'd come save her, but hoping he'd stay away.

"Shit smells good. Let's fuckin' eat before that asshole comes and ruins our meal."

George took two plates out of her cupboard—not an easy feat with the zip tie still on them—and set them on the counter, wanting to keep close to the hot water, waiting for any opportunity.

"Almost done."

She served them the two steaks and the greens and was just reaching for the big pot of boiling pasta when the boss man looked toward the back door, head cocked.

"That him? Or just that sniveling, little Olson fuck?"

"Not sure, man. Might be Meathead. Want me to go check?"

"Let me go," said George, her mouth moving in a mad attempt to distract them even as she went for the pot of boiling water. If it was Clay they'd heard, then she could help by keeping their attention focused on her. "Let me go, and I won't say a word. You can—"

Faster than he looked, the big man slapped George hard across the face before grabbing her and holding her tight against his body. "You think I'm lettin' you go? I'll fucking tear you apart. And then, when that asshole gets here and sees you, bleeding from every hole, I'll make him watch while I do it again."

"No!" George screamed as Ape dragged her away from the water and her only chance at escape. Her body thrilled with fear, but also with a secret curl of triumph. If he was focusing on her, then Clay was safe.

Assuming that had been Clay at all. She hoped it wasn't, for his sake.

Somewhere, deep down, she did something she hadn't done since the days before Tom died. She prayed, not for herself, but for Clay. Over and over again, the mantra the only thing she had left. *Please don't let Clay come. Please, God, keep him away. Please don't come. Please don't come.*

20

IT HAD ALL COME TO THIS—TO THIS MOMENT, TO HIS actions right here, in this place. His woman's house, with those fuckers who had their hands all over her. Silently, he moved in close, eyes flicking between the ground and those cheerily glowing windows. For once, he was glad she didn't have curtains back here.

He squinted as he approached. Two guys: just Ape and Jam. Good, although there might be a third up front. Fine. He could handle three. They might be mean as fuck, but he had justice on his side. He'd kill them if he had to. If it was the only choice, he'd blow them all sky high before he'd let them touch George.

Here he was, no plan, just apeshit insanity. He got close enough to see her stirring something at the stove. Her face was pale and worn, but she looked whole. He didn't realize how tightly he'd been wound until he saw her there: safe, whole, even now lighting up the room from inside, and fuck, he loved her so much it hurt.

There was someone close to the porch, he realized as he drew closer.

Shoving the gun into his pants, he picked up the first thing he found—a piece of clapboard siding—and stalked the man slowly, calmly. He'd take this one down and keep the element of surprise.

From inside, the sound of voices got louder.

Ape spoke, and she responded, the words not yet clear. He was right up next to the guy, a Club prospect he dimly recognized, when the sounds separated themselves into words.

The sharp sound of flesh hitting flesh, followed by Ape saying, "You think I'm lettin' you go? I'll fucking tear you apart. And then, when that asshole gets here and sees you, bleeding from every hole, I'll make him watch while I do it again."

Something blew in his mind, and he lost it in an entirely new way—like bits of his brain had exploded all the fuck over the place and there was nothing human left inside but anger and the need to kill. But even so, he held back.

Until he heard George's screamed "No!" and then it was on.

He swung the board and hit the prospect on the side of his head, watching him go down. Not dead. Good, not dead, but incapacitated, because he wasn't like them. He wasn't a murderer, damn it.

The hinges squeaked as he yanked the screen door open. *Should have oiled them* came the surreal thought as he charged across the porch, secrecy gone now that they'd hurt her.

He got to the inner door next, swung it open, and he was inside.

"Stop right the fuck there." The words halted his

progress, each one an ice pick in his heart. Frozen, he took in Ape with George by the stove, noting the way the man held her by the hair, keeping her head tilted back at a painful-looking angle. Water bubbled madly not a foot from where they stood.

Ape's other hand reached behind him and came out with that little fucking ax. Slowly, viciously, Ape ran the blade down her body, from neck to breast and back up to the hollow beneath her throat. It was sharp, Clay knew. Sharp enough to slice, and George let out a noise, a mewling sound more devastating than anything Clay'd ever heard, when the asshole pressed the blade into her perfect, unmarred skin.

"Drop the gun." Ape smiled. "And the…board." This last was said with a half chuckle.

Rage and something else mingled in Clay's head in a way he couldn't take the time to decipher. Slowly, carefully, he dropped both weapons, tamping it all down, using that moment to get his thoughts straight. Forcing calm. He was smarter than these fuckers. Smarter, better trained. And he had a whole lot more at stake.

"You always were a stupid fucking superhero of a know-it-all cocksucker, weren't you?" Ape went on before hawking a thick, slimy one right onto George's wood floor. "Always knew we shouldn't trust you."

Tightening his fist, the fucker pulled George up harder against him, drawing a thick, dark drop of blood from her neck and sending Clay's pulse into overdrive. "You here for *this*?" the asshole went on, voice setting fire to Clay's nerves as he shook George's head by the hair. His thick knuckles were tight enough to whiten the skin along her scalp. "You know you got a rat in your organization, Special Agent?"

Clay didn't answer. None of this mattered; the conversation was just distraction. All he wanted was George.

Outside, the sky belched a mighty roll of thunder—it shook the house, made it feel as unstable as the pit of Clay's stomach. The air was electric with expectation. He wanted to go to George, to comfort her, but that was the worst thing he could do right now. He'd already shown his hand—shown them how important she was to him. That had been a mistake. He knew them. He knew them so well.

They wanted him, needed to kill him, because without him, the case against their bosses was a whole hell of a lot weaker. But they wouldn't let George go no matter what—not when they knew how much hurting her drove him crazy. They'd do horrible things to her, unspeakable things. And Ape, Clay knew, would take pleasure in it.

"So, Indian. Nice cover, man. You had us fuckin' snowed right till the end. Had no goddamned idea you were ATF, right, Jam?" he asked. Over his shoulder, the other Sultan slid out of the hallway.

"Yeah, man."

"You got nine lives, motherfucker? How the fuck'd you get outta there with the bullet holes in your back? I mean, I saw it with my own goddamned eyes." The hate spewing from Ape was toxic. Clay could almost smell it on his breath, mixed with the cigarettes and bourbon and body odor.

George stirred, but Clay let his eyes catch hold of Ape's and latch on. No more looking at George. He needed to forget she was there, or he'd do something stupid.

"How much'd you pay Olson to tell you where to find me, Ape?"

"Fuck, man. Took you long enough. You're as dumb as you look. Special Agent Clayton fuckin' Navarro. Jesus Christ, a goddamned *spic*." Behind the stove, Ape laughed, and Clay's hatred concentrated on that sound. That stupid, evil sound. He held himself back from pouncing, since the man still held George. "All this time, us laughin' about how dark you were. Callin' you Indian and shit, and you were a filthy wetback. You and your wetback sister."

Clay tightened up, his breathing uneven, which was bad, dangerous as hell. He couldn't get out of control. He couldn't. It took everything he had to keep his face blank. *Everything*.

Behind him, on the screen porch, Clay caught movement. The prospect coming to, or the sheriff arriving on the scene? His eyes flicked to Jam, who didn't look quite as sure as Ape was. He was the wild card in the room.

Ape said, "You know, Indian, I feel like I might actually remember that little bitch?" Something dulled in Clay's vision, cutting out whoever was behind him, Jam skulking around the edges. "She had the tightest little—"

"I'll fucking kill you, you motherfu—"

"You know what happened to your sister, man?" Ape cut in, and Clay hardened himself to what was next.

Words, just words, he repeated in his head. Over and over again. But the words hurt worse than bullets. Those words tore him apart.

"What happened to that stupid fuckin' whore is nothin' compared to what I'm gonna do to this sweet, innocent, little bitch right here." Ape smiled his rotten-toothed grin, and Clay felt it, that next jolt of fear or adrenaline or whatever it was he'd been waiting for. Through the fucker's words, he let it fill his body, let it take him over, let it calm him and harden him and give him that dose of power he needed to do what he had to do. Because he was a cop, yes, but also a man—an honorable man—whose job it was to save the life of the only woman he'd ever loved. And that was exactly what he planned to do, even if he died in the process.

⤟

George heard the words, knew the man holding her by the hair was talking about her, but couldn't quite connect the two. Cut her, he'd said. He wanted to cut her. And the things he was saying to Clay about his sister…

"I'm gonna fuck every hole in her body—maybe slice a couple new ones to stick my dick into. And then—"

He pulled her hair tighter, bringing tears to her eyes, then tighter still. With a twist of his wrist, he rubbed her face into his sweaty neck. She gagged and tried to pull back, which only made him laugh and grind her face in harder, the blade of that ax ever-present at her throat.

The man was talking, taunting Clay, pushing him, and throughout his filthy tirade, her fear multiplied tenfold. George, a victim to God and the fates. Standing here, letting it happen, just letting it all happen to her, the way it had happened with Tom. Because who was she to fight the inevitability of what was to come? She'd lost against God once, right? So…

Around her wrists, the zip tie cut into her skin.

The man loosened his grip, stupidly forgetting, maybe, that she was an actual person and not some blow-up doll. In those few seconds, where everything in her life came together—images, feelings, the memory of her impotence against the inevitability of death, George recognized something new. It wasn't God she needed to look for in this moment. No doctors to beg, no miracle drugs to put her energy into. No faith to bank on.

She wasn't helpless here, a tiny David battling a big and omnipotent Goliath. No, here, right now, in her home, on her turf, with her hands tied in front of her, George held the power.

She closed her eyes against the feel of this big, filthy man, shut her mind to the reality of Clay paralyzed in front of her, and remembered the way he'd slammed his hands to his hips while they'd made love, breaking the plastic at his wrists.

She reached inside, gathered every tiny cell of her being, every bit of her strength and her will to live. With a deep rush of breath, she opened her eyes, met Clay's, let her gaze slide to the side to show him the pot boiling on the stove, and then, through a wash of tears, took the time to tell him how she felt, mouthing those words she hadn't yet had the courage to say aloud.

I love you.

George loved him. The truth of it exploded into him. It was all Clay needed.

Big and frightened but whole, her eyes flicked down to the right, and though he wanted to follow their path, he held back, unwilling to give Ape a clue to whatever she was trying to show him.

The stove he understood, with a white-hot jolt of

hope. A big pot of something, yellow flames licking at the bottom.

Her lips moved over the words again, and she smiled. *Smiled.*

With a single, calm blink of his lids and a slight tightening of his lips, Clay gave it right back to her.

I love you, he tried to say with his gaze. *I love you and I'll die for you.*

And then she moved, his kamikaze girl. She became a dead weight and dropped, unexpectedly heavy in Ape's arms. The asshole fumbled, his eyes following her for a second or two before flicking back to Clay, then back and forth, and while he vacillated, George made her move.

With a pull and a yell, she wrenched her arms back, and fuck if she didn't bust through that flimsy little piece of plastic as if it were nothing. She darted for the water—his baby was fast—grabbed it and flung. The splash wasn't as wide as Clay would have wished, but it got Ape in the face.

With a scream, the fucker staggered back as George scampered away, and Clay was on him. An elbow to the face jarred Ape, and Clay followed it with an uppercut that flung his chin up and sent an arc of blood through the air.

With a groan, Ape put his fist into Clay's belly, full of brute strength, and fuck, the guy was huge. It took a beat for Clay to get his breath back, another for him to stand up again and get some space. He'd forgotten how powerful the fucker was. But he wasn't fast. With a bellow, Ape came at him again, going for his face, but Clay sidestepped, part of him sucking in the near miss, letting it drive him back and then forward, his whole body in this one. A strike to the temple—surgical in its precision—and another to the monster's kidney, and, oh yeah, that connected. He felt the man's pain in the breath he spat out, the groan he couldn't get enough air to put a voice to.

Fuck, yes, this was it. Taking advantage of Ape's doubled-over position, Clay reached for the back of his head, gripped the greasy hair, and jerked him down to his knee. Ape's nose broke. The crunch of bone was audible. From there, Clay's inner beast took over, pummeling flesh and breaking bones like he'd never done in his life, his training a thin veneer over the savage animal inside.

Another strike, this one laying Ape flat out on the ground, where he rolled into a defensive little ball. But fuck, he deserved this. Deserved to be beaten into oblivion. Deserved a horrible, bloody, shattered death. He kicked the man, wanting to tear Ape apart, to make him suffer on the floor of this room. This house that had never seen violence before.

He paused, breathing hard, blinking past the sweat that poured down his face. Running a hand over his eyes, he was surprised to find blood there. Had Ape gotten a hit in?

He blinked again and focused back in on Ape.

You're no better than him if you finish him off, came the voice that had led him to this place.

He shook his head, exhaled on a hard, painful puff of air, and took in the rest of the room. George was nowhere to be found. Good. He needed her gone, out of harm's way.

Another swipe of Clay's arm cleared the blood from his eyes and the confusion from his soul. Ape was still alive, but he was down for the count. It was better this way.

He listened for a split second, hoping to hear some kind of backup but getting only the not-so-distant roll of thunder instead. Then came a soft scuff of a boot. Clay whirled toward it, ready, only to come face-to-face with Jam. *Jam.* Fuck, in all the confusion, he'd almost forgotten he was here. Jam lifted his hands and backed away from whatever he saw in Clay's face, a .38 pointed down between them.

Everything stopped.

"Got an offer to make, Indian. One-time deal," Jam said, gun trained at the floor.

Clay waited, muscles tense.

"I clean this mess up, and you'll never hear another thing from the Sultans. Nothing. Ever."

"Why would you do that?"

"Never liked how the brotherhood was run. Never. But I need it, man. Can't go back to being a civilian. Not after…" He swallowed. "Not since Afghanistan. Got a record now too, so…I need this. I need the life. You get that?"

"*Fuck*," Clay said, because he understood, more than he could ever explain. "Yes."

"I take care of this, and we're gone. Done. You go to trial against Handles and the other assholes you got inside. You win your medal or whatever the hell it is you're gettin' outta this or… *Oh, fuck. Right.* Carly." He shook his head, and Clay tightened up, ready for anything. "I didn't know she was your sister. I didn't know."

Clay pushed the image of his sister away and glanced around George's home, this place they had desecrated with their stupid club filth. "How do I know you're not coming back?"

"Don't give a shit about you. Or your woman. You did me—did us all—a favor, gettin' rid of the guys you put inside." Jam's eyes flicked down to Ape. "And him. I'll clean this up."

"I can't let you do that, Jam."

"Look, you fuckin' asshole. Don't you give me that holier-than-thou crap. I didn't know she was your woman, okay? I thought she was just some snatch and—"

"Shut the fuck up."

Jam raised his gun and took a step back, pointing it toward Clay. "I was a sniper in Afghanistan. Did I ever tell you that, man?"

"Yeah, Jam. You told me."

Jam's Adam's apple bobbed as he swallowed. "Had more than fifty kills to my name. So what the hell's one more, you know?"

"This is different."

"Different? Ya think? I was one of the good guys back then. Here? Here, I'm just a one-percenter. Just a fuckin' outlaw."

"You could change that. You don't want to do this, man."

"No!" He shouted. "'Course I don't wanna do this, but what choice are you givin' me? I won't go to prison, man. I can't do it. I've killed before, and I'll fuckin' do it again if I have to." He raised the weapon and aimed it straight at Clay's head. A kill shot, especially this close.

Clay opened his mouth to say something, anything to

stop the guy, but before he could get out the words, the shot rang out—deafening in the enclosed kitchen.

For a surreal instant, Clay thought he'd been shot again. But he knew how it felt, and this painless normality wasn't it.

Slowly, things came into focus: Jam, propelled backward, but still holding on to the .38. By the door stood a woman, her weapon raised—a snub-nosed revolver—and behind her, George, white as a sheet, eyes only for him.

Everything was quiet. That hollow vacuum a gunshot left in its wake. He'd *felt* it last time, almost stronger than the impact initially.

"Don't move," she said in a no-nonsense tone of voice.

"You Jessie?" Clay said.

"Yeah."

Jam moved, and she shot him again, in the arm this time. It sent his gun flying.

From the front door, behind the women, came the instantly recognizable shout of law enforcement arriving on the scene. Clay watched, ears ringing as Jessie threw her hands up. He shouted, "Back here."

Suddenly, the room was swarming with Blackwood Sheriff's Department deputies, their dark uniforms filling up the spaces. Taking over.

Taking over so Clay could let go.

Fuck, it was crazy how quickly the adrenaline drained away when you no longer needed it. Like the scarecrow from *The Wizard of Oz*, Clay felt boneless, like he could slide to the floor, skeleton liquid. Just one thing kept him up. His gaze searched the controlled chaos and noise of the room.

George.

He met her eyes, and when she smiled, Clay's bruised heart cracked wide open.

There was something desperate in Clay. George could tell as soon as he touched her. Those rough fighter's hands grasped her face, hard, and he kissed her even harder.

And, oh Lord, that kiss, after all the certainty of death, was like getting a second chance. It was a second chance for him.

She leaned in to whisper, "You okay?"

He huffed a breath onto her lips but didn't answer right away.

"Now that I got you, yeah."

"Sorry to interrupt." That was the sheriff, Steve Mullen, standing a couple of steps away. "I got quite the crime scene here. Just need a word, Special Agent Navarro."

Clay nodded, gave George's hand one last squeeze, and moved a few steps away.

She watched, not even tempted to help as EMTs arrived and took three men away. Outside, there was some kind of manhunt going on. The one outside had gotten away.

She watched as her home was ransacked—in an impressively orderly fashion and for only the best reasons—and caught snippets of conversations. They hadn't called in the feds, apparently, although Clay stuck around. Watching him become official and totally in his element was really lovely to behold. And hot. Totally hot, the way he suddenly took charge and called out orders.

After an interview with one of the deputies, she retired to the screened porch and watched from a distance, a stranger in her own home.

Jessie stepped out to join her. "You okay?"

George thought about it. *Was she okay?*

"Yes. I think I am." She raised the bottle she'd pulled from a kitchen cupboard. "Care for a glass of cooking sherry?"

"Hell yes. From the bottle is fine, if you don't have an actual glass."

"Here. Share mine."

Jessie took a long swig, refilled the glass, and handed it to George.

"Seriously, though. You feeling all right? You've had quite a night."

"I'm completely unfazed by this." George threw back the sherry. She'd have a headache in the morning, but fuck it. "Which I'm sure means I'm in shock. It'll hit soon."

They passed the glass back and forth, refilled it, and did it again. "You can't possibly be okay with all these people in your house?"

George stilled and looked inside, past Jessie.

"I'm alive. He's alive." She glanced at Jessie. "You and Gabe are safe. Does anything else really matter?" Pushing back a wave of hysteria, George went on. "What would I have done if you hadn't shown up right then, Jessie?"

"Oh, no. Don't you dare cry, or I'll let loose and then we'll never stop."

"I'm not." She sniffled and wiped her nose. "You saved his life. You were amazing. What would I have done—"

"Okay, stop it right now. First of all, I'm trained in firearms"—Jessie motioned inside—"and in how to deal with lunatics like that." She leaned in and put a hand on George's arm, squeezing just enough to be comforting. "George, you were *restrained*. Zip-tied, for God's sake. And you got out." On a huffed-out breath, Jessie shook her head. "Do you have any idea how big a deal that is?"

"I just—"

"You just nothing. You kicked ass. The rest of us… Clay? He's trained for stuff like this." Jessie wrapped an arm around her and squeezed. "You kicked ass." Jessie turned to look into the kitchen. "You know, he's gonna get pretty caught up in all of it."

George watched Clay for a few long seconds. "I know."

"So. The patient. The one you felt bad about feeling bad about. The guy I warned you against?"

George huffed out a half laugh. "Yeah."

Jessie surprised her by saying, "I think you made the right choice."

"Yeah?"

Jessie grabbed the glass from George and took hold of her hand. "You did good, George. You did good."

George nodded and let the other woman pull her into a hug. She fought back tears that she'd rather cry on her own.

Later, after Jessie left and the crew in her house thinned out, the sheriff approached George at her spot on the porch. "Sounds like you had quite a night," he said. "You tell my guys your side of things?"

"Yep."

"Might need you to come down for a recorded interview."

"Sure. Of course."

"You doing all right?"

She smiled. "Oddly, yes."

Clay chose that moment to step out, his eyes glued to her.

"Sheriff tells me I'm not welcome at the crime scene," he said.

"No?" She looked between the two men. "Isn't this a federal case?"

"Mr. Navarro is a witness in what happened tonight. Just like you. Anyway"—Steve stood up— "we'll be here for at least twenty-four hours or so. Be a long night." He glanced at the yard. "Or day. More likely. It's gonna be a long day. You all should skedaddle."

With a start, George turned to look out. A fresh pink light suffused the garden. She wished the air were fresh enough to go with that glow.

Steve asked, "What's the plan, Agent Navarro?"

"Well, ATF's gonna have to—"

"I talked to your SAC on the phone. I've heard all about the fed's plan. I'm asking you about yours."

It was when Clay swallowed and didn't look at George that she felt the queasy weight settle in her stomach.

"What's next, Clay?" she repeated—a whisper, just for him.

"Head back to Baltimore."

George's head started shaking before he'd finished the sentence, but Clay went on. "You've got the most to lose here, George. I can't...I can't keep putting you in danger like this. It's my presence here that made this happen. It's because of me that—"

"You're leaving?" Her voice came out shrill and harsh.

He nodded.

"After all of this? You want to pack up and take off? Back to your…what? Undercover life? Your job?"

"My life's in Baltimore. I need to get this as far away from you as possible. No matter what happens here, after tonight, it'll never be safe and—"

"*Fuck* safe," George spat, in a voice she'd never heard herself use. But damn it, she was tired and filthy and she'd been through a whole hell of a lot.

"George, you're not—"

"*No.* No, I'm helping, because this is my problem now too. Not just yours. Don't you see that?"

Clay's face—his beautiful face—was hard and drawn, his brows lowered into a straight line, his jaw tight and rigid. He wanted to argue, she'd bet, but she'd argue him into the ground.

The sheriff said something, and George couldn't even be bothered to throw a glance his way—she couldn't pull her attention away from Clay.

"This is *my* house, Clay. These men attacked my house. And it's my *life*." She hesitated, and then, with a giant sigh and a *fuck it* of a prayer, went on. "*You* are mine. You're *mine*, and I'm not letting you do this alone. What do you think happens when you leave? Huh? You think I just go back to what I had? To who I was? And you just go back there? To Baltimore? And whatever it is you do up there?" Another pause while she girded herself to go on. "No. No, you're not leaving. I'm not letting you go."

His brows lifted and then they settled, relaxed, his mouth loosened, his eyes lost a set of lines. "You're not?"

"No."

"I've got to go back. Got to testify and—"

"You think you could love me?" Lord, what was she doing? It was probably exhaustion.

But without hesitation he said, "Yes."

"Do you want to be with me?" she went on.

"You know I do."

"Then stay with me, Clay. Don't give this up. Don't give it up out of duty or a need to keep me safe. You've fulfilled your duties, Agent Navarro. And I understand the dangers. I'm okay with the risks. You go testify, do what you need to do to make things right, but come back to me. I won't break if you stay." With a hiccup of emotion, she went on. "But I might if you leave."

"You see what I'm like, George. This is my fucked-up life."

"I know."

"You're okay with this?"

"*No.* No, I'm *not* okay with *that*." She pointed at the law enforcement's orderly mayhem, examining every inch of her home. As if it were only natural, he sank into the empty space beside her, and she put a hand on the hot cotton covering his chest, patted her fingertips over his heart, and said, "But I'm good with *this*."

She tilted her head back, so close his breath heated her skin as his eyes flicked over her face, seeking, she thought, some kind of confirmation, some sign of strength; she did her best to give it to him.

"Stay," she whispered, finally wrapping her arms around him and begging with her body, her heat, her heart. "Stay with me."

21

A FULL TWENTY-FOUR HOURS WENT BY BEFORE THEY could return to George's house, and it had been another twenty-four since then, but the clarity in Clay's brain had yet to disappear. There'd been some fuzzy moments, like when he'd buried his face in his woman's neck, or after they'd fucked in their bed at a local B&B. He'd awakened wrapped up in her, close and warm and sweaty, her eyes still soppy wet with tears. Those moments had been soft and blurry at the edges, but what blurred them wasn't confusion or pain or any of those other things he'd drowned in for years—it was happiness.

His happiness.

Love, apparently, didn't have the hard edges he'd learned to associate with it.

Love wasn't pain. That was probably the lesson here, although it might be a little while before he truly took that one on board and made it his own.

Right now, though, Clay felt sort of…at peace with things, which wasn't entirely comfortable when strife was your constant MO. And yes, it was all new—as new as the henhouse he'd built today to surprise George. But new was okay, and sometimes, adjusting wasn't so much painful as it was a voyage of discovery.

The knock at George's door surprised him, and he hesitated before glancing toward the front of the house, thinking about Tyler and whoever else might come back to turn his life upside down.

After a few seconds, he walked through the kitchen, down the hall, and to the open front door.

"Evening, Clay," the sheriff said, smiling through the screen, six-pack in hand.

"Come on in, Sheriff."

He led the man to the back porch, where they each snagged a can and popped it open.

"You doing okay?"

"Yes, sir."

"Good." Steve looked around. "Place looks good."

"Can't take credit for that."

The dark eyes focused on his. "No?"

"Take it this isn't police business, since we dealt with all of that already." He lifted his beer. "Also this."

"No, son" was all Steve said.

"What can I do for you?"

"Well, first of all, we got the kids' class tomorrow. Just wanted to make sure you were gonna be there."

Clay sighed. "Look, man, you don't have to—"

"I know I don't. Now just…hold your tongue for a second and listen, will you?"

Clay nodded and did as he was told.

"I got something I want you to know about."

"What's that?"

"Had an interesting conversation today."

"Yeah?"

"Talked to your boss—"

"Ex-boss," Clay cut in.

"Right. Special Agent in Charge Jean McGovern." Clay waited for the old man to get to the point. "Has a lotta good things to say about you, son. She mentioned, very much off the record, she's been working closely with Internal Affairs on some issues out of her field office—Baltimore." He took a long, slow swig. "Said she had concerns that a certain field agent had gone rogue, working for personal gain rather than for the agency."

"Okay," said Clay with a sense of foreboding. *She means me.* He looked over the yard and waited for the sheriff to go on.

After a big inhale, Steve met his eye and said, "Guy who left the scene the other night? Special Agent Tyler Patrick Olson, ATF?" Clay's throat closed up. He waited. "Boat blew up. Late last night. Fishing off the coast of Virginia. Early prognosis, entirely off the record, is suicide. Your boss was reticent with the details, as you can imagine." He looked at Clay. "What's your take on that?"

Something drummed in Clay's ears, so hard, he could barely hear himself ask, "Anyone else on that boat?"

"Doesn't look like it."

"Any word on his wife and kids?"

"My understanding is that his family is safe."

A breath in, a big swig of beer, and Clay nodded, pushed back the questions, no matter how hard they burned. Tyler did this to himself. Homicide or suicide, whatever it was, he'd made the choice. That didn't make it any easier to swallow.

"McGovern claims you been having some issues. Psychological, she said."

"Also off the record?" Clay asked with a wry twist to his mouth.

The sheriff answered with a chuckle. "Yeah. Said you'd been shot. Shrink wants you on meds for PTSD and—"

"Not doing the meds, sir. Don't care who—"

"Slow down, kid. I'm not going to force you to do anything. It's not why I'm here."

"Then why are you here?" Clay asked before adding a belated, "Sir?"

Steve sipped at his beer. He was almost dainty in contrast to Clay's slugs. "I thought you might want to stick around." He slid a sly look at Clay. "'Course I'm not too keen on an ATF agent walking around in my community with untreated PTSD. Hanging around good citizens like the doc here and not taking care of yourself."

After a brief moment of irritation, Clay looked at the garden and the sky and the beer in his hand, and he let it go. "Think I'll figure it out," he said through tight lips.

"Not trying to tell you what to do, but I've seen people come back from places and—"

"I'm good," Clay said. It was probably true.

"You sure 'bout that?" The man turned to Clay, sharp eyes focused right at him. "Wouldn't want you hurting yourself. Or anybody else." He leaned away, reached into a pocket, and came out with a folded up piece of paper. "We're a small town, but we got us some top-notch shrinks and—hold your tongue and let me finish, son." Clay's mouth snapped shut. "You feel things getting out of hand, don't wait until it's too late. Don't wait until you're so far gone you can't go back. Give one of these people a call; take care of yourself. If I'm not mistaken, you'll be staying here with the doc, which means you've got more than your ass to worry about now. And all I'm doing is making sure everybody comes out good. You feel me?"

The paper, white against Steve's dark skin, shook slightly in the few beats it took for Clay to give in and take it. Without a word, face so red he wished he could hide it, he pocketed the list, unsure whether to be pissed or grateful for the man sticking his nose in where it didn't belong.

After a few moments of uncomfortable silence, the man spoke again. "Anyone tell you I was the first black sheriff they ever had in Blackwood?"

"No, sir."

"First one in this part of the state. Been a while, of course. Now they got lady sheriffs and everything," the man finished with a grin.

"Well, that's real—"

"Not done."

"Okay."

"You know the most important things I learned on the job?" Steve held up his beer, stopping Clay from trying to answer what was, clearly, a rhetorical question. "No rule book has all the answers in it. Not one right way to do things. You got to be smart, and you got to be fair. That's what matters. It isn't about being a man of the law so much as being a *man*. A good man." He looked hard at Clay now, waiting for some sign, some understanding.

"Yeah. Yes. I get that."

"Thought you might." Steve's eyes flicked over him before the sheriff took another deep slug.

"Anyway, all I'm saying is that you don't have to look the part around here to get the job. Although," he said with a wink, "it's always a good idea to know the right people."

"Whoa, Steve, I'm not trying to—"

"Yeah, well, I am. I've been at it twenty-five years and I got myself a girlfriend and all I want right now is to enjoy life. Been looking for someone to pass the torch to. Wasn't ready to retire till the right man—or woman—came along." Another sly look. "Wondering if maybe I found him."

"Look, you've known me two weeks. I can't—"

"Come to work for me. I'm low on deputies. When the time's right, I'll campaign for you. They'll vote you in. I can retire. Your lady can keep her man, and you can stay here and feel useful again," Steve said, crushing his can before setting it down. "I think everybody'd be getting pretty much exactly what they want, don't you?"

Clay finished his beer and hesitated before accepting another.

"Why? I'm not the kind of—"

"You're me." The sheriff's words stopped Clay with a surprised blink. "You're the guy who figured he wasn't worth a damn. People think you're the bad guy, the monster, 'cause of the way you look, but inside"—he flicked Clay's chest before leaning back, the wicker creaking under him—"you're solid."

The man's dark eyes on his were steady, trusting. It

felt good to have that kind of confidence pointed his way. Someone who got it.

Christ, don't let me cry.

Clay set his beer on the table, got up, and went into the house, ran some water into a glass, and slugged it back. For about thirty seconds, he stood by the sink, waiting for the buzzing to subside, until he remembered it was already gone. Slowly, he sucked in one breath after another, waited, waited, and… Nothing. No buzz, no frantic scream, no mashed-up, frenzied thoughts. Instead, there was just…him. Him.

With a big, honest breath in, he went back out onto the porch and had that second beer with the sheriff before waving him off. He stayed out there alone for a while after that. Alone in a house that felt like home.

Something caught Clay's attention—or, rather, the lack of something. He left the porch, stood on the steps, and stilled, head cocked, eyes roving over the yard. The *quiet* yard.

No cicada opera. A couple of insects sawing out their tunes here and there, but the loud, overwhelming cacophony was gone. Here one second and gone the next. *Gone.*

And with that silence came clarity. His mind, fuzzy and painfully blurred for so long, felt suddenly bright and clean.

Christ, could he do it? Could he stay?

What the hell would he do with himself here? He could work on George's place, fix the shit that needed fixing, do that summer martial arts camp for the kids… but eventually he'd just be the loser camping out in her bed, bringing nothing to the table. That wouldn't work for them long-term. He needed a job. Did he have it in him to be a cop?

Inside, he heard a creak and turned around to see George standing in her work clothes.

"Cicadas are gone," he said, oddly choked up.

A hushed "Oh" fell from her lips. She came out and joined him on the top step, her eyes filling with tears before they overflowed and ran down her cheeks on a sob.

Hesitantly, he put an arm around her, relaxing when she sank into him.

"But you're still here," she said. "I left work, sure you'd be gone, and then I saw your truck, and now—"

"Not going anywhere, baby," he said, taking her in his arms. "I'm home."

⁓ large ornamental flourish ⁓

Overhead, thunder rolled, finally here. George kept her head on Clay's shoulder and stared at the sky, willing the storm to break. She wanted something to ground this bright, hopeful feeling.

"Got a job offer," said Clay.

She stilled and stopped hoping. "Did you?" A flash of lightning got the chickens squawking, and George's chest tightened.

"Yep. Right here in Blackwood."

"Okay." The tightness in her chest became a flutter, which she ignored.

"Not exactly an offer. More of a suggestion, which I guess is a start."

"Oh my God, Clay." She lifted her head and smacked him on the shoulder. "If you're going to string me along, I'll turn around and go right back inside."

"No." He smiled. "No, stay, baby. Stay. I just… I need to ask you a question."

"Ask away." A drop fell on George's head, heavy and warm, but still, they didn't move.

"If…you know, the hormone thing you did. If it worked and you're pregnant. I guess… It's early, and we don't know where we're going with this, but…would it be so bad to have a baby with *me*? Instead of… I mean, I know I'm still pretty fucked up, but…"

"No," she whispered. "No, it wouldn't be bad at all."

"I've been diagnosed with PTSD. I mean, I was, before. I thought you should know that."

"I…I figured."

"You're not afraid of that? Of me?"

"Are you kidding? I trust you with my life."

"Good," he said, looking away. "Few nights ago, before all the shit went down, you also asked what or *who* I'd want to be? In the future. If I had one."

She thought back and remembered the urge she'd had to know him then. Such a short while, but it seemed like ages ago. "Yes, I remember asking you that."

"Well, this is it," he said, taking hold of her hand, his voice competing with a closer growl of thunder, immediately followed by a sharp, angry flash above them and a patter of raindrops. "This, right here with you. I want to be a man you'd love. That's what I want. I want to feel needed; I want to keep this small town safe. I want to make a baby with you one day. I want to make you smile and lose that sad look you get."

"I look sad?"

He shrugged in answer, rain dotting the fabric at his shoulders.

She clasped his hand back, loving the rasp of his skin against hers. "I don't feel sad now."

"No? You looked a little sad coming up here."

"That was when I still thought you'd be leaving me."

"What if I were the Sheriff of Blackwood? Would you still want me then?"

"Really?" she said through a giggle, her hand going to his face, suddenly wet from the pelting rain. "I told you. I want you here. I want you with me."

"God, I want you, George. I'm…I'm bad at this stuff, but I love you so much." His arms pulled her into a hard, soggy embrace. "So much it fucking hurts."

"I love you too, Clay," she said, letting him take her lips, loving the heat of his tongue, the smell of him and sodden earth, together more elemental than anything in the world.

"So, you're okay with me just…you know, hanging out?"

"Hanging out?"

"I keep trying to picture going back there. The old job. So weird, 'cause it's what I am, or was. What I did and…I doubt you'd like Baltimore, anyway. And I've got to be wherever you are, George." He paused and looked up at the sky. "Besides, this place sort of grows on you, you know?"

"Yes," George said, laughing. "Yes, I know exactly what you mean."

Clay might have said *I love you* again after that. At least, his mouth formed the words, but George couldn't hear a thing because the heavens opened up and gave them everything, deafening them. She put her lips to his and felt the rightness of this kiss. Hot and elemental, sweet and so full of love. Their tongues touched and danced as they sipped at each other, sharing rather than taking.

George laughed as Clay nipped at her lip. She laughed with the sheer joy of being alive and loving him. The joy of second chances, third chances, and in a strange way, coming back from the dead.

Water fell, sheets of it, washing them clean with the strength of waves, nothing so paltry as the patter of raindrops. The sky, alive with thunder and lightning, was angry and beautiful and so unbelievably inconsequential compared to what was happening right there on earth, where love reigned harder, stronger, and fiercer than anything the world could throw their way.

Read on for a sneak peek at the next volume in the Blank Canvas series.

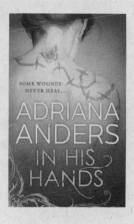

Dark and moody Luc Stanek craves a quiet life. But when a desperate woman lands, bloodied and branded, on his doorstep, he finds himself pulled into her world… and determined to save her no matter the cost.

Abby Merkley joined the Church of the Apocalyptic Faith as a child, and the brands marring her skin mark her as little more than the charismatic leader's property. Only Luc is able to see her for the woman she truly is. Determined to win her freedom, Abby and Luc will fight the only family Abby has ever known…for a future neither is certain can be theirs.

THE BOLT CUTTERS DIDN'T, AS PROMISED, SLICE THROUGH the fence like butter, but they did the job. Judging from the way the sun cleaved through the bare trees, casting long skeletons of shadow, it was close to noon.

Which meant she had to hurry.

Peeling back the chain link wasn't easy the way her hands were shaking, but she managed to do it without cutting herself. Thank the Lord, or else Isaiah would wonder what she'd gotten into and send someone scouting.

Abby's wool coat had to come off before she could slide through the hole, carefully avoiding the gleaming edges of fresh-cut metal. And for some reason she couldn't quite explain, she undid the ties at her chin and threw her bonnet down as well. She walked through the vines on the other side of the fence, gazing at row upon row of bare branches. Which made her worry. Would Grape Man have work for her without grapes on his plants?

He had to. He *had* to.

As she drew closer, something else occurred to her:

What if he wasn't here? She hadn't seen him drive through. But then, she'd walked the half hour to the back fence, which would have given him plenty of time to leave without her knowledge. The thought had her racing messily between the army of dry, brittle-looking plants, crucified on the mountainside.

The smell of woodsmoke was the first sign that he wasn't far. He was home, at least—thank goodness.

Past a wood shed and through the open picket gate she went. She climbed the three porch steps, breathless, her sopping hem hugging her calves uncomfortably. Before she had time to stop herself—because if she stopped, if she thought this through, she wouldn't do it—her knuckles rapped on the door.

Out of breath, face prickly hot and the rest of her body chilled, Abby waited.

Nothing. No shuffling, no footsteps, no sound at all besides the creaking floorboards beneath her feet.

She turned and scanned the buildings: the henhouse with its little yard full of chickens, two older shed-like structures, and that big refurbished barn to crown it all. Was he all the way up there?

Abby tromped back down the sagging steps with a renewed sense of purpose, ignoring the chafe of shoes that had seen better days—shoes that weren't made for running.

Ladies aren't meant to run, Hamish used to say. She swallowed back the memory. He'd been gone for weeks now. And a good thing too. Nobody deserved the pain he'd endured in those last days.

Nerves buzzing, she circled the cabin, which looked a lot worse up close, and went through the back gate and up the steep slope to the barn. Everything felt strangely off, like stepping through a mirror and seeing things the wrong way around.

The barn, it appeared, was the only building he had worked on since taking over—the only thing, besides the vines, that the man seemed to care about. It was enormous and built right into the boulders that crowned the mountain. It had fresh boards and a perfectly straight door that hung slightly ajar. Tentatively, Abby knocked on the thick wood. Too quiet. He wouldn't hear a thing from inside, but she felt hesitant, weighted. There were no grapes on the vines, and all was quiet inside the barn. Just a few months ago, the place had been a hive of activity.

Five months ago, while Hamish was dying and Abby barely had time to glance outside, much less spy on the neighbor.

This place, so silent now that she desperately needed help, intimidated her. But nothing would be worse than going back without accomplishing her goal.

"Hello?" She forced her voice out, pushing the door farther open and hating how small she sounded.

"Anyone here? Mister…"

She stopped. *Mister Grape Man*, she'd been about to say, but that would be strange, wouldn't it? "Hello?" she called louder, urging herself to move farther in. One step, two, through a dark vestibule hung with metal equipment. Tall boots lined one wall, and across from her stood a locked door.

This roadblock gave the turmoil in her belly nothing to do, nowhere to go. Weighted by a new sense of hopelessness, she turned and walked back outside.

From this height, everything splayed out beneath her looked like toys. The cabin was like something she'd played with as a child, but the man, when she eventually spotted him, looked nothing like the squat, happy farmer from that same foldaway barnyard. Her stomach twisted, half excited, half terrified as she tripped her way down the rocky slope.

She was close when the man finally noticed her. Close enough to feel tiny in comparison to his towering, long-limbed frame. Close enough to see how graceful his movements were, despite his imposing size. Close enough to see his eyes widen in surprise and his high forehead crease into a scowl. From the top of his unruly hair and unshaven face over the faded work clothes, which strained immodestly over shoulders and arms, to the tip of his muddy boots, everything about this man loomed as darkly foreboding as the mountain above.

She took him in for a beat or two, waiting for some sign of kindness from this man whose size did nothing to allay the fears she'd plowed through to get here. To offer the hope she'd depended on to counter the many, many risks.

He offered no welcome at all—no neighborly hello or hand raised in greeting. Abby almost stepped back, intimidated. But there was no choice. There'd be no leaving here without a job. Judging from the entrenched look of his frown, she'd have bet those immobile lips hadn't twisted into anything resembling a smile in years. As she forced herself to step forward into his shadow, the lines around his eyes deepened. *Make that decades.*

"Good morning, sir," she forced herself to say in her

friendliest voice. Surely he'd hear the cracks beneath the surface, that edge of desperation.

He opened his mouth, but before he had a chance to say a word, she soldiered right through. "My apologies for disturbing you on this…" She glanced at the lowering clouds, as broody and gray as his frigid eyes, and blubbered on. "I'm Abigail Merkley. Abby, I mean. *Abby* Merkley. I'm looking for work, sir."

He squinted at her outstretched hand in a way that was decidedly unfriendly, and for a good few seconds, it appeared he might not accept. Her first handshake ever, rebuffed.

He relented after a bit, carefully setting down the tool he used to prune the vines and sliding his palm against hers. She hadn't expected this when she'd held out her hand. She'd remembered the fish man at the market, the way he shook hands with his best customers. He'd told her it meant something. A connection, a promise. A *covenant*. Setting out this morning on the half-hour walk to the fence line, she'd planned this shake. Firm, businesslike. Secure. *Confident.*

The reality was nothing of the sort. It was… Well, goodness, the handshake wasn't a meeting of equals, the way she'd pictured it. It was consumption, one hand swallowed by the other. And it did things to her. Made her feel the difference in stature quite keenly. There was also the matter of how alone she was out here on this mountain. No one knew where she was—not a solitary soul—and here she'd gone and put her hand into an ogre's. Walked right up to him and offered it up.

He didn't scare her nearly as much as what lay on the other side of the fence, though. He should have,

but…what was it about his face? Not the unexpected translucence of those eyes nor their chilly distance. He didn't trust this, she could tell. He was angry, maybe, at her intrusion, but there was something else. Something sad or hopeless about the man, apparent in the purposeful squaring of those wide shoulders—an effort, she thought.

"Work?" He uttered his first word as his other hand rose to hers, chafing it in a way she'd have bet was subconscious. The word sounded off, chewed away at the *R*. His voice, deep and growling, was not what she expected. It made her want to clear her throat for him. "What work?"

She was ready for this question. She'd watched him, after all. Cutting and moving, cutting and moving. "I could help out here," she said brightly.

"Here?" He dropped her hand like a burning coal and shifted away.

"I've seen you pruning. Last year, you hired people. I figured—"

"I do it myself," he cut in. This time, she heard it: an accent. Not that thick, but different from any she knew. The words stayed close to the front of his mouth. As he spoke, she understood those deep-cut parentheses framing his lips.

"Oh." Disappointment tightened her chest, a sense of urgency making it hard to breathe. "I can learn," she said. When his expression didn't budge, she begged. "I'll do it for less than you paid the others."

His eyes lowered before meeting hers. "Where's your coat?"

Why on earth did he sound so accusatory?

"I don't…" She glanced back up the mountain, to where she'd left it in a pile by the fence, too afraid to rip it on the jagged metal edges she'd crawled through to get here.

He wasn't going to do it, was he? He wasn't going to give her the job that might save Sammy's life. This wasn't the man. This wasn't the day. This wasn't the mountain. Quite possibly not the lifetime. Was there any point?

She ignored him and turned back, taking in the view— different from the church land, with its westward-facing view. It was rockier here, steeper and more interesting. The sky in this direction pulled out all the stops, its high-contrast clouds cut off right over the seam of the mountains, saving their drama for these richer folks.

This side had begun to represent a way out, a better life for Sammy. Today, it had lost its glow, soured by anguish and despair and the almost audible ticking of the clock. *Get him out, get him out, get him out*, it chanted in time with the panicked beating of her heart.

Sucking in a big, icy breath, Abby looked right into that unforgiving face and said, "I would do most anything, sir."

She meant it too.

Acknowledgments

There are many people to thank for their help on this book. To Stephanie Snell, of Charlottesville Skin and Laser; Gordon Emery, of Cville Jiu-Jitsu; to my favorite lawyer, Joe P.; and to the Charlottesville Police Department's Brian O'Donnell—thank you for sharing your knowledge. All errors are my own. To Callie Russell, Radha Metro, Madeline Iva, Kasey Lane, Corey Jo Lloyd, Mollie Cox Bryan, and Joanna Bourne—thank you for reading me and advising me and providing me with much-needed perspective. I adore you all. Thank you to my parents and my husband, whose unflagging support made writing this book possible. I couldn't have done it without you. And finally, thanks to my agent, Laura Bradford; to Mary Altman, whose edits are always spot-on (she just gets me, you know?); and to the incredible team at Sourcebooks. You are all amazing.

About the Author

Adriana Anders has acted and sung, slung cocktails, and corrected copy. She's worked for start-ups, multinationals, and small nonprofits, but it wasn't until she returned to her first love—writing romance—that she finally felt like she'd come home. Today, she resides with her tall French husband and two small children in the foothills of the Blue Ridge Mountains, where she writes the dark, emotional love stories of her heart.

Adriana loves hearing from her readers! Visit and sign up to get news at www.adrianaanders.com or follow her on Facebook at www.facebook.com/adriana andersauthor, Twitter at www.twitter.com/adrianas boudoir, and Instagram at www.instagram.com/adriana .anders.